W9-CBX-114

THE SILENCE OF STONES

THE SILENCE OF STONES

A CRISPIN GUEST MEDIEVAL NOIR

Jeri Westerson

This first world edition published 2015
in Great Britain and 2016 in the USA by
SEVERN HOUSE PUBLISHERS LTD of
19 Cedar Road, Sutton, Surrey, England, SM2 5DA.
Trade paperback edition first published
in Great Britain and the USA 2016 by
SEVERN HOUSE PUBLISHERS LTD

British Library Cataloguing in Publication Data

Westerson, Jeri author.
  The silence of stones. – (A Crispin Guest medieval
  mystery)
  1. Guest, Crispin (Fictitious character)–Fiction.
  2. Stone of Scone–Fiction. 3. Great Britain–History–
  Richard II, 1377-1399–Fiction. 4. Suspense fiction.
  I. Title II. Series
  813.6-dc23

ISBN-13: 978-0-7278-8562-3 (cased)
ISBN-13: 978-1-84751-671-8 (trade paper)
ISBN-13: 978-1-78010-725-7 (e-book)

Typeset by Palimpsest Book Production Ltd.,
Falkirk, Stirlingshire, Scotland.
Printed digitally in the USA.

To Craig, my cornerstone.

ACKNOWLEDGEMENTS

A huge thank you to my agent Joshua Bilmes for finding Crispin a new home. Thank you also to Severn House for giving it a chance, and to Faith Black Ross for her careful editing and nurturing. Grateful thanks, as always, goes out to my ever-loving and long-suffering husband Craig. There's a reason he makes his own beer, wine, and mead. And another huge dollop of thanks to my readers who love Crispin and keep me going.

ONE

London, 1388

The columns rose to impossible heights, casting irregular shadows upon the crowded nave of Westminster Abbey. Courtiers stood in the front nearest the rood screen, with the rest of the rabble in the rear. Crispin Guest stood amongst them. Not with the courtiers, as was his birthright, but with the rabble, as was now his curse.

He glanced at his apprentice, Jack Tucker, a rangy boy and now his match in height, though the lad was only fifteen. Crispin watched him push his ginger locks away from his freckled cheeks, as he had done thousands of times before. The boy's eyes darted here and there, taking in the garlands and candles, the painted runners and gilded ribs of the vaults. Jack had watched with fascination the triumphal procession that had led them to the church for the Feast of the Holy Virgin's Nativity, and he seemed just as captivated by the pomp and ceremony of London's court. Yes, King Richard was there, Crispin noted, far in the front being catered to by the abbot of Westminster himself, William de Colchester. The sheriffs, too, were in attendance, William Venour and Hugh Fastolf, soon to relinquish their service to the men beside them. Crispin presumed the sandy-haired men with thin, pasty faces to be the newly elected sheriffs Adam Carlylle and Thomas Austin, but as to who was which, he hadn't a clue.

Crispin found his own gaze roving. The muttered prayers of Abbot William did not reach the rabble in the back, though the songs that came from the monks in the quire did rise and fall, echoing into the shadowy spaces. Candle stands and great coronas filled with beeswax columns lit halos on the floor and over the crowds, but it was still dim in the corners and under the painted pillars.

Crispin detested crowds. Anything could happen in a mob of people. And glancing at Jack, with the beginnings of red whiskers now prominent on his spotted chin, he knew better than most what a cutpurse could do in such a throng. Being in a church made no difference.

Still, better safe than sorry, and he put his hand on his scrip and pushed it along his belt until it sat snug and secure against his belly.

He hadn't any intention to be in Westminster today. After all, it was two miles from their home in London. And feast day or no, he was seldom in the mood for pompous displays. But Jack was of another stripe. The boy loved the saints and the trappings of their celebrations. A devout boy was Jack. Crispin smiled again, remembering the lad's pleas. And no local church would do, for he had heard of the splendor of feast days at Westminster Abbey, the king's church, and he wanted to see it for himself. And besides, he had told Crispin, 'There will be cakes, master, or so I have heard.'

And then Jack insisted that if they were to see a procession, then Crispin should strap on his sword. What better occasion, he declared. At the time, Crispin thought it just and acceded to it. But now he wasn't so sure. He laid his left hand on the hilt, fingers testing the leather and twined wire on the grip. It gave him comfort, but the proximity to the king and his consorts made Crispin uneasy. He acquiesced too often to Jack's whims, succumbing to vanity. And vanity didn't belong in a church. Yet his sword was merely an ornament today, just as the courtiers wore their blades. If there was trouble, he couldn't even draw it. His dagger would be more accessible in such a tightly-packed crowd. Not that he would need it.

He let out a breath and peered forward between bare-headed men and kerchief-coifed women. King Richard, resplendent in robes of white and trimmed in ermine, sat beside his wife, similarly clad. Her hair was encaged in gold netting that sparkled in the candlelight. They both wore crowns.

Lancaster was still in Spain, trying to win his own crown, but the news was not good on that front, at least that was the rumor Crispin had heard. He hadn't heard from Lancaster's son, Henry, for a long while. No sightings, no visits, as was expected. As he had hoped. Henry had no business consorting with Crispin, and the less of that the better, though there was a pang of regret at that thought. He was here, Henry, sitting not too far from his cousin the king. He was seated next to Nottingham. The two were part of a group of lords formed in the last two years to oversee the king, to rid him of his favorites, and to see that justice was done as far as the purse strings were concerned. Richard had promised, at the point of a sword, to be guided by their good counsel, but Crispin was far too suspicious of Richard's duplicity to completely believe in that.

Even so, he drank in the sight of Henry. He hadn't seen him in nearly a year. A stocky youth with auburn hair and a well-trimmed beard. He seemed the opposite in every way to his effete cousin. Crispin had been a household knight in Lancaster's estates, and he had often taken charge of Henry when the young boy's governor was unavailable. But Henry wasn't a boy any longer. He was certainly a man. Definitely Lancaster's son.

The scent of incense wafted over the crowd, and Crispin closed his eyes, inhaling. It reminded him of holy things, as it was supposed to, and with the sounds of chanting from the quire and bells being rung, he did feel the presence of God.

He opened his eyes and spied again the king and his court. When Crispin was a part of court, he had looked forward to such feast days. He used to sit with those others, drinking in the piety and feeling himself privileged to enjoy such a place in the house of the Lord. He hadn't realized then what vanity it was to believe that he deserved it and that those in the back – where Crispin now stood – were somehow lesser in God's eyes.

Today was different. Vanity did not blind him as it once had with the trappings of royalty and nobility about him. Today he could simply *feel*.

Closing his eyes again, he felt Jack lean against his arm. The boy trembled, and Crispin opened his eyes to slits to observe him. Jack's hands were clasped tightly before him in prayer. And he intoned the Latin along with the monks. The Feast of the Virgin's Nativity seemed especially important to Jack. For all men who had lost their mothers, he supposed. He seldom thought of his own mother or of the day of *her* birth – August the twelfth – but it seemed suitable to think of it now. He should visit her tomb back at his old estates at Sheen . . . but, with an unpleasant jolt, he remembered that the private chapel where her grave was, along with the entire manor house, had burned to the ground five years ago.

He swallowed down the regret – so many regrets – and turned his gaze again toward the figure of the king. Lank, graceful, Richard sat in his royal chair, face raised toward the abbot with a steady gaze. His beard was trimmed to a line running along his jaw and on his chin, and his hair was coifed to just below his ears in a decisive curl. His intense gaze was focused on the statue of the Holy Mother that had been brought in with the procession. Festooned with flowers, the sedate figure seemed to look back fondly at Richard.

Had the lords of Henry's army tamed the king and his spending ways? Had Richard learned his lesson and put aside his favorites? Would he be the king everyone hoped he'd be? Or was he the king Crispin, when committing treason all those years ago, suspected he would turn out to—

The thundering boom reverberated throughout the church. Everyone froze, caught up in sudden terror at the inexplicable sound. Then the crowd suddenly surged, and women and children screamed. Abbot William stopped his chanting and whipped around, perplexed.

Crispin's hand was on his dagger hilt, and he strained his neck to see what had happened. Had the roof fallen in? Was anyone hurt?

A puff of smoke billowed up beyond the quire. It looked to be coming from St Edward's chapel. A fire?

As soon as the crowd saw the smoke, more screams echoed up to the ceiling and bounced about between the Purbeck marble columns. People began pushing their way back, trying to escape the church. Crispin was jostled this way and that while he shoved himself forward. Jack was right beside him.

'What was it, Master Crispin?' asked the boy.

Crispin spared him a glance. 'I don't know. Let us find out.' He shoved harder, shouldering his way between panicked people with Jack pushing men aside just as hard. On his toes, he saw that the quire was blocked by the rood screen and a gate. The king and his courtiers were making their way toward the north ambulatory, and Crispin moved in that direction as well.

People moved past him in the opposite direction, pulling him back like a strong tide. 'Move your sarding arse out of my way!' Jack shouted at the crowd, and suddenly red-faced, he becrossed himself, glancing apologetically toward the large crucifix at the end of the quire.

All at once the way was clear, and they plunged into the brief opening. Crispin rushed forward down the ambulatory, boots slapping the tile floor. The crowd was far behind him now, squeezing themselves through the west doors to escape with cries rising and falling. He dismissed the sound as irrelevant while his eyes scanned ahead. He and Jack moved past the north entrance with its webbing of scaffolding nearly blocking the way.

He gained the archway to the Confessor's chapel and stopped. Jack promptly ran into him. 'What is it, master?' he asked in a hushed voice and peered over Crispin's shoulder.

The king and his courtiers had gathered about the stately shrine of St Edward. The tomb rose up in two tiers atop an ornate stone plinth with arches running along its longer sides. The king and his courtiers blocked the view, but they were studying something at the foot of the shrine. Crispin longed to draw closer but dared not.

'I don't see no fire,' Jack whispered.

'No,' answered Crispin just as quietly, and the relief he felt eased the tension that had wound his muscles tight. But there was still the remnant of smoke rising from the front of the crowd of men.

'Is it St Edward's shrine, master? Is something amiss with it?'

'I can't tell, Jack. I can't see past the courtiers.'

Just then the crowd parted for Abbot William, and Crispin could finally see. The men were looking at the Coronation Chair that stood opposite the shrine, and Richard stood before it, body sagging, breathing hard. His agitation was obvious, especially when he curtly gestured for some courtiers to escort the queen away. He looked up and tried to smile at his wife, but his misery was plain on his face. And then he spotted Crispin.

Crispin straightened. He thought he had been well hidden in the shadows, but when the king's glare did not abate, he realized how wrong he'd been. Richard stalked decidedly toward him.

'God's blood,' Crispin hissed and got down on one knee. Jack followed suit slightly behind him.

'Guest,' Richard snarled. 'What are *you* doing here?'

With head bowed, Crispin stared only at Richard's delicate slippers. 'Sire, I came only to the feast day celebration.'

He could hear Richard's tense breathing over his head and then his clipped, 'Stand.'

Slowly, Crispin did. He raised his eyes to the king. Richard was taller than him now, and the fact surprised him.

The king's lips twisted into a sneer. 'You came all this way to be at Westminster . . . for a feast day. Are there no churches on the Shambles?'

The other courtiers watching from a distance might have laughed at Crispin's distress at any other time. But they must have guessed their king's demeanor and kept silent.

'We . . . wished to see the celebration at Westminster, majesty.'

'And to witness my humiliation!'

'We . . . I . . . came to help, sire.'

'Help? *Help*? Yes, the *Tracker*.' He spit the title with vehemence.

'The *Tracker* helps all of London, does he not? Well then. Behold, Master Tracker. Look your fill!' He thrust his trembling arm forward toward the chair. The courtiers stepped farther back, leaving the chair alone in a pool of candlelight.

Urged thus by the king, Crispin had no choice but to move forward under the glares and suspicious gazes of the knights and noblemen. The sheriffs were there as well, and the new sheriffs whispered hungrily to each other, all the while keeping their eyes fixed on Crispin.

Jack's tentative steps were right behind his master. Surely the king could not blame Crispin for whatever was wrong.

He looked at the chair, King Edward I's Coronation Chair, with its straight back rising to a triangular point with two tall finials at its shoulders, its carved arms and gilt lions for feet at each corner. The back was painted a dark blue with birds and scrollwork in gold leaf. And the cushion was a dark velvet, so dark it looked like the night sky. All that was left of the explosion was a wisp of smoke curling upward. Nothing seemed amiss. The chair was in good order. The Stone . . .

'God's blood,' Crispin whispered.

The Stone of Destiny, the rectangular Stone that fitted neatly in a niche made for it beneath the seat, the Stone that Edward I had captured from the Scots nearly one hundred years before and put in the chair to show his dominion over them, was gone. In its place was left only a hollow and scattered bits of plaster.

TWO

Crispin glanced toward Richard.

'Yes, Guest. You've marked it well. The Stone of Destiny is gone!' Richard reared toward him. 'What have you done with it?'

'Sire? On my honor, I had nothing to do with its disappearance.'

'On your honor? As if that can be relied upon.'

Crispin gritted his teeth but said nothing.

Richard looked him over with disdain. Crispin knew the precise moment he noticed the sword at his hip. Richard's eyes widened, and he jabbed a finger toward it. 'What is *that*? How dare you! Your sword was taken from you, and you have the gall to wear one in our presence?'

Folly, vanity. He began to regret ever listening to Jack that morning.

'Surrender it at once!'

Hesitating too long brought down Richard's wrath. The king signaled to his knights. 'Remove the sword from that man,' he ordered.

Crispin stepped back and drew it. The king's eyes rounded further, until Crispin turned it in his hands and presented it hilt forward toward the king. He said nothing, even as he glanced toward a pale Henry Derby, as he watched over the shoulder of Nottingham.

Richard grabbed the hilt before his knights could reach it. They stopped as the king read the inscription etched onto the blade: *A donum a Henricus Lancastriae ad Crispinus Guest–habet Ius* – A gift from Henry Lancaster to Crispin Guest – He Has the Right.

Richard jerked his head toward Henry who paled still further. Turning, Richard presented the sword blade toward his cousin. 'My Lord Derby,' he said, voice tight. 'What is this?'

Henry stepped out into the open. 'As it says, sire. Master Guest saved my life, my house. He earned his reward. And I ordered the inscription to be there to prove his right.'

'Only the king may confer such on the likes of a traitor, my lord.'

'Forgive me, sire. But he did the house of Lancaster *and* the kingdom a great service. It needed a proper reward. Would you have me go back on my word?'

'And yet you would make me go back on mine? Did I not forbid this man to ever carry a sword again?'

'Your grace, much time has passed. And Master Guest has proved his loyalty . . .'

'To you. Not to me.'

'To you as well, my liege. To the crown.'

Richard's jaw worked as he tightened his hold on the sword hilt. Crispin groaned inside. If Richard broke this sword too how could he bear it? He had lived so long in ignominy, so long. The sword was something special. Denied to him for eleven years, this gift from Lancaster's son was at least some recompense for his exile. It wasn't something he flaunted in London. On the few occasions he'd found it necessary to brandish it in the last year, its appearance was always met with deep suspicion, but no one could deny the inscription Henry had caused to be there on the blade.

Richard's eyes flicked toward Crispin and locked. Still holding the sword forth, he sauntered toward Crispin as if ready to stab him with it. 'Do you think you deserve this, Guest? Do you think you deserve to wear a sword after your traitorous deeds?'

He swallowed. His mouth had gone dry, and his lips seemed to stick together. 'No,' he whispered gruffly.

The king was taken aback. 'By my life. Did you say "no"?'

Slowly, Crispin nodded. 'Your grace. I *know* I do not deserve it . . . after . . . everything.'

It was the truth. Though he valued the gift, though he felt a part of himself restored by it, it was a bitter offering. For it could not erase the guilt nor the deaths of the other conspirators who had not been as fortunate as to have benefited from the love and trust of the duke of Lancaster. The duke had not begged for *their* lives.

Richard glowered, assessing the blade. It was an old sword. Probably garnered from Henry's weapon's stores. Not a particularly handsome blade. It was well worn and even the braided wire twining round the leather grip of the hilt was tarnished and rubbed down flat in places. No jewel sat atop the pommel. No foliate carving ornamented the crossguard. It was a serviceable sword, suited to any man-at-arms. Perhaps Henry had chosen it purposely for that reason. Its only ornament, in fact, was the etched inscription along the blade, the newest thing about it.

King Richard took a breath, took another. Crispin had saved *his* life, too. And the king had offered to restore his knighthood and lands, if only Crispin would grovel for it. He could not make himself do it, had refused it. And there wasn't a day gone by when he didn't repeat that moment in his mind, allow it to play differently. Would it have been worth it to give up his last scrap of honor?

Richard edged the sword forward. Perhaps he was thinking of that time, too. The blade was nearly at Crispin's gut when he stopped. 'Take it,' he growled. 'Take it, damn you.'

He had no choice but to grab it by the blade. When he did, Richard stepped closer and, with the sword held tight to his side, slid it forward across Crispin's palm, slicing two thin lines. 'Swear to me in your own blood that you will be loyal to the crown.'

Crispin hissed at the sharp pain and watched his blood drip upon the church floor. He gripped the sword tighter, raising his gaze defiantly once more to the king's.

'I do so swear, your grace, to protect England's crown, its people . . . and you, my king.'

Richard's languid lids lowered over his eyes. He held the sword tightly for another long moment before slowly letting it go. Crispin carefully pulled it in, grabbed the hilt with his bloodied hand, and sheathed it smartly.

Richard continued his pointed inspection of Crispin's person. When he spoke, Crispin at first thought he was addressing him, but decided it must have been directed toward the abbot. 'We need a place to talk. Where can we go, Lord Abbot?'

'The chapter house,' said Abbot William steadily. Crispin did not know the abbot well, but he knew he was a cool man who had faced emperors and popes on his many missions for the abbey while he served as archdeacon. One irate King of England surely could not fluster him.

He gestured for the king to follow and turned on his heel, his cassock flowing over his slippered feet.

The king cast a glance over his courtiers and said in passing, 'Only Guest. And his servant.'

'But, sire!' cried his chancellor.

Richard never broke his stride and called over his shoulder, 'Must we repeat ourselves?'

It took only another moment more of the seething men's eyes upon him before Crispin strode forward, aware of a trembling Jack at his elbow.

A kerchief was thrust into his bloody hand. He looked down.

Jack had gotten it from God-knew-where, but Crispin was grateful and clutched it tight to sop up the blood.

He followed Richard at a good distance, back through the south crossing, along the east arcade, and to a narrow passage that opened into the octagonal chapter house. Upheld by one center pillar, the vaulted ceiling was a riot of stone ribs and cross-ribbing. The large space was surrounded by reticulated windows, tall and arched, illuminating the room with bright autumn sunlight. Crispin squinted from the difference between the dark cathedral to the suddenly lit space.

Stools and benches were arranged in a circle, facing the abbot's chair at the pillar, and Richard made for that center chair. Abbot William had come in with them, and he waited on the king's pleasure in the doorway as to whether he was to vacate his own chapter house or not.

Crispin stood before the king as Richard sat, leaning his elbow heavily on the chair arm. He pinched his lower lip between two fingers and stared at the tile floor. Crispin could hear Jack's panting breaths behind him. He longed to comfort the boy but didn't know how, or if he could. He hadn't a clue as to why the king had taken them aside with only the abbot for a chaperon.

Stealing a glance at Abbot William, Crispin saw only the monk's austere features. If he had met Abbot William on the street, he would have taken the man for a merchant, for he had that kind of face, with fleshy cheeks, round nose, and prominent chin. The abbot's pale blue eyes skimmed Crispin. No more than that. Crispin had had a lifelong relationship with the abbot's predecessor, Abbot Nicholas de Litlyngton, but with Colchester, none at all.

The king cleared his throat. 'There was . . . an explosion of some kind.'

Crispin nodded.

'Was the Stone demolished?'

Crispin looked first at the abbot, but the monk merely gazed at Crispin. The king continued to stare at the floor.

Crispin sidled closer. 'The . . . the chair would have likely blown up with it, your grace. There was no damage to it, as far as I could see on so cursory an inspection.'

Richard nodded, still glaring at the floor. 'And so. It was stolen.'

'It . . . would appear so, your grace. And something similar put in its place.'

Richard turned his head at last and fixed Crispin with the same glare he had bestowed upon the floor. 'They say . . . you find things.'

Crispin nodded, breathless that he now knew where this was headed.

'Our army lost a battle not too long ago. In Scotland.'

'I . . . had heard the news. At Otterburn . . .'

'Yes,' Richard hissed. 'First it was these damned lords peering over our shoulder, bringing an army against us. My dear cousin at its head! No peace, no safe harbor from them. Our counselors routed. Ex . . . executed.' His voice broke on the last, face anguished. 'You almost got your wish, Guest.' He flicked his fingers toward his head. 'This crown, so solid a thing, did not feel as solid a year ago. It was brittle, like frozen steel. Easily shattered.'

Crispin wanted to look away from the torment in the king's eyes, but knew he could not afford to offend.

'We are the anointed of God.' He gestured toward his person. 'And yet we were to heel to these lords like a hound. A *hound*!'

Richard breathed heavily, breath clouding in the cold and empty chamber, despite its brightness. Abbot William, accustomed as he was to waiting, stood by unmoving, emotionless, offering neither comfort nor counsel.

'Wolves, all of them,' Richard went on hoarsely. 'And now this. I tell you, Guest, I cannot stomach one more loss, one more blot against my good name. If the Scots rise up and rebel, England will lose them, lose that which my ancestor King Edward I gained. I cannot risk it. The Stone *must* be returned to *me*!'

'I see,' said Crispin quietly.

It was as if Richard suddenly realized Crispin was there. His pronouns changed back again to *pluralis majestatis*. 'It is more than a symbol of our dominion over the Scots. It is the very seat of power. The throne on which the crown is conferred. If *we* lost it, what would be said about *us*?'

Crispin said nothing. What was there to say?

'Do you understand, Guest? We want it found. We want *you* to find it.'

'I . . . will try.'

'Try?' He shot to his feet. '*Try* is not an option.' Jack, hoping to appear as small as possible in Crispin's shadow, suddenly caught Richard's attention, and the king strode toward him. Jack cowered back, but Richard grabbed him, and the boy let out a yelp. He slung his arm around Jack's neck, slamming him to his chest, and drew his bejeweled dagger. Crispin made an involuntary step forward before he froze.

'Your majesty, please!'

'Maybe you need an incentive, Guest.' Richard snarled over his shoulder toward Colchester, 'Go and fetch my guards. Quickly now.'

The abbot hurried to obey and disappeared through the chamber door.

Richard glared, his teeth visible with a grimace. 'And so we are alone. Now is the time. You can slay me as you had wanted to twelve years ago. It would be easy. Oh, you'd never escape this room alive, but it could be done.' He raised the knife blade to Jack's throat, and the boy tightened his lips over a whimper. Richard glanced down at the boy in his grip. 'Is it this you fear? Is this what keeps you at bay? This boy?'

'No, sire. I have no wish to dispatch my king.'

'So you say. But here is your chance.' He lowered the knife and held it at arm's length. 'Be a martyr.'

Crispin shook his head. 'I have no such desire, your grace. It appears you do not know me, after all.'

Richard frowned. 'Do I not?'

The king's guards clattered in, with guisarmes held forth. Their mail shimmered in the bright light.

The blade was back at Jack's throat. 'Harken unto me, Guest. You will find the Stone in three days. You will recover it for us, for the kingdom, or this boy will die the death of a traitor, for what else is he who consorts with traitors?'

Heart hammering, Crispin stepped forward, even as the guards lowered their spears toward him. 'Your majesty,' said Crispin softly. He swallowed. 'I beg you . . .'

'Three days, Guest. Before the Commons meet again. We will not appear weak without the Stone back in its place beneath the Coronation Chair before our own parliament. Do you understand us?'

Crispin stared into Jack's terrified eyes. 'But . . . surely you must realize that the Stone was taken some days ago.'

'That is your concern, not ours. Find it in three days or the boy dies.'

THREE

C rispin watched helplessly as Jack was marched away by the guards. The boy looked back once, eyes wide with terror. Crispin aimed a glare at Richard, whose smug expression made him tighten his fist so he would not be tempted to draw sword or dagger. He could not in the end, for he *had* meant his oath.

Besides, a guard had remained behind.

'Sire, please . . .' Crispin pleaded.

Richard paid him no further heed and swept out of the chamber, followed close by his guard. Only William de Colchester stayed and watched Crispin dispassionately.

'The king,' he said after a long pause, long after the echoed steps of the king and his guard had died away, 'does not appear to like you much.'

Crispin slowly counted to ten in his head. He decided he would very much like to strike the abbot, but knew he needed the man's help to investigate.

'Yes,' he bit out, turning back toward the exit. 'I need to see the Coronation Chair.' Without waiting for the abbot's permission, he stalked toward the door and passed through it. The king and his retinue – and Jack Tucker – were already gone, leaving only the new sheriffs and some monks in the church. He tried not to think of Jack, of where they would take him, and what might befall him if he failed . . . No. He *could* not fail. Must not.

Taking a breath, he approached the chair, but the sheriffs stepped in his way. One put his hand on Crispin's chest to bar him from moving forward.

'That's quite close enough,' said one. 'Who are you?'

They looked alike. They could have been brothers, for all Crispin knew. Both with light hair, both of medium height, medium girth. Same pale faces and somber eyes. He bowed to them both. 'I am Crispin Guest, my lords. Do I have the honor to meet Sheriff Carlylle or Sheriff Austin?'

The man straightened his green houppelande and postured. 'I am soon to be Sheriff Carlylle. Crispin Guest, you say? Ah! Fastolf and Venour warned us about you.'

The other, in a blue houppelande, came up beside his companion. 'So this is Guest.' He looked Crispin up and down. 'I suppose you mean to trouble us immediately, ever before we take office.'

'It is urgent, my lords. The king himself commissioned me to investigate this matter.' He gestured toward the chair.

Carlylle stepped aside. 'Far be it from me to interfere with the infamous Tracker. Especially when he is so commissioned.'

Crispin didn't have time to decide whether he was sincere or not. He pushed ahead and knelt immediately before the chair. A shadow passed over the floor and he turned. William de Colchester stood, hands within his cassock sleeves.

Crispin reached for the white fragments surrounding the area, the shattered remains of . . . something.

'My Lord Abbot,' he said, picking up one of the shards and eyeing it closely. 'When did you last see the Stone in its place?'

'Only moments before I went out to accompany the procession.'

'An hour or so ago, then, would you say?'

'Yes. Or so.'

The shard was chalky and had shattered completely. He looked about and the largest piece was only the size of a child's hand. He retrieved one and turned it. One side was painted a mottled gray color, while inside was white. He sniffed it. Lime plaster.

'I doubt that you looked very carefully.' He placated with a gesture before the abbot could protest. 'Oh, I mean no disrespect. But doubtless you have passed the chair many a time and gave it only a cursory glance. The Stone would lie in the shadow under the seat here.' He pointed to the rectangular space designed to hold the Stone. 'You would have assumed that the object was in fact the Stone of Destiny, as you expected to see. But this—' He showed the abbot the shard. 'This would have appeared just enough like the true Stone to pass the musters. It looks to have been a false stone made of plaster. Look here.' He handed the piece to Colchester and stood.

The abbot examined it carefully. 'Amazing. Diabolical.'

'Yes. It means the Stone was replaced with a false one. But it is difficult to say how long ago that was. I fear the Stone might be long gone.' And if that were so, then Jack . . .

'Then why this performance, for want of a better word?' asked the abbot. 'Why explode it while all were present? If the perpetrators wished harm to the king, then why not make an attempt upon his person?'

'Why indeed? Perhaps because they wanted more to discredit than to physically hurt. Detonate their stone at a time when most of court was here.'

'And such a demonstration of fire and destruction! How was it achieved?'

'Explosive powder. The same used for cannons and for gonnes. But it meant that the instigator was present to fire it off.'

'He could have easily been disguised as a monk,' said the abbot thoughtfully.

'Precisely what I was thinking.'

Abbot William nodded toward Crispin. 'I am beginning to see what our late brother Nicholas de Litlyngton so liked about you, Master Guest.'

'We were friends.'

'It is good to have clever friends.'

'*Without friends no one would choose to live, though he had all other goods.*' He turned a sheepish expression to the stone-faced abbot. 'Forgive me, my Lord Abbot. It is my custom to quote my favorite philosopher, Aristotle. I often do so without thinking, I'm afraid.'

'An interesting habit,' he said and tossed the plaster shard away. 'How will you proceed?'

He sagged and touched one finial of the chair's back, before running his hand through his hair. 'I don't know. Has the abbey received any threats? Any letters?'

'None that I have been aware of.'

'Who would have been responsible for cleaning the chair? Surely someone applying polish to the wood would have noticed a difference in the Stone on close inspection? It might give us a better idea as to when the switch was made.'

Colchester nodded. 'I will ask the chamberlain.' He turned and motioned toward a dark corner and only when a monk emerged from the shadows did Crispin realize he had been there all along, waiting on his abbot . . . or protecting him from Crispin, no doubt. 'Fetch him immediately.'

The abbot went back to his stoic stance of waiting, hands crossed over each other. Crispin could not stand immobile. He strode to the chair instead and walked around it as far as he could. The chair was situated opposite of Edward the Confessor's tomb. Candles on stands were positioned at each corner of the sepulcher, flickering their bright light.

Leaning over to examine the chair's chipping paint, the scratches from the explosion, Crispin shook his head in wonder. If more powder had been used, it could very well have blown up the chair. The thief either knew his business well or was extraordinarily lucky.

It wasn't long that a monk came striding toward them. His hair was nearly as red as Jack's, and he bowed to his abbot and looked down his nose at Crispin. 'My Lord Abbot,' he said with a distinct northern accent. Crispin narrowed his eyes.

The monk glanced past him to the chair, and he seemed to startle back.

'Brother Crìsdean, could you tell me when was the last time you cleaned the Coronation Chair.'

'Och, look at it!' He staggered forward, nearly shoving Crispin aside, and knelt before the chair. 'What happened?'

'Were you not at the Mass?' asked Crispin.

He picked up a few shards and scrutinized them. 'I was not. Someone had to make certain the refectory was ready for our royal visitors. My Lord Abbot insisted.'

'When did you last clean the chair, Brother?' Crispin said again.

He turned then, wild puzzlement on his features. 'What difference could it possibly make?'

'More than you think. The Stone—'

'The Stone! Jesus, the Stone!'

Crispin sighed. Was it an act? Had the man only just now noticed the absence of the Stone? And, if so, would he have noticed a difference when he last cleaned the chair?

'Just so,' he said mildly. 'If you could tell me . . .'

Abruptly, the monk turned his back. 'What happened, my Lord Abbot?'

Abbot William was the very image of patience. He shrugged a careless gesture toward Crispin, and the monk reluctantly faced him again.

'As I was saying,' Crispin went on. 'When was the last time you cleaned this chair? Did you notice anything amiss?'

'Yesterday,' he said in bewilderment.

'And the Stone. Do you recollect whether you saw anything strange about it?'

'No. On my life. It was the same as it always was. I wiped its surface as well. It was the Stone. The same. The iron rings were there.'

'Iron rings?'

'Yes.' He seemed to come out of his stupor and raised his face to Crispin's. 'The iron staples and rings, used for carrying the Stone. It has always had them.'

'I see. I have never had occasion to be that close to the Coronation Chair, nor to scrutinize the Stone before.'

'Naturally.' His accent seemed to thicken the more irritated he became.

'And where do you hail from, Brother *Crìsdean*?'

The monk raised his chin. 'And why would you care?'

'Because the Stone was stolen and a false one in its place was blown up to most dramatic effect. And the perpetrators were most certainly Scottish rebels.'

'Oh, I see. And the first Scot you come across is the guilty one, eh? Such a fine reputation you have, Master Guest. Surely I should be dragged away forthwith in chains!'

'Now, Brother,' warned Abbot William. 'No one is accusing you. Nor are we set to drag you away in chains. Master Guest was merely exercising his considerable skills of observation.' A flicker of a smile curved his lips but was instantly gone again.

'You may very well wish to mock me,' Crispin snarled. 'But I have been tasked with finding the Stone, and for this my apprentice's life hangs in the balance. It is hardly a laughing matter, my Lord *Abbot*.'

The abbot closed his eyes and bowed. 'Indeed. Forgive me, Master Guest. Is there more you wish to ask of my monk?'

So much more, he thought. 'No more for now,' he said instead.

The monk acknowledged them both with a bow and pivoted before hurrying away. He looked back once over his shoulder to glare at Crispin, but the shadows soon swallowed him.

The abbot looked back at his retreating monk curiously. 'You don't suspect him, do you?'

'I suspect everyone,' Crispin growled. He raked his fingers through his hair again. Something like this was difficult enough without the added complication of Jack's incarceration. 'How long has he been a monk here, Father Abbot?'

Colchester's normally blank features twisted in a frown. He slipped his hands inside his sleeves. 'Less than a year. He came from another monastery. In . . . in the north.'

'If I were you, I'd keep an eye on him.' Crispin turned to leave.

'Where do you go now, Master Guest?'

'I must follow a trail that is a day old. I am grateful it is not older.' He glanced over his shoulder. 'Please. Pray for a swift outcome. For Jack Tucker's sake.'

'That I shall, Master Guest. And for you as well.'

Crispin ducked his head in thanks before he walked in stiff strides down the ambulatory and past chattering groups of men still lingering in the nave.

When he stepped outside into the abbey's courtyard he breathed deep. What the hell was he to do now? *Organize your thoughts, Crispin.* He breathed again. Perhaps it would be best to seek out the place where the gunpowder might have been acquired. There weren't likely many places. Perhaps the Palace. Perhaps the Tower. He had to think. Whom could he ask? Lancaster? But he was still in Spain. Henry? He might know. He could send Jack to get a message . . .

How much he relied on the boy. How accustomed he had become to having him beside him. Stoking his fires, fetching the water, caring for him. And now . . .

Goddamn Richard! What was the man thinking? He was frightened, that was certain. And like a frightened beast he lashed out where he least should. If only . . .

A loud caw startled him. He looked down. A large raven had lighted on the path before him. 'Shoo! Begone!' He waved his hand at the bird, but it only hopped back a few paces before opening its dark beak again and crying its raucous call.

'I haven't time for this.' Crispin made a wide berth around the bird, but the raven hopped to stand before him again. It cawed once more, opened its wings, and flapped till it lighted on a fence post.

Crispin attempted to skirt it again but was bombarded with a cascade of caws. The bird hopped farther along the fence as if it was leading him.

Crispin looked around. A trained bird? Someone's idea of a jest?

He drew his sword halfway from its scabbard before he thought better of it. Was he to be seen on the street swiping at a bird? They'd think him mad. He took a step forward, and the bird cut him off.

He stepped to the side and was rewarded with hoarse cawing. He stepped the other way, and the bird took flight ahead of him. *What madness is this?*

Just to test it again, he made tracks in the opposite direction, and the bird was back, soaring over his head and alighting on the roof's eave before him. It scolded, glaring with tiny beady eyes.

'I'm a fool for certain,' he muttered and pivoted, returning to the path the bird seemed to want him to take.

Just as he made to skirt the bird again, it darted forward, landed on his scrip, and plucked at it, nearly getting to his money pouch inside. 'What the hell?' Without its prize, the bird flapped and called, flying off. But something clicked in Crispin's memory. He still felt the fool, but he trotted after the bird now, keeping it within his sight as it wheeled across the rooftops.

The bird flew ahead but waited for him on posts, ale stakes, and roof tops when he fell behind. 'I'm following, damn you,' he muttered, wondering why he was wasting his precious time on this when urgent matters awaited. But each time he tried to abandon the bird, it pursued him, sometimes so close he feared it would bite him. He sent up a silent prayer for patience and followed down more winding lanes. He felt more and more foolish until the bird seemed to be homing in on somewhere in particular.

At the end of a lane, the way was blocked by a ramshackle house with slate shingles, many of which were missing. The bird flew straight through the open doorway, and Crispin rested his hand on his sword pommel. 'Well! Let us excise this mystery forthwith.' He marched forward and didn't knock as he bent to pass under the low lintel.

The room was dark and vacant, except for a stool and a table with three legs. The hearth was cold, and shadows slanted over the walls. A ladder stretching up to a loft stood to his right. He heard a rustle, and figured it was the bird settling on a perch in the loft. 'Well?' said Crispin. 'Is anyone here?'

'Only me,' said a gravelly voice behind him.

FOUR

Crispin turned, fully expecting the sight of the old man with a tattered eye patch over one eye. He folded his arms over his chest when the raven lighted on the old man's shoulders.

'I'll be damned,' said the man in a roughened voice. 'Is that Crispin Guest?'

'It is, you old thief. This can't be the same bird from all those years ago.'

The man chuckled and rubbed his gray chin stubble. 'Och me, no. Sir Ingram has long since passed. This is Lady Agnes.' He raised his finger to the dark bird, and she nibbled affectionately on the digit. 'And a right smart *fitheach*.'

'Your "Lady Agnes" tried to pilfer my purse. You wouldn't be up to your old tricks again, would you, Domhnall?'

'Me? Ah, Master Crispin. An old man such as m'self?'

'How else did she get into the habit of seeking out purses?'

'They like shiny things. Coins, jewelry.' He shrugged. 'I canna seem to break her of the habit.'

'Of course not.' He looked around the barren room. Small, few bits of furniture, a sputtering fire in the mostly broken hearth. Crispin usually only concerned himself with the hardened criminal, those willing to commit violence, rape, or extortion. He had always been inclined to let the petty thief off with a warning. And Domhnall had been no exception. His trained bird had done much thievery over the years, but the man had been clever and had done Crispin a favor or two, and so Crispin had been willing to look the other way.

He shuffled his feet on the dusty floor. 'You're a northerner, aren't you?'

Domhnall lowered himself to a rickety stool and fed the bird on his shoulder scraps of dried meat he pulled from a pouch at his belt. It looked to be nearly the only food on the premises.

The man squinted his remaining eye at Crispin. 'That had a very accusing tone to it, sir.'

'Forgive me. I had not meant it to come out that way.' He crouched to be at the man's height, looking him in the eye. 'It is just that I seem to be plagued of late with your countrymen.'

'Oh? How so?'

How much to say? 'Something of great import was stolen. I have reason to believe that Scottish rebels had something to do with it.'

'Rebels, you say? Well. That is something, then, isn't it? Do you think I'm a rebel?'

'I wouldn't put it past you . . . but no. I do not.'

He chuckled again and lifted the bird from his shoulder with a finger. Its toes wrapped about it as he lifted higher and shook his hand, sending the bird flying to its perch. She cawed once at Crispin, as if he had something to do with it, and commenced grooming her feathers. 'I'm too old for such nonsense in any case. And too set in my ways to return to Scotland. I've no family and my clan has long forgotten me, no doubt. No, Westminster is now my home.'

'I am glad to hear it. Would you care to make some coin?'

The old man's jovial features suddenly turned to a scowl. 'Just because I am an old man doesn't mean I'd betray my countrymen and king. That's the Scottish king I speak of, in case you didna get my meaning.'

'I understood you, Master Domhnall. I feared my request might put you at odds with your countrymen.' He rose and bowed. 'My apologies. Forgive this intrusion, then.' Crispin turned to leave.

'Wait.' Domhnall rose slowly, grunting. 'Och, these old bones. And with another winter coming on, too. Maybe you'd best explain, Master Crispin, and then I'll tell you whether you insult me or not. After all, a full coin purse can go a long way to assuage my indignity.'

Crispin gave the room another glance before walking to the man's meager fire. 'Very well. I shall have to trust you even as you put your trust in me. The Coronation Chair at Westminster has lost its Stone.'

'Eh?' The bushy brows over Domhnall's hazel eye and eye patch gradually rose. 'Do you mean to say . . . God's toes. The Stone of Scone has been liberated?'

'*Stolen*, yes.'

Domhnall offered a sly smile. 'Ha! Well.' He shrugged. 'There's a difference of opinion, then.'

Crispin grimaced, thinking of the empty space under the chair. 'The king is not best pleased.'

'No. I reckon not.'

'And as a consequence has taken my apprentice hostage. I have three days to find it or he'll kill the boy.'

Domhnall's smile slipped away. 'Oh.' He hobbled forward toward the raven on its perch and petted the dark feathers. The bird, for her part, seemed to coo at his ministrations. 'Oh, that is a harsh thing.'

'Yes,' he said tightly.

'I always admired the fact that you took him in, Master Crispin. Him a lowly cutpurse. One of our own, so to speak. No, Jack doesn't deserve that.'

'You see my dilemma.'

'Aye.' The bird left the perch to light upon his shoulder again. She gently toyed with his eye patch. 'I'd no see harm come to young Master Jack,' he said, lightly batting the bird away. Lady Agnes sat back, eyeing Crispin with the cock of her head. 'What sort of help would you be needing?'

Crispin sighed with relief. 'I would mostly need you to keep your ears and eyes open.'

He tapped the eye patch. 'Only the one left, but it's as good as two.'

'And report to me if you hear anything of this plot. But Master Domhnall, our time is very short.'

'Isn't it always, bless the Lord? And yet, plots there are aplenty on the streets of London and Westminster. Those men that hold the Stone might be reasoned with.'

Crispin laughed humorlessly. 'My friend, you have a very naïve view of the world if you believe that. Why, by God's grace, would they wish to do so?'

'For money, of course. Many a high and mighty ideal can be swayed thus.' Crispin gave him a withering look. 'Oh, not you of course, Master Crispin. Who has not heard the tales of the Tracker?'

'Do you mean to say that they hold the thing for ransom? That all the king need do is give them their bag of gold and they would relinquish it? I think it far too valuable to trade it for gold. In many men's eyes, it represents the king's foot on the neck of Scotland. You cannot put a price on that. It can be a banner for open rebellion, and Richard knows it.'

'You know a great deal of such matters for a southerner.'

'I was a warrior, remember? My head was bent over many a map of strategy. Only a fool would bargain the Stone for money when so much time and preparation went into its theft.'

'There's a saying in my country, Master Crispin: *Cùm do chù ri leigeadh.* "Hold back your dog till the deer falls." There's more here than meets the eye.'

'How do you reckon that?'

'It's hiding under the thatch.'

'Your metaphors are aggrieving my head.'

'Tell me how the Stone was taken.'

Crispin gauged the old man again. The cagey bastard knew more than at first appeared. 'It was replaced with a fake some days ago, and the fake exploded during Mass.'

'Ah!' The man scrubbed at his chin again. 'It was no to be a secret until it was discovered gone, then. They could have left the fake there for days, months before it was discovered. But no. They wanted this to strike fear in King Richard's heart. They wanted to let all the kingdom know what they were about. This is not the work of mere rebels but of a man of wealth with long arms.'

Crispin nodded. 'A lord.'

'Aye. And no just any laird. What of all the uprisings in the north of late?'

'Yes, what of them?'

Crispin waited for more, but the man simply shuffled back to his stool and sat.

'I will think on it, Master Crispin. And I will let you know.'

Dismissed, Crispin saw no other course but to leave. He reached into his scrip, wincing from the cut on his hand, and pulled out his money pouch. Taking two coins, they were suddenly snatched out of his hand by a snapping beak and the whoosh of dark wings.

Domhnall laughed and accepted the coins Lady Agnes dropped into his open palm. 'Now you see, that is a fine servant.'

'Yes. As is Jack Tucker.'

The old man blinked his rheumy eye. 'I have no forgotten, Master Crispin.' He tucked the coins into his own pouch and gave the raven a bit of dried meat. 'You can rely on me.'

Crispin bowed. 'I thank you, Master Domhnall.'

'If I were you,' called the old man just as Crispin reached the threshold, 'I might ask at the Keys Tavern. It is known that many of my countrymen favor the place.'

'The Keys. And whom do I ask for? Rebels?'

'Och no. Give your name. They'll know who you are and your purpose.'

Crispin gave him a nod of thanks and passed through the open door.

Once on the street he searched about, trying to get his bearings. Where was he? That damned bird had led him there from Westminster Abbey. He glanced above the rooftops and reckoned in which direction the Strand lay. It was a main thoroughfare between London and Westminster. There. That was the direction. He took a few steps, looked back at the strange hovel, and moved forward. Domhnall was a tough old bird – as tough as the birds he trained. And Crispin knew he was as good as his word.

The streets were bustling. Men and women shopkeepers busied themselves, dusting off their wares. Young apprentices hurried, carrying wooden pails of water, or fetching bundled sticks for fuel. Dogs followed the boys, either chasing them in fun, or looking for scraps. A beggar or two stalked in the shadows. Westminster was very much like London in most respects.

He made it to the Strand. In one direction lay Charing Cross and the palace. In the other was this alehouse. He set off east, looking for the ale stake and the sign of the keys.

The road was full of carts, those being pulled by people and many more being pulled by donkeys or oxen. Days were always busy along the hectic thoroughfare. Crispin found himself walking behind a man holding up a rack of roasted meats, and when the scent of them reached him, he realized he couldn't recall the last time he ate. He leaned forward to tap the man on the shoulder when a hand closed over his arm.

He whirled about, hand on his knife hilt. A man with a heavy swath of fur at the shoulders of his cloak smiled affably at Crispin. 'You are Crispin Guest,' he said in a northern dialect.

'Yes. Who are you?'

'The answer to a prayer, no doubt. Consider this your lucky day, meeting me.'

Crispin took a step back and studied the proud man skeptically. He was tall, broad-shouldered – though it could have mostly been fur – with a ruddy complexion and hair, and too confident an air about him. 'I ask again, who are you?'

'The name's McGuffin. And I have a feeling you'll want to be talking to me.'

'Do you? As soon as my business with this other is concluded, then we'll talk.' Crispin gave him one last appraisal and turned his back.

The man called after Crispin. 'Is it the Stone you're after?'

Slowly, Crispin turned.

McGuffin smiled and rocked on his heels. 'I have food and drink, too. Come.' He gestured and turned back toward Westminster.

Crispin looked up the street to what he thought was an ale stake, and then back to where the tall Scotsman was stalking up the street. With a weary sigh he strode forward, following the Scot.

FIVE

J ack Tucker stared mournfully at the door that shut him in the dark little room. He was inside the palace, this he knew, for there was many a time he and Master Crispin had crossed that forbidden threshold, sometimes on their own, stealthily, and sometimes with the help of the duke of Lancaster or his son Henry of Derby. He well remembered the long corridors and winding stairs. But he had no idea where exactly he was this time. All he knew was the meager hearth, the tiny window that he could not climb out of, and the barred door, with its great iron hinges that could not be undone.

'You're in for it now, Jack Tucker, and that's a certainty.' But he was also certain that Master Crispin would succeed. In time. He hoped. The man had never failed before. Well . . . seldom.

Would Richard really do it? Would he truly execute him for Master Crispin's failure? He gnawed on a fingernail and paced the short length of the room again, tugging his cloak tightly over his shoulders for warmth. No one had seen fit to bring him food, and he was hungry! But the hollowness in him warred with the feeling of butterflies and fear that ate at his gut. Had he been forgotten already? Would there be anything left to find once Master Crispin accomplished his task?

Jack equally prayed for his deliverance and cursed Richard's foolishness. Master Crispin would have investigated had Richard only asked. 'Slud!' He probably would have investigated anyway since it was in his nature that he could not leave a mystery alone.

Where was the sarding Stone? If it was Scottish rebels – and who else would it be? – then they could be over the border by now. And where would that leave *him*?

He shivered. 'Dead, that's what,' he whispered.

'Boy!'

Jack stared at the door. Someone had hissed at him through the wood. He stepped closer. The voice again. 'Boy! Are you in there?'

'Er . . . aye. Aye, I am. W-who are you?'

A key scraped in the lock, and the door whinged open. Too late Jack thought to ambush the guard. He was forced back away from the door instead and looked up to see . . . a lady of middle years.

Gowned in finery from the fox fur on her collar to the long drape of her embroidered skirts, she stood on the threshold, a lantern in her hand. Her small mouth was pursed, and her hazel eyes appraised him critically.

It took Jack far too long to remember his courtesy, and he bowed to her. 'My lady,' he squeaked.

'You are Crispin Guest's boy?'

'I am his apprentice, my lady. Jack Tucker.'

She smiled. The apple of her pale cheeks pinked. 'Jack Tucker is a fine name.'

He straightened. He liked her immediately.

Her smile vanished as she glanced back over her shoulder. Jack could see that she was alone, and even *he* knew a lady in the palace unescorted by a lady's maid was not a good and proper thing. 'We must hurry. I have permission to take you to, er, better lodgings. But I wish to avoid any difficulties.'

Jack looked back into the dank room, with its open window letting in the damp, its meager fire, already sputtering and likely to go out. But where was she taking him? Could he trust her? Did he have a choice?

He girded himself, nodded, and walked out. She closed and locked the door after him, tucking the key into the scrip at her belt.

'Come with me,' she said sharply, 'and don't tarry.'

Jack followed meekly. They climbed stairs from the undercroft to a dark corridor, lit only occasionally by oil lamps in wall niches. Not a well-used corridor, then. Little wonder he had been forgotten. He supposed it could have been worse. He could have been in a dungeon cell as he had been in Newgate, not nearly as clean or warm as the room he had just relinquished, and that was saying something.

He looked over her skirts, her veil. It was all he could see of her from behind. She was tall and stately, that was all he knew, for he longed to ask who she was but knew he had no right to do so.

The corridors brightened with more candles and oil lamps. She led him to some apartments that seemed familiar. Were these close to Lancaster's rooms? And the king's? Richard wouldn't like that. Jack ducked his head and looked around carefully, as if expecting the king to leap from the shadows.

She took a key from her scrip, fit it in the lock, and opened the door. A maid rushed to greet her.

'My lady! What—' And then she saw Jack and frowned. 'Who is this?'

'He is . . . our guest. Please lay the fire in the squire's room.'

She bowed to her lady and hurried to fetch a servant for the task. The lady blew out the candle in the lantern and set it on a table. She moved past an archway toward the hearth, whose warmth Jack could feel from the antechamber. She warmed her hands before the fire and finally turned her head toward Jack. 'Have you eaten, Master Tucker?'

His face reddened when his stomach did the answering in a loud grumble. He shook his head. 'No, my lady. I have not. Not since yesterday.'

'By Saint Katherine,' she sighed. 'Then you are quite lucky I found you when I did. Oh, Mylisant,' she said, as the maid returned. 'Please fetch Master Tucker here some victuals. Boys are always hungry, are they not?'

Mylisant hastened to comply and hurried past Jack before disappearing out the door.

'Come, come, Master Tucker. There's no need to stay out there. Come closer to the fire while we wait for food. Would you have wine?'

Jack crumpled the hem of his coat in his fingers before realizing he was doing it and let it go. He stepped haltingly through the arch. 'I . . . I . . .'

'Do pour us both some wine, Master Tucker. Just there.' She gestured to a sideboard where sat a flagon and several goblets made of silver.

Jack took a breath and walked with more purpose to the carved sideboard. By the rustling of cloth behind him, he reckoned that the lady must have taken a seat.

He grasped the flagon in his trembling hand. Closing his eyes, he composed himself. *You can do this, Jack. You've done it many times for Master Crispin's guests*. He opened his eyes again, poured the amber wine into the goblets – making certain he only poured himself a little – and brought them both to the fire. He bowed as he handed it to the lady.

'Thank you, Master Tucker. My, Crispin has taught you well. Where did you come from? Where did Crispin find you?'

Jack rocked on the balls of his feet. He held the goblet but did not drink, not until she took her first sip. It was only after he drank a little that he realized how dry his mouth had become. It was fine wine, far better fare than could be gotten at the Boar's Tusk. He cleared his throat. 'Master Crispin . . . he, uh, found me. On the streets. I, er . . .' He lowered his face. 'I was a lowly thief, my lady.'

'Dear me.' She looked at him anew from over the rim of her goblet.

'Aye.' He changed his weight from one foot to the other. 'But I don't do that no more . . . *any*more,' he added, screwing up his face in concentration. 'Master Crispin, he taught me to read and write. I am accomplished in Latin, French, and a bit of Greek, though the latter still don't make much sense to me.'

Her eyes glittered as she drank. 'I've always had trouble with languages myself.'

Jack blinked. He never imagined that the nobility had trouble with anything. 'And he's been teaching me arms practice,' he went on. 'I can use a sword!' He smiled, but it was short-lived. 'Master Crispin only has the one. His was taken away some years ago . . . as you probably know. But he wears a sword again, my lady, given to him by Lord Derby! It was a fine thing when he done that, my lady. My master. He deserved it. He was loyal to the house of Lancaster. And to England . . . and its king.' He said the last sourly. He couldn't help it. He wasn't adept at hiding his feelings behind subtlety, not like others he knew. Not like that cool and detached Abbot of Westminster Abbey.

'Of that I have no doubt,' she said quietly.

She continued to study Jack. He took a few sips of his wine while his eyes traversed the room, spying heavy curtains, a painted wall of a garden scene, the sideboard, a coffer, a small table, a tapestry, another two chairs, and by one of them, an embroidery stand with a cloth stretched across it with threads in many colors hanging free below it. Behind it stood three doors, probably leading to more antechambers and bed chambers.

'I wonder, Master Tucker, if you know who I am.'

Jack clutched the goblet between his hands. 'I'm sorry, my lady, but I do not. I would remember you in my prayers.'

'I am Lady Katherine. I used to be the governess in the duke of Lancaster's household.'

Jack rattled the name around in his head, trying to figure out if Crispin had mentioned her before. When it struck him of a sudden. 'Lady Katherine Swynford?' he muttered. Of course! Lancaster's longtime mistress. No wonder the rooms were familiar. They were next to Lancaster's apartments. And he well recalled what Master Crispin had said of the lady, how he disapproved of such conduct from his mentor. Jack was set to disapprove of her as well, except . . . Except that the lady had rescued him, or at least, removed him to a place where the waiting would be more comfortable. And he couldn't find it in his heart to disapprove at all. It would be like condemning the Madonna herself.

The lady seemed to have seen Jack's dilemma on his face. 'I see. Crispin *has* told you about me.'

'He . . . he . . .'

'I can imagine what he said.' She sighed and set her goblet aside. Jack felt awkward, standing, his empty goblet still clutched in his hand against his chest. 'He never approved of me and his grace. Well, to be honest, I never would have approved of such a thing myself. But love is . . . what it is.'

'Aye, my lady.'

She touched a ring on one of her fingers fondly before studying Jack anew. 'Have you found love yet, my young friend?'

He stared at the floor. 'Ah, me? No, my lady. It's a rough life on the Shambles. My master taught me to be wary.'

'The Shambles,' she repeated softly.

'Aye, my lady. That is where we reside. In the shadow of St Paul's.'

'I see.'

Jack spun the goblet's stem in his fingers before stepping toward the sideboard and setting it down. He stared down at the cupboard, at its intricate carvings of vines and grapes. 'What's to become of me? The king. He said . . . he said . . .'

'How did you ever get into this predicament, Master Tucker?'

He shook his head. 'Damned if I know,' he muttered, and then looked up, aghast. 'Oh! I beg your pardon, my lady!'

She smiled. 'There's no need. I've raised four sons, you know. Their language can be very . . . colorful.'

'But there's no call for me to be more lowly than I already am. Master Crispin would be ashamed.'

'And that matters to you?'

'Oh, aye!' He rushed toward her and knelt on one knee. 'I'd never have him ashamed of me, my lady, or have cause for him to be shamed. He's had enough, hasn't he?'

'I daresay he has. Despite what he has felt for me, I have always been charmed by Crispin. Let me think. Yes, I met him when he was . . . well, about your age.'

Jack smiled and rose. 'Truly?' He edged closer. 'What was he like back then?'

She settled on her seat. 'Well, he was quite a serious boy. I suppose losing a mother at such a young age as he did might make one serious. His father was often absent, but a mother and a mother's love . . . well. And he quite understood the responsibility awaiting him; his lands, his title. Servants and tenants. But it wasn't all serious brooding. He laughed, too. And played. With Lancaster's sons and . . . mine. He was talented with dance and song—'

'Master Crispin?'

'Yes, of course. He was quite accomplished in courtly ways. But nothing could quite divert him from his arms practice and horse-manship. He was a sight to behold on the lists.'

'Aye. I saw him myself.'

'Did you? How is that possible, Master Tucker? I do not think you could have seen him, for that was longer ago than you were born.'

'Oh, er . . .' Jack realized his mistake too late. Only a handful of people were to know about that particular incident of three years ago. His foolish loose tongue!

'Never mind,' she said kindly. 'But I was diverted. I was asking about *you*.'

'Oh.' He dusted off the knee of his stockings. 'Well . . . his majesty isn't fond of my master . . .' He looked back at her and her raised brow. Of course she would know that. All of court knew that. 'And at the Mass for the Holy Virgin this morning, the Stone of Destiny was stolen.'

'Yes.' Her solemn expression told him she knew this, too. Did not all of London and Westminster know of it by now?

'And the king, knowing my master's occupation, exhorted him to find it. And as surety, he – the king, that is – kept me as hostage. And worse.' He swallowed. Fear crept up his throat again. 'If my master fails to accomplish it before Parliament convenes in three days, I'm . . . I'm to die. As a traitor. But, my lady, I'm no traitor!

I never said naught against the king. And Master Crispin, he done naught, too. If only the king would see reason. Master Crispin would have felt honor bound to undertake the search. The king didn't have to . . . have to . . .'

Shameful, hot tears coursed down his face. What sort of man was he to weep in front of this woman? He turned away to hide it, but she was suddenly there beside him, and in the next instant, her arms enclosed him, and he found himself weeping into her samite gown.

Ah the feel of it! Her soft arms encircling him, the pleasant scent of her, like a garland of flowers, and her tender cooing. The sensations came from long ago, of his own mother's arms, and he wept that much more for thoughts of her.

Finally, he pushed himself away and smeared his hand over his face. 'Forgive me, my lady,' he said roughly. 'I have every faith in Master Crispin's abilities. Indeed, I have been his servant now for nigh on five years, and he seems to work miracles. But I have never been in such a position before. It . . . it doesn't seem right.'

'Dear Master Tucker. Of course it isn't. But his majesty . . . has a troubled association with your master, I'm afraid.'

'Aye. That's saying a mouthful.' He blinked away the wet of his lashes. 'But what of you, my lady? Will you not get into trouble for helping me? I wouldn't want that heaped upon my sins.'

'You mustn't vex yourself over that, Master Tucker. I can look after myself. But I couldn't leave you in that awful place. No matter what the king says.'

He shook his head and leaned against the sideboard. 'Oh, it's a sore thing. The Stone gone missing. My poor master. How will he ever find it? It might be long gone by now.'

'It might be.' She stood beside him. 'Surely you know how Crispin does his "tracking." What would *you* do?'

Yes, concentrate on that. Then the other fears could be swept aside for now. 'Well, it was a curious thing it being blowed up like that.'

'Yes, very curious.'

'And it wasn't the Stone at all. It was something made to look like the Stone. To hide the fact that it was already gone.'

'But if that were true, why call attention to it? Would it not be better to hide the fact that it had gone missing?'

'It might. Except that the Stone is mixed up in courtly matters.

The Scots were proud to have stolen it and bided their time. Maybe once it was back in Scotland, then it would be safe to shout it to the rooftops.' His heart hammered. If that were the case, then he was a dead man already.

'To embarrass the king.'

'Aye. And quite a show they made of it.'

She took the flagon and walked back to her goblet with it. Jack rushed after her. 'Here, my lady. Let *me* do that!'

'Nonsense, Tucker. I do know how to pour my own wine. Please sit down.'

She poured it and picked up her goblet, gesturing for Jack to take the seat opposite her. He did so gingerly, edging downward with the thought that he'd suddenly have to jump up again. And as soon as his bum hit the seat, the door swung open and a servant came in with a tray. Jack did jump up and offered to serve Lady Katherine.

'We will serve each other,' she said, motioning to the servant to place it on a table between them. Once the servant left, Jack took his place again and reached for the meats only after she had her own in hand.

He chewed thoughtfully. He did wonder at the strange and startling way the Stone was exploded. 'I wondered at it, at the way it was done. The Stone, I mean.'

'We must let Crispin do his work and await his word.'

'Aye, I suppose. There isn't much I can do to help him from here.' He swallowed the last of his food. 'My lady, are you certain it is well my being here? Where Master Crispin is concerned, his majesty's heart is hardened as much as Pharaoh's was. And I would see no harm come to you in your kindness.'

'I have friends at court. It is all well, Master Tucker. Now, perhaps if you have finished your repast, you will see to your new lodgings.'

'Aye, my lady.' He wiped his hands down his coat and followed her to the door she pointed out. It was a smaller door than the other two. When he opened it, he found a small but comfortable room . . . with a bed! He backed out of it. 'Oh no, my lady. There must be some mistake.'

'There is no mistake. We call it the squire's room, for many a squire has taken his ease in there when he was not attending his knight. And since your knight is otherwise occupied, it is fitting for you.'

'But my lady . . .' He peered in again. 'It is too rich for me.'

'Nonsense, Tucker. Go in. You must seem to be locked away to satisfy the king.'

'But there is a casement window . . .'

'And do you argue as much with your master?'

He offered her a sheepish smile. 'I am afraid I do, my lady. I thank you.' He stepped in the doorway again and stopped. 'And I will think on the problem of this missing Stone. It might be that we *can* help Master Crispin.'

'How so?'

'It seems likely to me – in order to accomplish such a scheme – that the culprits would have had to have help from the inside, so to speak. From the abbey or from court.'

'From court?'

'Aye. There are many who would embarrass Richard and not just the Scots. He might have enemies within. And that is something we are in a unique position to study further.' He ducked his head. 'Oh, begging your pardon, my lady. If it pleases you to do so, that is. It might be risky.'

She smiled. 'It might be interesting. I should like to help, at any rate, Master Tucker.' He nodded and went inside at last. She closed the door after him as he looked about the small room, but he noticed that she did not lock the door.

SIX

Crispin followed McGuffin back into Westminster and to a humble cottage just off the main bustling streets. His hand was never far from his dagger hilt, and he was just as ready to make use of his sword. Every now and then, the man would look back at Crispin, just to make certain he was still there. He'd smile, nod his head, and continue on. But once he reached the cottage he stopped at the threshold and gestured to Crispin to precede him.

There was no point in backing out now. He drew his sword – happy to have the length of steel with him – and kicked the door open.

He didn't quite know what he expected to find. The Stone, perhaps, sitting in pride of place on the table situated in the middle of the floor. Dark men plotting in the shadows.

What he found instead was a congenial gathering of northerners – four of them – crouched over their cups, laughing and singing, a fire crackling behind them in the hearth, and an aroma of food that made Crispin's belly groan.

The men stopped their laughing and drinking and turned as one toward Crispin and his brandished sword. Feeling foolish, Crispin sheathed it again and stood with his fists at his hips. 'Very well, McGuffin. I am here. Where is the Stone?'

The men looked to McGuffin who closed the door and carefully barred it.

Crispin's hand returned to his knife hilt. 'Am I a prisoner now?'

'Not at all, Master Guest. We simply need to talk with you without interruptions.' He strode into the room. 'Give the man some food and drink. He hungers.'

Some of the men cleared the way at the table and others brought forth a platter of meats and cheese. McGuffin grabbed a flagon and filled a cup with ale and thrust it toward Crispin. 'Drink, man. And sit. We'd talk with you.'

Crispin held the cup but did not drink. 'McGuffin . . .'

'Sit!' His large hands covered Crispin's shoulders and forced him down onto a chair. Crispin splashed his ale onto the table, but none of the men seemed to mind. They encouraged him to eat as they were doing, grabbing handfuls of the cooked flesh – pork, by the smell of it – and shoving it into their mouths.

McGuffin sat beside Crispin and gestured toward the hunks of pig. 'Go ahead, Master Guest. Feast with us.'

Crispin couldn't force the issue, not when he was outnumbered as he was. So he reached for the roasted meat and tore off a hunk. He bit into the juicy flesh and sighed at the taste. It had been a long while since he'd had anything as tasty and succulent as this.

He chewed for a while, eyes scanning the room. At the plump women who served them with jovial faces, at the men in their own jocularity, and the surroundings that spoke of money but not wealth.

When his gaze finally turned, the man was watching him. He leaned on the table, his cup never far from his mouth, hovering. 'I see your mind working, Master Guest. Good. I like a thinking man. This lot.' He waved his cup at them. 'I'd be lucky if two of them could summon the wits to outsmart a dog.'

Instead of anger and fighting words, the men swatted at him good-naturedly and laughed.

Crispin ate and drank, keeping his own council. He tried using his left hand, as the cut to his right palm stung, but it proved too clumsy, and he didn't wish to appear weak in these men's eyes. When he was satisfied and had wiped his mouth and hands on the tablecloth, he sat back with his ale and fastened his eyes on McGuffin's. 'Now what?'

'Now . . . we tell you about ourselves.'

The men suddenly stilled. Crispin's grip on his cup tightened. They wiped their faces, filled their own cups, and attended McGuffin.

'Now then,' said the Scot. 'Though it is true that we well know about the Stone's disappearance – who in Westminster or London does not? – alas, we had nae to do with it.'

Studying the men, Crispin could see they had nothing to offer. He slid his gaze back toward McGuffin, but kept his face impenetrable.

'Not for lack of trying, mind you. Oh, we applaud the scoundrels that did it, but we no ken them.'

'This was only a few hours ago. How could you have learned of it so quickly . . . unless you were somehow involved?'

He looked at Crispin and laughed. 'Ah well, "involved" is a verra loose term. Let us just say . . . I am *acquainted* with the idea of it.' The others chuckled in recognition. 'I am an affable man, Master Guest. I'm a loyal vassal and do my duty to my king. And I'm certainly no fool. And surely you'd no deal with a fool, would you, Master Guest?'

'I don't know. Would I?' He stared pointedly.

McGuffin laughed heartily at that, slapping Crispin on the back. 'A good jest indeed. No, Master Guest, I'm no fool. But I do know something of the Stone's disappearance. Aye.' He looked around as if worried the others would hear, and yet when he leaned in toward Crispin, he spoke just as loudly as before. 'Aye, we know about the Stone. And we know about you. And we've a mind to hire you, you see.'

'Hire me. For what?'

'Well now. It's not exactly as the Tracker might be used to. You see, we'd like to pay you. Pay you in good English coin.'

'To do what?'

'Why . . . to look the other way.'

Crispin forced his brows to stay where they were. 'To bribe me.'

'Och, such a feeble word that is. Does it no sound appealing to you, to gain coin just for getting out of the way?'

Crispin stood, his chair skidding back.

'Verra well, Master Guest. Sit down. Let us take another tack.' He gestured toward the chair.

Out of curiosity, Crispin sat and listened.

'If no to look the other way, then at least for another task. You see, we need to move something out of London. Something precious, and we canna afford to be followed, and we canna afford to be stopped. So we might need the expertise of a man with your . . . credentials. You see, you know the streets and alleys of London. You're an asset in many ways.'

'So now you wish to smuggle something out of the area.'

'Aye.'

'About . . . so big?' Crispin gestured something about the size of the Stone.

McGuffin smiled. 'No so big as that, Master Guest.'

'It isn't merely because I know London's streets. You could get any number of henchmen who wouldn't raise a question at all if you waved enough money under their noses. Why me in particular?'

McGuffin canted forward again. 'You are known to us, Master Guest. Indeed, to all of London and beyond. Twelve years ago, you committed treason and lived. We have to assume you've no love for King Richard still. That makes you the most logical man.'

Crispin rose again. 'You must think me a great fool indeed.'

The room fell silent.

'I am loyal to my king now,' he went on, 'no matter what transpired twelve years ago.' He heaved a sigh, composing himself. Quietly, he offered, 'I know what it means to your countrymen, but this simple act of thievery will mean the death of an innocent boy. Surely . . . surely some mercy is mete here. Surely you can see that a precious life means more than . . .' Their faces, so full of mirth before, had suddenly hardened into carved stone. When they had risked so much to steal the thing, there could be no mercy, not for a mere boy such as Jack. He conceded it to himself, but in the back of his mind, he began to scheme how he could steal it back.

He lowered his head and rubbed the rawness out of his eyes. 'I cannot help you,' he said wearily. 'I cannot turn a blind eye or help you in any way. I must succeed in this. You must understand.'

'We do, we do, Master Guest,' said McGuffin. His conciliatory tone gave Crispin fleeting hope. Perhaps they could be reasoned with. Perhaps . . . he could make some sort of bargain with him.

'However,' McGuffin went on. 'There is one small problem. We were so fairly certain that you would *not* help us . . . that we may have done something bad. Something that, on the face of it, would seem extreme. We truly wanted your help, you see.'

'And I told you I cannot. My apprentice's life hangs by a thread . . .'

'Och, aye, that is a shame. We didna anticipate that. But surely you must know, as a knight yourself, that sometimes the footman must be sacrificed for to win the battle. It is like chess. Do you play chess, Master Guest?'

'Yes.' He narrowed his eyes. What was his meaning now?

'And so. 'Tis also true on the chessboard, that the pawn is sacrificed for the greater good of the game.'

Crispin clenched his jaw. 'Jack Tucker is not a pawn!'

'Oh, but he is. King Richard has declared him so.' He pointed a finger in Crispin's face. Crispin didn't like it. 'We've heard about your apprentice, and Jesus-on-a-cross it's a shame. But our task matters more than him, or you, or me. And to that end, we had rather hoped you would help us. And if not for your own honor, than for the sake of the life of another.'

'Wait. What are you talking about? Jack Tucker is . . .'

'It's no about him. It's another. It's a sad fact, Master Guest, that when a man is well-known for holding his honor dear and for protecting the weak – as any knight should – that it shows the chink in his armor, so to speak. Your weakness, Master Guest, is your kindness. And as any good warrior knows, one must take advantage of any weakness when one is at war.'

He paused and the meaning sank home. Crispin edged forward, itching to draw his sword. 'What have you done?'

'We are . . . entertaining a friend of yours. She is in good health, never fear. But she is our guest until you complete your task.'

Crispin stiffened. 'Who? Who have you taken?'

'Her name is Eleanor. A woman of your longtime acquaintance, I gather?'

Eleanor? The wife of the tavern keeper Gilbert Langton? Crispin's oldest friends on the Shambles?

He trembled with the effort to control himself. 'I warn you now – all of you – if you have harmed even one hair on her head, your lives will be forfeit.'

'I swear by Saint Andrew himself that she is well.'

'And when did this happen? I left them but not a day ago.' He let out a laugh he could scarcely dredge up. 'Ha! I don't believe you. I want proof.'

'Och, Master Guest. We are wasting time.'

'It is my time to waste. Show me. Show me she is well.'

'How are we to do that?' cried one of the men, a ginger-haired, round-faced fellow. 'He'll ken where we have her.'

'Aye,' muttered McGuffin. 'That's a quandary.'

'No proof,' said Crispin with a smug raise to his chin, 'no help.'

'We could hood him,' said another with burly arms and a thick, dark beard.

Crispin stepped back. He had no fondness for being blindfolded.

'Aye,' said McGuffin with a nod. 'That will do.'

'That certainly will *not* do!' Crispin protested.

'You want your proof, then that's the only way.'

'You can bring her here.'

McGuffin ran a hand up into his hair, mussing its already unruly locks. 'Aye, well. Might do.'

'You'll bring her here, then? Safe and sound?'

McGuffin looked at his fellows, and they silently seemed to agree. 'Alec,' he said to the swarthy man with the beard. 'Go and fetch her.'

'Me?' The cup in his hand was full, and he indicated it with some annoyance.

'Aye, you. Make haste. Master Guest hasn't got all day.'

The one called Alec sneered at Crispin, and Crispin sneered back. The man grumbled as he took his leave, exhorting his fellows to leave his ale alone until he returned. As soon as the door shut behind him, his friends laughed and took turns downing the contents from his horn cup.

Crispin strode across the room, folded his arms, sat on a bench with his back to the fire, and waited.

Time crept by slowly. Church bells tolled None in slow, droning gongs. McGuffin's men, who had been so jovial before, were more subdued and now spoke in low murmurs, leaving Crispin out of the conversation. That was fine with him. His mind churned with strategies. Was Eleanor well? How had she fared? She must be frightened and Gilbert panicked. Crispin would very much like to do these men harm for daring to hurt his friends, but any vengeance would have to wait. For all McGuffin's caginess, it was obvious they had the gall to want Crispin to help them smuggle the Stone from London. He was already branded a traitor. What had begun twelve years ago would certainly culminate into a long-delayed execution for this. Richard would never understand that he had been coerced. He wouldn't care. And frankly, Crispin wouldn't blame him.

Best to see first that Eleanor was in good health, negotiate her freedom, and then figure out how to appease both these brigands and the king.

Meanwhile, where *was* the damned Stone?

With a surreptitious glance about the room, he saw only one coffer which was big enough for the Stone, but there was also a door leading to yet another room and he knew not what was behind that sturdy barrier.

The serving women had dispersed a while ago. Were they servants or the wives of these men? Did they all reside here in Westminster, or was this a rented cottage? Time enough to discover that later.

He brooded over his thoughts until a sharp knock sounded on the door. Crispin stood as did the other men.

The door whinged open and Alec stepped in, pulling on someone. He yanked harder. Crispin stopped himself from intervening just as a woman stumbled through the doorway.

Crispin expected the gregarious and plump figure of his friend Eleanor Langton, the tavern keeper from his favorite ale house, the Boar's Tusk. But this slender person who staggered forth was certainly not her.

He kept his mouth shut until the woman turned around. Her frown soon turned to surprise and Crispin's own face surely reflected the same emotion.

He looked the woman up and down. She wrenched her arm free from Alec's grasp and stomped hard on his foot. He howled in pain and hopped about the room. The men laughed and the edges of Crispin's mouth fluttered into a smile.

Fists at her hips, the woman threw back her head, gauging the men around her, and then Crispin again. 'Faith!' she said in a roughened and smoky voice. 'Is this any way to treat a lady?'

Crispin couldn't help it. He burst out laughing. Relieved tears teased at his eyes.

McGuffin stomped forward. 'Och! What mischief is here?'

Crispin gathered his laughter and heaved a cleansing breath. 'Mischief? No mischief.'

'No mischief?' said the woman. She gestured with a delicate hand. 'These ruffians have detained me without so much as a "by your leave." Verily,' she said with a sigh, 'I should have known you'd be involved, Crispin.'

He bowed. 'An unfortunate set of circumstances, I assure you. My apologies.'

McGuffin was no fool, as he seemed fond of telling Crispin, and he appeared to sense something afoot immediately. 'What goes on? Is this not your friend, Eleanor?'

'No,' said Crispin, the same time the woman gave an emphatic, 'Yes!'

McGuffin looked from one to the other. 'Well? Which is it?'

Crispin couldn't help but chuckle again. 'It's yes *and* no. "Eleanor" is certainly one name used. But perhaps I had best introduce my acquaintance . . . John Rykener . . . who sometimes goes by the name "Eleanor" to, er . . . ply his trade.'

McGuffin's eyes bugged.

Rykener straightened his skirts. His voice dropped nearly an octave. 'Greetings, gentlemen. How can I be of . . . service?'

SEVEN

'What, by Saint Andrew, is this?' cried McGuffin.

'That's what I'd like to know,' said Rykener. He shook a finger at Crispin. 'It's not safe being your friend, is it?'

Crispin shook his head. He felt better. There were two of them now. And he knew John was a good companion in a fight, even though he spent his time as a 'female' embroideress . . . though more often as a whore. Crispin set aside his usual distaste, not only for John's chosen profession, but at his preferred clientele.

'I don't understand . . .' McGuffin looked from one to the other and then turned an accusatory glare on Alec.

The man threw his hands up. '*What?*'

'You canna make certain that the woman you abduct *is* a sarding *woman?*'

'I never had to make certain before!'

Crispin crossed his arms and moved between them. 'Gentlemen, please. Clearly you have made a grave mistake. See what comes of trying to coerce me? Now. Let us talk plainly about the Stone.'

The men all looked at one another. Besides McGuffin and the disgruntled Alec, there were three more men. None of them had a sword, and Crispin was fairly certain that with his blade he had the advantage of them. And now, with John at his side, he felt the odds were even better.

'All this fighting over me,' sighed Rykener. 'It's quite flattering.'

'Hold your sodomite's tongue,' sneered Alec.

Rykener postured. Wiry though he was, Crispin knew him to be quick and strong. 'I certainly will not. I'm the one who was abducted, after all.' He turned to Crispin. 'Crispin, are we leaving this place?'

'In a moment, John.'

'Oh no you dinna!' McGuffin blocked their way to the door. The other men moved from their places and slowly approached, surrounding them. 'There is still the matter of your helping us.'

'Helping you smuggle the Stone to Scotland? I think you are dreaming, churl.'

'I tell you it's no the Stone!'

'Of course it isn't. That's why you have gone to so much trouble to bring me here, to abduct this man.'

'I *thought* he was a woman!' wailed Alec.

Rykener examined his nails. 'It's no fault to you, sir. I am good at what I do.' He raised his face and smiled a lurid grin. 'Want to see?'

The man fell back, becrossing himself. Rykener laughed.

'Behave, John,' said Crispin but wasn't certain if he meant it.

'I'm behaving as best I can for a man who was snatched off the streets for evil purposes. That's a day's worth of fees I've lost, mind you.'

'He's lost a day of fees,' said Crispin to McGuffin. 'What do you plan to do about it?'

'Me? Well . . . naught! You don't seem to understand the dynamic here, Master Guest.'

'I understand it perfectly well. You have attempted to coerce me by means of an illegal abduction . . . of the *wrong* person . . .'

Alec stomped his foot. 'I *thought* he was a *woman*!'

Crispin went on, ignoring him. 'And you held him against his will, thereby causing him to lose the means of his livelihood. I think you owe him recompense.'

McGuffin, mouth agape, suddenly crossed his arms over his chest. 'I'll no pay it.'

'Very well. But don't be surprised if you are called before a judge and forced to pay it. Then everyone will know how you were fooled.'

McGuffin flustered. 'Pay his . . . but he's a . . . and you would have *me* . . .'

Rykener tapped his lip with a finger. 'I think I've lain with a lawyer recently. I could call upon him. Prepare a suit against you.'

Scrambling at his scrip, McGuffin grumbled his oaths. He withdrew some coins and slammed them on the table. 'Here's your devil's fee, sodomite!'

Rykener sauntered toward the table and scooped them up. He winked at McGuffin. 'Much obliged, I'm sure. And much thanks to you, Crispin.'

'The very least I could do, John.' He bowed. 'Now let us leave this place.'

'Hold!' McGuffin moved back in front of Crispin. 'We haven't concluded our business.'

'Oh yes we have. I have no intention of helping you.'

'But I tell you again, we no have the Stone!'

Patience brittle and snapping, Crispin withdrew his sword. He aimed it at McGuffin's chest. 'God's blood, sir! You have the Devil's own gall. I will leave this place and I will not help you. I must find the Stone to help my apprentice. If you haven't got it, then tell me where it is!'

McGuffin's face reddened. 'I wish I knew. For I would surely help the bastards that stole it.'

'Then we have nothing to discuss.' He pushed John over the threshold and made to follow.

'Master Guest!' McGuffin pleaded. 'You plotted against your own king!'

Crispin spun, trembling with the force of his emotions. 'And don't you think I've regretted it every day of my life since then?' He seethed but drew back. 'And I *have* learned my lesson. I suggest you do the same.'

'I need your help, Master Guest, and it appears that you need mine as well. Can we not come to some agreement?'

'Do you know ought of the Stone of Destiny or not?'

McGuffin breathed hard, eyes darting from Crispin, to John, to his men, and back to Crispin. 'All this . . . for your apprentice?'

Crispin raised his chin. 'He's a very good apprentice.'

McGuffin grunted, nodding. 'You are a strange man, Master Guest.' They stared at one another for a long while. Too long for Crispin's liking. He was about to turn away when McGuffin said, 'You might ask after a man named Deargh. And that's all I can say. But beware. He's . . . dangerous.'

He swept both men with a glare before backing through the doorway and shutting the door tight. Crispin heard the bar being dropped behind it.

John turned to him. 'You do know the most interesting people.'

'Don't I.' He had to think. Now what? McGuffin might not know where the Stone was but he was involved in some other plot that he wanted Crispin to turn away from. That did not bode well either.

'Crispin,' said John gently at his side. Crispin looked at him and scowled. He hated him in his woman's clothing. 'What is amiss? Where is Young Jack?'

'Don't you have some proper clothing to change back into, John?'

'I'm far from my lodgings here in Westminster. Come. No one

knows who I am in this town.' He took Crispin's arm. Crispin wrestled out of it on the pretense of sheathing his sword.

'Very well . . . but stop taking my arm!' He pushed him off a second time.

Rykener laughed. 'It's one of the many things I like about you, Crispin. You are so right and proper, yet you befriend thieves and whores and tavern keepers and . . . *embroideresses*.'

Crispin shook his head. 'I'm sorry you got involved, John. They didn't mistreat you, did they?'

'No, they were perfect gentlemen. Perfect *Scottish* gentlemen. And so. What, by God's grace, is going on?'

They walked slowly, avoiding the muddier puddles where they could. Crispin found himself instinctively helping John over the worst of it simply by virtue of his woman's clothes, which caused no end of jeering from Rykener. Despite his embarrassment, Crispin explained the disappearance of the Stone.

After a long silence, John studied Crispin's face. Their eyes met. 'Bless me, I wouldn't be in your shoes, Crispin Guest, for all the gold in England. Poor Jack. What on earth are you going to do now?'

'I don't know.'

'I suppose it's best, then, to seek out that other Scottish fellow, that Deargh that McGuffin spoke of, eh?'

'Yes. I suppose I must.'

'I'd like to go with you. I promise to be good.'

Crispin squeezed his eyes shut. 'John . . .'

'Truly, Crispin. And you owe me, at any rate. Getting dragged into your folly. I'm only glad I wasn't Madam Langton, after all. I did spare her that distress.'

'Well . . . you have me there.'

'Then I can go?' He clapped his hands. 'I've always wanted to see you at work.'

'It's not a particularly safe place to be, at my side.'

'I know that. I did rescue you once.'

'And, for that, I am grateful.'

Rykener quickly scooped up Crispin's arm and held it tight, making Crispin unable to free himself without making a scene on the street. 'And I see you have a shiny new sword now,' he said close to Crispin's ear. 'There's a story there, I'll warrant.'

'John,' he hissed. 'I told you to behave.'

'I am behaving. You should see me when I am not.'

'I think I'd rather pass.'

They walked on along the Strand at its busiest hours. None had given way to late afternoon. Crispin watched with trepidation as carts came and went. It would be simple taking the Stone out of Westminster. If it was still here. The king should have had all carts and wagons checked, but it was far too late for that now.

He wondered what it was that McGuffin and his men wanted smuggled out of Westminster if not the Stone. He said it was smaller. If smaller, did he truly need Crispin's help?

He shook the thought loose with a toss of his head. Didn't matter. Crispin needn't concern himself over it. He was well and truly out of it, with his own problems to think about.

He and Rykener walked along, with John squeezing a death grip of his arm. 'Must you clasp so tightly, John?' he whispered. 'I fear my arm will be dead by the time we get there.'

'Oh, sorry. I did not want you to shake me off. And a lady needs an escort in such a dangerous highway.'

'You are not a lady!'

'But *they* don't know that.' He gestured toward the men along the road, some of whom did look rather rough.

Crispin sighed for not the first time.

Ahead was an ale stake, leaning into the lane, and beyond it the sign of the keys. Crispin nodded toward it. 'The alehouse Domhnall spoke of. Might we find this Deargh here?'

John loosened his grip, perhaps realizing that Crispin not only needed his wits about him but his sword arm as well. 'What will you do?'

With each passing hour, Crispin appreciated Jack Tucker more and more. His quiet and thoughtful scrutiny of how to approach a job, his quick wit and ability to jump at a problem with little prompting, his ability to be silent and not ask so many questions!

'I will do what I need to and ask for this Deargh. And, when I have him alone, exhort him to hand over the Stone.'

'That doesn't sound very exciting.'

'I'd rather it not be, if truth be told.'

'I thought you ate, slept, and breathed excitement. There is no end of the tales of the Tracker on the Shambles. I've heard quite a few stories. I wonder how many of them are true.'

'None of them, I'll warrant.'

'And I wouldn't take that wager. I know you, after all.'

Crispin gave John a warning look before he proceeded under the carved keys and through the door.

The room was remarkably warm. And little wonder. It was smaller than the Boar's Tusk's hall, and many more people were crowded into it.

The room was filled with noise and the smells of spilled ale and roasted meat. He threaded his way through the tables and toward the fire where it was almost too warm. Raucous men and women played dice in a corner, while others drank their cups together at worn tables.

He felt fingers clasping his cloak and turned to see not Jack Tucker – the Jack Tucker of an earlier day when he was still a young boy and not the fearless and accomplished young man he was now – but an anxious John Rykener.

Crispin wended toward a man who looked to be the tavern keeper, tending a roasted pig over the fire.

'I beg your pardon, good sir,' said Crispin with a bow. 'But might you know of a man named Deargh?'

'Eh?' said the man, cupping his hand to his ear. 'It's noisesome in here.'

'Indeed,' said Crispin a bit louder. 'Do you know of a man here named Deargh?'

'Deargh? There's no Deargh here.'

'Are you certain?' The place echoed with brogues. It made sense he'd be here.

The tavern keeper looked at Crispin skeptically. 'Never heard the name before. But you might ask Fergus. He's the man playing dice in the corner. The bald one. He knows everyone what comes and goes.'

'I thank you.'

Crispin backtracked through the clustered bodies and headed toward the corner. A crowd had gathered to watch the dice players, and they were laughing and crying out with jeers and catcalls.

The bald man, Fergus, crouched on the wooden floor, casting the bone dice into the corner. His sleeves were rolled up over brawny and hairy forearms, and his bald head sheened with sweat. A woman nearest the corner was leaning on her thigh, her leg propped up on a bench, revealing a good, plump length of stocking-covered calf. When she laughed, she exposed a mouth of missing teeth.

Crispin watched for a while, getting impatient as the man continued to throw. As long as he kept winning, he kept playing.

'Master Fergus,' Crispin called suddenly above the noise.

Startled, Fergus cast badly. The crowd 'awwed' at his loss. The man turned angrily toward Crispin. 'Who said that?'

'I'm afraid I did. My apologies.' And he bowed. Everyone fell silent. Clearly Crispin was the outsider and all glared with suspicion on their ruddy faces.

A hand slammed his chest and wadded his coat in a fist, lifting Crispin to his toes. Fergus leaned in and rose to his full height . . . which proved substantial. 'You made me lose.'

His onion breath was as powerful as his arm. Crispin blinked at him.

'I dinna like losing,' the man growled.

'Unhand me,' Crispin warned.

He studied Crispin. 'Or what?'

'Or *I* won't greet you,' said John, moving forward. He cocked his head and offered a sultry smile.

Crispin stared at him. What was the man doing? But he well knew what he was doing. He simply didn't wish to believe it.

Fergus turned his attention to John and clearly liked his small chin and petite mouth. And with his softened voice, Crispin supposed John passed very well for a woman. But it was a dangerous game. If the man grabbed him in the wrong places . . .

He lowered Crispin and fastened his attention on John. 'And just who might you be, fair lass?'

'I'm Eleanor,' said John, lowering his chin demurely. 'And this hasty fellow is Crispin Guest. You might have heard of him. He is also called the Tracker. And he wanted so to ask you a question. So much so that his impatience cost you that pot. He does apologize.'

Fergus never looked at Crispin. All of his attention was focused on John. 'That's forgotten. I've won a fair lot today. Enough to buy a comely maid some ale.'

John giggled and pulled his veil over his cheek. 'You are a sweet one, aren't you? Isn't he a sweet one, Crispin?'

'Like honey,' Crispin grunted.

Fergus rolled his eyes and gave Crispin his attention. He seemed to know he would get nowhere with *Eleanor* if he did not answer Crispin's fool question. 'What is it you want?'

'I am looking for a man by the name of Deargh.'

Fergus crossed his arms over his wide chest. 'I know every man who comes and goes in this place. Even more so than the tavern keeper. And a wench or two,' he added, smiling and chucking John's chin. John obliged him with a girlish titter. 'But I've never heard of this Deargh.'

Crispin glared. 'Are you certain?'

'Are you mad? This lovely lady has assuaged me from kicking your arse. You'd think you'd be grateful I answered that much.'

Crispin turned toward John. 'Oh yes. Very grateful.' When he looked up, everyone else was staring at him, too. 'I don't suppose anyone else has ever heard of a man named Deargh?'

They all shook their heads and slowly returned to their dice-playing. Except for the woman leaning on the bench. She stepped down, straightened her skirts, and walked toward Crispin.

'Looks like your friend is occupied,' she said, tilting her head toward John, who had allowed himself to be enfolded in Fergus's arms. *Dear God, be careful, John.* 'Maybe you need a bit of company. Some sport.' She smiled. She seemed to have only a few teeth in the front of her mouth, both upper and lower, making her resemble a horse.

'Ah. Yes, well. Since I cannot find the, er, the man I was looking for, perhaps it is best I go now.'

'Och now. You wouldn't want to disappoint a maid, now would you?'

He doubted very much she was a maid, but he was certainly wise enough not to say that aloud. He glanced over his shoulder at John, who was slowly being drawn away toward the back of the room. Should he rescue him? John could probably take care of himself, but Crispin didn't want to chance it.

He bowed to the toothless woman. 'If you will excuse me.'

He followed the couple to the rear and grabbed hold of John's arm. 'Come . . . er, *Eleanor*. I think our business here is concluded.'

'Don't you know when to make yourself scarce?' said the man. 'She disna want to go with you.'

'Perhaps we should let the lady decide.'

'Perhaps this,' said Fergus, drawing back his fist and swinging toward Crispin. Crispin ducked, and Fergus's fist hit home to the unlucky man standing beside him. Down he went, but he popped back up just as quickly.

'By the Mass!' He swung at Fergus and this time John ducked. Fergus's reflexes weren't as good, and he hadn't gotten out of the way at all. The fist hit his jaw but only knocked his head back. He narrowed his eyes and grabbed the man by his cotehardie and tossed him backward. The man cascaded into a group just raising their cups to each other. The cups flew, spraying several others with ale, and those men jumped back, glaring at those who had lost their cups and were scrambling over each other on the floor.

One man tipped his cup deliberately over the head of a man below him, who didn't take kindly to the gesture, and yanked the standing man's leg so that his feet flew out from under him.

The place collapsed into a melee.

Crispin tightened his hold on John and stumbled away with him toward the entrance.

Men fought one another. Stools sailed overhead. Beakers smashed on the floor. A dog barked and skipped from group to fighting group, nipping at fingers and bums.

John's wild eyes found Crispin's. They ducked flying debris and men being pushed over tables, feet high in the air. They side-stepped a particularly nasty engagement where two men had pulled their daggers but fortunately were too drunk to do any serious damage to one another.

Just as they reached the entrance, John was yanked away from Crispin's grasp. Fergus had returned and dragged John into the midst of the tavern. Rykener looked back at Crispin with widened eyes.

'Dammit,' Crispin muttered. He shoved his way through, grabbed Fergus by the shoulder, and spun him. 'The *lady* isn't interested.'

Nose bruised and dripping with blood, Fergus didn't bother answering. He drew back his fist, but Crispin leaned in, balled his own fist, and punched the man's belly hard.

Fergus doubled over with an expelled, 'Oof!' and John wrenched away from his grip, scrambling behind Crispin and glaring at Fergus over his shoulder.

Crispin turned, but Fergus wasn't done. He dove forward, shoving his shoulder and head into Crispin, and he and John tumbled backward into a servant with a tray. The tray's contents scattered and splashed everyone near it.

Crispin shook his head and looked up, finding that same toothless woman blinking down at him. 'Now you've gotten on Fergus's bad side,' she said, shaking her head. She glanced up in time to see

Fergus barreling down on them and yelped while skittering out of the way, skirts flying and pimpled bum exposed as she went.

Crispin rolled out of the way. Still on his back, he jabbed his feet and shoved them into Fergus's chest, whose head was down like an ox's, pushing stubbornly forward. Crispin pushed harder, but Fergus kept coming. Until John broke a jug over his head. Ale spilled around the man's eyes and cheeks, blending with the blood from a cut on his bald pate.

John wrestled Crispin to his feet and pulled on him. 'Come on! Let's away!' Crispin staggered after him and they made it through the door at last. They stumbled into the lane and looked back, even as more men hurled through the door, still fighting into the street.

Crispin and John exchanged glances. They didn't have to speak as they both suddenly cut up the road and back to Westminster, away from the fracas.

They finally stopped and leaned against a stone wall, catching their breaths.

Crispin thought John might be hurt, might be crying at first, but the man was laughing instead. 'That was the stupidest affray I've ever had the misfortune to be part of.'

Crispin wiped his face with his hand and looked at his palm. No blood. Just ale. He nodded and stood up straight. 'I have to agree with you.'

'Ah, Crispin. It's never a dull moment with you, is it?'

'You thought it would be boring.'

'I must confess.' He smiled. 'I shall never underestimate a simple task that involves you ever again.'

'Hmpf,' Crispin grunted, straightening his coat.

'Where to now?'

'How about you return to London and let me continue with this investigation.'

'Oh no, Crispin! I'm having a marvelous time. And without Jack, well. Perhaps you need someone seeing after you.'

'John . . .'

'Please, Crispin. You look like you could use a friend.'

He ran a hand over the back of his neck. 'But with you . . . looking like that . . .'

'What's wrong with the way I look?' He felt his coif, which had gone askew, and restored it to the center of his head. After all, he didn't have long hair like a woman to tuck up into it, and that would surely give the game away. 'Is my gown all right?'

'It's . . . it's fine. But I'd rather you were in tunic and stockings.'

'But this is better. I'm in disguise.'

'It's not better!'

'Hush, Crispin.' John looked around, but the passersby ignored them. 'You'll spoil everything.'

'God's blood, John! This is not a game. My . . . Jack Tucker is in danger.'

'I know.' He grew solemn and blessedly silent, merely watching Crispin, waiting for him to decide what next to do.

'I must go back to the beginning,' Crispin muttered at last. What had he been about to investigate when he left Westminster Abbey? 'Explosive powder.'

'Explosive powder? What is that?'

'It was used to destroy the fabricated Stone. I was about to investigate where such powder could be obtained.'

'Explosive powder is generally used for what?'

'Cannon. Gonnes.'

'For . . . gonnes?'

'Yes.' Crispin moved toward a shop wall and leaned against it. He felt as if he were running in circles, getting nowhere. He scrubbed his face with callused palms and rested his head back against the plaster. Gray and overcast, the sun made no shadows along the street edges.

'Hmm,' said Rykener, resting beside him. 'I know of a man who is a gonner. He and I . . . well.'

Crispin kept his eyes fixed on the sky.

'He will help me if I ask him. Shall we go . . . but no. I should go alone. I do not think he would like my bringing someone along.'

Crispin pushed away from the wall. A break at last! 'I need to know where one might easily obtain the powder. Can it be bought? And where?'

He nodded. 'How shall I find you? Your lodgings on the Shambles?'

'Yes. I pray to God I shall be safely delivered there soon.'

'Be careful, Crispin. For Jack's sake.'

'I will try.'

Rykener made his way down the rutted road toward London, his skirts disappearing amongst the crowd. He glanced worriedly over his shoulder toward Crispin.

Thoughts of his lodgings sounded good to him, until Crispin thought of how empty they would be without Jack. That boy had truly gotten under his skin. He supposed he was more than an apprentice when it got down to it. He considered Jack something like family. And why not? He was not a lord to bequeath his worldly goods to heirs. He had no heirs *and* no goods. Save for his sword now, and his family ring. And a certain thorn from a religious relic. Perhaps even more valuable than sword and ring combined, but knowing Jack, he would never part with any of it. No, he could give the boy little else for his years of service . . . except his life. Yes, now was the time to use all his wiles and find that wretched Stone. 'I wish I'd never heard of the Stone of Destiny,' he muttered, stepping out into the street.

He had to clutch at hope. He had to believe that the Stone was still within reach. Still in Westminster or London. And if it was, he would find it. And rub the finding of it in King Richard's face.

EIGHT

J ack opened his door, still surprised that it remained unlocked. He'd spent the better part of the day simply staring out the window into the walled garden and listening to the sounds of the Thames as it rushed by, with its many boats and fishermen shouting to one another across the churning water, casting up the earthy smells of moss and fish.

But after some hours at a leisure he was ill used to, he jumped up from his post and squinted into the next room. He had to be put to something useful. This idleness seemed only to add to his frustration.

'Oi!' he called out softly. 'Is anyone there?' Perhaps a servant was about. He could ask them and perhaps be put to work, sweeping or setting the fires. For there were rooms yet to explore in the warren of apartments that connected Lady Katherine's with Lancaster's.

Jack turned his head around the door and spied a young servant looking back at him with horror. Jack looked down at himself to check for . . . well, he wasn't sure. Something horrible, but could identify nothing that would make the boy look at him like that. The lad wore a coat with the arms of someone on his breast. Jack surmised it might be the Swynford arms.

'Er . . . boy. Can you—?'

The servant yelped and darted away through one of the ante-chamber doors.

Jack leaned back against the archway. 'God's blood,' he murmured, using Master Crispin's favorite oath without thinking. 'He's a skittish one, isn't he?' Listening, he couldn't detect anyone else about, and so he made his own way to the hearth and urged the flames with a poker sitting beside it.

Looking around, he could find little in the way of dust or untidiness. He supposed Lady Katherine's servants were competent enough. In a corner of his heart, he wished that perhaps they weren't *so* tidy. There was little for him to do.

A door opened and he jumped back. Was he supposed to leave his little 'squire's room'? He wasn't sure.

Lady Katherine swept in, looking much the same as when she'd left him hours before. The coif on her head fell around her face in gentle folds, and though a mature woman, she was still quite lovely in his estimation, with a small mouth, wide, thoughtful eyes, and gently arching brows. Her brown hair, slightly wavy, was pinned up under her coif but still showed at the nape of her exposed neck, in the French fashion.

'Master Tucker.' She gave a little bow and, belatedly, he scrambled to bow back. 'I'm afraid you startled one of my servants. He wasn't made aware that you would be our guest.' Her eyes held amusement.

'Begging your pardon, my lady, I didn't know no one was about. And I also didn't know . . . if I was allowed to leave the room. The d-door . . . it wasn't barred.'

'I have no intention of locking you in, Master Tucker. I promised to keep you here but not to shackle you.'

'And for that I thank you again, my lady.' Rolling on his heels, he pressed his hands behind his back. 'Might there be something I can do, my lady? I was not brought up to be idle.'

'Ah, I see. Boredom brings you forth.'

'Aye. My master taught me never to be idle. *Our characters are a result of our conduct.* So says Aristotle.'

She laughed, pressing her fingers to her lips. 'I had forgotten how Crispin was so enamored of the philosophers. I see he has passed on this liking to you.'

'Oh, Aristotle is wise, my lady! Did you know he has a saying for all of man's foibles?' Jack shook his head. 'I don't wonder why my master holds such store in him. And Aristotle being dead all them centuries, too.'

'It is a wonder,' she agreed.

'But er . . .' Jack looked around the sunny room. 'There doesn't appear to be anything for me to put myself to, my lady. I would happily clean, but your rooms are well kept. I commend you on your servants' competence.' He didn't mean to sneer, but he felt his face configure that way.

Her lips twitched into a smile, and she seemed to try to hide it behind her veil. 'I'm sure they will be happy to hear that. I don't suppose you play chess, Master Tucker.'

He brightened. 'Oh, but I do! My master has taught me.'

'What an efficient master. Crispin is training you up as a proper squire, I see.' She moved to a sideboard and opened one of the cabinet's doors, removing an ornate box and setting it on a table between two chairs.

'I can't be no squire as my master is no knight.' He rolled his eyes. 'Ah, look at me. Parroting his words back. He is always saying that. But Master Crispin will always be a knight in my eyes, even though I never knew him as such.'

'Yes,' Lady Katherine agreed softly. Opening the box, she began taking out the finely carved chess pieces and rolled out the checkered leather board onto the small round table.

Jack sat opposite her and waited for her to finish setting up the board. She took white and he waited again for her to make the first move. They played silently, with Katherine making soft compliments on his moves from time to time. It never occurred to him to try to lose.

In the end, he managed to win, and when he lifted his beaming face he found a smile on her face as well. 'You are very good, Master Tucker. I commend you and your master on his tutelage. I never could quite get Henry to play fair or to enjoy the game.'

Henry? He realized she must have meant Henry of Bolingbroke, Lancaster's son.

'Master Crispin is very patient. He is always correcting me in my play, my swordsmanship, the way I speak.' When he looked up again, her eyes seemed saddened.

'These past twelve years,' she said softly, 'they must have been very hard.'

'Aye, my lady. I don't think there's a day that's gone by when my master hasn't felt the sting of it. I try to ease his burden, but . . . well. I can little understand myself the extent of what he has lost.'

'I've no doubt that your presence in his life has comforted his troubled soul.'

'I only pray that that is true, my lady.'

She sat quietly, examining the board, or so he thought. When he measured her gaze, it was unfocused, looking past the knights, queens, and kings. 'If only we could help him.'

Jack realized she might be speaking more broadly, but his mind was focused on the trouble at hand. He scooted to the edge of his chair. 'Well, I've been thinking about that. If the Stone is very important to the Scots, so it must be Scots what took it. And took it in a spectacular manner, the most of which was designed to embarrass the king.'

She slowly nodded. 'Yes. I should think that was certainly part of it.'

'And so. If that is true, then this whole thing is a Scottish plot. What might have set them off at this time? My master and I get so little news from court.'

She leaned in, talking quietly, always with an eye glancing toward the closed doors. 'I don't suppose it is any secret that King Richard hasn't enjoyed the last two years under the guidance of his lords. Those led by Gloucester and Henry.'

Jack nodded. Master Crispin had said as much. They were sent to London to set the king aright about his favorites and how the royal coffers were spent. In fact, it had kept all of London on tenterhooks, wondering if any of the five lords – the duke of Gloucester, the earls of Arundel and Warwick, Lord Derby, and the duke of Nottingham – would try to seize the throne for themselves. Richard had holed himself up in the Tower when they marched into London last year, with Henry Derby in the lead. Master Crispin had been nothing but tense the entire time. Indeed, all of London was so until it had all settled and Richard had come out of his tower, still the king but with less power than before. But even now, with the earl of Nottingham and Henry still breathing down Richard's neck, there was still no easy rest for the king. He had said as much himself before he had snatched Jack by the point of a blade.

It was rumored that Henry was more disposed toward his cousin the king, whether because of guilt at treating one anointed by God so, or because he feared to act this way toward his kin, but the tongues of London also claimed that Henry *wasn't* warming to Richard. Jack thought rather that Henry remembered their childhood friendship and wanted something of that back. But whenever Jack brought it up, Master Crispin would only grunt his reply. Jack could only shrug. Master Crispin surely knew more about court politics than he did.

Katherine spoke again. 'And Richard has not warmed to their guidance. Any excuse to embarrass him puts Richard at a disadvantage.'

'But to steal the Stone? Even that seems risky.'

'Just so. Then that leaves the escapade in the hands of the Scots.'

'Why would they strike at this time?'

She placed one hand near the one that rested on the edge of the chessboard-table. 'There has been rebellion in the north. As I understand it, the Scots did not renew a truce with us, a clear signal that they wished to wage war, or so I have been told. And there have been many battles, many skirmishes. We have lost several of them. The latest was only last month, in Otterburn, in Northumberland.'

'That must have hurt the king dearly.'

'It was a blow to all who stand with the king and England.'

'Who are the players, my lady, so that I might understand it?'

'Did not Crispin explain it?'

'He, er, might have. But sometimes, when he speaks of such things, it is only the sound of the wind to me.' Jack reddened. 'I will try to fathom it this time, I give my oath.'

Katherine smiled. 'I do believe you, Master Tucker. Well, then. As I understand it, Sir Henry Percy, the earl of Northumberland's son, had just taken over the defense of the border.' She placed a white knight on a black square 'But there is a reason they call him "Hotspur,"' she said with a shake to her head. 'He engaged with Sir James Douglas of the Douglas clan—' She slid the black knight to another black square, facing the first knight – 'against the advisement of others. He and his army were routed. Over fifteen hundred English lives were lost and captured to their Scottish five hundred. It was foolish and wasteful . . . and it embarrassed the king.' She tipped the white knight, and he toppled several pawns.

'Ah! Then perhaps this Sir James—'

'No. He was killed at the battle.'

'Oh.' Jack glared at the chessboard, suddenly seeing lines of men-at-arms and mounted knights. The sounds of battle assailed his imagination, and he could almost picture it all in his mind.

'Percy was captured,' she went on. 'But Douglas's right-hand man survived.' She picked up another black knight and clutched it. 'John Dunbar, earl of Moray. I should think that this victory might have riled the Scots into greater fervor. The marches are such dangerous places.'

'And is he still in Northumberland, my lady? This earl of Moray?'

She shrugged, replacing the white knight on the board. 'I don't know if anyone knows his whereabouts. But it is said he is clever and treacherous.'

Jack rose. 'A message should be sent to my master. This is valuable information he could use.'

'And are you to deliver this message, Master Tucker?'

Jack jolted. Dammit! He had been ready to fly and suddenly remembered his wings had been clipped. He sagged back into his chair. 'Faith! I cannot.'

'But nothing prevents *me* from doing so.'

Jack's hopes soared again. 'Would you, my lady? Oh, but my master's lodgings are on the Shambles. You . . . you shouldn't go there.'

'Nonsense. Every woman has the right to shop for meat. That is what one does on the Shambles, does one not?'

Slowly he nodded. 'Aye. You could. And my lady, can you tell Master Crispin that all is well with me? That you are taking fine care of me.'

'I will.' She rose and called out for her lady's maid. Mylisant popped through the middle door and frowned upon seeing Jack, as she always seemed to do.

'Make ready to ride. We are going to London.'

Mylisant curtseyed. 'Yes, my lady.' And she rushed off with Lady Katherine to find cloaks and footmen.

Jack felt more at ease now that he was helping at last, though little he knew what good it would do Master Crispin in the end if the Stone was in Northumberland.

He paced again, from one side of the room to the window on the other.

He stopped abruptly when he heard noise outside the apartments in the corridors. Marching men. And suddenly there was a pounding on the door.

Jack dove for the squire's room and scrambled to shut the door just in time, as he heard the maid, Mylisant, hurry to the antechamber door and open its locks.

A man bellowed to see Lady Katherine. Jack dropped to his knees and peered out the keyhole.

Lady Katherine strolled in, sedate and unperturbed, long gown trailing after her.

'What is the meaning of this disturbance, Captain?' she said sternly. Jack could well imagine her saying the same thing in that same tone to her erstwhile charges; to Crispin, when he was Jack's age, if he had been rough-playing with Henry Bolingbroke.

The captain of the guard bowed. 'Forgive me, Lady Katherine. But I was given to understand that the prisoner was broken out by you. His majesty is very displeased.'

'His majesty gave me permission to house the hostage Jack Tucker in more amenable surroundings.'

The man, clad in armor, head covered in a visor-less bascinet and aventail, shook his head. 'That is not the message the king conveyed to me, Madam.'

'It is the message he conveyed to *me*, Captain.'

The captain sighed and shuffled his armored boots. 'Lady Katherine, perhaps it is best that you divorce yourself from these dangerous proceedings. The king *explicitly* commanded me to make certain of the prisoner's whereabouts. I think it is best that I take him and let you sort it out with his majesty at a later time.'

'I do not think it best, Captain. I think that I should talk to the king myself now.'

The captain raised his chin and looked down at her. 'I will not debate it.' He turned to his guards and gestured them in. 'Find him,' he said to them.

Jack clutched the door. He should surrender himself before harm came to Lady Katherine. He rose and reached for the handle when a loud voice arose from the open doorway.

'Hold! What, by Christ, are you doing molesting my governess!'

Jack knelt to the keyhole again and pressed his eye to it. Henry Bolingbroke himself walked through the door, shoving aside some of the king's guards. He stepped into the room and stood with his fist at his hip, facing the captain. Garbed in a long, crimson houppelande with his family arms embroidered riotously over the material, Jack thought that Henry seemed more intimidating than that captain of the guard with all his armor. Henry little resembled his dark and stoic father Lancaster, but instead – so it was said – took after his mother the Lady Blanche, with his ruddy hair and husky build.

The captain was clearly ruffled. 'My Lord Derby, I was sent by the king—'

'I know that my *cousin* sent you,' he said, gleefully emphasizing the royal relationship. Henry, as well as Jack, could plainly see how it discomfited the captain. 'But *I* am telling you that there has been an error. Surely the king could not have made conflicting orders.' He turned and bowed decorously to Lady Katherine. 'My dear Lady Katherine.' He bent to kiss her cheek. 'Surely you spoke directly to the king himself on this matter?'

She nodded demurely, allowing the soft veil to flutter about her face to great effect. 'Of course. I never should have had the nerve to steal one of the king's hostages without his express permission.'

'I thought as much.' He turned to face the captain. 'And you, sir. Was your audience with the king in person?'

The captain scowled. 'No, my lord. I received a missive—'

'Ah well!' Henry slapped the man's shoulder. The captain cringed. 'That is all settled, then. Plainly the message was somehow muddled. I will speak to my cousin the king without delay and clear up this misunderstanding. You are free to return to your duties, Captain, as are your men.'

The men, poised in the room, looked from Henry to their captain. It was clear that Henry held greater sway. They bowed to him and exited smartly out the door.

The captain, tight-lipped and taut, stiffly bowed to Henry, then to Katherine, before turning on his heel and marching over the threshold.

Henry strode to the door and pushed it shut. Jack saw him relax his shoulders, and he suddenly looked like the congenial man he always appeared to be in front of Crispin. 'My lady, you do get yourself into fixes. You know very well that the king gave you no such order.'

'He might have done,' she said with a shrug. She straightened Henry's collar affectionately. 'Had I asked him.'

'Lady Katherine,' he sighed. 'Ah me.'

'And how did you arrive in so timely a fashion, Henry?'

'I happened to overhear the guards discussing it. Imagine my surprise to discover that *you* were harboring him. Of course I should have known.'

She lowered her eyes. 'You are quick to find me guilty.'

He laughed. 'Truly? Very well, tell me the miscreant *isn't* here, then.'

Jack shoved the door open and raised his chin. 'I am no miscreant, my lord,' he said defiantly, if not a bit shakily. 'I am the king's hostage for no other reason but that he hates my master.'

Henry smiled. 'And there is Jack Tucker, Crispin's right-hand man. How goes it, Master Tucker?' He took two long strides with an outstretched hand and met Jack in the middle of the room, grasping his hand in a tight grip.

Jack stared down at their clasped hands in awe. Why was Henry Derby shaking his hand like an equal?

Henry tightened his grip and pulled Jack closer. 'And though it is true that King Richard does not favor Crispin . . .' He leaned toward Jack's ear and said in a rough whisper, 'it is best not to say that aloud.'

'I . . . I beg your pardon, my lord.'

He released Jack and waved his hand in dismissal. 'Never mind. What's done is done. There is time to make certain you are safe. I suggest moving you to my lodgings across the corridor. It might be safer there. But you must keep out of sight as it is next to the king's lodgings.'

Jack gulped. 'Aye, my lord. You are being very kind to me. I don't know that I deserve it except to keep my master happy, God bless him.'

'I was on my way to see him, in fact,' offered Lady Katherine.

Henry raised his brows. 'Were you? Well then. While you are on your mission I shall sequester Master Tucker. And you can honestly reply once the king's guards return – and they will – that he is not here. I don't think the king would dare search *my* lodgings. I must say, I am surprised he sent men to search yours. Especially since I thought you were lodged at our estates with my wife.'

She turned her head slightly. 'And so I was. You know I find her most charming and your little Henry a joy, but I felt the need to visit Westminster to see to the duke's household here. I expected a speedy trip and an equally speedy return. Nothing controversial was on my mind, I assure you. As for the king searching my lodgings, well. As you well know, I am only Lady Swynford, governess to Lancaster's children, all of whom are grown and at their own affairs. The king does not consider me to be unassailable.'

Henry narrowed his eyes but nodded at the truth of it. 'Be that as it may . . .' He turned to Jack. 'I think we are both tasked with making sure young Jack here is kept from the king's eye. For an old friend's sake.'

Katherine turned to study Jack, hands folded one over the other. She gave him an encouraging smile.

Jack looked from one to the other gratefully. Not in a thousand years would he ever have thought he would be in such company. Not if you had paid him a bag of gold.

NINE

Crispin trudged heavily back toward London. There was no speeding his journey. It would take a quarter of an hour, no less than that. Too much time to think. But maybe Rykener had discovered something from his . . . paramour? He shuddered. He liked the man well enough but couldn't understand his tastes. Yet he was a reliable friend, and Crispin trusted whatever information John could glean. If that explosive powder was procured in Westminster or London, then that would offer a valuable clue, somewhere for Crispin to search instead of the void that lay open to him.

The Strand became Fleet Street, and he had only just passed White Friars. Ludgate was ahead and he'd be home in no time now.

A gust of leafy wind caught his cloak and billowed it like a sail before he cast it back with a flick of his arm. Autumn was just around the corner. Even summer had not been as warm as summers before it. Every season seemed like winter these days. Crispin shuddered in anticipation of the season to come. Fall was difficult, but winter was always much harder. He had hoped they could enjoy the warmer days for a little while longer, but it was not to be. Was it even likely that Jack had a window wherever he was housed? The boy was used to a certain amount of freedom. Four walls did not sit well with him. He was more of a wild thing, like a cat, needing his time to roam. Crispin sent up a silent prayer – and an apology to Jack. Surely he would not be in this predicament if he had not come to know Crispin.

Walking along the familiar path with his solitary thoughts and weary to the bone, he almost didn't notice the man flagging him down from the alley. He slowed and looked back over his shoulder. Yes, the man was waving at *him*, a gangly fellow in an oversized green cotehardie. 'God's blood,' he sighed and turned, trudging toward him.

The man greeted Crispin with an awkward bow. 'You're Crispin Guest,' he said in a coarse whisper. 'I seen you many a time on the Shambles.'

'What of it?' he answered gruffly.

'It's like this. I know of certain men who have been desperate to talk to you. Certain men who might have something you wish to find.'

He clenched his jaw. 'And what might this "something" be?'

The man glanced quickly this way and that. 'It isn't exactly the sort of thing a man can talk about on the street, now is it?'

Crispin grunted and turned away. A hand reached out to clutch at his arm.

'Now, now, good master. You give up too easily.'

'I'm tired, I'm hungry, and I have no more patience.'

'Very well, then.' The man sidled closer. Crispin watched his prominent Adam's apple bob on his scrawny neck. 'It's . . . the *Stone*.'

Crispin looked him over. 'And who are you?' The man's accent was clearly from London. He was no northerner.

'I'm a messenger what keeps his business to himself, for that is how coin is earned. I've been instructed to tell you to go to the Boar's Tusk. Do you know it?'

Crispin snorted. 'I have some acquaintance with it.'

'Then I suggest you go there now. Or this Stone they speak of might be permanently lost.'

Could this man be trusted? Was he walking into a trap? Of course it made little difference at this point. He knew he would have to go.

'Thanks,' he tossed over his shoulder.

'I hope it's worth it!' called the man after him before he ducked away into the shadows and disappeared amongst the travelers on the lane.

Crispin said nothing as he continued down the way until he could pass under Ludgate's arch and cut up to Paternoster Row to the Shambles. Walking, he cast a longing glance toward his lodgings. Below, the tinker Martin Kemp was sitting outside at his table full of wares. In his leather apron-covered lap, he hammered delicately with a pointed hammer onto the curved bottom of a cauldron. His head was bent forward, and strands of his dark hair hung over his face, escaping from the leather cap he often wore.

Crispin did not hail him but instead raised his eyes yet further to the floor above, to his own lodgings and its closed shutter. Had Jack been home, the fire would be sending puffs of smoke from the slanted chimney above, but there was nothing coming from that rickety brick structure. The hearth would be cold, the place dark.

He put those thoughts aside as he strode on as the street changed to West Cheap. He approached Gutter Lane to his left, but as he made to turn up that lane to his favorite tavern, there was a tug on his mantle.

He jerked away from it, hand immediately covering his scrip. When he turned, he spied a short, squat man, wearing a bulky cloak of a thick woolen weave. 'Crispin Guest?'

'Yes? What is it? I am on my way to meet someone.'

'I think you'd best come with me.'

Another northerner, by the sound of his accent.

'And why should I care to do that? I told you. I am meeting someone—'

'At the Boar's Tusk. Aye. But you don't want to be talking to them.'

He turned fully, appraising the man. 'Don't I?'

'Och, no. For they no have the Stone. Me and my lot, on the other hand . . .'

Crispin closed his eyes, breathing harshly through his nostrils. 'Are you trying to tell me that *you* have the Stone and not these others I am to meet?'

'Aye. That's it. Will you come?'

He opened his eyes. 'Where?'

'It's no too far.'

'*Where?*'

'A chapel.'

'A chapel?' He shot the man a hard look before sighing. 'Lead me, then.'

The little man waddled ahead and Crispin surveyed the street, surreptitiously looking for other men lurking and ready to pounce on him. Every shadow was a danger, in every archway lay a trap.

They turned down Bread Street to Trinity and there, tucked away amongst the overgrown brambles of a churchyard, lay an abandoned chapel, its ancient crumbling stone going back to King John's time.

The man climbed over a fallen tree limb and looked back at Crispin as he headed for the door.

Vaguely, Crispin wondered how in Heaven he chose who to believe in all this. He knew he was desperate, but the wrong move could cost Jack his life. He decided he had to trust his oft reliable instincts. If he couldn't trust those, then he was doomed indeed.

He stepped over the limb and met the man on the mossy steps. The man's gaze met Crispin's once before he knocked solemnly on the door. They waited.

It was only a few heartbeats until someone opened the door and peered out, face encased in a hood. 'You've brought him!'

The little man pulled himself up to his full height – which wasn't much – and raised his chin. 'I have.'

The man inside pulled the door open. 'Come in, Master Guest. Come in!'

With all the dignity he could muster, Crispin stepped over the threshold into the dark chapel. Men had gathered over a brazier at what had once been the sanctuary. They turned and stared as he walked down the short nave.

He stopped just short of the sanctuary steps. 'Well?' he said, looking around the disheveled place. The sky was visible above the crossing where the roof had fallen in. Broken beams lay where they had landed God knows how many years ago and were covered in a layer of dust, dried leaves, and bird droppings. In fact, the rafters fluttered with settling birds, with flapping and the occasional downward drift of feathers.

The five men gathered about Crispin, and he was at the same time repulsed and amused by their awestruck expressions. 'Who is in charge, and where is the Stone?' Crispin asked without preamble.

The squat man who had retrieved him raised his stubbled chin. 'I am Findlaich. And I speak for these sons of Scotland.'

Crispin squared with him. 'Good. I weary of wasting my time. What do you want in exchange for the Stone?'

Findlaich traded worrying glances with his fellow. 'I think you have the wrong idea, Master Guest.'

Crispin felt a headache coming on. He pinched the bridge of his nose and clenched his eyes shut. 'The Stone. Where is it? I am thin with patience.'

'We had our orders to take the Stone.'

Crispin slowly opened his eyes. Orders? Now they were getting somewhere. 'Orders from whom?'

'Ah,' said Findlaich, pointing a finger at Crispin. 'That, I canna tell you. But the Stone was ours to take, and by King Robert, we stole into Westminster.'

'I say again,' said Crispin, feeling his blood course within. He opened and closed his hands. 'What do you want for it?'

'It's no that simple, Master Guest.'

With blood bubbling over, Crispin lunged and with one smooth move, grabbed the man by the bunched shoulders of his cloak, unsheathed his dagger, and yanked him up so that they were eye to eye, dagger to throat. He heard the sound of blades being drawn all around him but didn't care.

'Listen, you brain-boiled, dull-witted Scottish boar of an imbecile. You will not play your games with me. I have had enough. Tell me NOW where the god-forsaken Stone is or—'

To Crispin's surprise, the man laughed. 'Och, here's a man for ye, lads. No pasty-faced English here.'

But instead of the good-natured laughter of McGuffin's men, they moved swiftly to Findlaich's side and pulled Crispin off him. One shoved him back and another held his dagger to Crispin's chest. Breathing hard and coiled to spring, Crispin steadied himself.

'We'd like to tell you our tale, Master Guest,' said Findlaich, 'if you will listen.'

Do I have that kind of face, Crispin wondered, *that seems to like to listen to tales?*

The other men stepped back, allowing Crispin some space, but only so much. He knew he wouldn't have time to lunge for Findlaich again before a beefy arm belayed him or a ham hock shoulder blocked his way.

'I'm certain you know the tale of the Stone of Scone, eh, Master Guest?'

'King Edward wrested it from the Scots . . . when he *trounced* them in 1296.' He took great pleasure in Findlaich's frown at the word 'trounced.'

'That may be so,' said the Scot with a rumble. 'But the Stone has a great history. It was once the stone that Jacob used for a pillow. *And Jacob rose up early in the morning, and took the stone that he had put for his pillows, and set it up for a pillar, and poured oil upon the top of it.* So you see, it has a long history of its holy and consecrated stature. The ancient king Cináed mac Ailpín originally brought it to Scone Abbey and there it sat, anointing king after king. Even old King John Balliol . . . before your Edward could steal it away. So you see, it has a long history to my people.'

'*Vae victis,*' said Crispin with a sneer. 'Woe to the conquered.'

'Aye, the spoils of war cannot be denied to the king and his army when they come knocking on the door. So it is ever thus. D'ya know what is said of the Stone? *Ni fallat fatum, Scoti, quocunque locatum, Invenient lapidem, regnare tenentur ibidem.'*

Crispin intoned, *'If Fates go right, where'er this stone is found, the Scots shall monarchs of that realm be crowned.* So?'

'So? You dinna see? It's no that English kings become the kings of Scotland, but that the kings of Scotland become the kings of England.'

Crispin snorted. 'Very pretty. Your own interpretation, no doubt. This is all very interesting but not getting us closer to a negotiation. I suggest you tell me where the Stone is and we shall see about your, er . . . *reward* for returning it.'

'Oh aye. Reward.' He scratched at his bearded chin. 'I well remember how King Richard *rewarded* Wat Tyler with a parlay on London green . . . and laid him low with a blade. Much reward he received with his head paraded on a pike.'

'And rightly so for rising against the crown.'

Findlaich laughed. 'So says you, Crispin Guest, the traitor who lived.'

Crispin drew in a sharp breath. His face instantly heated. He longed to draw his sword, but more information was needed. He could not kill this man who had hidden the Stone, else it might never be recovered. He breathed, gaze steely against the sharp eyes looking back at him, measuring.

'Is that all then?' Crispin grit out. 'History lesson over?'

'All but the recent history. We were asked to do this thing, Master Guest. Oh, there is pleasure in the doing, but it wasn't our idea, you see. Coin was exchanged.'

'How much?'

A furrowed brow rose.

'How much do you want, dammit?'

'Well, I wish we were in a position to bargain with ye, Master Guest. Nothing would give me greater pleasure, I assure you. But . . .' He walked toward the brazier and stretched out his hands toward it. The light flickered over his features in golden flutters. The cold was deep inside the little chapel, with its stone walls, stone floors, stone roof. It held the cold to it like a mother holds its babe. But Crispin was used to cold. Used to ceaseless nights of it, and days, too. He didn't move. But he gathered himself like a horse waiting to spring into a gallop.

Nothing more seemed forthcoming. He looked around again.

Where could the damned Stone be? Anywhere, he reckoned. Anywhere hidden in plain view in a stone building with its stone walls falling down around it. His gaze moved more critically over the debris on the floor, under the skewed arches, into the shadows.

'Are you working with McGuffin?' asked Crispin. 'There's no use in lying to me.'

The man fiddled with the clasps of his cloak in studied insouciance. 'What has he told you?'

'Precious little. But I already surmised he was working for a great lord.'

'The Mormaer,' said one of the men in hushed tones.

'Wheest!' hissed Findlaich. The man shrunk back.

Mormaer? What sort of thing was that? He'd have to ask Domhnall when next he saw him. Yet it was plainly something to strike fear in the faces of these Scotsmen.

The men looked at one another anxiously, in fact, and they gestured to Findlaich, speaking in their strange twisted tongue.

Findlaich questioned his compatriots, but they all shook their heads. With a conciliatory posture, he opened his hand to Crispin. 'I may not speak to you of the Mormaer at this time, Master Guest.'

The Mormaer? Crispin wracked his mind, trying to remember if he had ever heard the name before, but came up empty. He had spent his warrior years in France, not Scotland. He had been thrust from court long before the latest uprisings began.

Findlaich raised his chin and looked down his bulbous nose. 'What's on your mind, Master Guest?' It had the tone of, *'What would it take to get rid of you?'*

'I have encountered others who claim . . . *they* have the Stone.'

Findlaich made a growling sound and swept his glance over his fellows. 'I'd be anxious to know who they are.'

'Indeed. But what does it matter if they don't have it?'

'Well, that's the thing, Master Guest. We have our orders. We were to take the Stone but no orders were given about what to do with it once gotten. And anyway, we don't have it. It was gone before we could get to it. With a verra interesting item in its place.'

'Somehow,' said Crispin, 'I knew you were going to say that.' He approached the brazier and warmed his hands over it, relishing the warmth on his face.

Tricked again. And the wrong choice made. Again. He should

have gone on to the Boar's Tusk as planned. Was that chance slipping away?

He rubbed his hands for another moment and turned. His strides were long down the nave, but footsteps followed him, and then someone ran to head him off at the door. A burly bear of a man furrowed his brow at him, body blocking his exit.

'We weren't done talking, Master Guest,' said Findlaich from behind him.

'Yes we were. You don't have the Stone so there is nothing else to say.'

'But you are a finder of lost things, are you not? They call you the Tracker.'

Crispin halted but did not turn around. He laughed instead, a harsh bark of a sound. 'Don't tell me you intended to *hire* me, too?' He did turn then, eyes narrowing. 'You whoreson. Don't you know why I am already looking for it? The king has my apprentice as hostage. If I don't find it and return it to the king, he will kill the boy! What the hell do I care about you?'

'Such haste and impertinence,' said Findlaich, shaking his head. 'I care not for what schemes the king's got brewing. I only know my own task. And that was to secure the Stone. But I no have it. And I shall be in peril if I do not do as my patron says. Yet, I might have an idea who does have that troublesome Stone.'

'And why should I trust you?'

'Well now . . .' He rubbed his shaggy chin again. 'There are things that I know that perhaps you do not . . .' Sagging, he shrugged. 'I wish no harm to your lad, Master Guest, but as you well know, men like us are at the mercy of our betters.'

Betters? Who would lead such an expedition for the Stone, he wondered. Who could? A Scottish lord, no doubt. But who? This Mormaer? *The* Mormaer, he corrected. The tribal nuances of northerners were a puzzle to him.

And anyway, how would the knowing of it help his situation? Well, all the pieces were necessary. Only a complete tapestry yielded an understandable picture.

He faced Findlaich, whom, he realized, had been civil to him. 'You will forgive me if I leave you now? For I have another appointment which might provide answers that we all seek. Pardon me if I do not invite you along.'

'To the Boar's Tusk?'

Crispin nodded. 'I realize I can't prevent you from coming . . .'

Findlaich raised a conciliatory hand. 'We'll no follow you, Master Guest. We can find out what transpires, at any rate. We *will* speak again. But be warned. You mustn't trust the others. They are dangerous men, despite what they might have told you.'

'And you? Am I to trust you?'

Findlaich spread out his hands. 'I have no harmed you or yours. I am a man doing my duty to his laird. But the others. They are only out for themselves. I would hire you, aye, but if you've no mind for it, then I wish you God's speed. But tread carefully. Danger awaits.'

Crispin bowed. He didn't doubt it. The hulking man stepped aside from the door and Crispin was allowed to leave. He took several steps out to the street, stopped, and looked back. No one passed through the door to follow. A small mercy, he supposed.

He retraced his steps back to Gutter Lane, and the sight of that ale stake jutting into the road made his heart leap with hope and the familiar. The wooden sign carved into the shape of a tusk, with its peeling paint, creaked back and forth with a gust. He pushed the door open and stood for a moment on the threshold, casting his gaze across the noisy tavern hall, looking for men who looked like they might be looking for him . . . when his eyes fell on Eleanor. A sudden squeeze to his heart propelled him in her direction. She was laughing with some men at a table, pouring their ale from a round-bellied jug, her sleeves rolled up to her chapped elbows. Her ash blonde hair escaped from her linen kerchief but she didn't seem to notice it swaying before her flushed face. Her intent was on the men, and when one said something to her, she threw back her head and laughed.

Crispin moved closer and stood above the table, simply looking at her.

She pushed away that errant strand of hair at last, and then rested a hand on the shoulder of the man who had made her laugh, whispered something low to his ear, and was greeted with *his* laughter. A strange feeling, something like jealousy, rumbled in Crispin's chest, but when her gaze lifted and beheld him, her genuine smile of affection dusted any other emotions away.

'Crispin!' she said, hurrying around the table. She enclosed him in a hug, and though he was not given to public displays of affection, he endured it without complaint. 'You have an anxious look about you,' she said, setting the jug on the table and pulling on his arm. She maneuvered him to his favorite spot before the fire, facing the door. 'Wine?'

He stopped her from shoving him to the bench and instead took both her hands to gaze at her critically. 'Eleanor, are you all right?'

'Eh? Why wouldn't I be?'

'Well, it was just . . .' But it wasn't her that had been abducted. They had gotten the wrong 'Eleanor' after all. He smiled. 'All is well, then?'

'Of course! Well, the price of wine is ruining us. That Flemish wine has flooded the market and I don't know that we will recoup our own losses. We've had to lower our own prices accordingly, mind, which will no doubt cheer you, but other than that . . .'

'I'm glad to hear it, Eleanor. About you *and* the wine.' He lowered to the bench at last and clasped her hand. He couldn't seem to let it go. Charmed, she sat beside him.

'Crispin,' she said quietly, 'what vexes you?' She looked pointedly at her hand in his. His face heated in embarrassment.

'Sometimes, I worry over you. And Gilbert. You have rough clientele at times.'

She laughed heartily at that and took back her hand. 'Rough? These?' Her gesture swept over the men and women who frequented the tavern. Perhaps they weren't the best or richest merchants, and there were many who could barely pay for meat and drink – much like Crispin himself – but very few ever created trouble. And if in their drunken state they did, the other customers would soon set them to rights.

He conceded it with a bow to his head. 'At any rate, have a care.'

'You must be involved in very sticky doings if you are warning us. And where is that young knave, Jack Tucker? I've seldom seen him out of your company.'

The good feelings that warmed his chest turned suddenly cold. 'Eleanor,' he said quietly, confidentially. 'He's . . . he's been seized by the king.'

'*What*?' she shrieked, earning Crispin's cringing disapproval.

'Eleanor!' he hissed between clenched teeth.

Heeding his warning, she leaned closer. Her voice dropped down in volume to match his. 'By the saints! What mean you, Crispin?'

Staring only at the scared wood of the table, he told the tale, punctuated now and then by Eleanor's squeak of concern.

'And there are men I am to meet here.' His eyes flicked from table to table, looking for anyone who might be waiting for him to be alone.

'Oh Crispin.' She brought the hem of her napron to her wet eyes. 'Poor Jack!'

'Yes. So it is urgent I get on with it. Eleanor, your presence here might be a hindrance to that.' His expression softened when he saw hers. 'I'm sorry. I know you want to help . . .'

She rose. 'And I can best do that by staying out of your way.' She reached down and squeezed his arm. 'You'll do it, Crispin. You shall. Never fear that. Jack's fate is in good hands.' With a stiff nod, she ambled away, but looked back worriedly over her shoulder.

After sitting quietly, still surveying the room, Crispin saw Gilbert approach. He said nothing, but the concern in his eyes was easily readable. He set down a horn cup and alongside it a jug of wine. He nodded to Crispin and left him in peace. It had to have been the quietest exchange the two of them had ever made.

Crispin shuffled closer to the table, grabbed the jug, and poured himself the dark Flemish wine. He took up the horn cup, gave the wine a sniff, and pleased with what he found, drank. He sat upright, not leaning his arms on the table as he was wont to do. In most instances at the Boar's Tusk, his posture told all comers to leave him alone. But this time, he wanted to be approached. And yet, as open as he made himself, no one seemed inclined to do so.

He poured more wine – relishing the sweetness of it against the Boar's Tusk's usual sharp fare – and watched the room under brooding brows. A half hour. An hour. Two. Plainly, no one was there who wanted to talk to him. Another false lead? Who was that man who had urged him to go to the Boar's Tusk? Was that merely a misdirection?

He mulled Findlaich's words of warning. He had no doubt that these men were dangerous. They risked their necks under Richard's eye to do this thing. If Richard even had an inkling Crispin was talking with them, he'd be thrown into a cell. McGuffin seemed genteel enough and claimed he wasn't looking for the Stone, but could he be believed? And Findlaich had talked of others. These that had wanted to meet him at the Boar's Tusk. Clearly, they were in competition with one another. But if Findlaich didn't have the Stone, then it must be with this third group.

'Fie on it,' Crispin muttered and pushed away from the table.

There was just the merest satisfying sottedness to his head from the wine when he rose that he left extra coins on the table. He left the alehouse without bidding his farewells to the Langtons. He was too tired for that. He felt as if he had run races in full armor. He'd start again tomorrow. He was in no mood or humor to think of any more solutions today.

It wasn't a long walk from the Boar's Tusk to his lodgings on the Shambles. Martin Kemp, his tinker landlord was still at his work at the little table under the shelter of a propped-up shutter, even as the sun dipped toward the rooftops.

He raised his face from his work with a smile. 'Greetings, Crispin!'

Crispin attempted a smile. 'Martin.'

'You've been quiet of late. You must be at another of your Tracker tasks, eh?'

'Yes, I must be.' He trudged toward the stairwell that hugged the side of the building.

'While you were out, those men came by.'

Crispin had just set his hand to the railing when he stopped. '"Those men"?'

'Yes.' He bent back to his work, delicately hammering nails flat against a tin patch on a pot. 'They were naturally curious as to when you would return. I wanted to let them in to wait, as I am accustomed to doing, but Alice insisted they did not. Said that most trouble upstairs comes when I allow your clients in. I can't say that she's wrong.'

'I think that was most prudent this time.' *And as much as I hate to say it,* 'Give my thanks to your . . . good wife.'

Martin snapped his head up at that. 'My . . . *good* wife? Dear me. Now I know trouble is afoot.'

Crispin offered him a genuine smile. 'Don't worry, Martin. Only the usual amount, I should think.'

As he trudged up the stairs, he noted silently that news of the Stone had yet to travel to the Shambles. Or at least Crispin and Jack's involvement in it. But who were the men who had come to see him? It seemed that three factions were somehow involved, and none wanting anything to do with the other. Were these the errant ones that had not made an appearance at the Boar's Tusk?

Unlocking and pushing open the door revealed the cold, empty room, just as they had left it that morning. Crispin unbuckled his sword and hung it up on the peg by the door and likewise his dagger sheath. He stumped toward the hearth and knelt beside it. Poking the ashes aside, he searched for any amount of remaining kindling, found some sticks, and dragged them forward. He rose briefly to retrieve the tinder box, reached in, and got flint and steel to raise a spark on the tinder and bits of straw he had snatched from Jack's straw pile. Soon a small fire was going.

He coughed from the smoke and withdrew to his bed. Pulling off his leather hood and casting it toward the table, he unbuttoned his cloak, draped it over the blanket, and after removing his boots, he climbed into bed and drew the blanket and cloak over him.

He slept a few hours before the pounding on the door awakened him. Dusk had fallen. He scrubbed at his face with a cold hand, cast a glance at the still glowing hearth, and pulled himself to his feet. Head still bleary, he yanked open the door and froze. He blinked stupidly, not quite believing what he was seeing.

Lady Katherine smirked and raised a brow. 'Has it been too long, Crispin? Do you no longer recognize me?'

TEN

Crispin swallowed and squeezed his eyes shut before opening them again. Clearing his throat he shook his head. 'My lady,' he said before clearing his throat again. 'I am . . . surprised . . . to see you.'

'No doubt.' She paused for a moment more before ducking her head. 'Will you invite me in, Master Guest?'

He grimaced and stepped aside. 'Yes, of course, forgive me.'

She signaled to her retainer at the bottom of the stairwell before striding in. Slipping off her leather gloves, she moved toward the table, looking around.

Crispin felt the pall of humiliation drape over him that she, too, was seeing where he lived. It was bad enough that Lancaster and Henry Derby had seen it. He felt as if all of court now knew, now saw.

He looked down and noticed that he stood in his stocking feet. Hurrying to the bed, he sat and hastily stuffed his feet into his boots again.

'I . . . may I offer you some wine?' He was almost certain he had some. 'Or . . . something. A chair?'

She swiveled and regarded him. 'I don't require anything, Crispin,' she said softly. It was that same voice. He remembered it, after all this time. Her gentle look, her calm voice. She had been governess to Lancaster's daughters but it was often that his sons would seek her out as well for comfort. Little they would get from their own harsh governors. And Crispin, who knew well before the children what she and Lancaster were to one another, had stood off at a distance, measuring her interactions, her intentions, looking for any slights she might offer the children or Lancaster's wives. He had looked for anything that might have shown any disrespect that would reflect badly onto his lord. But she hadn't. She had always been demure but firm, running the nursery like a chatelaine in a castle.

'Very well. Er . . . forgive me, Lady Katherine, but, er, what exactly are you doing here?' *God's blood!* She didn't want to hire him, did she?

'Tactful as always, Crispin.'

He shook his head. Dammit. 'I . . . I didn't mean anything by it
. . . I . . . I . . .' She had always had that effect on him, making
him act like a fool, like a school boy who had been caught at some
mischief, even though twelve years separated the last time they had
even seen each other let alone talked.

Pressing her lips together, she shook her head, desperately control-
ling a smile. He scowled. Nothing had changed in the last twelve
years. Not for her. She was still Lancaster's mistress, as far as he
knew. He was no prude, but he had never liked the fact that she and
Lancaster . . . well. It was unseemly.

She turned and stood before the fire, warming her hands. She did
not face him as she spoke. 'I see you still do not approve of me,
Crispin.'

Crispin straightened, remembering himself. 'It is not for me to
approve or disapprove of you, Lady Katherine.'

'And yet,' she said with a sigh, 'you always make it known.'

He bowed his head.

'I am on a mission of mercy. And to bring you information . . .
as concerns Young Jack Tucker.'

He snapped up his head and moved swiftly toward her. 'What?
What has happened?'

'Nothing has happened, Crispin. Oh, I am saying this badly. I
merely came to tell you that he is in good hands. Henry has taken
over my duties in succoring him.'

He blinked, slowly processing her words. 'Henry is . . . and you
were . . .'

'I wasn't at the abbey when it all transpired, but I certainly heard
about it. I made it my personal task to seek out Young Jack and to,
well, rescue him from the cell in which he was housed. I feared for
his safety there, for it is a forgotten place and other prisoners have
not been kept well, I am afraid. I took him into my lodgings, but
it was soon discovered what I had done. Henry intervened and took
Master Tucker to his own lodgings for safekeeping.'

'And what . . . what did the king make of that?'

'That I do not know, but my instincts tell me he won't be best
pleased.' She pulled out the chair and sat, arranging her skirts about
her. She settled her hands in her lap and merely looked at Crispin
for a long time. 'You look well, under the circumstances.'

He paused before pulling out the stool and sitting across from
her. 'And you look ever lovely. I hope all is well with you.'

She smiled and inclined her head in a bow. 'All is well. The children are grown, but now they have children of their own. I am still busy.'

'And . . . his grace, the duke? I hope . . . I take it he is well?'

'Yes. He writes to me.'

Crispin scowled, though he tried not to. 'I . . . do not hear of him.' *There is no one to ask,* was left unsaid.

'I know. But be assured, Crispin, he does think of you. Often.'

He would have given anything to stop the hot flush to his face. 'He . . . should not.'

'Do you presume to tell the duke what to do, Crispin? *I* certainly do not.'

They sat in silence for a time. He could not draw his gaze any higher than the table, but he noticed out of the corner of his eye that she freely perused his lodgings. Finally her gaze settled on him again. 'I have seen more cheerful rooms.'

He coughed. 'Yes. So have I.'

'Be of good cheer, Crispin. Master Tucker has great faith in you. And so do I.'

His embarrassment should have lessened but didn't.

'And Master Tucker wished for me to impart information to you. He thought it important that you should know about John Dunbar, earl of Moray.'

Frowning, Crispin searched for that name in his memory. 'I do not know of a John Dunbar.'

'I had heard that he was one of the lords instigating the uprising in the north and was there at the latest battle at Otterburn only a month ago.'

'Yes,' he said slowly. 'I do seem to have heard something of the kind. How does this name help our cause?'

She shrugged. 'It was only that Young Jack deemed him important. I believe he felt that this earl might have instigated this latest outrage in Westminster.'

'Earl of Moray, you say?' He rose and began to pace across the room. 'He is in Northumberland, is he not? Is it known where he is now?'

'I do not know. Does it matter? When my lord of Gaunt wishes something accomplished, he need not even be in the country for his wishes to be carried out. It can also be so with this Scottish lord.'

'Yes. You are right, of course.'

'Jack wishes to do all he can to help. He has advised me to tell you that he, too, will be investigating.'

Crispin stopped and whirled to face her. 'What? He is under no circumstances to investigate.'

'He insists he can help—'

'I forbid it! The fool!' He recommenced pacing. 'Is he not in enough peril already?' He turned again and pointed a finger at her. 'You tell him that he is to keep low and out of trouble.'

Lady Katherine fussed with her gown's sleeve. 'I am surrounded by men who cannot be commanded one way or the other,' she muttered.

'Tell Jack—'

She rose. 'Master Guest, I have the distinct impression that the apprentice is just as stubborn as the master. I can relay your message, certainly, but I have no hope of it ever being obeyed.'

'Madam—'

'Crispin! May I offer only a small portion of advice?'

He blinked, breathed, and settled his shoulders. 'Of course.'

'Move slowly. Think. Assess. *Then* act. This has always been your greatest fault.'

He had forgotten that she was one of the few who watched him grow from someone of Jack's age to manhood. And she had raised sons, her own as well as Lancaster's. She would naturally know how men react. Yet always before, he was reluctant to take her advice. He had scoffed at her and her relationship, at the bastards she had given birth to. He grasped those old feelings for a few moments more . . . before letting them go. Who was *he*, after all, to take the high moral ground, he who had committed treason?

He could see that she was only trying to help him. And her relationship to Gaunt and Gaunt's to her were none of his affair, and never were. And, in fact, it seemed to be an enduring love, one that had not been deterred by time or circumstances. His fusty convictions on the matter were becoming gray and worn through, like old fabric.

He shuffled uncomfortably. 'I am doing my best, Madam.'

She smiled kindly and something shivered in Crispin's heart. He opened his mouth to say – he knew not what – when the door burst open.

John Rykener, still in his woman's clothing, spilled into the room and rolled across the floor until he hit the table, legs flailing from his skirts.

'Dammit!' he cried, rubbing his head. 'Damnable table.' He looked up with a sheepish smile for Crispin until he noticed Lady Katherine. Rykener scrambled to his feet and straightened out his clothes. 'Forgive me,' he said. His voice was suddenly gentle and light, more like a woman's than a man's.

Crispin shot a look toward Lady Katherine. By the astonished expression upon her face he could tell she had not been fooled. Crispin dropped his face into his hand. 'Lady Katherine, may I present my friend . . . John Rykener. John, Lady Katherine Swynford.'

'Oh bollocks,' John whispered before curtseying.

Lady Katherine drew herself up with all the aplomb she had garnered from years at court. 'It is a great pleasure to meet one of Crispin's friends . . . Master, er, Rykener.'

'The honor is mine, Lady Swynford. Please . . . forgive me my uncouth words and . . . well, my appearance. It is a long tale . . .'

'Of that I have no doubt.' She turned to Crispin and grasped his arm. 'I must go. Be at peace. Jack is in good hands. And please, Crispin, take care, but do so in all haste.'

'*Festina lente*,' he murmured.

'Precisely. Fare well. God keep you. And you as well, Master Rykener.'

'My lady.' Rykener bowed and quickly moved to open the door for her.

She gave Crispin one last glance over her shoulder before she was gone.

Red-faced, Crispin turned on Rykener. 'Thanks much for that, John!'

ELEVEN

J ack saw very little of Lord Derby, but he saw far too much of his servants. There was no idleness in Henry Bolingbroke's apartments. The servants set Jack to work for his keep immediately, and he was happy to finally feel useful. But as dusk settled over Westminster, the steward left him alone at last, and Jack was once more on his own.

He walked the lonely rooms like a shadow. He had been told by the servants through their mistrustful glares, that the young lord's family resided elsewhere on their lands far from Westminster. That was where Lady Katherine was supposed to be as well, but Jack got the impression that Lady Katherine did very much what she liked. Despite her being Lancaster's mistress – something that seemed to displease the pious king – she appeared to be well-liked and roamed freely throughout court, even in Lancaster's absence.

A fact that Jack was mightily grateful for.

He cast about, peering into cupboards, prowling into coffers, and dragging out the beautiful fabrics of Damascene and embroidered velvets, holding them up to the golden light from the windows. He whistled in appreciation, knowing he held in his hands bags full of marks. Carefully, he replaced them, closing the lids again. *Them coffers should be locked*, he mused, ticking his head at thoughts of the steward who had earlier pushed him about most rudely.

Wandering farther, he found another parlor and a door. Looking around, he tried the latch and was surprised to find that it, too, opened. 'If Master Crispin were in charge,' he muttered, 'all them doors would be locked.' He shoved it open and walked out into a walled garden.

He took in the little pathways, the small, trimmed shrubs, the flowers nearly at the end of their blooming, and the trees, their leaves shimmering from the breeze off the Thames just over the wall.

He breathed deep. Master Crispin always said that Jack would become 'squirrelly' if he remained indoors too long, and it was true. Winter was the hardest, for it was bitterly cold outside and yet Jack found himself stealing down the deserted alleys and haunting archways.

He needed the air. And there was plenty of it in the garden as the day slowly faded in that secluded place.

But amid the chirping birds and the scramble of a mouse into the underbrush, he heard a faint sound of someone weeping. Stealthily, he searched within the garden, but his ears led him to the wall between this and the next apartments. He gauged the wall and reached up, finding a handhold. Pulling himself higher, he carefully placed each foot into crevices in the stone, and in that way, like a spider, he scaled the wall and gingerly peered over the top to the next garden.

A young woman, face in her hands, was weeping softly. She sat on a carved bench under a beech tree. Her gown was of fine samite and silks with an embroidered cloak covering her shoulders and flowing down to her feet. She was young, and of what Jack could see, beautiful.

Jack secured himself to the wall and hissed, 'Demoiselle!'

She instantly stopped crying and raised her head, searching for the voice.

'Pssst! Up here!'

She turned wide, moist eyes on him, blinking. Jack's heart leaped at the tender sight of her.

'Lovely Demoiselle, why do you weep?'

She wiped her nose with the back of her hand and sniffed. 'You would not understand.'

He liked the way she cocked her head and her odd little accent. He could not tell from where she hailed. 'Oh, I might understand more than you think.'

She looked steadily at Jack. 'Who are you, boy?'

'I'm just a man what sees a lady in distress. And as a proper and genteel man, I offer you my services. How can I help?'

A smile flickered at her mouth. 'You are kind. But my troubles are great. I doubt the likes of you – despite your, what was it you called it? Ah, your "proper and genteel" ways – could possibly help me.'

'But, my lady! What is a man if he cannot help his fellow man, and the weakest of them? For Woman is to be succored and cared for. So my master says.'

'Your master sounds like a kind and sensible man.'

'He is, my lady. Ever so. And he has taught me his ways. So come now. What can I fix for you? Surely it cannot be such a trial as you make it.'

A deep sigh raised her shoulders. 'There is much you do not know.'

He grasped the edge of the wall and settled himself. 'Help me to know.'

She sniffed again and turned her head, staring distantly into a small grouping of white-barked trees. 'Something . . . has been stolen.'

'Oh?'

'Yes. Something of great value. And I very much fear that I shall be in grave circumstances because of it. Because . . .' She paused and then whispered, 'Because of my husband.'

'Oh, my lady. This grieves me greatly. And a great knave it is that has stolen this thing from you. Are you certain that it isn't merely mislaid?'

She nodded, the tears coming again and streaking down her face. 'I fear the worst,' she rasped. 'That they did not merely steal it but wish to do me further harm by extorting me for its return.'

Jack was suddenly enraged. That such a lovely and innocent woman should be so abused! He longed to pull his dagger and show the knave a thing or two about courtesy to a lady. But he calmed himself and straightened his shoulders – as much as he could while clinging to the top of a wall.

'And so you see,' she said softly, 'I am quite alone in this. I have not even told my maids. In truth, I do not even know why I am telling you.' She gazed at him, searching his face. 'You seem like a dream, like an angel come to save me.'

'No angel I, my lady. And no dream either.'

'I do not know why I find it easy to speak these things to you. But you have a kind and open face. Has anyone ever told you that before?'

Jack flushed and lowered his eyes a moment. 'Ah, no, my lady. I have never been called such.' He smiled with what he hoped was a reassuring expression. 'But you have seen the truth of it. God must be shining down on both of us to reveal it to you.'

'Maybe you *can* help,' she muttered. 'Maybe . . . there is a chance . . .'

'My lady, you do not know how lucky this encounter is. For my master is a man who has years of training in finding such lost objects. And as his only apprentice, I have learned these fine skills m'self.'

She looked up again. 'You have? Praise God!'

'Oh, aye! We have recovered many a lost item, big or small. The great and the lowly. My master is well known for these skills throughout London.'

'Oh? Such a fine thing and a skilled master. What is your name, sir?'

He tried to bow but nearly lost his footing. She made a squeak and rose partway before he recovered himself and chuckled. 'Never fear, my lady. I am as sure-footed as any goat.'

'Then should I call you that? My Goat?'

He laughed. 'Ah, my lady. Is that any name for your savior?'

She sobered quickly. 'You are right, sir. I should not jest.'

He did not like that solemn look to her face. It was much more beautiful when a smile lit her eyes.

'My lady, if it pleases you to call me "Goat," then who am I to naysay you? "Goat" it is.'

She did smile at that, and Jack's heart warmed. But her smile soon faded. 'How can I ever tell you what has transpired? How can I ever say?'

'Well, as my master says, it's best to begin at the beginning and then I can see how it all lies.'

She opened her mouth to speak, but the door to her garden burst open and a gaggle of lady's maids spilled out. 'My lady, you must come inside,' said the oldest, in the same strange accent as the young woman.

'Oh, but . . .' She looked up helplessly at Jack.

He smiled and waved her off and gave her the thumbs up. She frowned at that, not seeming to understand, and cocked her head beguilingly.

'My lady, please!' cried the lady's maid, grabbing the woman's elbow and lifting her to her feet. Jack could see that she was a delicate creature and not too tall.

Still she hesitated, seeming reluctant to leave Jack. He tried to convey that he would be back with gestures and head nods.

'My lady,' said the impatient maid. 'Your husband the *king* awaits!'

Jack's heart seized and his jaw fell slack. They ushered her away at last. She glanced once over her shoulder toward him with a hopeful expression before the door closed on her.

Jack's hands slipped, and he slid none too gently over the rough stone wall back down on his side of the garden. He fell in a heap and stayed there a good long time until the smell of wet earth filled his nostrils and the sun set over the rooftops of Westminster.

TWELVE

'Peace, Crispin. Must you pace so?'

Still red-faced with embarrassment, Crispin moved restlessly about the room. Did he not live in poverty enough to embarrass himself? Must his associates make it worse? 'And why are you still in those clothes, John?' he growled.

'I didn't have time to change . . . and Stephen likes me in them.'

'Spare me the details.'

'Well, if you will ask . . .'

'What did you find out? About the gonne powder?'

'Ah, well then. Stephen has agreed to talk with you tomorrow and tell you about obtaining the stuff.'

'Right.' Crispin rubbed at his face. Pangs of hunger clawed at his insides, the first he had felt in a while. He turned toward the pantry shelf and saw a coney hanging upside down by its feet and silently blessed Jack. 'Will . . . will you sup with me, John? My apprentice has left us a rabbit. And though I am a poor cook, it will be sustenance.'

'I have a way in the kitchen. Will you let me cook it for us?'

'Is there no end to your talents?'

'So many,' he chuckled. 'It is why I am so sought after.'

'John, details. Leave them out.'

John laughed outright at that but pulled down the coney, whipped out his dagger, and began to expertly skin the beast.

The rabbit was roasting nicely over the fire, and John and Crispin enjoyed the wine from their bowls. John had chopped the turnips along with their greens into a pot and had added an onion and a bit of butter and wine. Crispin thought it smelled heavenly, and his stomach growled equally in appreciation.

John leaned over and poked a pronged fork into the roasting flesh and declared that it was done and commenced tearing off the hindquarters and placing them on a wooden platter. He spooned the turnip and onion mixture onto the platter as well and placed it upon the table.

'There! A supper fit for a king.'

'Or only his servants.'

Crispin offered John the first choice, and the man stabbed a leg with his knife and brought the steaming meat to his lips. He took a bite and smiled, closing his eyes in ecstasy. 'Quite tasty, if I do say so myself.'

That was good enough for Crispin and he, too, dug in with his knife.

With his mouth full, John leaned into the table. 'What did you discover from those men in the tavern?'

Crispin speared a turnip and turned it, glaring at the cube. He was weary of turnips but when he took a bite it seemed to have a whole new flavor from what he was used to. John *did* seem to have a way in the kitchen. 'Those men never turned up. I was waylaid by yet other men. I tell you, John, there seems to be a wider conspiracy afoot. Or the left hand does not know what the right hand is doing.'

'Eh?'

'These factions. There seems to be little organization behind it. And though they know about one another, no one seems to have the Stone or know its exact whereabouts. It seems to be a conspiracy of fools.'

'And yet the Stone is just as gone as before.'

'Yes. It is serious. But the question is, do any of these men truly have anything to do with the Stone or are they using me to find it for them?'

John lowered his food to the platter and stared. 'That is diabolical indeed! Who would be so devious?'

'This is no mere prank. A lord is involved. Though it does me little good if he is in Scotland.'

'Then I would not worry over him but over his underlings, for *they* are the ones who are here.'

'Yes.' Crispin brought the wine bowl to his lips and drank, brooding. 'Have you ever heard the term "Mormaer"?'

John shook his head. 'I can't say I have. What is it?'

'I don't know. Some Scottish term or title. I shall have to seek out my Scottish spy in the morning.'

'Crispin! A Scottish spy! You are full of surprises.'

They talked as they ate, and when they were through and had cleared the platters and bowls and stirred the fire to something warm and pleasant, Crispin looked up at his visitor. 'It is late. You should stay.'

John's slow smile made Crispin immediately regret his choice of words. 'Why, Crispin!'

'You know what I meant, damn you! The straw. Over there! Jack isn't using it.'

John pulled off his gown at last and stood in his shift to unbraid his hair. 'Straw? Ah, this takes me back.' He laid his gown on the straw and sat atop it, using the folded blanket beside it to cover his feet and legs. 'You keep your apprentice on straw? Does not Jack deserve a cot at the very least?'

Crispin had divested himself of cotehardie and boots. He sat on his own rickety bed in stocking feet and his chemise. Frowning, he pulled his legs up and tucked them under the blanket. 'He has never complained.'

'Well he wouldn't now, would he? He's a proper apprentice, isn't he? And he adores you. He'd never complain or expect more than he gets, I suspect.'

Crispin lay back, resting his head on his laced hands, and watched the hearthglow waver on the ceiling. 'I . . . I suppose I never thought about it.'

'Bless me, I adore you, too, but you are sometimes a dense man, Crispin Guest.'

'That I am,' he said wearily.

He fell asleep later than he wanted, to thoughts of where in London to find a proper cot for his apprentice . . . and worrying that the boy would never come home to enjoy it.

Crispin awoke early, earlier than the snoring Rykener, and nudged him with his foot to awaken him. 'Get up, John. I have porridge.'

John yawned and stretched. 'What a quality host you are, Crispin.'

Crispin grunted in reply, tossed last night's wine from the bowls into the fire, and spooned barley porridge into each.

After they had eaten and made ablutions – John insisted on shaving first, holding out his hands and displaying his women's garb in explanation – he and Crispin left the lodgings just as the bells tolled Terce.

'We are early to meet him,' said John, pulling his cloak about him to ward off the chill wind.

'Does he live nearby?'

'Yes, but—'

'Let us go, then. We're wasting time.'

'But he won't like my making an appearance at his lodgings during the day.' Crispin gave him a look that made John roll his eyes. 'Very well. It's just down here on Dyer's Lane.'

Rykener led the way past merchants at their tables and boys with carts. A spotted dog trotted ahead of them, seeming to be on his own hurried business. John came to a dyer's shop and stepped through the door. The place smelled of acrid odors, and every surface seemed to be spattered in one way or another with a color. Crispin peered through a large open archway where apprentices were busy at vats, either stirring them with wooden stirrers the size of spades, or carrying bolts of muslins and wool.

A man carrying a burden of bolts backed out of a storage room and called over his shoulder, 'I shall attend to you shortly, Madam and Good Sir.'

'We'll wait,' said John in his softened voice.

The man whirled, his bolts flying out of his hands. Wide eyes raked over John, and the man's suddenly blushing face took in Crispin as well. 'Good Christ!' he hissed. His head jerked over his shoulder, searching out his apprentices who were still busy in the other room. 'Christ Almighty, John! I told you I'd meet you!' he whispered, looking John up and down. 'You could have at least changed your clothes . . .'

'That's what I keep telling him,' said Crispin. 'This is urgent, sir. Can we talk now?'

'Now?' He winced, thinking, until he noticed his cloth scattered upon the floor. 'Curse you, John Rykener.' He bent to pick up the bolts.

'That's not what you said yesterday,' said John, stooping to help him.

The now sweating man cast a guilty glance at Crispin. 'For God's sake, John. Your friend . . .'

'Knows well who John Rykener is,' said Crispin. 'Come, man. Put your cloth away and come now to talk. Please.'

The man nodded and collected his bundles from John. He stuffed them on a shelf and grabbed his cloak from a peg by the door. 'I'm going out!' he called loudly to the back.

If his apprentices heard, they did not signal such, but only continued their vigorous work with the dying vats.

The dyer shoved John toward the door, frowning. Crispin followed. Without another word the man led them to a tavern. Inside was darker and smokier even than the Boar's Tusk. They trailed through the long tables and found a spot near the back.

After the tavern keeper brought them a jug of ale and three cracked and chipped beakers, John leaned in. 'Stephen, this is Crispin Guest. Crispin, my friend, Stephen.'

Stephen nodded to Crispin, hunched over his cup, and drank a dose.

'Master Stephen, I do not know if John imparted to you the seriousness of my quest, but . . .'

'I know who you are, Master Guest,' said the dyer, still hunching low. He was John's height and lank build, and wore a neatly trimmed brown beard. He cast his eyes about, but there was no one near enough to overhear them. 'I would not have my association with . . . with *Eleanor*, here, get around. Get my meaning?'

'I have no wish to divulge such information, Master Stephen.'

John rested his chin on his hand and watched the two of them silently. Occasionally he lifted his beaker to his lips, took a sip, and set the beaker down again.

Crispin encircled his beaker with his fingers but did not drink. 'I was given to understand that you were a gonner, Master Stephen.'

Stephen wrung his hands. 'I am. That is my brother's dying shop, and I assist him when I can. It is the family business. And I have not been required by his majesty's army for some weeks. When we are near London again, sometimes we are housed with the garrison at Westminster and sometimes we are allowed to go back to our businesses.'

'I see. But as you know, I was wondering about explosive powder.'

'Yes, so John, er, Eleanor said.' He licked his lips. 'There is a man who makes the stuff, as far as I can tell. He makes it for the king's army, but I happen to know he sells some on the sly as well.'

'And how do you know?'

'Because he asked us gonners if we wanted to buy our own. You see, some of us are not men of business. Some are men of opportunity, so to speak. Mercenaries. I can well see how such a thing can prove beneficial if, say, one were to try to break into a rich man's house. You can blow up a wall if you are skillful.'

'Indeed. Will you tell me who and where this man is?'

He glanced at John, and almost imperceptibly, John nodded. 'Well, yes. I can tell you. Or show you, if I must.'

'It is much appreciated, Master Stephen.'

'Anything to get you out of my hair,' he muttered.

Rykener, who was sitting across from the man, slipped from his bench, shot around the table, and scooted in next to Stephen. 'And do you want me out of your hair as well, Stephen?' he whispered.

All wide eyes again, Stephen took in Crispin before he cringed and lifted his red-faced gaze to John. 'You know I don't,' he said quietly.

John grinned from ear to ear. 'Neither do I want the same.'

Crispin coughed lightly. 'Gentlemen?'

'Oh dear,' said John with a laugh. He moved away from Stephen and grabbed his cup still sitting across the table. 'We're making moon eyes at each other in front of the Tracker. What *will* he think of us? And he has much important work to do. Stephen, will you tell him where he can find the man he seeks?'

'Yes. Yes, of course.' He explained to Crispin that the man could be found on Trinity and Le Reol. A shop without distinguishing signs or marks, between a tyler and a pavior.

'Much thanks,' said Crispin, leaving coins on the table. He rose and, with a nod to the men, headed toward the door. He was almost outside when someone grabbed his arm.

'You're not leaving without me, are you?' said John.

Crispin glanced back to the wary dyer, clutching his beaker, eyes darting about the room. 'I had every intention to do just that.'

'But I am going with you.'

'No.' Crispin grasped John's wrist and yanked it from his arm. 'You are not.' He pushed open the door and stepped outside. His destination was beyond St Paul's, mid-city. He set out again when John trotted to head him off. Walking backward in front of him, John pouted.

'But Crispin, I'm the one who got you the information.'

'And I thank you for it.'

'I want to help.'

'You can help by staying out of the way.' He used his arm to nudge John aside none too gently.

'But, Crispin! I can be useful.' He slid in close up against him and wrapped his hands around his arm. 'So you said last night.' He said it purposely loud enough so that those standing close by turned to look, eyes assessing both Crispin and Rykener.

Crispin gritted his teeth. 'I'm going to kill you,' he said under his breath.

Rykener squeezed his arm and smiled into his face. 'No, you're not,' he purred.

'Yes, I am,' he hissed. He looked around and sighed. 'Very well . . . but let *go* of me.'

Rykener carefully unwound his hands and strode happily alongside Crispin, who glowered whenever anyone looked his way.

They cut down Old Fish Street that became Trinity. Crispin raised his head to look at the signs. A basket maker, a wheelwright, a chandler . . . finally a tyler and there the pavior, and in between no sign at all. Crispin stopped and studied the plain door. 'This must be it.'

'It's exciting, isn't it?'

Crispin gave him a withering look. 'It's nothing of the kind. Now wait here.'

'Not on your life.'

'Then for God's sake, John, please be quiet.'

Rykener nodded, but the light leaping in his eyes gave Crispin enough reason to worry. He knocked on the door anyway. They waited until a bolt was thrown back and the door creaked open. A man with a bluntly sculpted face peered at them from the gloom. 'Well then?' he asked in a roughened voice.

Crispin bowed slightly. 'Are you the man who makes explosive powder?'

The man sucked on his teeth. 'Who wants to know?'

'I am Crispin Guest, sir. I am also known in London as the Tracker.'

The man's eyes widened. 'What . . . what do you want with me?'

'I would speak with you on a matter of some urgency.'

The man scowled and looked down at his feet. At last, and with a reluctant shake of his head, he pulled the door open wider and stepped aside. 'In, then.'

Crispin walked through and John followed. The man eyed Rykener but closed the door after them and bolted it for good measure.

The place was dark and close and had the unpleasant odor of sulfur permeating its timbers.

John stumbled against a stool and scoffed. 'Can you not light a candle, man?'

'No, I can't. There is great danger in candle flames and my work.' He eyed John most peculiarly. Crispin thought he knew why. In his clumsiness, John had neglected to use his 'Eleanor' voice.

'At least open a window,' said John, more softly this time.

The man stomped to the window and pushed open the shutter, letting in light and a fresh gust of air. 'Better? Now what do you want?'

'I have it on authority,' said Crispin, 'that you are in the habit of selling your explosive powder to individuals.'

'What of it? It isn't against the law.'

Crispin stood taller than the man and made certain to make a point of looking down at him. 'No, it isn't against the law. The letter of the law, that is.'

'You make little sense. State your business or be on your way.'

'Let's not be hasty. I need to know if you have sold any of this powder to any northerners of late.'

'Northerners?' He scratched his jaw where a weedy beard shadowed his chin. 'Yes, come to think of it. There was a group of northerners just a sennight ago. They paid good English coin for it, so I explained how to use it and they were on their way. They only bought a small amount.'

'Did they say what it was for?'

'No. They paid their money. What did I care?'

Crispin ticked his head. 'A man should take better care of his soul, sir. *The man who does not rejoice in noble actions is not good.* Little did you know what mischief would come of their purchase.'

'I can't be the conscience of every man.' He strode to the door and threw the bolt. 'I told you what you wanted to know. Now I must be back to my work.'

Crispin didn't budge. 'Can you describe the men?'

He shook his head and shrugged. 'They were like any other men. Except they were northerners. Could barely understand their speech.'

'There was nothing distinguishing about them? Tall or short? Broad or thin?'

'We-e-ell.' He scrubbed at the back of his head. He stared distantly, attempting to think, or so Crispin hoped, when he shot his hand forward, pointing out the window. 'There goes one now!'

Crispin leaped toward the window, eyes scanning the people on the street, trying to discern if anyone looked familiar to him. 'Are you certain?'

'Yes.'

'Well, which one, man?'

The man went to the window, standing shoulder to shoulder with Crispin. He pointed at a lordly-looking man in a mustard-colored cotehardie. 'That's him there.'

Crispin turned on his heel and grabbed for the door latch. He flung the door open and tore across the threshold. 'You there!' he cried.

Several people turned, looking curiously at Crispin. When the man in the mustard cotehardie turned, his eyes blazed, and he broke into a run.

I hate it when they run. Crispin took a breath and pelted after him, but he was overtaken by a blur in a skirt. Before he could register what was going on, John Rykener leaped and felled the man in a hard tackle to the mud. The man skidded a few feet on his face.

John turned a mud-spattered smile to Crispin with the man struggling beneath him, swearing all manner of Gaelic oaths. 'I got him, Crispin! I *got* him!'

THIRTEEN

Jack had slept fitfully all through the night. He could not get it out of his head that he had been speaking to the queen! And in a most disrespectful manner. *Oh, Jack. It's like you're asking for the gallows.* But Queen Anne had seemed like any other young lady: sad, frightened, desperate. Like many of Master Crispin's clients, truth be told. Didn't she deserve the same help as any other?

'And I *would* help if I could . . .'

He cringed on his cot, even as the weak sun of morning threw gray light into the small servant's room. *You're a coward is what you are,* he admonished. He had almost spoken it aloud but remembered that there were other servants snoring softly around him. Sitting up, his gaze swept over the curled bodies of boys in the employ of Henry Bolingbroke. He cast his blanket aside, and as quietly as he could – for he knew that arrogant steward would be in any moment to awaken them all – Jack slipped off of his cot and tiptoed toward the door. He gently pulled it open and left the little room.

He breathed free again, standing in one of many parlors. Without thinking too hard about it, he went to the hearth, and set about building up the fires. But even as he worked, the face of that gentle woman – *the queen!* he reminded himself – kept creeping into his thoughts.

She was distressed, and didn't *he* know about getting on the wrong side of King Richard! What could this missing thing be that clapped her in such danger? But how could that be? All the kingdom knew how much Richard doted on his wife, even as childless as she remained. She could simply be imagining her distress . . . yet, it had looked real enough to him.

God's blood, he *wanted* to help! He could do nothing for himself holed up as he was, but he might be able to do something for the queen. Still, he needed advice. Whom could he ask? Henry was a busy man, and Jack did not feel that he could approach him. Lady Katherine, on the other hand . . . But she was in her lodgings across the corridor, and he was supposed to be in hiding. Still, it was early yet. Perhaps he could make his way over there, await her.

He liked that plan. And with no one around he decided to chance it.

Stealthily, he passed through the archways to the main parlor, first standing against the wall and peering carefully around the corner. A servant was laying the fires, but as soon as he had accomplished his task, he disappeared through another door. Jack saw his chance.

He trotted silently across the chequerboard floor and grasped the latch. Gently, quietly, he turned the key in the lock and pulled it open. Face pressed against the jam, he searched up both ends of the corridor. A guard paced down at the far end and Jack waited until he had turned away before he darted forward and pressed himself against the walls and made his way to Lady Katherine's suite.

He tried the door, but naturally it was locked. He had only moments until the guard had a chance to spot him, so he dropped to his knees, withdrew his lockpicks, and began to drop the pins one by one. They fell easily to his skillful ministration, and he was in with the door closed, before the guard ever blinked in his direction.

Inside he looked around. He could wait there in the outer parlor, or he could try to find her. Hubris had gotten him this far. He reckoned it might as well take him all the way forward.

There were several bedchambers in the apartments, but he wasn't certain which one was hers. Not being the burglar kind of thief, he wasn't used to creeping about into bedchambers.

He stood in the antechamber and folded his arms. *If I were the duke of Lancaster, I'd want a grand bedchamber.* Before him stood a wide door, carved in intricate detail. *But if I were his mistress, I would not be in it, as it would not be my place. And so, I would be close, but not too close.*

He passed the closest bedchamber and went toward the third. He rubbed his cold hands together and grabbed the latch. Locked. It took only moments to break through, and he slipped in with his back to the door. The large bed had its curtains drawn. The hearth glowed from banked coals, but a lady's maid – a very young one – lay nestled in an alcove by the hearth. How was he to get rid of her?

All thoughts fled when she started to stir. Jack darted under the bed as the maid yawned and stretched.

He peered out from under the bedframe to watch as she rejuvenated the fire, grabbed the jug, and quietly left the room to fetch water.

Once the door snicked closed, he slipped out from under the bed and stood before the curtains. If he were wrong . . . But also, what if he were right? Would she endorse such an intrusion? He moaned. And here he imagined he had thought it through.

'God help me,' he murmured, grasped the curtains, and opened them a sliver. Someone lay in the bed under the blankets. 'Lady Katherine!' he hissed. 'Please, Lady Katherine. Awake!'

Slowly she stirred but then froze. Without warning, she threw herself forward and faced Jack, a bejeweled dagger in her hand.

Jack fell backward onto the floor. 'My lady, it's only me, Jack Tucker!'

'Master Tucker?' Bare feet emerged from the side of the mattress and then the lady in her shift, bending to peer at him. 'Holy Mother! What in Heaven are you doing here?'

'Well . . .' He lay on his back like a turtle and felt, under the circumstances and looking at her poised dagger, that perhaps he had best stay there.

She scrambled out of bed, still brandishing her knife, and with a face full of fury stood over him.

'Forgive me, Lady Katherine. But I . . .'

'Get under the bed,' she demanded.

'But I—'

'*Get under the bed!*'

And then he heard the approaching footsteps, too. He swooped under just as the door opened.

'My lady,' said the maid. Jack stared at her feet in their pointed shoes and at Lady Katherine's bare ones. 'Where are your slippers? Let me fetch them for you, Madam.'

Scurrying feet, a hand reaching down and grabbing fur-trimmed shoes shot through with foliate embroidery, and then the maid knelt, offering them to the lady to slip on. Once she did Lady Katherine dismissed the girl.

'But my lady . . .'

'Warm some wine, Joanna. I will sit by the fire while you prepare it.'

The pointed shoes shuffled out of the room. The door closed, the bedclothes were cast aside, and Lady Katherine's face was glaring at Jack once more. 'Master Tucker?'

He slid out the other side and stood, brushing off his coat. 'I apologize, Lady Katherine. I did not think . . .'

'Boys your age very seldom do.' She huffed an exasperated breath and tugged on a fur-trimmed gown. She stepped purposefully toward the hearth and seated herself in a tall wooden seat, adjusting the cushion behind her. 'Quickly now, Master Tucker, what is it? Are you in danger?'

'Danger? Oh no, Lady Katherine. Not me, at any rate. I came to ask your advice.'

'And a simple note would not suffice?'

'No, no it wouldn't, I'm afraid. This is a delicate matter.'

He stood with his back to the flames, warming his backside. He hated to admit how good it felt. No wonder Master Crispin so regretted being tossed out of court, when there were fires and warm bedchambers and plenty of food and wine to be had.

'Well?' she asked, arranging her robes around her and fluffing the collar up around her jaw.

'Ah. Well, you see, yesterday I went out to the garden. His grace the earl has a wonderful garden, my lady, as wonderful as the duke's. And so I went out to take in the air and I heard a woman weeping. That's not a thing I can simply ignore, so . . . so I went to investigate. I climbed the wall, you see, to see what the matter was.'

'Most imprudent,' she muttered under her breath.

'Aye, that might be so, Madam. But I did, and I saw a young woman weeping most piteously. So I asked her what was wrong and befriended her, for she looked like she could use a kind face. And she was grateful . . . was this lady. And said that something was stolen from her and then, well, I might have boasted a bit about my master and me and how we find things.' Jack becrossed himself and flicked his eyes heavenward, beseeching forgiveness from on high.

She ticked her head. 'That was most gracious of you, Master Tucker. Noble, to wish to succor a woman in distress.'

'Aye. That was my thought. My master trained me so. And . . . so . . . I offered to help, to do as she wished. It's a point of honor, my lady.'

'And you wish to fulfill this oath.'

'Aye, that I do. But . . . then I discovered—'

They both glanced at the door and Jack dove for the bed again, pulling his feet in just as the door opened.

The maid set down a metal jug of steaming wine. She poured some into a silver goblet. 'It's a bit hot, Madam, so let that cool but a moment.'

'I shall. Thank you, Joanna. You may withdraw until I call you.'

'You . . . do not wish to dress?'

'In a moment. Let me enjoy the wine first.'

'Oh. Yes, Madam.' She seemed to hesitate before turning and walking out the door.

Jack poked his head out from under the bed again. 'I hadn't thought to hide under beds till I was a bit older.'

Lady Katherine hid a smile behind her hand and fussed with the goblet, blowing gently on the steamed wine. 'Is that something Master Guest taught you as well?'

He smiled sheepishly, feeling his cheeks warm. 'My lady. I'm speaking indelicately. I forget where I am.'

'No need to apologize, Master Tucker. It is good to have young people speak their mind to me again. It is very refreshing. But you were saying . . .'

'Oh! Well, I discovered that the lady over the garden wall . . .' He swallowed through a hard lump in his throat. 'The lady . . . is the *queen*.' He whispered the last and wrung his coat hem in his hands.

She sobered. 'Oh dear.'

'Aye. What am I to do?'

'Oh, Master Tucker. You and your master are well suited to one another.'

He couldn't disagree.

'I need not remind you how dangerous that could be, associating with Queen Anne. The king, after all, visits those quarters as well.'

'Aye, Madam. I am painfully aware of that. That is why I seek your advice. I made a promise to her, an oath. Is it mete that I should break it?'

She took a sip of the wine, swallowed, and then set the goblet to her thigh. 'No, Master Tucker. It is never proper to break one's oaths.'

'That's what I was afraid of.'

'Does she know who you are?'

He brightened. 'No! She called me an ekename: Goat. On account of my climbing the wall.'

'I see. Well, that is something. She doesn't know who you are or your association with Master Guest . . . and I would keep it that way.'

'That sounds a bit like I'm to talk with her again.'

'You made an oath, Master Tucker. Though it will not be easy to fulfill, you are bound by your honor to try.'

'Aye. Well then. How am I to contact her?'

'I shall help you there. I will send a message to the queen and tell her to meet me at Henry's lodgings. And there you will explain yourself.'

'Aye, my lady.'

'And now,' she said, rising. 'How to get you out of here?' She thought for a moment, staring at Jack the whole time, before she nodded. 'I am afraid I will be soiling one of my favorite shifts for you, Master Tucker.'

'Oh, my lady!'

'Never fear. A soiled shift is a little thing to the great deed you are to perform. It's best you get under the bed again.'

Puzzled, Jack complied and watched, wondering what he was supposed to do.

Lady Katherine stood staring into the fire for a moment when she picked up her goblet and deliberately poured it down her front. 'Joanna! Come quick!'

The maid scurried in.

'Look what a clumsy oaf I am, Joanna.'

'Oh, my lady. Let me get this off of you before it stains.'

Lady Katherine turned deliberately toward the door so that the maid stood with her back to it. Jack got the message quickly and slid smartly out from under the bed, and keeping low to the floor, made for the door. Lady Katherine winked at him as he finally slipped out.

He tiptoed through the antechamber, to the parlor, and out the main door and waited against the wall for the guard to disappear before trotting back toward Henry Bolingbroke's lodgings.

Once back inside he leaned against the door and breathed. 'Blind me with a spoon,' he gasped. A fool! A fool, to take such chances. It might have been wiser to simply forget his oath, but Master Crispin was too good a tutor.

It was early, but Jack was too agitated to simply wait for news. He set himself to work, and when the steward finally arrived, he was surprised when Jack was already at his tasks.

'Very good, Master Tucker. You are more industrious than the earl's common retinue.'

'Thank you, Master Waterton, but I am the product of my own master's industriousness. *In the arena of human life the honors and rewards fall to those who show their good qualities.* So says Aristotle. So my master teaches.'

Waterton's look of astonishment was almost comical. 'Indeed! I had heard of the qualities of Master Guest's philosophies but it was not in accord with his indictment of treason.'

Taken aback by the steward's harsh words, Jack lowered his face, feeling his master's shame. 'While it is true that a man's deeds are the mirror of his qualities, Master Crispin's intentions were never selfish. And he has paid the price many times over.' He lifted his eyes and looked Master Waterton in the face, for he didn't wish to imply that he was ashamed of his master by his manner.

'Well said, Master Tucker. Should you ever find yourself in need of employment, I would be happy to recommend you to his grace's household.'

'Oh! Master Waterton, that is a great honor. But I would never leave Master Crispin. You see, he needs me, sir.'

Waterton nodded with only a flicker of his lips. 'So he does. Carry on then, Master Tucker.'

Jack watched the man depart and continued the tasks he knew he could fulfill.

But as each hour struck, he kept glancing toward the main door, wondering when the queen might arrive. Would she? Surely it was better to concentrate on who stole that wretched Stone from Westminster Abbey. After all, if it could not be found in – he ticked the days off on his hands – two more days! – he would be doomed.

Two days. Would it be possible? Sometimes Master Crispin found stolen objects within hours. But this was more than a simple stolen item. This was a conspiracy, and that meant the hands of many men. The Stone could be anywhere, and suddenly two days did not seem enough time to find it.

A knock on the main door startled him and he froze, listening hard. A woman's voice! He crept through the antechamber and stood near the archway. Indeed, it was Lady Katherine.

'Forgive this intrusion, but I would speak to Lord Henry.'

The servant dithered. 'Lord Henry is not within.'

She pushed past him and entered into the warm room, with its tapestries and painted murals, dark wood sideboard and cupboard, and cushioned chairs by a merrily burning hearth. 'Then I will wait.'

'M-Madam. It is not known when his grace will return.'

'I am in no hurry. Do me the favor of fetching me warmed wine. I feel a chill. And, er, two goblets. One never knows, does one?'

Jack had seen that same expression on many an apprentice when their masters asked an unfathomable task of them. This servant was no different as he passed Jack hiding in the shadows. As soon as he was gone, Jack peered into the room. 'My lady!' he whispered.

'Come in, Master Tucker.' She watched him approach and stand over her as she sat. 'I have sent a message to the party in question, and she will arrive shortly.'

The servant returned and stiffened upon seeing Jack. Jack straightened and looked down his nose at the man. The servant set down a tray with a flagon and two goblets, all the while eyeing Jack with deep suspicion.

'You may go,' said Lady Katherine. 'Young Jack here will attend to me.'

The servant did not change his expression of suspicion as he left the room, but at least he did leave. Jack breathed again.

'Lady Katherine, I'm sorry for putting you through this.'

'I took responsibility for you. And I mean to see it through.'

'To the bitter end, eh?' He sagged. 'What . . . what will happen if Master Crispin can't . . . if he can't . . .'

She leaned forward and took his hand, holding it firmly between her two warm ones. He suddenly hoped he had washed it thoroughly enough this morning. 'Master Tucker, I've known Crispin a very long time. And I know once he has been set to a task he will fulfill it with all haste and skill. You must not give up faith in him. With his last breath he will defend you. I have seen it in his eyes. You are more important to him than any of the many servants he used to have.'

He swallowed. A ball of warmth filled the hollow place inside him. 'Truly?'

She smiled, squeezed his hand once, and then let it go.

He stepped back, took the flagon, and poured her wine, handing her the goblet with a bow. She took it with a nod of thanks and sipped.

They waited. Lady Katherine patiently amused herself by examining the tapestry across the room while Jack stood, hands behind his back to keep from fidgeting.

Half of the hour had passed and longer when a timid knock sounded on the door. Jack shot a look to Lady Katherine, and she calmly nodded to him. He rushed to the door, steadied himself, and opened it.

The anxious young lady – the queen – stood in the doorway, her lady's maid at her side. Her face snapped into surprise when she beheld Jack and a gasped 'oh!' released from her parted lips, but she quickly composed herself and turned to her maid. 'Please await me without.'

The maid, the older one he had seen in the garden, did not look as if she thought this a good idea, but she nevertheless bowed and stepped back away from the door.

Jack bowed low and opened the door wider for her to enter. He closed it after her, and she entered into the parlor and found Lady Katherine standing to greet her.

'It was so good of you to come, your grace,' she said, curtseying and gesturing toward a chair.

Queen Anne gave the room a cursory glance before she made her way to the chair, her gown's hem fluttering behind her, and sat. She gestured for Lady Katherine to sit as well, and both women faced one another.

Jack stood numbly for a moment before he scrambled to fetch the queen a goblet of warmed wine and presented it to her with another deep bow.

She took it graciously and studied Jack with a curious expression.

'I was puzzled, Lady Katherine, by your missive.' She spoke again with that same strange accent Jack could not identify. He knew that the queen had come from some distant country, but he didn't know where that was.

'The matter is . . . complicated, your grace.'

Queen Anne held herself differently in these surroundings, Jack noted, than she had in the garden. Among the autumn trees and faded foliage, she had seemed more at ease, more herself, but here, in this parlor, she sat stiffly, looking at Lady Katherine from the corner of her eye. Jack reasoned that the queen followed the dictates of her husband in all things. And he knew King Richard did not approve of Lady Katherine and her continued relationship with the duke of Lancaster. Perhaps the queen and Lady Katherine didn't have much of a rapport at all. The idea of it saddened him, for here was a family. The duke was the king's uncle, after all, and it seemed as if they all ought to be closer. On the Shambles, families might argue, but they all came together for meals, for festivals, for chatter over a beaker of ale. It seemed that the nobility were less content than those Jack had known on the streets of London. It made no sense, for surely wealthier people must be happier than his lot in places like the Shambles.

The queen flicked a glance at Jack before turning back to her goblet again.

'Perhaps,' said Lady Katherine, eyeing the both of them, 'it would be easier if we allow your . . . "Goat" . . . to explain himself.'

This time the queen turned her full attention to Jack and he shrank a little. Her blue eyes were wide and he again saw the distressed maiden in the garden beseeching. He licked his lips. 'Your grace, I . . . forgive me for speaking so liberally to you yesterday in your garden. I did not know who you were.'

A faint smile lightened her face.

'Ah. Then there is nothing to forgive. For you gave me honesty where others would have simply flattered, or worse, dismissed my worries.'

'Never that, your grace.'

'You're a sweet boy, my Goat.'

Jack's face scorched.

Lady Katherine rose. 'I think I should leave you to it. You have much to discuss.'

Jack reached out. 'Oh no, Lady Katherine!' He turned quickly to the queen. 'If you will pardon, Lady Katherine has been a friend to me, your grace. And she is a most discreet lady. Perhaps you might wish her to stay. I can do much to help you but she might be able to succor you. For it is said that a secret shared is a burden lifted.'

The queen looked from one to the other and offered a quick nod. Smoothly, Lady Katherine recovered her seat. They all fell silent again.

Jack remembered the many times clients had come to Master Crispin and him, burdened so heavily from their anxieties that they found it difficult to talk. He did what Master Crispin did and gentled his expression. 'Sometimes, your grace, it is easier to begin at the beginning. That way you can go through it all step by step,' he urged with a friendly nod.

She sighed, laying her hands in her lap and looking at them. 'Very well. I . . . there was this . . . object. In itself, it seemed innocuous. But once it was taken, it was explained to me how the king, my husband, might misconstrue. It might put me in bad stead with him.'

Jack stopped her with a raised hand. 'I see you are reluctant to name this object. We will let that lie for now.' He could hear his master's words in his head as he parroted them. 'But tell me. When was it exactly you noticed that it was missing?'

'It was the day of the explosion in the abbey.' She paused to briefly touch her lips with trembling fingers. Clearly, the event, though two days ago, was fresh in her fears. 'I had it on my person. When the explosion happened and with all the confusion, I was jostled this way and that. Many people moved around us, and it was later that I found it missing. I thought at first that it had dropped in the abbey. I went myself later to search, but it was not there. And then that evening I received the first letter.'

Jack's heart sped. 'And your grace, do you have that letter?'

She shook her head. 'No. I burned it immediately. And every subsequent letter.'

Jack sighed. A great pity, that. Their only clue. 'Did you recognize the hand of the letter?'

Again she shook her head.

'What exactly did the letter, the first letter, say?'

'It . . . it told me how this . . . this object . . . might be taken by the king. How careless I was in commissioning it. And how silence on the matter might be maintained with a "small remuneration." I did not understand it at first. Your English is sometimes strange to me. But when the second letter arrived, I was made to understand that I was to supply this miscreant with a sum of money.'

'How much?'

'One thousand marks.'

Jack choked, coughed, and smoothed down his coat once he had control of himself again.

'Yes,' she said with a trembling sigh. 'It is a very great sum.'

Jack wrung his coat hem until he realized that he had returned to an old habit and placed his thumbs between his belt and body, as Master Crispin was wont to do. 'What did he say would happen if you did not pay?'

'He would show the . . . object . . . to the king. He said it would intimate that I had been unfaithful. But nothing could be further from the truth!'

Lady Katherine stretched out a hand to grasp the queen's. Jack knew that such intimacy was usually reserved for maids and always initiated by the higher ranking noble to a lower. But in this case, the queen seemed only to notice the much-needed comfort. For she was in peril just as much as Jack was. Infidelity in a queen was an act of treason.

Jack girded himself before he asked, 'But could you not explain to his majesty that this was not the case? That this . . . this object was not meant in that way?'

'How could I be certain? He is a kind and generous husband.' He could see the truth of it in her eyes, and possibly *only* through her eyes, for he had seen precious little evidence of the king's generosity himself. 'But it would test the bounds of any man, any *husband's* pride.'

'I see. Well then. Will you not tell me what this thing is, lady? For it will be nigh impossible for your Goat to find such a thing if he is not to know whether it is the size of a pea or that of a horse.'

Her teeth dug into her lower lip, reddening it to a rose color. She was beautiful and tender in her distress. Jack was of the opinion that Richard did not deserve such a queen.

'Well . . . if I must say. It is . . . a piece of jewelry. A brooch. I had it commissioned to look like his majesty's arms – the lions of England, the fleur de lys of France, the martlets and cross of Edward the Confessor – but . . . it was artlessly done and if it is whispered in your ear, they somehow look like the arms of another courtier. I know it is a plot to embarrass the king, to make him look weaker in the eyes of his subjects. To hurt me is to hurt him. My Goat, can you find this brooch?'

'I . . . I will do my best, your grace.'

He worried at his own lip as the queen rose and thanked him. She exchanged pleasantries with Lady Katherine, but it was plain she wished to depart as soon as possible. Once she had gone, Lady Katherine returned to Jack's side. 'A simple thing, then. The theft of a jewel.'

'And extortion,' said Jack absently. 'But that is not what troubles me. What if the explosion and theft of the Stone were but a distraction? A way of stealing the brooch from the queen?'

'But that is absurd. How can the two things be related? It's so outlandish!'

'My master has taught me to think in patterns, my lady. And though it might be coincidence it might also have served as a planned opportunity.'

'Let us pause and suppose, just for the sake of argument, Master Tucker, that this is so. The perpetrator would have had to have known that the queen carried the brooch on her person.'

'Aye, he would. And so he would have known when the explosion was to happen, you see?'

'But then . . . only the conspirators knew that.'

'Aye. You see the problem.'

'It seems fantastic that they might be working together.' She shook her head but paused. 'It . . . would have to be from the inside. Someone from within the palace.'

He nodded. 'If we suppose that they were, then we can imagine the rest. Master Crispin has taught me that anything suspicious must not be discounted. And so my proposal is this. If one plot did not work, then another was set to go in its place. Now that both have gone forward we have three problems to solve. Who in the palace is a traitor, where is the Stone, and who has it?'

FOURTEEN

The man bucked beneath Rykener as he pressed the miscreant's wrists to the mud. 'You damnable woman!' the man cried over his shoulder in a thick northern brogue. 'Get off!'

Letting his wrists go, Rykener grabbed handfuls of the man's cloak and hauled him to his feet. The man swung at him, but John managed to pull the man's swinging arms behind him and had him secured until Crispin arrived.

'Well done,' said Crispin, looking the muddied man over.

'Who are you?'

'I'm a man who doesn't like to be trifled with. And you sir, and your ilk, have been trying my patience to the limit.'

The man spit the mud from his lips and squinted. 'Och, I'll wager you are . . . Crispin Guest.'

'How very astute.'

The man tried to wrench his arms free and sneered back at John. 'Call off this bitch of yours. She's as strong as an ox.' He seemed to notice the spectacle they were making. 'For God's sake, man. To be bested by a woman . . .'

'Well there's where you're wrong.'

John twisted the man's arms up just once more before letting him go. He patted the man's shoulders. 'Don't feel too badly. You were bested by a man, after all. Albeit one wearing women's clothes.'

The man spun around and glared, eyes sharpening on John's flat chest and smirk.

Before the man could gain his senses and flee, Crispin grabbed his cotehardie at the neck and hauled him close. 'I want to know where the Stone is. And I think you can enlighten me. That would be better than a dagger in the gut, wouldn't it?'

The man sobered. There was plainly nowhere to run. 'Very well, Master Guest. I . . . *I* don't know where it is . . .'

'I'm beginning to think that no one does. And yet it vanished into thin air. With *your* help.'

The man had the nerve to crack a smile. His eyes flicked toward the shop. 'Oh, I see. The man who sells the powder has a loose tongue.'

'He doesn't like the idea of a blade at his throat any more than you would, I imagine.'

'You have me. There's no need for threats. Aye, I supplied the means to blow up that plaster Stone, and it worked perfectly.'

'Too perfectly, as no one seems to know where the real one is now.'

The smile faded. 'Aye. Well. That was *not* part of the plan.'

'So I gathered.'

The man straightened, pulling his shoulders back. 'You have only yourself to blame. You've been avoiding us.'

'What the devil—' Crispin frowned. 'I've been avoiding no one. It is only chaos from Scotland. None of you have enough brains to scrape together a cogent plan, one that can be followed. If you have some new information I would be pleased to hear it.'

'You were to meet us and you didna.'

'At the Boar's Tusk?' Crispin shook his head. 'I tried. Are you Deargh?'

'He is the man who leads us.'

Crispin rubbed his forehead. 'Very well. I am prepared to talk with him now. You will take me to him.'

The man seemed to mull it over and finally nodded. 'Aye, that's likely best. It's back to Westminster, then.'

Crispin gestured for the man to lead, and with all the dignity of a man covered in mud, he set out back to Trinity Street as Crispin and John followed.

John elbowed Crispin as they passed through Ludgate, some minutes later. 'I have to say,' he said quietly so that only Crispin could hear, 'you lead a very exciting life.'

'You should have seen it before I was exiled to the Shambles.'

John shook his head. There was mud on his cheek and his coif was somewhat askew. 'Despite your hardships, my friend – and I do not mean to diminish them – I have a feeling that you are a much more interesting man now.'

Crispin snorted. Interesting indeed! What had this life made him but bitter and morose? True, it had given him a heretofore unknown empathy for those of the lower classes, for he saw how they struggled – how *he* struggled – from day to day to merely put food on the table. And sometimes there was none. There was many a time that he went to bed with a belly aching and hollow. But that hadn't been the case for some years. When had that tide turned? Could it

have been when Jack Tucker wormed his way into his household?
With that second mouth to feed, perhaps he had spent fewer coins
on drink. He scowled, thinking. Perhaps. And yet he often got just
as drunk. He knew damn well that Jack had supplemented their
larder by cutting purses or pilfering the occasional bird from the
poulterer. But not lately. Not in the last few years as the boy grew
into manhood. He was fifteen now. And Crispin well remembered
his years at that age. Jack was the quickest study he had ever seen,
like a cloth ready to soak up anything under it.

And where was he now? Not in a dungeon, thanks to Lady
Katherine. He sent up a prayer of thanks for that. Even though
imprisoned, his lot was better, at least for the moment.

And John had gotten him thinking about a bed for the lad. He
supposed it was high time he did something about that.

He nearly ran into a snuffling hog being led to market back toward
London and he looked around to notice that they had just passed
under the Temple Bar arch, being waved through by the porters,
and were almost within spotting distance of Charing Cross.

London was now behind them, and Westminster before with a
smattering of shops along the Strand that opened to the vista of the
more crowded shops and houses of the central city, such as it was.
Farmland and plains rambled beyond the perimeter, much as it did
outside the city limits of London.

Westminster Abbey's bells tolled Sext, and Crispin looked up
into the cloudy sky, happy to feel a little noon sunshine warming
through.

Crispin thought they would head to the Keys, but their man
instead led them into the middle of the city, down crooked streets
growing narrower.

'Where are you taking us?' said Crispin at last, eyeing the lanes
and fenced dead ends with suspicion.

'It's just down here,' said the man, though with his darting glances
and nervous gestures, he didn't look too certain.

The man moved quickly now, weaving through the men and
women along the road, putting distance between himself and Crispin.
'What the . . .'

And before Crispin could utter another word, the man broke into
a run. He picked the perfect moment, for just as Crispin tried to
give chase, a boy with a herd of sheep turned the corner, and Crispin
and Rykener were blocked from moving forward.

'The churl!' cried John. 'Why did he run? I thought he wanted to speak to you, to meet with you?'

Crispin pushed ineffectually at a blackface sheep that bleated at him as it shoved forward. 'Did he? Perhaps not. This scheme has got more twists and turns than a labyrinth.'

'What do we do now?'

Crispin measured where they were and headed without speaking toward one of the many narrow lanes. Wet laundry hung in arcs of heavy lines, crossing over one another, fluttering listlessly in the smoky gusts.

They ducked under a particularly low-hanging drape of white linens where they reached a door. Crispin knocked gently and stepped back.

'Come in, the door's unbarred!' came the call from within, and mere moments after was followed by a raucous caw, startling John. Crispin pushed the door open and moved into the dark space. Flint struck against steel, sending a spark, lighting briefly the cold and now familiar room.

Domhnall with Lady Agnes on his shoulder knelt at the renewing fire and squinted at Crispin. 'Welcome back, Master Guest,' he rumbled.

John becrossed himself.

Domhnall gave Rykener one look and turned back to his smoking fire. 'Why does that man wear a dress?'

'You have a sharper eye than most men,' said Crispin, 'even with only one.'

'So I've been told. Get on, girl,' he said to the raven, sending her to her perch.

'Forgive our hasty intrusion,' said Crispin. 'We were led astray, I'm afraid. Though it is just as timely.'

'Now who's speaking in riddles?'

Crispin conceded it with a lopsided grin.

The man poked at his fire, but it didn't seem to coax much of a flame. 'It's good you've come. I have some information for you.'

He rose with a grunt and shuffled toward his stool, smirked once toward John, and sat, easing himself down with a groan and creak of joints. 'Och, it's a hard thing, old age. At least you've got your Jack Tucker.'

'I am trying to assure that I do.'

'Ah yes. Sorry. I forget. Well now. I have a name for you.'

'Yes?'

'John Dunbar, earl of Moray.'

'So. I have heard this name. He is behind this, then?'

'Aye, so it is said on the streets. He's got henchmen here doing his will. But he's wicked clever.'

'So clever that he tells his henchmen to do only so much without telling the others what they are doing?'

'Aye, he could be. Then no one could tell the whole plot under torture.'

John made an audible swallow.

'I see,' said Crispin. 'Diabolical. I have another name or title for you. What of 'Mormaer'? Have you heard that before?'

Domhnall smiled grimly. 'Aye.' He lifted his gnarled hands toward the fire. 'The Mormaer is the Great Steward. The Mormaer of Fife has the great honor to crown the kings of Scotland.'

'And what has this Mormaer to do with this theft?'

Domhnall chuckled. 'I should have thought that this was obvious. He has everything to do with it. The Mormaer of Fife is the chief of the Clan MacDuff. And I should think it might be no surprise to you that the present clan chief is John Dunbar, earl of Moray.'

Crispin studied Domhnall and his self-satisfied grin. 'I suppose all this does your heart glad, Master Domhnall, that all will soon be set aright in Scotland.'

'A wee bit,' he said, smile fading. 'But nothing will be set right with a mere Stone. Scotland must be free of the English. Of your lords and your castles. And don't roll your eyes at me, Crispin Guest, for I know you are of Welsh blood and the same has happened in Wales as happened in Scotland. But we will never stop fighting for what is ours.'

Crispin reddened at the reference to his Welsh heritage. Few knew of it and fewer ever mentioned it.

'I can understand without agreeing, Master Domhnall. *It is the mark of an educated mind to be able to entertain a thought without accepting it.*'

Domhnall waved his hand dismissively. 'Our King Robert is just now showing his claws, Master Crispin. In Otterburn and the Marches.'

Crispin looked down his nose at the old man. 'Nothing of that concerns me as much as the return of the Stone.'

Domhnall nodded slowly, licking his lips. 'Aye. For Jack's sake.

But how do you know you can trust me, Master Crispin? After all, it would do my heart good to best the English and steal the Stone.'

'I don't know.'

Domhnall looked into the fire, a ghost of a smile on his dry and scored lips.

'Call it my gut instincts. You have never deceived me before. *Between friends there is no need of justice.*'

Domhnall poked at the fire, bushy brows shadowing his eyes. '"Friends," eh?'

Crispin shrugged. 'I suppose.'

The old man nodded and laid the poker down. 'That is why I didna fear to tell you about these rebels.' He settled on his seat and swiveled toward Crispin. 'It is said there is also one who is no exactly earning his martyrdom.'

'Eh? What is your meaning?'

The bird suddenly twisted toward John. She dove and pulled at the purse at his belt.

'Ow! Help Crispin! I am being attacked by a devil bird!'

'By the Mass,' swore the old man. 'Wheest! Lady Agnes! Leave the gentleman's purse alone. He's our friend, and we don't steal from friends.'

The bird stopped flapping at John's face and soared across the room to her perch again. She clacked her beak at Rykener without an ounce of apology.

John drew back in alarm. 'By the Blessed Virgin!'

'She'll no attack you again.'

'She's only a trained bird, John.'

Rykener checked on his scrip still secured to his girdle. 'Trained! Such industry, to be sure.'

'Aye. She's a good bird. Mostly brings back jewelry.'

John perked up. 'Truly? How long does it take to train a bird?'

Crispin shot him an exasperated, 'John!'

'As I was saying, Master Crispin,' Domhnall went on. 'There's one of the Mormaer's henchmen with no good intentions for the honor of Scotland. He is in it for himself, for gold. So it is said. And a man who is in it not for honor is a verra dangerous man indeed.'

'I see. But who?'

He shrugged. 'They no said. That's for you to ferret out. But have a care. We do not know who is the deadliest of these henchmen of the Mormaer. They all verra well may be.'

'I know they are dangerous. The very nature of the scheme makes it so.'

'Each deadly sin leads to another. I think greed is foremost, and where there is greed, there is envy, and soon, murder.'

Crispin paused. Domhnall's words fluttered in his head like gnats. 'And how is it you know one is greedier than the others, that they all aren't working for the Mormaer? Two were certainly keen to warn me of the other in just that way.'

Domhnall's smile rose slowly. 'You *are* a suspicious laddie.'

Crispin smiled back. 'It keeps me alive.'

'So what does it mean, Master Crispin? That the word on the street was . . . planted?'

'It would seem so.'

'Why, in Heaven's name?'

'For me to discover? To confuse? To hide the truth.'

John crossed his arms over his chest and smirked at Domhnall, nodding his head toward Crispin. 'He's good, isn't he?'

'Verra good,' Domhnall agreed.

'I expected to be lied to,' Crispin went on, lost in his own thoughts. 'But why seek me out? Would it not have been more prudent to lay low, stay out of my view?'

John snapped his fingers. 'They *wanted* you aware of them?'

'That explosion would certainly have gotten my attention, whether I had been present at the abbey or not. But again, why?'

'To "plant," as you say, this false information,' said John. 'They knew you'd be a threat.'

'Flattering, but frustrating.'

'So the story that none of them had the Stone might yet be false.'

'It's still possible that one of them does have it but is attempting to misdirect me.'

Domhnall shook his head. 'I dinna think so. For if any had it, would'na they be gone at once?'

'*I* certainly would be,' said John.

Crispin rubbed his stubbled chin. 'John, we need to split up.'

Rykener frowned. 'But I like working with you, Crispin.'

'You are still working with me, just separately. I need this of you, John. It's for Jack Tucker, after all.'

He sobered. 'Of course. For Jack.'

'I need you to seek out McGuffin.'

'What? The rogues who abducted me?'

'So many puzzles,' said Domhnall sagely.

Crispin agreed. 'I need you to find out what they want, what exactly they were after. I don't think they are a deadly assembly, but be on your guard anyway. I will seek out this Deargh and return to talk to Findlaich. I feel if I can just get enough information from all three gatherings I can put the pieces together and find that damned Stone.'

'With all haste, Crispin.' John hesitated, seeming reluctant to leave. Finally, he offered a clumsy nod to the old man, gave Crispin a stern but worried look, and then hurried out.

Crispin stood before the grim fire. 'I thank you for this information, Domhnall. I know it can't be easy to . . . well, your own countrymen . . .'

'I know you'd scarce believe it, Crispin, but I do value my honor almost as much as you do your own.' Crispin nodded. 'I grieve that I canna tell you more than this.'

'You have done well.'

'With information that you had already gleaned. But I shall dig deeper, Master Crispin, never you fear. There is more to discover. The deceptions are deep within the weeds.'

'It is much appreciated.'

'Don't forget, Crispin, when all seems lost, one must go back to the beginning.'

Crispin rubbed his eyes. 'Yes. That is an inevitability.' He stopped and looked up. 'The beginning. In the chaos I have neglected the beginning. Thank you again, Master Domhnall. You are wise.' He dug into his scrip, raised a coin in his hand, and watched as Lady Agnes spotted it, lifted from her perch, and smoothly snatched it from his fingers before depositing it with her master.

Domhnall laughed, raised the coin in a salute, and dropped it deftly into his money pouch.

Crispin left the hovel and stood on the street, searching. He had to find this Deargh. But he needed to return to Westminster Abbey first.

Crispin skirted past the scaffolding and approached the Coronation Chair. The church wasn't empty. It was never truly empty during the day, what with folk kneeling and beseeching favors in prayer, others searching for employment, and monks keeping a wary eye on all of them to be certain they didn't make off with a candlestick or two. But no one was near the Confessor's tomb.

He glared at the empty chair, blaming it for its hollowness. But this was useless. The Stone did not lose itself. The fact was, it was gone and he was a man who finds lost things. 'So think, Crispin.' His voice echoed in the cavernous space. The flames at the Confessor's tomb flickered, and the chair stood stoically empty.

None of these men needed him to find the secreted Stone or do some other such nonsense as McGuffin spouted. It was all to keep him busy. Perhaps while the real culprit did the deed? So was there more to it than simply stealing the Stone? What plots were unfolding at court? The thought was more worrisome than a missing Scottish relic, but how could he convey that message to the king? No, once more, Crispin was on his own.

Days ago the true Stone had been replaced with a false one. And despite conniving by McGuffin and Findlaich and this yet-to-be-discovered Deargh, it all started here. Though anyone could come and go at all hours, the abbey church was patrolled at night by the porter and others. Therefore, the most logical culprits would have to have come from within. Which meant monks.

Was it really a coincidence that Crìsdean, the caretaker of the Coronation Chair, was a Scotsman? Crispin had no time for the benefit of the doubt. 'Occam's razor,' he muttered. 'The simplest answer is most likely correct.'

He glanced once more at the chair and turned abruptly to approach the cloister gate. Ever before he arrived at the bell rope, a monk behind the gate saw him and ran – he presumed – to get the abbot.

It wasn't long before the stately Abbot Colchester strode from the shadows. 'Master Guest,' he said from behind his monk as the gate was unlocked. 'Have you news?'

'No, my Lord Abbot. I have returned to investigate. I wish to speak to Brother Crìsdean again.'

'We can meet in my lodgings.' He turned to go, but Crispin stayed him.

'My lord, I would prefer to stay by the chair. I think . . . much can be gleaned by such proximity.'

The abbot cocked his head. 'As you will. Fetch Brother Crìsdean,' he said to the monk. As the monk left, the abbot led the way to the Coronation Chair.

Crispin walked behind him, watching the straight shoulders, the noble bearing of the abbot. Though the man did not come from nobility, he had certainly learned a thing or two as he rose in the ranks in the monastery. Certainly his travels had been tutor enough.

Instead of standing as Crispin expected of the man, he walked slowly around the chair. 'Truth to tell, Master Guest, I have never much thought about this, dare I call it, "sacred object." For does it not seat the anointed by God? It was here, part of many sacred objects, but seldom used as are the others. No, it has been taken for granted, and I vow when this is concluded not to do so again.'

'You can scarce be blamed for taking it for granted. Much as you would a pillar or archway. It has always been there, will always be there.'

'But we have a habit, does Man, of taking that which we see every day with a certain amount of disdain in its monotony. Only when there is chaos do we find it golden. Only when it is lost do we feel the loss.'

'Did not Jesus preach of the ninety-nine sheep and how precious the one that was lost?'

The abbot turned to Crispin and measured him a long time. 'Are you sermonizing to me, Master Guest?'

'Not at all, Father Abbot.'

But when Colchester turned away again, a smile flickered at his mouth.

It wasn't long thereafter that the sound of feet approaching grabbed their attention and they angled toward the sound.

Brother Crìsdean, short in stature but thickset, ambled toward them. He appeared more subdued than he had the other day when Crispin first spoke with him. He bowed first to the abbot and gave barely a nod to Crispin. The monk's gaze seemed not to want to land on him.

'Master Guest will ask you some questions, Brother Crìsdean,' said the abbot.

With head bowed and hands clenched together Crìsdean waited. Crispin made him wait. The longer he waited the twitchier he became. Finally, after a long pause, Brother Crìsdean looked up, contempt on his face. 'What are your questions? I have my duties to perform.'

Crispin began. 'How do you feel about the king?'

The monk's laugh was yanked from him like a sneeze and seemed to surprise him. 'Such a question! He is the king.'

'*The* king not *my* king?'

'What difference does it make? You're splitting hairs.'

'A fine distinction. *Is* he your king . . . or is it Scotland's king whom you follow?'

He implored Colchester. 'Must I put up with this harassment, my Lord Abbot?'

'Yes, you must,' the abbot replied impassively.

The monk took a step back, blinking his astonishment, but he scowled, seeming to understand his predicament a bit better. 'King Richard,' he said between clenched teeth, 'is my king.'

'Good to know.' Crispin folded his arms over his chest and peered down his nose at the man. 'How do you feel about the Stone of Destiny?'

'These are foolish questions, my Lord Abbot. If this is how the Tracker operates, then the Stone will never be found.'

'You know nothing of me. But someone does. Someone has been trying to misdirect me. I think you know something of the Stone's whereabouts, Crìsdean. And I think that you are as much a part of this plot as any of the conspirators.'

The monk trembled. His fury was clearly splashed over his face. 'He insults me. He calls me a . . . a . . . conspirator! I am a brother in Christ!'

'You're a Scotsman, and you had your eye on the Coronation Chair from the beginning.'

'You're mad!' He implored the abbot again. 'He's mad, my lord. Please!'

The abbot blinked slowly. 'Do you have a point, Master Guest?'

'My point? This man—' he pointed directly at Crìsdean '—knows more than he will say on this matter. I accuse you, sir, of plotting to steal the Stone. Where is it?'

'There is no call to accuse me, Master Guest. None at all. I am innocent.' He wrung his hands. 'God help me, I am innocent.'

The way the monk twisted his sleeve cuffs in his hands, the fact that he would not look up at him, caused a rush of anger to stiffen Crispin's shoulders. He leaned in to Crìsdean, 'I will give you exactly one day to tell me what you know – for I can tell that you do know something – or I shall inform his majesty's guards, and trust me, they know how to get a man to talk.'

Crìsdean's eyes fixed on Crispin. He breathed raggedly, his fear clearly visible in his widened pupils. The monk's mouth worked, but nothing came out.

Walking toward the chair, Crispin stared down at it. 'You did not work alone. The Stone is a heavy thing. Would you die or suffer torment to keep the other safe?'

'But . . . but . . .'

Crispin whirled. 'But what?'

It was there in his eyes. Crisdean was ready to crack. It was one thing to protect an innocent. Another to protect a fellow conspirator. If he were innocent there would not be such fear in his darting gaze. He would cleave to his faith that God would protect his righteousness.

None of that was there in those watery eyes.

'*One* day,' said Crispin sharply. He took in the Confessor's tomb, other distant monuments steeped in shadows, and felt as if he would burst with ire if he didn't leave this place. There were no clues, no leads to take him from one post in the abbey to the other. He knew the abbot certainly must have led a search already into all the recesses that he was privy to and that Crispin could only dream of. The dormitory, the refectory, the kitchens. So many hiding places. How could one merely search and find it? True, it was no small thing, but a clever man with a well-thought-out plan could do it, could hide it almost anywhere. What other choice did he have but threats?

Crispin didn't acknowledge the abbot but turned away instead. He'd said all he needed to say, and he marched down the tiled floor of the church, down the north ambulatory, where he shoved open the door and trotted down the steps. On the street he cursed the sky, raising his hands with a cry so raw and so frustrated that he wasn't certain if he had even formed words.

If the abbot had not stood there, Crispin would have thrashed the man within an inch of his life. He *knew* something! It was evident in his eyes, the way he held himself. He *knew* something, dammit! And while he kept his council, safe and sound within the abbey precincts, Jack was suspended in Purgatory where he did not know whether a reprieve awaited or death. How could this be happening to him again?

He clenched his fists and stopped his restless pacing. 'Control,' he hissed. 'Must not lose control.'

He breathed, staring upward toward the spire, the church rooftop. He had given the man one day and he would wait. And the monk would relent, for he had no other choice. Face the torturers or face

Crispin. Which was the better part? The man would confess and give up the other.

The idea of wine or ale seemed very good to him, and he threw himself forward to search out an ale stake.

The people on the streets were dwindling as the day wore on. They were returning to their houses, seeing the workday come to its end.

But there were not so many people on the streets that he did not notice the little man. To be fair, through his ranting, he hadn't noticed him at first, but caught his movement through his peripheral vision; that stuttered, jerky movement, the hesitant steps that shadowed his own.

He walked on, still looking for that ale stake, and when he found one, he turned quickly to duck inside the alehouse.

The small twitchy man sat a few tables behind him.

Once served, Crispin took only a cursory drink of the ale before he rose, making as if to leave. But he circled and found himself behind the little man, who was looking about, presumably trying to catch a glimpse of Crispin.

Crispin leaned over him, placing both hands on the table on either side of him. Close to his ear he whispered, 'Are you by any chance looking for me?'

The man froze at first before he slithered about and tried to slip away. Crispin clamped a hand to his shoulder. 'I think you are following me.' He slid onto the bench beside him. But he canted forward and angled, not quite facing the table. 'If you have something to say you had best say it.'

The man wet his lips with his darting tongue. His dull gray eyes flicked once to Crispin's before he lowered them again and kept them directed toward the table. 'M-Master Guest . . . I meant no harm . . .'

That northern accent again. 'Good. Then you have a message.'

'Aye. If it please you, you are to come with me.'

'Why?'

'To meet Master Deargh.'

'You simply could have said so. Well, if you are to lead me then there is no time to waste.' He stood and hovered over the man.

The little fellow rose shakily to his feet. He looked up once at Crispin again before he ducked into his stooped shoulders and shuffled toward the door.

The man said nothing more as he hurried in skipping strides through the muddied lanes deep into Westminster. There wasn't much to the city. In fact, it could be more characterized as a village, with its sparse shops, houses, and wharfs. A suburb of London, it had yet to embrace the grandeur of that noble city. But Crispin had no doubt that someday it would. Its shops were serviceable, its houses for servants and shopkeepers, with a few noble houses for those that could not be retained within the palace walls, were sure to spread out like a tributary of the Thames.

The little man stopped at an inn and did not hesitate to go inside. Crispin followed, alert and engaged with every shadow, every dark corner. He followed the man up the stairs, across a gallery, and up to a chamber door, where the man knocked. The door opened, and the man standing in the doorway glanced at Crispin with an almost bored air.

Inside the room, Crispin noted that it was an antechamber, with another door toward the back. Men stood in one clutch at the other end of the room and, when they parted, revealed a table at which a man sat, playing at cards by himself. After a moment, he set the cards down and looked up. His dark brows lowered over brooding eyes and he took in Crispin with a calculated inspection. The man with the mustard-colored cotehardie who had tussled with John Rykener. There was still mud stains on his chest.

'You are Master Deargh?'

The man gestured to the empty seat in front of him. 'Take a chair, Master Guest.'

FIFTEEN

Jack found his prison too confining. For one, he quickly realized that any sort of investigating would be severely hampered by the necessity of his staying indoors. And two, he needed to talk to the queen again.

He could not pester Lady Katherine. Surely she had her own tasks to attend to. He knew he was also keeping her from traveling back to Essex to be with Henry's wife and child, and he did not know how much longer he could depend on her beneficence and her presence. It was time to act on his own.

Suddenly he heard the admonishing voice of his master in his head, just as clear as if he were standing in the room with him. *'Don't do anything foolish, Jack!'* he heard him say. But with an apology on his lips and a prayer sent heavenward, he knew that he had no choice but to be as foolish as his master well knew he was.

Where would the queen be at this hour? He hoped against hope that she might be in the garden. With a quick look around to make certain no servants saw him, he made for the door to the little outdoor space and ventured outside. No one was about on Henry's side and he quickly went to the wall separating them. He climbed, using a twining vine here, a tree branch there. When he was at the top with a view of not only the churning Thames and all the business of boats and skiffs spearing their way over the squat whitecaps, he saw the queen's garden laid out before him. Carefully trimmed trees were situated in squares surrounded by low hedges whose flowers had only just gone to seed. Little paths and even a fountain delighted the eye. It all must have been a sight in the spring when it was in full bloom.

He knew he'd have to chance it. He swung his legs over the wall, measured how far it was, and leapt down.

'I can hear you well, Master Crispin,' he muttered when he landed. 'There's no need to shout.'

He crouched down, measuring where he was and scanning to see if he could catch sight of anyone in the distance. It was a large garden, larger than Henry's or even Lancaster's, which was very large of itself. It was a luxury extended to the wealthy, to the royal. He recognized it as a fine thing, though all he could think about was the work it took to get it this way and maintain it. A score of gardeners probably made a fine living at it, and Jack wondered idly how much they earned at such a task.

He would have a better chance of not getting caught if he found the door and stayed clear of it while still keeping it within view.

Skirting the path for his own way through the foliage, he maneuvered himself behind a late-flowering plant and watched the portal, hoping it wouldn't take long.

'You there!'

Jack froze. Maybe they didn't mean him?

'You! Boy, I see you.'

God's blood! He slowly rose, standing amid the bushes like a lonely sunflower.

A maid frowned at him and stomped toward him. She wore the horned headdress that the queen had made popular, its veil fluttering behind her. 'What are you doing here? You are not a gardener.'

'Am I not?' He tried to chuckle, but his throat was thick with fear. 'Aye, well. No. I . . . I . . .' He shrugged. 'Demoiselle, I am a harmless lad. Truly. And you would scarce believe my course should I explain it to you. But might you tell your mistress that . . . that her "Goat" waits without?'

Her eyes widened and a smile replaced her scowl. '*You* are Goat?' Her manner changed. She slid toward him almost seductively, eyes full of brightness and warmth. 'Master Goat, I must say, I approve.'

He was not mistaken. She was all but leering at him. He tried a smile. 'Now, now, demoiselle. You must, er, deport yourself. Wouldn't do to, erm, delay my meeting with the . . . with your mistress.'

Disappointment swept over her features, but she offered a dimpled smile in return. 'Well, there's always later.'

'There is indeed!' he said with a wide grin, and brushed down his coat. In his head, he thanked Master Crispin profusely for procuring Jack his stylish new cotehardie of blue.

With a kittenish smirk, she wheeled and passed through the little arched garden door and Jack waited, smoothing down his hair and wiping at his face to make sure no crumbs marred his cheeks.

When the door opened again, the queen emerged. He bowed low and she reached forward to grab his hand. 'Not here. Let us go farther in.' She dragged him and finally pushed him to a bench, hidden by trees, bushes, and a trellis covered in yellowing leaves.

She sat beside him and Jack held his breath. *Jack Tucker, you are sitting next to the Queen of England. Did you ever!*

'Why have you come, my Goat? Have you found out anything?'

'I am sorry to say, your grace, that I have scarce begun my investigation. I have more questions to ask of you. I was afraid that I . . . that I was overcome by your presence and that of Lady Katherine, and my tongue was tied.'

'Oh.' She sank but lifted her chin to face him. 'What do you need to know?'

Jack rubbed his palms over his thighs, trying to dry their dampness. 'I need to know the names of those who were closest to you while you were in the abbey. Can you recall?'

Her expression turned thoughtful. 'There was my Lady of the Chamber, Margaret, John Lincoln of Grimsby, Sir Baldwin Raddington, Henry Derby, and assorted retainers and monks.'

'Who was closest to you when the explosion happened?'

'I don't remember. There was such confusion.'

'Try, your grace. It is a matter of some importance.'

She screwed up her face, thinking. 'When . . . when the explosion occurred, we all got to our feet. My lady's maid was beside me, but she was soon crowded out by the monks and the king's household guards.'

'And . . . are you acquainted with these knights, your grace?'

'What do you mean?'

'I mean, was any of them a stranger to you?'

'Oh, I see. No. Not that I could recall . . . Wait. There was one man. I did not recognize him.'

Jack squirmed excitedly. 'What did he look like? Did he speak?'

'He was dark-haired, with a dark beard. I saw little of his face with his helm and aventail.'

'Did he say anything?'

'I do not think so. Perhaps . . . yes, perhaps he said simply, "Your grace, come with me." But then the king was beside me in the next instant.'

'What did his voice sound like? Did . . . did he sound as if he was from London?'

'No. Not as Londoner's speak.'

'Perhaps . . . a northerner?'

She bit her lip, angling her head in thought. 'I . . . yes. He could have been.'

Another damned Scot! They were crawling all over England, apparently. 'Was there anyone else beside you, your grace? Anyone besides this knight?'

'John Lincoln, but he was quickly thrust to the opposite side of his majesty and I.'

'And who is he, my lady, for I am not as familiar with the court as I might be.'

'Why, he is the king's secretary. And the Keeper of the Jewels.'

'Keeper of the Jewels?'

'Yes. There are many official pieces that the king must wear for certain ceremonies, as well as his personal accouterments.'

Jack's mind whirred. What if this man wished to help bring down the king? Could he be trusted? He had the keys to the wealth of the kingdom. Maybe he had a bone to pick with Richard. One never knew.

But this other knight. This was suspicious. How could Jack ever find him? And in almost the same instant he wondered, a spark of an idea lit in his mind.

'Your grace, we need to find this knight, this guard. I propose that you ask the captain of the king's guard to assemble them in the courtyard for your inspection.'

She looked at him aghast. 'But I have never done such a thing.'

'But . . . you are the queen. Can you not order it?'

She smiled gently. 'You have a very unique perspective of what I can accomplish as queen.'

He reddened. 'Forgive me, your grace, but I know so very little about you and what you may do. I assumed too much.'

'Never fear, my Goat. All is not lost. Perhaps I may send my lady's maid to inspect them. She can concoct a story to seem plausible.'

'That would do very well, your grace. Does she . . . does she know . . .'

'No. But she is discreet and will do what I ask without question.'

'If this can be done soon and with all haste, I might be able to get somewhere. That is . . . I can pursue this line of attack and find your jewel all the quicker.'

'You are a marvel, my Goat! Such ideas! I pray you can help me.'

'But we must be swift about it, your grace. We cannot delay.'

She jumped to her feet. Jack scrambled to do so as well. 'Lady Margaret!' she called.

And the dark-haired beauty that had at first caught Jack appeared. She curtseyed to her queen and smiled at Jack. Jack could not resist grinning back.

'Lady Margaret, Goat and I have an assignment for you.'

'Your grace?'

'It is a secret thing. You mustn't tell anyone you are doing it and for whom. Do you understand?'

Her bright face paled. 'Yes, my lady. Of course.'

'Very well. Then you are to go to the king's guards. Look at each one of them and tell me if any of them are from the north.'

'My lady?'

'Can you do that?'

'Oh,' said Jack, 'and especially if they are knights you do not recognize. Perhaps newly come to court. And they would have been in Westminster Abbey when the explosion happened.'

She looked equally perplexed at Jack but nodded. 'Yes. I can do that.'

'Then go now,' said the queen. 'With all haste and get back to me. Then you can get a message to my Goat. He is in the employ of our dear cousin Bolingbroke.'

She nodded. Jack could see the new determination on her face. She spun and hurried away.

'That is my signal to leave, my lady.' He bowed low to her and headed back to the wall.

She called after him, 'God keep you, my Goat.'

He walked backward, looking at the figure of the queen as she caught a falling leaf from the tree above her and studied it in her palm.

He almost took the main path but remembered in time to travel through the bushes along the Thames-side wall. He broke through the hedges and turned a corner . . . and found several guards waiting for him.

SIXTEEN

Crispin sat facing the muddied man. 'You simply could have said. Why did you evade me?'

Deargh reached across the table to pour Crispin some wine into a ceramic goblet. Some sloshed onto the tablecloth, which absorbed the golden liquid.

'I wanted the measure of you. A traitor.' Crispin scowled. 'A former traitor, then. A mystery, more legend than man. A disgraced knight. I wonder if anyone truly knows you.'

Deargh sipped his wine and studied Crispin over the rim.

Crispin leaned back in his chair and crossed his arms over his chest. 'It's interesting . . . how you happen to know me.'

'Who has not heard of the Tracker?'

'In London, yes. In parts of Westminster, even. But in Scotland?'

Deargh chuckled. 'Some news travels farther than others. A man who was once exiled for treason and who now catches criminals and finds lost relics? That is the stuff of legends, Master Guest.'

Unconvinced, Crispin studied him. 'Where is the Stone?'

'You don't waste words, do you?'

'I have my reasons.'

'Aye, your apprentice. Word travels quickly from court.'

'So it would seem.'

'I would tell you to keep out of it as no your business, but I have the feeling that would be wasted breath.'

Crispin leaned on the table. 'It is my business. The king has made it so. And so have your compatriots.'

'Commissioned by Richard personally.'

'You seem to know a great deal of the doings of the English court. One wonders if you have spies there.'

Deargh grabbed his goblet again but did not drink. Instead, he turned the stem in his hand and stared into the tawny liquid. 'Every court has spies.'

'No doubt. But let us get down to it. I've been tasked to find the Stone, and you have been tasked to take it. We are at the same task but at cross-purposes,' sighed Crispin. 'There must be some mutual agreement we can come to on the matter.'

'I doubt that, Master Guest.' Deargh drank.

Crispin threw himself back into his chair. 'Can you at least tell me *when* it was taken?'

'I canna say.'

'If you have heard anything about me of late it is that I don't have time to waste.'

'I know you are a fair man. And negotiating with you would be a reasonable enterprise.'

Hope surged in his chest, but he was careful not to show it on his face. 'So you mean to return the Stone for a ransom?'

'Possibly. But it is worth more than money to my countrymen.'

'Was this *your* plot, then, or devised by another? A lord, perhaps?'

'I am a laird, Master Guest. In Scotland. You think of us as barbarians, but we have lands and manor houses and courtiers . . . and wealth. Just as the English do. And great honor to be appeased.'

'Yes, and you win battles and lose them. Just as we do. So is the Stone for sale or isn't it?'

Deargh leaned back, matching Crispin's posture. His eyes quickly flicked over his men standing in the perimeter of their table's candle glow. 'It is no for me to say. I am merely an errand boy. My superior would have the Stone and gave instructions as to when and how to obtain it.'

Crispin waited. The man was hedging.

Could it be? This couldn't be happening. Heart sinking, Crispin loosened the arms over his chest. 'You don't have it either?' he ventured.

Deargh sucked on his teeth and looked down at the table. 'Alas.'

Pushing himself noisily away from the table, Crispin rose. 'Then why am I even bothering to talk to you?'

'Because you have an apprentice dangling by the end of a rope and if I do not find the Stone of Scone for my laird, I shall be in the same predicament.'

'When I find it, I am not finding it for you.'

'You might. With the proper persuasion.'

Crispin rested his hands on the table and inclined forward. 'Mark me. I have no patience for thieves, murderers, or extortionists. And I've had it up to here with Scotsmen. Take your threats and shove them up your arse.' He turned toward the door, even though Deargh's men blocked the way.

'How will you proceed without my help, Master Guest? You only have two days left. Maybe less. Will your pride kill your apprentice?'

Crispin knew he could not draw his sword in time to cleave Deargh's men and escape harm to himself, so he let it lie. His sword hand twitched and finally curled into a fist instead. Without turning he said over his shoulder, 'Well?'

'I don't think it is any surprise to you that there are . . . factions . . . interested in the Stone of Scone.'

'I have met the others, yes.' He turned to face Deargh. 'All seem equally incompetent.'

Deargh smiled. 'Perhaps.'

'Who is this lord you are all working for? For I have no doubt that this is one scheme, one master, with many little helpers. I would even postulate that he chose these three separate groups thinking if one failed then surely one other would succeed. Alas, his confidence seems to have been entirely misplaced.'

Deargh's smile faltered. The insult had at last struck home.

'He is a man you would have had little acquaintance with, Master Guest.'

'The earl of Moray, you mean?'

The man's eyes flew wide. 'You *are* a man who "tracks" information, aren't you. Would that we had hired you at the outset.'

'Except that I have no interest in getting on the wrong side of King Richard. Again.' Crispin looked at the wine, felt a dry scratch in his throat, and pulled out the chair. He sat, cupped the goblet, and drank. 'Who is this John Dunbar, anyway?' he asked, wiping his lips with the back of his hand. 'Or should I say "Mormaer"? Does he think he will make himself king by sitting upon the Stone?'

'Many a man has been made king for less.'

'True.' Crispin drank again and held out his goblet to be refilled, only he held it out to Deargh's men and waited.

A shadow grudgingly moved forward. He was a tall, broad man – as all these Scots seemed to be – and grabbed the jug with a ham-fisted grip before sloshing the wine into Crispin's cup. Crispin didn't so much as acknowledge him as he drank again.

'John Dunbar is a verra great laird and warrior. He is my clan chief.'

'Oh? *Clan*, is it?' Crispin pictured them as fur-wearing, woad-painted savages, dancing before a bonfire. 'But he would be king?'

'He would only return the Stone of Scone to the sons of Scotland where it belongs.'

'But he wouldn't mind a little ransom instead, eh?'

Deargh shrugged. 'An army is an expensive thing, Master Guest.'

'Naturally. How much gold, for the sake of argument, might his grace the earl be willing to accept to give up Scotland's honor?'

The table wobbled as Deargh shot to his feet. 'You had best curb your tongue, Master Guest,' he snarled, his calm slipping away at last.

Crispin gazed up at him mildly. 'Or what?'

'Or you'll no get my help to find the Stone.'

'*Your* help? It seems more like you need mine.' Crispin took a last gulp of the fine Flemish wine, set down the goblet, and stood. 'I think I've got all I need.'

'What? What mean you?'

'I mean, I've got the information I require. Good day.'

'You'll go nowhere until I tell you you can.'

Crispin sighed and stuck his thumbs in his belt, rocking on his heels. 'Have you sent a ransom demand to his majesty?'

'Well . . . no.'

'And you won't until you actually have the Stone or know its whereabouts. And so you truly have nothing to bargain with. And you have told me much that I didn't know before. All in all, a good meeting. Now, if you will excuse me, I will continue my search.'

When Crispin turned his back on the Scot, he was still facing the man's henchmen. They glared, making a wall to block the door. It must have been some silent gesture from Deargh that made them move at last, for they reluctantly parted, allowing a path for Crispin to make his escape.

He shouldered past them, making certain to bump them as he went. He was nearly at the door when it burst open and McGuffin and his men pushed their way in, forcing Crispin back. *God's blood*, Crispin sighed.

'Aha!' cried McGuffin. 'I should have known. Deargh, you piece of shite.'

Deargh cast his goblet to the floor, shattering it and splashing its contents upon the nearest men. 'By the rood! You lackey, McGuffin.'

'I'm no lackey, Deargh, not as you are. So what have you told him, eh? Everything, no doubt.'

'He didn't need to be told. He sussed it out for himself.'

'Oh he did?'

'Yes,' said Crispin. 'You are all oafs and easy to manipulate.'

'Eh? Who are you calling an oaf, Master Guest? Here I am saving your sarding hide—'

'My hide didn't need saving. I was about to leave.'

'McGuffin,' said Deargh wearily, 'I'm sure you'd like to continue to believe you are important in the scheme of things, so you'd best get on with it. Out with ye.'

'I *am* important.' He dug into his scrip and dragged out a folded parchment. He snapped it open with one flick of his wrist and flattened it on the table before Deargh. 'See here. A letter from his grace himself, *with* his seal!'

Deargh dove for it and smacked it out of the way before Crispin could get a good look at it. 'You fool! Don't wave that about in front of the Tracker!'

'By all means,' said Crispin mildly. 'Don't mind me.'

By the look on Deargh's reddened face, Crispin would have wagered anything that Deargh had a letter just like it.

'It's nothing he doesn't already know. And who are you calling a fool?'

'You, you fool!' Deargh now had his hand on his dagger hilt and McGuffin, just as red-faced, had reached for his.

McGuffin's men growled, facing off with Deargh's.

'Gentlemen,' said Crispin, raising his hands between them. 'It seems that the two of you should unite for this one course. Surely you will both be able to find the Stone if you work together.'

'I told you!' cried McGuffin to Crispin's face. 'I'm no looking for the sarding Stone!'

'What?' Deargh scrambled around the table. 'Then what have you been charged with?' He gestured for his men to retrieve McGuffin's parchment from the floor.

But Crispin was faster. He was able to skim it before it was snatched from his hands by McGuffin himself.

'Here!' said Deargh. 'Let us see that.'

'I don't think I will,' said McGuffin, stuffing it back in his scrip and giving Crispin a sour eye. 'It seems we *have* given the Tracker too much information as it is.'

Deargh clenched his fists and snatched a glance at Crispin. 'I'm no working with this lowland fool. I have greater work to do. And you, Master Guest. I suppose you have no intention of helping us for the sake of your apprentice.'

'You would be right. In all truth, I believe you will slow me down. Good day, gentlemen.' He shoved McGuffin roughly aside and pushed the door open himself. He trotted down the inn's gallery steps and marched across the hall amid stares from the occupants, no doubt privy to the loud goings on in Deargh's chamber.

Outside in the fresh air, he breathed hard. He had only gotten a glimpse of McGuffin's letter but the man hadn't lied. It had nothing to do with the Stone of Destiny, and everything to do with some sort of jewelry.

What the devil was going on? He decided he would very much like to meet this John Dunbar face to face . . . and stab him good and hard in the gut.

SEVENTEEN

Jack ducked. The arm that had reached out to grab him caught only air. He threw himself backward into the foliage with the cracking of twigs and the flailing of leaves.

The knights dove in after him, but he squirmed away on his back. Gauntlets poked through the branches in front of his face, and he tried to meld into the ground as much as he could, but he escaped each grasp, each closing of fingers like claws.

Rolling, he desperately scanned ahead, looking for options. An open path. No good, it was too open. Then a wall with a dead end. No good either. The gnarled tree would have to do.

He tore through the brambles, leaves exploding around him, and leaped for the rough bark of a tree like a squirrel. And very like a squirrel, he used both hands and feet to scale the knotted trunk until he gained the first outstretched limb. He stood on it and looked down, but some of the knights were already following him up the tree, though as encumbered as they were by armor it wasn't as easy.

Looking up, he spied another heavy limb and climbed for it, gaining height with each step. He could see far over the walls now, both into Henry Derby's garden and beyond to the busy Thames. Lambeth Moor spread out east across the river, with its green and rusty plain broken up by occasional right-angle hedges and grazing cattle. If the river were closer he'd make a dive for it, but it was a stony embankment that shouldered the outer wall, and he had no desire to land upon that!

No, he'd have to either make for Derby's wall or the queen's chamber, and by the looks of things – what with knights climbing after him and more coming through the queen's door – neither seemed like a viable option.

Merciful Jesus, he prayed, *I got m'self into a fix now. If You can see Your way to offering me a path to freedom, I'd be very obliging.*

His feet looked too close to the climbing knights and so he had no choice but to go higher. He knew he would soon run out of limbs thick enough to hold him . . . 'Ah!' His eyes followed the path of a long branch above. It reached upward, shooting toward the sky, but if a weight were attached to it – say about Jack's weight – it might just carry him over Derby's wall. If it didn't break first.

He looked down. The angry face of a knight sneered back up at him. 'Get down here, you gawby lop!'

Jack kicked his way higher, dislodging a clump of dead leaves, cobwebs, and an old bird's nest. It cascaded downward and landed on the knight's face. He batted at it with a yell and nearly lost his grip. 'I'll bray you good when I catch you!'

Jack didn't wait. He shimmied higher, wrapping his legs around the narrowing branch. The higher he climbed, the more the branch shivered and tilted. Just as he hoped, it began a slow swooning bend toward the other wall. He inched still higher, for he needed that length to get him over the barrier.

'Stop at once!'

The garden hum of bustle and shouting came to an abrupt halt. Jack risked his precarious balance to look down over his shoulder. The queen! She stood on her porch and, with an imperious air, glared down all the king's guards who had gathered. And with a lump in his throat Jack saw that there were many more than he thought.

'I command you to stop,' she cried again.

'But your grace, that man—'

Jack's branch was dipping lower toward his goal. His feet were mere inches from the wall now and all he need do was leap. He took one last look over his shoulder and gave a grateful smile to the queen.

'What man?' she said, and Jack released the branch and dropped hard on the other side of the wall. The branch slashed back like a whip.

He heard their complaints and shouts but he left it behind him and ran through the garden to the door. He grabbed the latch and threw it open . . . and came to a halt before Hugh Waterton, Derby's chamberlain. His face was dark and his hands darted out to grab Jack by his chaperon hood.

'What are you doing?' he demanded.

'I . . . I . . .'

A loud banging on the main door made them both turn. Waterton scowled down at Jack again.

'Master Waterton, I swear by Jesus's precious blood that I was on an honorable errand. I swear! Lay me hand on a saint's bones and I will swear the same.'

The door banged again with, 'Open up in the name of the king's guards!'

'I just need to . . . hide, Master Waterton. I beg you. His grace Henry Derby himself would vouchsafe for me. He would, sir.'

He could see it in the steward's eyes. The man plainly did not want to believe him, but something compelled him to do so. Or so Jack thought. Waterton cast a glance back in the direction of the door and its echoing pounding. He curled his hand tighter in the cape of Jack's hood and dragged him forward. 'Come with me.'

They stalked past frightened servants, staring aghast at the main door through the many doorways. 'Master Waterton,' cried one as they shouldered past him. 'Should we open the door?'

'No! I will be there anon to open it myself.' He shoved Jack forward into a chamber Jack had never in before. Waterton strode to the bed, bent over, and pulled out a truckle bed. Designed for a servant to sleep near the master, it had only a thin mattress stuffed with straw.

'Get in.'

Jack complied immediately. Waterton barely gave him time to lay flat before he shoved it under the larger bed again. 'I need not tell you to stay quiet.'

Jack becrossed himself, albeit tightly as there was little room to move. In fact, his nose was pressed up against the under ribs of the bed above. He listened as Waterton stomped away. The banging had not ceased, and the shouting on the other side of the door had grown louder. Jack cringed down and awaited his fate. Either he would stay hidden or . . . Or King Richard would make good on his threat.

Waterton must have opened the door for the noise level rose to a crescendo. Jack closed his eyes and prayed. Surely it should not be so trying doing a good deed for his sovereign queen!

'You're mistaken,' he heard Waterton say, far too close to the room. 'He made his way out the door. You must have just missed him.'

'But he was here?'

'That is the truth, my lord.'

Master Crispin had always said that if one must lie, stick as close to the truth as possible.

Men stomped with heavy boots throughout the apartments. Doors opened and slammed.

Until the voice of Henry Derby thundered from the entry. 'What, by God and St George, is this?'

Muttering and sounds of obeisance – Jack knew them well – a woman's scream, and the calling out to the guards.

The door opened to the chamber and Jack froze, holding his breath.

The call to the guards came again, but the knight hesitated. Jack could hear his armor clanking from the doorway. The knight moved into the room, each heavy footfall growing closer. Jack heard him try the coffer, but it was locked. He opened a sideboard with a squealing hinge. The footfalls approached the bed and stood there a long time.

The call again.

The knight swore under his breath and spun on his heel, his footfalls falling away with distance.

Jack breathed shallowly and waited. He would have to make very certain that no guards remained before he made a move.

And just as he thought that he had waited long enough, he heard the hurried footsteps of two men enter the room. Before he could gird himself, the truckle was pulled out and he was dragged to his feet in a strong grip.

'By my mother's bones, Jack Tucker!' shouted Henry Derby into his face. 'Do you mind explaining what you thought you were doing? Are you not in enough peril?'

Waterton stood beside Henry, glaring at Jack with just as much fire as the young lord. Jack's throat constricted with fear and for a moment nothing would come out. But with some hard swallowing he looked the man in the eye. 'I am heartily sorry, your grace, for inconveniencing you—'

'Inconveniencing me? You and Master Guest are nothing *but* an inconvenience.' He shoved Jack away. Jack stumbled to right himself and straightened his coat and hood.

'I know it, my lord. No one knows it better than me and Master Crispin, and that's a fact. But we are both bound by our honor to do what is right, and he apprenticed me as a Tracker and that I will do with my last breath, sir.'

'Tracker? What nonsense is this?'

'Our vocation, my lord. My master is the Tracker and I his apprentice. In tracking. I was only doing me job.'

Henry folded his arms over his chest. 'Doing what job?'

Jack bit his lip. 'Er . . . I may not say, my lord. It is a matter of confidentiality.'

'Confidentiality?' His fists were now at his hips and he leaned into Jack, too close for comfort. 'Master Tucker.' His voice was low and deadly. 'I will not have the king's guards in my household. I cannot give them an excuse to look into private matters, do you understand me?'

Jack swallowed, his throat constricting again. He nodded.

'So whatever it is you think you are doing – tracking or no tracking – you had best stop it now. Are we clear?'

'But . . .' he managed to squeak.

Derby's nose was up against Jack's. 'Are . . . we . . . clear?'

'Yes, your grace,' he whispered.

'Good.' He pulled back and straightened. 'If I hear of any more disturbances, I will return you to the dungeons from whence you came. My generosity only goes so far.'

Jack said nothing, which seemed to suit the young lord. He gave a nod and turned smartly, hurrying away and out the suite's door.

But before Jack could even think about relaxing, Waterton had him by the collar. 'I am charged with keeping order in the earl's chambers. When anyone – servant or guest – displeases him, it is up to me to make it right. But you, Master Tucker, have gone far beyond inconveniencing my master. You put him in danger, and he already lives on the knife edge of it in his current position. You will not discommode him again.'

'Y-yes, Master Waterton. I understand, sir. I am sorry for everything . . .'

'You will stay in your room, Master Tucker. You will not leave it. And to make certain of that, I will lock you in.'

'Oh no, Master Waterton! Please don't do that.'

'Come with me.' Fisting his hood's cape again, he dragged Jack along back to the servant's room.

'Please, Master. Don't do it. I can't be useful locked up.'

'On the contrary.' He opened the door and pushed Jack in. 'You will be at your most useful if you do not cause this family further harm.' He slammed the door and a key scraped in the lock, shutting it tight.

EIGHTEEN

A woman came running down the lane toward Crispin, muddied skirts held up, exposing spattered stockings. But of course it was no woman but John Rykener. Out of breath, Rykener stopped before Crispin and bent over, breathing and clutching his thighs.

'Bless me!' he gasped. 'You are a hard man to find. I was trying to warn you—'

The door opened to the inn and out stepped McGuffin and his men. As soon as he spotted John he pointed straight-armed at him. 'You!'

John stomped his foot. 'You are no gentleman, sir!'

McGuffin trudged toward John and glowered over him. '*I'm* no gentleman?'

This began to draw the attention of the people along the street. Crispin slowly stepped back out of the way.

'You treated me most foul when all I wanted was a little information. After all, sir, you and your men did handle me roughly.'

'Here! What's this?' A man with a hay fork over his shoulder came out of the gathering crowd and approached McGuffin, who was squaring with Rykener. 'Demoiselle, should I call in the law?'

Rykener's demeanor changed immediately. His face softened, and he smiled at the man. 'Oh, you are kind, good master, to wish to help. But this . . . this *miscreant* can do me little harm now.'

McGuffin's face blared red. 'I'm . . . That . . . Oh! I'll no forget this!' He stormed off up the lane, followed quickly by his retainers.

Seeing no more than a common row, the crowd dispersed on its own. Rykener curtseyed to the man with the rake and hurried toward Crispin, taking his arm even as Crispin protested.

'I had been trying to warn you about McGuffin,' said Rykener, walking down the lane with Crispin who finally shucked him from his arm. 'He said he would find you.'

'What did you say to him?'

'I told him that he had to help, that his soul was in peril because of it. I might have even blasphemed a bit. Called him a few names.'

'I appreciate it, John. Did you learn anything new?'

'He swore every oath he knew that he had nothing to do with the theft of the Stone, that he was charged to some other purpose – I could not find out what – and that I was never to return to darken his door.'

'It might interest you to know that I did find out what *he* was up to, at least. He is supposed to be in charge of secreting a stolen piece of jewelry belonging to the queen.'

'Our queen?'

'Yes, presumably. Why this has anything to do with the Stone's plot, I do not know, but it is the same plot, for it was fashioned by the same man, John Dunbar, earl of Moray.'

'Just as you said to Master Domhnall. Should you not have pursued that cause simply to find the Stone?'

They wove their way down to Charing Cross and stopped at the stone steps. 'Though I think I believe McGuffin when he says he has nothing to do with the Stone's disappearance, I am beginning to think I should have.' Crispin stepped up onto the steps and sat. The shadow of the arched monument angled away from him, and he could enjoy the sun as it warmed the wool breast of his cotehardie. John sat beside him, arranging his skirts. 'We know where he is, and he is safe there for the time being.'

'But now you are certain of this John Dunbar.'

'He is not my concern. He is far from here. The immediate threats are these three factions. And I have met Deargh.'

'Oh! And is he the danger that Master Domhnall painted?'

'Perhaps. He wanted to hire my help and was disappointed that it was not for sale.'

'Just like McGuffin.'

'Yes. But I am fairly certain that there are at least two monks at the abbey who were at the heart of this conspiracy and one might just be ready to crack. I told him that I will allow him one day to decide whether he deals with me or the king's inquisitors.'

'How did he react?'

'Like a guilty man.'

'Oh dear. I wish Jack Tucker were here. He'd know what to do. Oh! I . . . forgive my wayward tongue.'

'I know. I wish he were here, too. He'd say something like,

"You're not thinking clear, Master Crispin—"' He did his best imitation of Jack's voice and accent. His chuckle was bittersweet. 'And he'd be right. I was so balled up in fear for that stubborn, annoying boy that I nearly lost my thread of thought. But it's back now. I think I shall return and see if that monk is good and marinated and ready to confess all to me.'

'What happened to giving him a day to decide?'

'John,' he said chuckling and shaking his head, 'I was never going to give him an entire day.'

The argument had been going on for the length of time it had taken to traverse the last few streets. 'John, for the last time, will you go home and change!'

'Crispin, there is no time. We are almost at the abbey.'

'Precisely. Do you go into a church dressed like that?'

'All are welcome at church, Crispin. The Almighty knows who I am, woman's clothes or man's.'

Grumbling, Crispin stalked forward up St Margaret's Street, leaving John to trot to catch up. They made it to the north door. Crispin hurried in under the cool stone, hastily dipping a finger into the font to sketch a cross upon his forehead and chest. He marched forward until he was almost under the crossing. The way was barred by a locked gate to the quire. He headed up the north ambulatory instead toward Edward the Confessor's chapel.

He slowed when he approached it. There, the tomb, and before it, the chair, devoid of its Stone.

'It truly is missing, isn't it?' John said beside him, voice echoing in susurrating whispers. 'I somehow thought . . .' He hugged himself. 'It gives me a chill thinking about it.'

Crispin felt it, too. 'I know exactly what you mean.'

He could see monks wandering in the distance, and others – merchants, clerks, lawyers, pardoners – all milling in the nave, looking for prospective employers. Still, even with all these, he approached the Chair unmolested. The chair, still a proud thing, was the worse for wear with its missing stone, like a gouged eye. The debris had long ago been cleared away. When had the Stone been taken? That was the important question, one that couldn't seem to be answered.

'Is it heavy, Crispin?'

He looked at John standing beside him in his women's clothes. The man had his fingers to his lips, brows bowed outward with worry.

'I imagine it is. A piece of granite to fit that space. It would take two men at least to carry it away. Rings or no rings.'

'Truth to tell, Crispin, I can't say that I have ever thought much about the Stone of Destiny. Does it . . . is it a fancy stone? Carved and all?'

'As far as I know it is not. I have only seen the one side of it, facing this way.'

'It must be very old.'

'It was said to pillow Jacob's head. So it *is* very old and has come very far.'

'Such a thing. Shouldn't it have been guarded, then?' He looked around, perhaps looking for those elusive guards.

Crispin followed his gaze, spying the finery of curtains, gold leaf, velvet cushions for his majesty, and the finery festooning the tombs. 'Well, the monks guard what treasures are here, either golden ones or the honored dead.'

'Perhaps *they* are not enough.'

Crispin nodded. He had a point. After all, here *they* were with no one questioning them. Slowly, he walked around the chair, then lifted his gaze to the tomb, and still higher up the walls to the arched ceiling falling away into darkness. 'Three factions, John. All having something to do with stealing the Stone, and not one of them has it.'

'You believe them now, then? That it isn't a farce just to deceive you?'

'Oh I believe it is a farce, right enough. But, if anything, it has rebounded upon them. They sought to confuse me but succeeded in only confusing themselves. I believe they were sincere in their belief that each faction was to take charge of the Stone and were confounded when that part of the plan exploded in their face.'

'So . . . they don't have the Stone? Any of them?'

'No.'

'But . . . each thought *they* were to be the recipients.'

'Yes. Except perhaps for McGuffin.'

'Then . . . what happened?'

Crispin scrubbed at his chin. 'What jewelry is it, I wonder, that McGuffin was to steal? Surely it was worth more than the mere selling of it, for why else would it have to do with the queen? Why that particular piece? And when was it taken? Was the taking of one to distract from the taking of the other?'

'Bless me, Crispin! What thoughts you weave!'

'Hmm.' He rested a foot on the step leading up to the chair, and rested his forearm on his thigh. 'John, if you were to steal the Stone of Destiny, how would you go about it?'

'What? Oh, I see. It's like a game.' He moved closer to the chair but still stayed behind Crispin to peer at it. 'Well, as you said, it's heavy.'

'Very.'

'And so I would need an accomplice.'

'True.'

'And then . . . bless me, larceny is hard!'

'Only for honest men.'

John smiled. 'You *are* kind. Well then. I think it should be at night, no? Is the church locked at night?'

'No, but certain gates and doors are. And there is a porter who patrols.'

'But he should be easy to avoid since it is just one man. All it would take is watching the schedule of the man for a few nights.'

'Just so. Or already knowing his schedule. Or perhaps even he was part of the plan.' Crispin rose higher, looking closely at the chair, almost close enough to touch. He had seen Richard crowned in that chair, but he doubted he would see his heir so crowned. Whoever that heir might be. At the moment, that would be Roger Mortimer, Earl March, the king's cousin. But Richard was young and healthy. He would certainly outlive Crispin. No, Richard's was the only coronation he would ever see, and a regrettable one it was.

'And so,' John went on, 'after knowing the schedule of this patrolling monk – assuming he wasn't part of the crime – I should wait until it was very dark and very late and steal into the abbey. We would take the Stone from out of the chair . . .'

'And replace it with one of plaster.'

'And . . . oh. And replace it with one of plaster . . .'

'Which contains a portion of explosive powder.'

'It did?'

'It did.'

John looked anew at the chair. 'And then my foul compatriot and I would simply walk out the door with it.'

'Put it on a wagon?'

'That would be most expedient.'

'And then simply cart it away. Anywhere.' Crispin stumped down the steps again and breathed in the incense-infused air. He watched the taper burn in its sconce at one corner of the Confessor's tomb. 'It could be anywhere, John, and none of these damned Scotsmen know where the hell it is. But why? How did this so carefully laid plan become so muddled? Why wasn't it accomplished?'

'Perhaps it was. Perhaps there is a fourth faction.'

Slowly, Crispin turned toward him. 'God's blood. You don't suppose . . .'

'For your sake, I hope it is not true.'

He smacked his forehead and paced, his steps beating a cadence in dispersing echoes. 'Why so many? Is it true? Did this Moray need to make certain that at least one of them would be successful? And yet. I had every impression that at least Deargh believed he was to carry out the rest of the plan. And he does not look to be a man to trifle with.'

'But that is not necessarily so. You see, Crispin, when I am working on an embroidery – especially a complicated one – we use many seamstresses. We each have a part to play, whether it is finding and sorting the thread, or making certain we follow one another in the pattern so it all looks the same. We all must follow through or the whole thing is ruined.'

Crispin studied John for a long time. So long it made John twitchy. He moved to Crispin's other side and stared at the chair.

'Then maybe something went wrong,' said Crispin. 'Deargh *was* supposed to get the Stone, but someone failed in their part of the plan.'

'Failed in what way?'

He shrugged. 'I don't know. No one seems to know.'

John sighed. His chin was raised and his eyes scoured the lofty heights of the ceiling and fan vaults. 'Then how are we ever to know?'

'We must find a way to discover it. That is how this tracking is done.'

He turned his gaze back to Crispin. 'It's very difficult, isn't it? What you do?'

'Yes, it can be.'

'But you are very clever, very tenacious. And I won't abandon you.'

Crispin was touched more than he could say by John's expression of fealty. He simply nodded rather than speaking, afraid his voice might crack. He moved on down the ambulatory and toward the crossing.

The bells suddenly rang above them. He felt their deep resonance in his gut.

Nearly Vespers. When had it gotten so late?

'John, I think I need to speak with Abbot Colchester. It might be easier for me to question this monk alone. Would you mind?'

'Oh. I see. Of course.' He looked down at himself, at his woman's clothes, partly torn and mostly muddy from his altercations. 'I truly shouldn't be here dressed as I am, should I? I . . . should go.'

'Return to my lodgings, if you will. There . . . might be food in the pantry . . .'

John smiled. 'I might be able to help you there,' he said, patting his scrip. He offered an encouraging expression before he turned and walked toward the colonnade of the north transept. Crispin watched him go, watched that willowy figure disappear into the gloom.

He passed through the crossing and headed toward the south transept toward a door to the cloister. He could find someone to take him to the abbot's lodgings. Even when he visited Abbot Nicholas, he had found an escort. It was simply good manners not to wander about in a monastery. But especially with the stoic Abbot Colchester, Crispin felt he needed that go-between.

He was nearly at the door when he turned at the sound of rapid footsteps approaching. Their drumbeat rang harshly on the tiled floor and echoed back louder and louder. He strained his eyes to see in the hazy light and saw a figure lit by the dim glow of the candles from the shrine. It stopped and he saw the head turn, searching. It seemed to spot him and tore forward, and it wasn't long until he realized it was John Rykener.

He skidded to a halt before Crispin, grasping his cotehardie with curled, trembling fingers. 'Crispin! Crispin, you must come!'

'What is it, John?'

'Just . . . just come!' He pushed away from him and ran back. Crispin followed, walking at first, then breaking into a run. He followed John's swift retreat and slowed when Rykener stumbled to a stop with legs flailing. He seemed to be looking down at something.

Once Crispin approached he could see it, too. A man was lying on the stone step of the north transept. Crispin knelt. Closer, he could plainly see that it was a monk. His tonsure shone bone-white in the fading sunlight, that which was not blood, for there was also a great gash in his scalp so deep that it showed a cracked skull and brain matter. A great deal of blood was pooled about him, but with even a cursory look about, Crispin could tell this was no accident. There was nothing for him to bash his head upon on his own.

John stepped away and retched into a corner. 'Oh God,' he whispered over and over. 'Oh God, save us. Save us.'

Avoiding the blood, Crispin maneuvered around the body to look at the face. Eyes wide, mouth agape, the monk had been surprised by his attacker. But Crispin was somehow not surprised at who it was. He would have liked to have talked to the monk one more time. But that was plainly impossible when Brother Crìsdean's brains were scattered upon the floor.

NINETEEN

Abbot Colchester strode out of the shadows to stand before the body of his monk. 'Master Guest,' he said breathlessly, 'who could have done such a thing?'

'My Lord Abbot, I must speak with you alone. I was coming to you to do just that when we discovered the . . . your monk.'

The abbot raised his eyes to Crispin. Usually, those blue eyes were cold, calculating how much to say, how much to dismiss. But now Crispin found them lost and muddled. The man had reasoned with popes and argued with dukes, but murder had never lain at his feet before this.

The abbot nodded distantly. 'Yes. Yes, we must talk. The sheriffs will be here soon. We must talk before they arrive.'

And so, thought Crispin, the abbot was not as muddled as all that when he had kept the sheriffs and their interfering ways in mind.

Colchester turned and walked back into the gloom, plainly expecting Crispin to follow. Before the abbot called to him, Crispin turned to John, who was clearly shaken by events. He took him firmly by the shoulders. 'J—Eleanor! Are you listening?'

Rykener blinked dazedly at Crispin. 'Y-yes. Yes, of course.'

'Go on back to my lodgings. I'll meet you there. Can you do that?'

John straightened, girded himself, and nodded. 'Yes,' he said softly. 'Take all the time you need.' He looked back at the body and shivered. 'You must stop this terrible thing, Crispin,' he whispered.

'I will do what I can.'

John gave him a meaningful look before slumping away. His steps grew steadier and faster as he hurried out into the early evening.

Crispin took a calming breath and trotted after the abbot.

He followed him not to the chapter house but to his lodgings, that all too familiar passage between cloister and out buildings. His predecessor, Abbot Nicholas, often had Crispin as a guest, where they played chess and drank wine and talked of politics and philosophy. He missed those days, missed the old monk and his wise advice. And wondered still at his deathbed words: 'You must forget what you think you know . . . Beware of what you find . . .'

Brother John Sandon scrambled forward, hoisting a lantern. It cast a glow over his worried countenance as he ushered Crispin forth into the chamber, barely after Colchester's steps.

The abbot did not sit calmly behind his desk as Crispin had seen once before, but instead paced, his fingers on his lips, eyes fixed a few steps before him.

Crispin stood, watching him until the man came to a halt on the other side of the room. Looking back at Crispin, the abbot's face was pulled taut with strain. 'This is no mere coincidence, is it, Master Guest?'

'No, Lord Abbot.'

'Christ preserve us,' he muttered. He dragged himself toward a chair by the hearth and sank into it. There used to be a similar chair beside it, one Crispin had occupied many a time with Abbot Nicholas, but the chair had been moved in favor of a small table and a chandler. A Psalter lay on the table, a ribbon marking the place where the reader had left it. There was no dog lying before the hearth either. Nicholas's greyhound, Sturdy, had left this earth not long after his master had.

Soft steps behind him made Crispin turn. Brother John had brought a folding chair and was placing it not too far from the little table. He gestured for Crispin to sit, and with a nod of thanks, Crispin did.

The abbot had encaged his face in his fingers, eyes closed. Perhaps he prayed. Perhaps he merely contemplated the horror of murder. Crispin waited respectfully as long as he could before saying, 'My Lord Abbot, we must talk.'

Colchester lowered his hand from his face and watched the flames rise and flicker in the hearth. 'Speak, Master Guest.'

'How well did you know Brother Crìsdean?'

'Not well. He was fairly new to the abbey. Less than six months now.'

'And was he the only brother who cared for the Coronation Chair?'

'No. He had assistants. There are few monks in our monastery that are alone at their tasks. We have so many souls here, you see.' He sighed. 'So many souls.'

'Then . . . it might be prudent for me to speak with them as well. I had come back to see if Crìsdean would now speak to me. I find that a threat is more than enough to extract the guilt from a man. But, as we saw, I was too late.'

The abbot looked up suddenly. 'Do you think . . . someone overheard you? Do you think that someone wished to stop Brother Crìsdean from confessing?'

'It is a possibility.'

His gasp was somewhat of a surprise. Crispin didn't think Colchester was given to fits of astonishment. 'Your apprentice Master Tucker. What will become of him?'

A spike of fear jabbed his heart, as it always did at the mention of Jack. 'So far he is well. But as you know, if I do not find the Stone by tomorrow . . .'

'God will help you, Master Guest. Your cause is just.'

If only He could do so a little faster. Aloud he said, 'Indeed, Lord Abbot. And so I am here at the beginning where it happened. If I could speak with those brothers . . .'

The abbot snapped his fingers and Brother John appeared from wherever it was he had been waiting. 'Gather Brother Crìsdean's assistants. Have them come here in all haste, Brother.'

The monk bowed and scurried out to comply.

The abbot dropped his face in his hand again and, with his expression masked, said, 'Perhaps you can fetch us a cup of wine, Master Guest. I suspect you know where it is.'

Crispin rose to comply. The wine was where expected – on the sideboard – and he poured from the silver flagon into two awaiting goblets, also of silver. He took the first and handed it to the abbot with a bow before returning to his seat to wait for the monks.

He marked the time by how low his wine was, how the fire diminished, and the light from the window as it changed from angled beams to dusky shadows.

The door opened, and he set down his cup and stood to face the monks.

Three men huddled together. One wept openly, the youngest, while the other two – both middle-aged men – kept their eyes lowered.

Abbot William rose slowly, like an old man. He slipped his hands within his scapular and nodded to his charges. 'My brothers, no doubt you have heard about the tragic end of our own Brother Crìsdean.'

'I can scarce believe it,' wailed the younger monk, eyes red, face streaked with wet.

'God have mercy, it is true,' answered the abbot, becrossing himself again.

'But I had only just talked to him, not more than half an hour ago,' said one of the older monks.

'And where was that, Brother?' asked Crispin. A time of death would surely help.

The monk merely studied Crispin, eyes darting between him and his abbot.

'This is Crispin Guest, Brothers. You are to answer his questions as if I asked them.'

They all bowed.

'And so I ask again, Brother—?'

'Jerome, Master Guest. Brother Crìsdean and I were checking on the stores of beeswax and oil. This we use for the polishing of wood. The quire stalls, the carrels in the cloister, staircase balusters . . . so many places where the wood must be cared for.'

'I see. And where was this?'

'In the stores room.'

'And . . . did anyone else see you there together?'

Brother Jerome blinked. 'I . . . do not understand your meaning, Master Guest.'

'He means,' said Abbot William, 'are there witnesses to your being together at such a place at such a time?'

'Witnesses? You surely do not think . . . you do not accuse . . .'

'Of course not, Brother Jerome,' said Crispin. 'It is merely to make certain of the time and incident.'

Jerome's expression had not lost its huffiness but he grudgingly answered, 'Yes. As a matter of fact there was. Brother Andrew.'

Crispin scanned the faces of the other monks. 'Which is Brother Andrew? Is he an assistant as well?'

'Yes. He could not be readily found. Perhaps he is preparing for Vespers.'

'How did Brother Crìsdean seem to you, Brother Jerome? Was he calm? Agitated?'

'I would say he was greatly agitated. His hand trembled so much that I asked him what the matter was. He kept muttering that he never should have had some sort of responsibility. And then suddenly he looked up at me and nodded. "Yes," he said, seeming to decide something. "I shall go to the abbot at once." And that was the last I saw of him.'

Crispin turned to the other two. 'And did either of you see Brother Crìsdean any later than half an hour ago?'

Both shook their heads.

'So sometime within the last half hour, Brother Crìsdean was dispatched,' muttered Crispin.

The youngest monk wailed again. 'Must you speak so callously of one of our own, Master Guest? He was mentor, brother, and father to me.'

'Yet you scarcely knew him,' said the other monk.

'Eh?' asked Crispin.

The other older monk stepped forward. 'I am Brother Lewis. Brother Crìsdean has been with us a mere four months.'

'A faithful cleric can do much within a briefer amount of time, Brother Lewis,' said the younger monk, sniffing.

'Brother Harold, you attach yourself where you should not. The Rule stipulates that no friendships should be established . . .'

The abbot raised his hands. 'Brothers, please.'

Brother Lewis stuffed his hands impatiently within his sleeves. 'Lord Abbot, it is proper to remind our younger brothers of the Rule.'

'But more fitting in chapter, is it not?'

They all fell silent at his admonishment.

'Nevertheless,' the abbot continued, 'now is not the time to berate. We have lost a brother in a most grievous manner, and Master Guest is here to assist us. Pray, Master Guest, what do you construe from this information?'

'I'm afraid I'll need more than this,' said Crispin. 'Where did Brother Crìsdean come from prior to his assignment here?'

Abbot William shook his head. 'I don't know. Brother John, do fetch Brother Thomas Merke. He keeps the records of the abbey,' he said to Crispin. 'He can tell us.'

Brother John escaped again and Crispin looked over the three monks. 'Is this other monk, this Brother Andrew, also one of Crìsdean's assistants?'

'He is,' answered Jerome. 'He is a true alchemist, mixing the compounds for cleaning the wood and for supervising the soap-making.'

Alchemist enough to know how to use explosive powder?

'Then I shall also need to speak to him,' he said to Colchester. 'How did the rest of you fare with Brother Crìsdean?'

They exchanged glances with one another. 'As well as anyone,' said Brother Lewis. 'We are all brothers here, working for the community.'

Crispin shuffled his feet, keeping his eyes withdrawn. 'That isn't exactly what I asked.'

'Well,' said Jerome after a pause, 'Brother Crìsdean could be . . . how should one say?'

'One mustn't speak ill of the dead, Brother Jerome,' said Lewis.

'I am not speaking ill of him!' He ruffled his scapular. 'I am merely pointing out a truth.'

'And that truth is?' asked Crispin.

'That Brother Crìsdean was snappish. And aloof.'

'That's not true!' cried Harold. His tears seemed to have abated at last, but he still dragged his hand over his eyes. 'It was merely that he didn't understand our ways. He was from the north, you know.'

'Yes, I did detect the accent,' said Crispin. 'I wonder if—'

Brother John returned with another monk, Brother Thomas. He had a ledger and a roll of parchments under one arm. 'This is all most distressing,' he said to no one in particular. He bowed to the abbot and then looked toward Crispin. Crispin had met him before when the abbot was first installed.

The abbot gestured toward the bundle under Thomas's arm. 'Are those the records, Brother?'

Thomas hurried to Colchester's desk and laid the parchments on the surface. Carefully he began to unroll. 'Yes, my Lord Abbot. I grabbed what I could and began looking through the records after they were requested and then decided to bring them all. Brother John here says that Brother Crìsdean came to us approximately four months ago.'

All the monks nodded their heads.

Brother Thomas licked his fingers as he thumbed through parchment after parchment. 'My Lord Abbot, I have checked and rechecked and it appears . . .' He let the parchments go and they fell back together on the table. He sighed and threw up his hands. 'My lord, I cannot find a record of him at all.'

The abbot drew back. 'What?' He rushed to the table and thumbed through the parchments himself. His fingers followed the entries made; he read line after line. He shuffled more, looking at the bottom of the pile and then each subsequent. 'Are *all* the papers here, Brother?'

'Yes, my lord, including the ledger there' – he pointed to a leather-bound book tied with a leather thong. He shook his head. 'But I cannot find record of him. It's as if he . . . he just *appeared* here.'

Abbot William scoured the frightened faces of his monks. 'Can anyone recall when he arrived? Come now. Surely someone knows.'

They exchanged looks again, the three. 'He . . . he arrived at the refectory at supper,' said Jerome. 'I recall that. He sat beside me. Afterwards, we talked and he discussed his new assignment caring for the Coronation Chair.'

'Yes, yes,' said Brother Harold with an anxious twitch. 'He came to me and asked me to assist him and soon I was assigned there.'

'Who assigned you?' asked Brother Thomas.

'Why, it was . . . it was . . .' He stared at the floor, thinking. 'I do not recall, Brother. I was told. By . . . Brother Crìsdean.'

Everyone fell silent.

'It appears,' said Crispin, 'that this scheme has been plotted for a very long time.'

The abbot glared at the parchments again. His expression was one Crispin had never seen him wear. Always he was the most measured and decorous. Now his eyes were somewhat wild. 'But how can such a thing be?'

Crispin glanced at the tiny careful writing on the parchments. 'With so many monks here it would take a clever man, one with the courage to carry through on such a daring enterprise. He may not have even been a monk at all.'

Harold gasped and threw his hands over his mouth.

Abbot William clenched his fists. 'I would speak with Brother Andrew.'

'I shall see to it at once!' said Thomas and ran from the room.

The abbot in his rage turned on Crispin. His nostrils flared with each blasting breath. 'This is outrageous! How could this have happened?'

'It is not the fault of any of your clerics, my lord. As I said, a clever and devious man need only force himself amongst you.'

'A wolf in sheep's clothing,' seethed the abbot. He marched to the hearth and stood over it, leaning with his arm on the stone mantel. 'How *dare* he?'

'If he was in the employ of who I think he was, then the stakes were very high. And he was paid very well. But somehow, he needed to be silenced.'

'He has paid the penalty for his foul deeds on this earth. God will mete out proper punishment as he stands in judgment.'

Crispin said no more. He waited again to talk to this Brother Andrew.

It took a long time. The bells for Vespers had long ago rung, but none of the monks moved. The abbot was particularly still, a statue staring into the fire, barely lifting his chest to breathe.

When at last Thomas returned he was sweaty and out of breath. The monks gathered around him. Even the abbot turned anxiously.

'We checked and rechecked, my lord,' said Thomas. 'But Brother Andrew is not here.'

'Impossible,' sputtered the abbot.

Crispin rested his hand on his knife hilt. If Brother Andrew was not present in the abbey then that meant one of two things. That he was missing because he, too, was murdered like Crìsdean and his body secreted somewhere.

Or . . . because he himself was a murderer.

TWENTY

J ack listened to the church bells all the next morning until the sun
climbed higher. First Prime, then Terce. The guilt from his actions
weighed heavily on him. He would not be the cause of the king's
wrath borne down on Henry or even Lady Katherine. And in the
midst of it he pictured Master Crispin's disappointed face. He had
never beaten Jack as other masters did their apprentices. His stoic
silences were far worse, berating with a mere look and a discontented
sigh. How Jack flayed himself because of those expressions!

But his promise burned fiercely within him, too. For the queen
sorely needed his help, and he had vowed to give it. What would
Master Crispin do?

Jack stared at the locked door and up at the small window above
his head. The glass sat in its own chamfered niche but was not made
to open, only to give light. He would have to break it to climb out
of it, *if* he could squeeze through, which he doubted he could.

The door, then. But it was locked from the outside. But was
the key in the door? He knelt and put his eye to the keyhole.
'Damn!' He could see clearly through the hole, which meant no
key. And he could see a servant approaching with a tray. His
stomach growled. It had been a while since he ate. He was relieved
that he would not starve to death.

But wait! The servant was to unlock the door. Jack concentrated
and expelled a 'Ha!' when the idea came to him. He lifted up his
coat, grabbed the hem of his chemise and fiddled with the edge.
Quickly slipping his knife free of its sheath, he sliced a thin length
of material from the shirt, returned his coat and knife to their places,
and wadded up the material in his fist just as the door opened.

The servant poked his head in. 'Sorry, Jack. Master Waterton was
tardy in telling us where you were. I thought you'd need a little
food about now.'

'Ah, Hubert. I knew you wouldn't forget me, lad.'

Hubert moved into the room and set down his tray. On it was a
bowl with slices of cold fowl, boiled onions, and sprigs of borage.
A good-sized beaker of ale was there as well. Hubert, a lank boy,

younger than Jack with a spotty chin and cheeks, smiled and wiped his hands down his tabard. 'Wouldn't forget you.'

Jack liked the boy and didn't want to get him into trouble, but it had to be done. With his hands behind his back and his back to the door, Jack casually crept closer to the lock. In his fingers he shredded the material and wadded it up good and tight. When he touched the lock at his fingertips, he felt for the lock hole and stuffed the wadding in, pushing it tight against the bolt spring.

'Am I to be locked in the whole day?'

Hubert's smiled faded. 'Well . . . that's what Master Waterton says. It's a shame is what it is, Jack. Why are you kept a prisoner here anyway?'

'It's a long tale, lad. One I may not be at liberty to say. But know this. I would not have harm come to Lord Henry or any of his retinue, including you, Hubert.'

'I know that, Jack. Everyone knows that.'

He sighed. 'Not Master Waterton. He was right angry with me.'

'You caused a stir, there's no denying it.' He smiled again. 'Never a dull moment in Lord Derby's employ.'

'Nor in the Tracker's either.'

Hubert moved close to Jack and Jack pulled his hands away hastily from the lock. 'You promised to tell me about more of your adventures with Master Guest.'

'Of course, of course. But, er, I would not keep you from your duties. Master Waterton has a sharp eye.'

'Oh, aye.' He bit his lip. 'I'll be back later then. Around Sext. I'll bring more ale and we can talk.'

'That's a plan, Hubert.' Jack nodded eagerly, hoping the boy would forgive him if he was not here to receive him.

Hubert moved around Jack to the door. 'Be at peace, Jack.' He held the edge of the door in his hand, and with an apologetic twist to his lips, pulled the door closed. Jack heard the key grind in the lock and waited until the footsteps receded. He put his ear to the door and closed his eyes, straining to listen for anyone near it. When he was satisfied that no one was about, he yanked on the door handle. He needed only to wriggle it a bit. The bolt had only moved a little in the lock and not into the door jamb. Pulling the door open only a crack, he cautiously looked around.

He glanced back into the room and at the full beaker. 'Be a shame to waste it,' he muttered, and stepped back quickly, took up the beaker, and drank most of the ale down. He wiped his mouth on his sleeve, checked the door again, and slipped through. Carefully he closed the door, and tip-toed toward the main antechamber.

He remembered well those knights who had cornered him in the garden. Especially the one with the northern accent. He hoped he could find him and then, somehow, get a message back to Master Crispin. If this brooch could be found, it could very well lead him to the Stone of Destiny. For with one day left till the Commons met, Jack was truly running out of time.

His destination was the main courtyard, so when he made it through the door of Henry's lodgings and out into the corridor, he followed his gut in the direction he reasoned Westminster Hall was. Keeping his hood up and his head down, he passed guards in the corridors, giving them a surreptitious glance as he passed them. None were his man.

As he reached the White Hall, more courtiers surrounded him, and it was easier to blend in. He straightened, trying to look as casual as possible, as if he belonged there, all the while trying to hide his face in the shadow of his hood and examining the guards he saw patrolling the doorways. But he knew he wouldn't fool anyone for long. Those guards had seen his clothes, after all. And as much as he tried to conceal his cotehardie with his cloak, he knew flashes of bright blue would give him away.

Passing through narrow corridors he finally arrived at the Great Hall. Pausing and taking it in – its armorial banners hanging in colorful tribute to the chivalry of England along both sides, the dais with the throne, and the many guards, ladies, and men seeking audience with nobles – Jack girded himself, pulled his hood down that much lower, and dove into the crowd.

The hall was grand on a scale to compete with any cathedral. He'd been here before, of course, in circumstances he would rather forget. But as he reached the main entrance and stood at the top of the stairs, looking down into the great courtyard and toward the garrison of the king's guards, it suddenly occurred to him that he could keep going. He was free! No one knew where he was. He could walk right out the front gateway and return to London and none would be the wiser.

He glanced back over his shoulder as court went about its business. No one was looking at him. No one noticed him at all. He'd be just another citizen making his way from court. And Master

Crispin wouldn't have to fret over him any longer. Free as a sarding bird!

But even as that thought made his spirits soar, they were just as quickly shot down as surely as if an arrow had pierced him.

He couldn't return to Master Crispin for that would be the first place they'd look. And they'd probably arrest his master for good measure.

Desperately he scanned over the wall toward St Margaret's Street beyond where people were milling, past the gate. He saw farmers with wagons laden with hay and young girls carrying pails of milk. Would they begrudge him his chance at freedom? Would any of them?

And it wasn't just freedom, but the *gibbet*. The king had said he would die a traitor's death for consorting with his master. He rubbed his neck, swallowing hard.

Yet that wasn't even the worst of it. For he had made an oath to Lord Henry that he would be good, and to Lady Katherine as well. In exchange for their caring for him instead of his rotting in a cell, he had made an oath on his very honor. And he had meant it. At the time.

And that was his choice. Hang or be loyal to his oath.

His heart thundered. 'Damn you, Master Crispin,' he whispered. 'I would never have been so muddled if you hadn't mixed up me head with notions of honor. I'd be a free man by now.' He strained his neck, looking toward the Great Gateway with its stone arches and gatehouse towers. That was the way to freedom . . . yet, with a sorrowful shake of his head, he knew he could not take it. Master Crispin had sowed in him such a deep concept of loyalty and duty that he could not, *could not* dishonor himself and his master by leaving those who trusted him to their fates . . . even though it could very well result in his hanging.

He rubbed at his neck again. 'It's a terrible thing, this,' he muttered. 'This . . . sense of duty. It's like to get a man killed.' He swallowed, wishing he could get to that beaker of ale again, before he slowly tramped down the stairs.

Sulkily, he headed toward the gatehouse where the guards were milling, head still full of his musings. He didn't mean to damn his master. Never would he do that! He asked forgiveness from God and also asked to find this guard. All he had to do was find that Scotsman and then . . . Then what? Find out his name, he supposed, and . . . He blew out a sigh, ruffling his wayward fringe. He wished

Master Crispin was there to instruct. He wasn't quite sure what he was to do once he identified the culprit.

He slowed his steps and tarried beside a horse trough. Clearly he hadn't thought this out. His only thought had been to get out of that locked room and find that damned guard. But his honor was at stake! This he knew.

He turned and abruptly ran into a broad man, nearly knocking him over. 'Forgive me, good sir! I did not see—' Brushing off the man, Jack looked at his face. 'Master Wodecock!'

Bill Wodecock, one of the king's stewards, pushed Jack back at arm's length. Jack tried to pull away, but the man clamped an iron grip over his arms. 'Jack Tucker?' He hastily looked around him. 'What are you doing out of confinement?'

'It's a long tale, Master Wodecock.'

'Is it?' He looked over his shoulder again and walked Jack backward until he slammed against the stone wall surrounding the yard. 'I should call the guards on you to take your hide away,' he hissed.

'Pray, sir, don't do that. I am on a most important mission for, er . . . a lady of some importance.'

'What? The Devil take you for your lies, boy!'

'On my honor, Master Wodecock.' That sarding honor again! 'I'm telling the truth.'

'I saw you heading for the gatehouse. You were stealing away.'

'No, master, I wasn't! I was on my way to see about a certain guard who might have done this lady a wrong. I swear by St Dismas, master!'

'By St Dismas indeed! You're a thief, Jack Tucker, and well I know it. And now you would steal the good grace of the king . . .'

'Have mercy, Master Wodecock. For I know the peril I am in. And yet I have no choice but to stay under the king's shadow for the sake of others. Wouldn't I be gone by now if I intended to escape? You wouldn't have stopped me, no matter your strength.' *Or girth*, he thought, measuring the squat and stout man before him. 'It is vitally important that I find this guard.'

'What nonsense you spout, Tucker. No doubt learned from your master.'

'But you know my master well and you also know that he is an honest man.'

'That doesn't make the apprentice the same.'

Jack pulled himself up and slapped down the man's hands from his cotehardie. 'You don't know me. Maybe who I was but not who I am. Call the guards if you don't believe me. Or be silent and help me. One way or the other, I am in God's hands alone, and I swear by that God who lords over all that I am telling the truth.'

Wodecock's glare followed up Jack's figure and down again, as if the soles of his shoes could tell the man anything about Jack's character. At last and after much grunting and sneering he placed his fists at his ample hips. 'Help you how?'

Jack's taut spine relaxed with relief. 'Aw now. You are a fair man, Master Wodecock. I will do right by you, sir.'

'Help you *how*?' he asked again, almost a bark.

'Well, I need to find a certain guard. But, er . . . they have seen me. Know what I'm wearing, you ken? So, erm, if say, *you* were to . . .'

'You want to send me on your fool errand? I'm a busy man, Tucker. And I don't have time for the likes of you!'

He pushed away from Jack to make his exit when Jack scrambled ahead of him, walking backward as the man moved relentlessly forward. 'But you're not turning me in, which must mean you believe me. Even a little.'

Wodecock kept travelling, but he was moving away from the gate-house. 'I believe in your master. Not so much in the apprentice.'

'Fair enough, for you seem to know my history. But Master Wodecock.' And he used his strength to push against the man's chest and stop his forward progress at last. 'You'd be helping Master Crispin.' He saw Wodecock's sneer deepen, and hastily added, 'and the king . . . and the queen. My business is intimate with both, master.'

'Ha!'

'It's true! For if you know why I am here, you know all. And this is something that will help. You must know about the Stone of Destiny,' Jack said quieter, eyes flicking over Wodecock's shoulder.

'Aye,' said the steward. 'Though I scarce believed it. Do you mean to tell me you are looking for the—'

'I am on my course, Master Wodecock. And I detected the sound of a northerner in the king's guards. I have reason to believe something suspicious.'

'Could you not have gone to Lady Swynford with this?'

'I would not involve her further. You see the difficulty.'

He growled, eyes narrowing. 'What do you want *me* to do?'

Jack sidled closer. 'Well, they know my attire, you see. If we go together and I wait outside, perhaps you could lure them out on some pretext.'

'Lure them out!'

'Shush, master! We are looking for a northerner. I would name him and send that name to my master.'

'You want me to go into the gatehouse. What if he is not there? What if he is in the palace at some other duty?'

'I searched the faces of as many guards as I could see . . .'

'Folly. All folly.' He scrubbed his chin with a beefy hand. 'Well . . . so be it. But you—' and he aimed a finger at Jack's face '— better be right.' He pulled up his belt and stalked toward the gatehouse. Jack followed at a distance but made certain to be near the archway and kept his ears primed.

Yet as the time passed, Jack began to worry. Had Wodecock slipped out without him noticing? Was he turning Jack in even as he waited like a lamb to the slaughter?

In a panic, he turned, but stopped at the sound of a boot on the stone floor.

It was Wodecock, and he was alone.

'Master Wodecock?'

'There was no one there with a northern accent, you fool. Your head's gone addled.'

'But he has to be somewhere.' He stared into the middle distance . . . and saw him. 'There!' He pointed at first before he thought better of it. The guard was talking to a lord, listening carefully to his instructions. 'We must get closer,' Jack hissed, and started out across the courtyard.

A strong hand closed over his shoulder and drew him back, making him stumble. 'Are you mad, boy? Your master surely did not teach you that! Striding across the ward as if you belonged. Now be still and follow me. Put your hood down over your face, close your cloak, and crouch a bit. Lean in to me as if listening to my sage advice that you'll never heed.' Jack did as instructed, staring at his feet but glancing up occasionally from under the low brow of his hood. As they neared the two, Jack heard the lord as he talked to the guard. It was the harsh accent of the north, right enough! But he couldn't make out what instructions he was giving the guard.

He inclined closer but Wodecock's hand seized him and pulled him back, yanking on his upper arm. He winced with a whispered, 'Ow!' in complaint.

'You are the most empty-headed apprentice I have ever met,' he hissed into Jack's ear.

'Master Wodecock, I—'

'You're a knob-pated idiot.'

He clamped his lips shut tight lest he insult the steward right back. But he couldn't help but softly ask, 'Why are you abusing me so?'

'Because, you brass-headed carbuncle, those aren't Scottish men. They're from Yorkshire!'

TWENTY-ONE

'Yorkshire?' Jack looked back at the two as they receded into the crowds of the courtyard. 'But *that's* in the north.'

Jack stumbled forward when Wodecock slapped his head. Jack rubbed the spot and scowled.

'It's Yorkshire. Aye, it's just as incomprehensible as Scot, but it isn't the same. You've made a fool of yourself and almost made a fool of me, too. What have you to say for yourself?'

'Well . . . I . . .' He sighed. 'I suppose I did make a mistake, master. It's easy enough to do.'

'Only for a sack of turnips like you.' He brushed off his hands. 'Go back to your hidey-hole, boy. Before they catch you.' He gave Jack a parting glare before he stalked across the courtyard back toward the Great Hall's entrance.

Jack looked back toward the guard and the lord and cursed. 'How am I supposed to know the difference?' he muttered. 'North is north, to me.' But as Master Wodecock receded, another idea rose up in his mind, and he found himself trotting after the hefty steward.

'That had better not be Jack Tucker on my heels,' he growled, not turning round.

'Er . . . it is, good master.'

The steward dug into the courtyard with heavier steps, head lowered. 'Are you mad? Go away!'

'But master! There is another man I must find. The Keeper of the Jewels. And I—'

Wodecock came to an abrupt halt, muttering murderously, until he spun and faced Jack. 'You will not be stealing into his chamber or any other. You will go back to your place of securement or, by God and St George, I will shout out right now in this courtyard who you are and that you are a thief. And then you'll see how quickly the king's guards can dispatch you.'

Jack swallowed. 'A little charity goes a long way, Master Wodecock,' he murmured.

Wodecock took a deep breath in order to call out, but Jack lurched forward and covered the man's mouth with his hands.

'Peace, good master! All right! I surrender to your good counsel . . . such as it is.' He huffed a sigh and released him. *No wonder my master is so sour all the time.* 'I'll go. Thank you for your help and guidance.' He bowed.

'Next time, boy, stay the hell out of Westminster. It'll be healthier for you and your master.' He gave Jack no further acknowledgement but instead trod forth as fast as he could away from him and up the steps to the Great Hall.

Alone again in the courtyard, Jack watched him disappear into the shadows of the archway and took one last longing glance at the Great Gate. *Farewell freedom*, he sighed and, making certain his cloak covered his coat, he trudged back toward the entrance of the hall and wearily climbed the steps.

What was he to do now? How could he possibly help the queen when he couldn't help himself? Yet was he to go to her and tell her that he had failed before he even tried?

He thought he had learned enough as the apprentice to the Tracker, foolishly assuming that he might be ready to do it on his own, but he found himself woefully inadequate to the task. He began to worry that he would never fully master it. Didn't Master Crispin have the advantage of him after all, with his being born into his nobility? His master knew how to talk to all kinds of people whereas Jack did not, *could* not, by virtue of his place in life. Who would talk to the likes of him? He'd be brushed off like so much dirt. How was he ever to accomplish it?

He moved across the Great Hall, going unnoticed by the many courtiers and hangers-on, servants and tradesmen. He glanced up into the rafters and trailed his hand along a pillar. Wasn't Master Crispin sneered at and berated for being a traitor – a word Jack would never dare utter in his presence? But it was true. He *had* committed treason and paid the price for it every day. He seemed to be disdained and disregarded as much as Jack was, yet he accepted it with aplomb. 'That's breeding,' he decided, something he lacked. Would he ever be good enough? Was Master Crispin's trust misplaced?

Jack took his morose thoughts through the corridors and almost failed to notice Lady Margaret when she stopped before him. He bowed to her and she giggled, offering him a rounded cheek and a grin. 'Master Goat! I was hoping to find you.'

'Lady Margaret. Alas. I was on my mission for your lady and I am afraid I have failed.'

'Failed? Oh no, you mustn't say that.' She brushed her fingers along his arm and he was cheered momentarily by the gentle touch.

'I am afraid it is true.'

'And I must confess the same, for the king's guards turned up no Scotsmen. Only a man from Yorkshire. Imagine making that mistake.'

'Heh. Aye, imagine it.'

Jack eyed the very public place they were standing, and gently took her hand to lead her to a more private area behind a pillar. 'Has she . . . has the queen confided in you in the matter?'

'I understand the gist of it now.' She glanced down at their joined hands, for Jack had forgotten to let it go.

He hastily tried to snatch his hand away with a muttered apology on his lips, but Margaret held it fast.

'There's no need. There is comfort in your hand. And . . . such a strong hand it is.'

'Oh.' Jack felt himself blush down to his toes. Lady Margaret was the very image of pink and modest virginity. Yet there was mischief in her eye as well, especially when she fluttered her lashes in that manner. 'Well, a man must be strong. To protect the women.'

'And do you have a woman, Master Goat? Many, I'll wager.'

His cheeks felt even hotter. 'Well now. I am a man of responsibilities. I haven't the time to while away my days on trivialities.'

'Trivialities?' She feigned offense and took back her hand. 'And so! A woman is nothing but trivial to you?'

'The playing of coy games, demoiselle, is what I meant. But I am an honest lad. And when I give my heart, it is for keeping.'

She gasped, forming her lips into an inviting 'O.' 'Bless me,' she said softly, moving closer. 'Such a . . . charming thing to say.'

'Aye. Well.' He shuffled. He would *like* the sentiment to be true, and one day it would be. But for now . . . He leaned in with the objective of capturing those soft lips and Margaret seemed intent on letting him, when she suddenly pulled back.

'You are wicked, Master Goat. You bewitch me.'

'Not as much as you bewitch me,' he said breathlessly.

'Oh, but my lady is sore afraid. We must keep our minds on that.'

'Our minds. Aye.' Jack straightened his coat and blew out a breath. 'So . . . Let me think this through. Queen Anne was in the church with all the rest.'

'And I was there beside her.'

'Aye. And she said that in all the confusion, you got pushed back.'

'I shall never forgive myself.'

'But I was there, too. There was the loud report, smoke, and much confusion. One could not be certain if there wasn't a fire. Many tried to flee.'

She shook out her veil, letting the soft material flutter over her shoulder, revealing a creamy, slender neck. '*You* were there?'

'Er . . . aye. In the back.'

'Intriguing,' she said. A smile crept onto her face once more.

She was far too beguiling for his thought processes. 'Well then . . . her grace told me of those that were sitting with her. Oh! Perhaps you can help see me to the Keeper of the Jewels' chamber.' Lady Margaret might be a far better distraction than the beefy steward.

'The Keeper of the Jewels? Why him?'

He sidled closer. 'Know you that the queen has lost a valuable brooch?'

'Yes. But though he sat with us, he was nowhere near my lady.'

He scratched his head, frowning. 'But her grace told me that she was seated near the Keeper of the Jewels and that she was ushered forth by a guard who told her – in a northern dialect – that she was to come with him . . .'

'Yes, the Keeper was near *us* but that is not what happened.'

He stared at her anew. 'Eh?'

'I clearly recall. I had been shoved back by one of those gallant men scrambling to get themselves to safety,' she said with a sneer. 'But it wasn't the king's guard who spoke to her. It was the monk that was sitting beside my lady, he was the one who took her arm and told her to follow him. The monk with the northern brogue.'

'The monk?'

'Yes.'

Jack blinked. 'Do you know the name of this monk?'

'Of course. I remember it well because it was the same as the saint of Scotland. Andrew.'

TWENTY-TWO

Jack's excitement made his hands shake. He clenched them into fists to steady them. 'Was he a Westminster monk or one from your household here?'

'That is difficult to say, for I did not see his face.'

'So he could have been a household monk?'

'Possibly.'

He took her hands in his, and her eyes brightened with tenderness. 'Lady Margaret, I must ask you to do me a great favor.'

'Ask it,' she said, breath coming faster.

'For reasons I cannot now explain, I am not allowed to leave the palace. Can you go to Westminster and enquire about a Brother Andrew? If he is there or if he is not, get word to me through Lord Derby's household. Will you do that?'

'Yes! Yes, of course. And what will you do?'

'I will see if he is not bound to St Stephen's chapel. Thank you, Lady Margaret.'

'Ah, Master Goat, I am so pleased it is you who is helping my lady. I know that all will end well.'

'Your prayers on it would do me good.'

He released her hands, but she stepped forward faster than he could prepare himself for, took his face in her hands, and planted a firm kiss to his lips.

When she drew back, she wore a satisfied smile. 'God be with you, fair Goat.'

'And to you, Lady Margaret.'

Jack watched her depart. She looked once more over her shoulder before she disappeared around the corner.

He whistled low and hefted up his belt. 'Jack, me lad. There's something of Crispin Guest about you yet.'

He shook his head. Business first. Looking around, he knew that St Stephen's Chapel was in that direction and headed there. Still keeping his hood down, he arrived at the entrance and peered inside. Candles blared on the altar and in chandlers positioned down the nave. Penitents on their knees prayed silently, heads bowed over their clasped hands.

Prayer seemed like a good idea, and he sent one skyward, flowing along with the scent of incense and the wispy smoke from the candles. He stepped inside and, finding the font, he dipped his fingers in and becrossed himself with the cold holy water. Just the touch of it calmed his thoughts and he ventured forward. Perhaps he could ask in the sacristy. He wasn't all that familiar with the doings of churches. Not that he hadn't spent time in them. As a former thief, he went often to church, but as he had done with Master Crispin all those days ago, he stayed in the back near the entrance. For though he had prayed hard to God and the saints, he didn't want to call attention to himself by trying to push his way forward.

He stood in the nave, thinking how he was to go about discovering who this Brother Andrew was. Eyes adjusting to the dark, he scanned the nave and rood screen. A monk knelt beneath the rood, and Jack screwed up his courage and carefully approached.

'I beg pardon, Brother.'

The monk slowly turned, looking Jack up and down.

'I am looking for a particular monk. And I know not whether he belongs to Westminster or to St Stephen's.'

The monk blinked slowly. 'Well then?'

'He's a northerner . . . a Scotsman, by the name of Andrew. Do you know him?'

The monk's brows flickered. 'Why do you want to know?'

'It's very important. You see . . .' Jack took a quick glance around and whispered, 'It concerns the Stone of Destiny, the one from the Coronation Chair.'

The monk's eyes snapped open to the size of mazers. He shoved Jack so hard that Jack fell back on his bum. Like a rabbit on the run, the monk took off in loud slapping footfalls across the nave. Those in prayer lifted their heads to look. A woman shrieked as she leapt out of the way.

Jack was on his feet in a heartbeat and gave chase.

The monk escaped through a door. Jack arrived just as the door fell closed and he yanked it open, darted through, and skidded to a halt.

He was in the cloister. An arcade with study carrels lay to his left with a greensward in the middle. He saw the feet and hems of many becassocked men in the carrels and no other sign of a running man.

Jack wiped his sweaty palms down his coat. He took a cautious step forward and peered around the tall wooden back of the first carrel's seat. A monk with dark hair and dark brows bending over a large tome looked up at him. 'What are you doing here? The cloister is only for the brothers.'

'Well . . . I . . .'

The monk snapped the book closed with a thump and stood. 'You must leave.'

'But . . . but Brother, I . . .'

He grabbed Jack's arm and pulled him toward the door.

Jack squirmed. 'There's no need for that! Why is everyone always manhandling me?'

But once they got to the door, a monk jumped up from one of the carrels and ran down the arcade in the opposite direction.

Jack swung, trying to go after him, but the monk held fast. 'Everyone is in such a hurry today,' the monk muttered. He opened the door and looked at Jack. 'Out!' He shoved and Jack stumbled over the threshold. Jack turned back toward the door but gave up when he heard a key turn in the lock.

'That's that, then.' But didn't cloisters have walls, like garden walls? He snapped his fingers and ran out of the church. There had to be a door to the outside. He hadn't remembered passing one on his way through the corridors to the Great Hall, but surely there would be one.

But he saw nothing. He'd have to go all the way around, through the Great Hall and outside.

He hurried, remembering to hide his face with his hood. Through the Great Hall he went once more and out to the courtyard. It was a wide expanse, still full of people and the king's guards. To keep his face turned away, he looked up at the outside of the Great Hall, pretending to admire its grandeur. When he saw he was clear of guards, he doubled his steps and turned the corner. There was the bell tower and then the walls to St Stephen's cloister. He stood a moment, measuring them and looking for ways to scale it.

A tree grew close to the wall about ten yards away and he made for it.

Looking around for prying eyes, Jack quickly climbed the tree. A branch stretched over the space between trunk and arcade roof but didn't quite reach. Even so, it would have to do. He crawled on his hands and knees across the branch till it got too thin. A good two yards to go. He got to his feet and wobbled unsteadily on the branch. With a quick prayer he took a breath and leaped.

Rolling, he landed on the terracotta-tiled roof. A few tiles broke as he landed and he righted himself, but once he was secure, he crept to the peak and looked over. A good view of the cloister and carrels. But where had that sarding monk gone?

He walked along the peak, crouching down in case he had to hide, going first toward the belfry and then turning round and heading toward the chapel.

Wait. Was that him? 'Oh, they all look alike!' he muttered.

A solitary monk passed through a door to a secreted space between the cloister arcade and St Stephen's chapel, where the buttresses almost hid another man from view. He appeared to be waiting, and when the monk came through the door, the man squared his shoulders. He was tall, noble, and dark-haired, while the monk was slender, pale, and auburn-haired.

The man looked about but seemed content that they were alone. 'A fine clandestine meeting place.'

Jack lay down on the tiles, barely peeking over the side so he could just glimpse them. He was grateful that the sound echoed and carried their voices quite clearly up to him.

'Just as you would have it,' said the monk in a distinct brogue. *Got you!* thought Jack.

He was certain this time that the man's accent was *not* from Yorkshire. Why was Westminster suddenly crawling with Scotsmen?

Neither looked familiar – the man was a stranger and the monk wasn't any he had known from Westminster – but they were plainly talking of what he needed to hear most.

'I told you this was trouble,' said the monk.

'Och, you're whingeing is tiresome, Brother,' said the man.

'It is *not* whingeing,' said the monk. 'Brother Crìsdean is dead and I do not intend to remain a target.'

'A target, you say?'

'Aye. I know it was one of the Mormaer's men, but I don't know who.'

'You're dreaming, Brother Andrew.'

Jack squeaked in triumph and then slapped his hand over his mouth.

'No, I'm not! I want protection. I want sanctuary!'

The man snorted. 'It's a little late for that, isn't it?'

'I'm damned,' whispered the monk. 'I never . . . I never should have . . .'

'You're being a woman about it, Brother. Calm yourself. You're doing Scotland's king a brave deed.'

Jack perked up. He dug his foot into one of the tiles to get a better look and felt it loosen. *Oh no!* He slapped his other foot over his ankle, holding the tile fast, but he knew that it was slipping and, in his now twisted position, he did not know how long he could hold his place.

'I fear, Laird McGuffin, that they will be after me next,' the monk went on.

'Listen to you. "After *you* next"? You have nothing to fear from these loyal men of Scotland, Brother. That's rather disingenuous of you.'

'Disingenuous?' The man's voice rang harsh in the echoing space. They both turned to look, but there was no one there. No one they could see, at any rate. Brother Andrew lowered his voice. 'Tell that to Brother Crìsdean as they lower his body into the ground.'

'There's no need to be so dramatic.'

'Are you going to help me or not?'

'I already told you. I have nae to do with the Stone of Destiny. My task was with the queen. Now. Have you something for me or not?'

Jack's eyes widened.

Grumbling, the monk withdrew a small parcel from the pouch on his leather girdle and handed it over. 'I now add thievery to my many sins.'

'Best keep up with your prayers then, Brother.' The one called McGuffin dropped the cloth-wrapped item into the pouch on his own belt and patted it. 'You've done well.'

The monk shook his head, seeming not to hear McGuffin's praise. 'I can't go back. I don't know who to trust. I had my orders but . . . but no one has contacted us. Only you. And with poor Crìsdean murdered . . .'

'Looks like you have a problem.'

Andrew whipped his head toward McGuffin and scowled. 'Oh, I have a problem right enough. And so do you and your compatriots. Crìsdean wanted to give it up, wanted to tell all to the abbot. If it hadn't been for . . . for his death, the whole game would be given away. And maybe it should have been.'

'Now, now, Brother.' McGuffin toyed with his cuffs. It looked as if he had already lost interest. 'No need to lose heart now when all is so close to being achieved.' He headed for the door.

'That's easy for you to say. You don't have this thing hanging over you.'

Andrew moved forward and caught him by the arm, but McGuffin looked down distastefully. 'You should'na contact me again, Brother.'

'Oh, I won't. I should not have helped you. I should have cleaved to the plan. But you've a silver tongue, haven't you?'

'Brother Andrew, you'd best take this up with your laird.'

'Maybe I shall. But I tell you this. It will be a dark day when I give up the Stone to just anyone. For it is secreted well and sound, and even an *each-uisge* himself canna find it. Just try to discover where the sarding Stone is now!'

'Language, Brother!'

The monk darted his gaze about the empty space and scowled. He pushed McGuffin out of the way and stomped away through the door.

Uh oh. They were leaving. And Jack needed to follow. But the monk was delving deeper into the cloister, and the man was creeping through the door, through a short passage in the arcade and out to the chapel in the opposite direction.

'God's blood!' Jack leaped up and ran back to the tree. The tile he had been holding in place slid down the roof's incline and shattered on the courtyard below. He stood on the edge of the roof, windmilled his arms catching his balance, and leaped. He barely caught the branch and swung for a moment, measuring how far down the ground was – too far – but jumped anyway.

He landed on a soft tuft of grass and rolled down the slight hill. Getting to his feet, he ran across the courtyard before he remembered himself and kept his head down and his legs moving swiftly but stiffly.

Jack knew he had a problem. For no doubt the monk could lead him to the Stone. But even as he made his way across the endless courtyard and then up the steps to the Great Hall, he knew he'd soon lose the man who seemed to have the queen's brooch.

His honor and the queen, or the Stone and his life?

'I didn't think it would be so hard being a Tracker.'

Just as he made it to the archway, a gaggle of female courtiers blocked the way. Jack hung back, bobbing on the balls of his feet. Silently, he prayed that they would hurry, but he couldn't very well plow through these noble ladies. When finally there was an opening, he darted through the hall, got to the corridor between the hall and St Stephens, and looked both ways.

The monk was gone, lost in the cloister.

'Bollocks!'

But then he spied McGuffin moving past him from the chapel, making long-legged strides toward the Great Hall. Well, better this than nothing.

He hurried forward to just behind the man. He passed again over the tiles of the great expanse, dodging the pillars, ignoring the fluttering of banners and the fact that once his master's banner had hung there just as proudly as the others.

The man called McGuffin moved swiftly and steadily ahead of him. He matched strides.

He'd cut hundreds of purses in his day. There was no telling how many. And he'd saved baubles and coins from all those purses for his retirement. Master Crispin had not made him donate them to the alms box, for he had understood about a man's need to put something aside for his old age, and he told Jack that he even admired him for such industry . . . though he made it clear that Jack was not to add to that cache. Not by thievery at any rate. And he hadn't. Only with his wages, which were poor indeed, but Master Crispin had done the best he could on that score. Jack could hardly complain when he had a roof over his head, food in the larder, and clothes on his back.

He rubbed his hands together. It had been years since he'd cut a purse. And a lad who was out of practice could easily get himself caught. He prayed to the Virgin for help and to keep his fingers nimble and his knife sharp.

The man slowed to survey the courtyard. He seemed to sweep his gaze from one end of it to the next. And there was a smug smile on his face. So! He thought he could best the king by this coercion, this thievery of virtue. And he was clearly a compatriot of those who had stolen the Stone. Jack had been right about that, at least.

Gloat, then, thought Jack. *It's your last chance.*

The man's attention was elsewhere – on a group of chattering ladies. They curtseyed to him and he bowed to them. Jack slid forward, flashed his knife swiftly to the purse's ties, and slipped away as discreetly as he'd arrived, pouch in hand.

Until something dragged hard on his hood.

When he turned, he looked into the scowling face of the man called McGuffin.

'Just what do you think *you're* doing, my lad?' He glared down at the pouch Jack hadn't been swift enough to secret inside his own.

Jack squeezed it tighter and blinked innocently. 'Are you speaking to me, good master?'

The man had not relinquished his hold of Jack's hood and wound it slowly around his hand, drawing Jack closer.

'Don't play the fool with me, boy. Give it back.'

Jack clutched the pouch tighter but resisted the urge to hold it behind his back. He girded himself and narrowed his eyes. 'I know what's in here,' he said in low tones.

The man's eyes widened. 'You . . . you don't know what you're talking about.'

'Oh, but I do. And so, *good master*,' he said with a sneer, 'perhaps *you'd* best step back away from *me*.'

'Who are you working for?' The hood was entirely wound about his hand and wrist now, and he yanked Jack in tight. 'For the Mormaer?' he whispered.

Jack shrugged out of his grip at last and stepped back. 'I am the queen's man. I'm for England. And you'd best step aside, for you have trespassed on the Tracker's apprentice.'

The man's eyes widened even more. 'The Tracker?' He looked around, obviously searching for him.

'He's not here, but never fear, for I shall warn him of you.'

Abruptly, the man barked a hail of nervous laughter. 'It seems I cannot escape the Tracker. But if he is not here . . .' He drew his sword. 'Then I need not worry over any interference. I doubt that a boy such as you would garner much sympathy after I take back my *stolen* purse.'

Uh oh. Jack blinked hard. He hadn't thought of that.

He drew his knife, but when he measured it to McGuffin's sword his blood ran cold.

McGuffin raised the blade and Jack cringed, taking a step back. His mind whirred with a thousand ways to escape, but none of them would get him very far. But with the blade rushing toward him, he froze. He gasped the beginning of a prayer.

A fierce clang, and he looked up to see the blade blocked.

Henry Derby's blade had stopped it, and his eyes, bright and wide, took in the two of them. 'What the hell is this?' he cried.

TWENTY-THREE

Henry swung, smacking McGuffin's blade aside. McGuffin stumbled back, arm lowered. 'I have no quarrel with you, your grace.'

'But you would brandish a sword on this boy?'

'He . . . he stole a purse from me!'

Henry swiveled toward Jack, but kept his sword at the ready. 'Did you?'

'I beg you to hear the whole tale, my lord,' Jack pleaded.

Henry scowled but then turned that scowl toward McGuffin. The Scot seemed to get the message and sheathed his own weapon. 'Perhaps this man will explain,' said Henry, sword lowered but still drawn.

The man looked from Henry to Jack and aside to where the men of the courtyard were beginning to approach. He offered a sudden smile. 'Now that I think on it, I could very well be mistaken. I will let the matter rest, if the boy will do so as well.'

Astounded at the man's gall, Jack grimaced.

But Henry was waiting. Would he let the miscreant go? Jack had the brooch in hand and the churl was not likely to bedevil the queen again.

He spread a smile over his teeth. 'Aye,' he said slowly. 'I'm sure this fine gentleman meant me no harm.'

Henry blinked. 'Meant you no harm?'

'Aye, your grace. He . . . er . . . merely bumped into me. And it is an easy mistake, thinking his purse was gone. No harm done.' Jack saluted McGuffin with a wink.

Henry took his time sheathing his sword. 'If the boy has no complaint then neither do I. But be careful next time, my lord, on whom you draw your sword.'

'I shall be, Laird Derby.' He bowed low, gave Jack one last narrowed glance, and sauntered – rather quickly, Jack thought – toward the Great Gate.

Jack's euphoria lasted only moments before Henry gripped his arm so tightly the blood drained out of it. Neither of them said a word as they traveled the corridors, Henry's grip remaining tight while Jack stumbled after.

When they reached Henry's lodgings he cast open the door and shoved Jack through. Tripping and rolling, Jack landed against the hearth. He heard the scrambling of servants' feet, but when he looked up they were alone. And Henry looked murderous.

Jack got up onto his knees. 'My lord, there is an explanation.'

'There may be, Tucker, but you have deliberately defied me. You deserve a beating.'

'And you may do so in justice, my lord. But before you do, I beg you to call in Lady Katherine.'

'Knave. Would you involve her in your misdeeds?'

'By the saints, I would not. But she knows what I have been about.'

'And why is it you cannot tell me?'

'It is a matter of some delicacy.'

'So you keep saying. But by God, Tucker! Delicacy or no, you are ruining me.'

'I beg you most humbly to forgive me, your grace. I would never willingly hurt you or your house. I am as loyal to it as my master is.'

Henry's eyes scoured him just as surely as he had used a hard brush. Jack felt the prickle all over, the prickle of suspicion, of disbelief and discontent. But he also saw the earl's eyes soften just that much, and the man took a deep breath, expelled it, and studied Jack some more. At last, he turned his face aside, seeming to argue with his angels, and threw his hands in the air. 'I don't know how Crispin suffers you.'

'He suffers greatly from me, I'm certain.'

'And yet he does suffer you . . . because he trusts you. And is there no man more loyal?'

'No, your grace. It is why I serve him.'

Henry nodded, shrugged. 'Very well. Waterton!'

The steward appeared smoothly from where he had been waiting in an alcove. 'Your grace?'

'Send for Lady Katherine. We will await her.'

Waterton bowed, but Jack had not missed the scowl he directed toward him as he left to his duty.

'Tucker. Serve wine.'

Jack bowed and scurried to comply as Henry unstrapped his sword, laid it on the table, and sat before the fire.

He offered the earl wine and then stood behind him as Master Crispin had taught him.

'No,' said Henry, after taking a sip. 'You will stand where I can see you, you knave.'

Sheepishly, Jack stepped forward, keeping his face lowered.

'You are a handful, are you not? It seems no one obeys me in my own house. Lady Katherine was to be in Essex with my wife, and I thought I told Hugh to keep you under lock and key.'

'He . . . he did, your grace.'

'What? Oh ho! Broke out, did you? You are a wily fellow. No wonder Crispin likes you so much.'

Jack's face heated. He did not know if it were more from embarrassment or pride.

He waited uncomfortably under Henry's gaze as the earl silently sipped his wine. Henry seemed amused by Jack's discomfiture, which, Jack supposed, was only just.

The door opened and Waterton led the way. Behind him was a stern-looking Lady Katherine. Jack winced. He had failed them all again. If he had only made it back to his cage before anyone had noticed! *Sloppy, that's what it was*, he admonished. *What would Master Crispin say?*

But more to the point, what would Lady Katherine say, for she appeared in a state. 'Lord Henry, I apologize again for this boy's misbehavior. It is my fault that he has fallen into your hands, and I beg your forgiveness.'

'No, Lady Katherine!' Jack cried. 'It isn't your fault at all. It's all mine. I . . . I can't be tamed. Lord knows Master Crispin has tried, but I am as wild a creature as when he first met me. The man is a saint, there is no denying it.' His voice caught and the tears flowed. He had no idea that they would come and he angrily wiped at his face. Here he was, nearly a man, and he could not control himself. He'd never become a Tracker at this rate.

'You are a handful, Master Tucker,' she muttered, reaching for him. She didn't seem to be able to keep herself from offering comfort. But he wriggled out of her embrace. No! He didn't deserve it! He had disobeyed and done the very thing Henry had warned him against. He was a danger to them. Better that he rot in a cell than do so again.

'You must put me back in the dungeons, Lady Katherine, for the Devil gets inside of me and I cannot keep my word.'

'Cannot keep your word?' She cocked her head. Her hands enfolded gracefully together. 'But you have been trying to do the deed assigned to you by the queen, have you not?'

Henry inhaled sharply.

Jack blinked away the tears and nodded, staring at the floor.

'No one blames you for trying, Master Tucker. And certainly, under the circumstances, she cannot blame you for failing.'

He snapped his head up. 'Oh, but I didn't fail. I have it! I mean, I have done the, er, deed for her majesty. If you would send me to her . . .'

Henry slowly rose. 'Wait. This miscreant was truly on a mission for the queen?'

Lady Katherine gave one nod. Jack thought he saw her wink at him.

He looked at Jack. 'And you . . . you accomplished it?'

'So he has said. Is it true, Master Tucker?'

'Aye, my lady, your grace. I have.' He stood a little straighter.

'I'll be damned,' said Henry.

Lady Katherine sniffed. 'Henry,' she warned.

'Pardon my language, my Lady Governess. But under the circumstances . . .'

'I suppose so.' She beamed.

'Erm . . . Hugh.' Henry turned to his steward. 'Could you get a message to the queen? Ask her most humbly if she might come to my chambers. That there might be something to her advantage— No. Tell her instead that Master Tucker—'

'Her Goat, your grace.'

Henry looked askance at Jack.

Jack blushed. 'Er . . . she calls me her Goat. She does not know my true name.'

Amusement glittered in Henry's eyes. 'Hugh, tell her majesty that her . . . *Goat* . . . has a message he wishes to convey to her personally. Will that do, Master Tucker?'

'Aye, your grace. I think that will do very well. Er . . . thank you, sir.'

'Don't mention it.' Henry tried to hide his smile when he faced his stunned steward. 'You'd best go, Hugh.'

The steward bowed. 'Yes, my lord.'

Henry watched him go distractedly. 'I don't suppose you can tell us what this mission was, Master Tucker.'

'I . . . no, your grace. I would if I were at liberty.'

'Yes. Yes, I suppose you would. You can be a tight-lipped fellow. That is a most useful trait in a trusted servant.'

'I try to be so, my lord.'

Henry snorted.

It took longer than Jack expected. He supposed, while he had been standing in one spot for over an hour, that you couldn't just summon a queen. Henry and Lady Katherine had fallen into light conversation. She had taken a seat by the fire with him and they had discussed small household matters, with Lady Katherine exchanging stories of Henry's wife and child.

Yet, the more time passed, the more anxious Jack became. Besides the queen, he had to get a message to Master Crispin regarding that McGuffin and Brother Andrew. It might mean they could find the Stone, and with the Commons meeting tomorrow, Jack knew he was out of time.

He wiped the sweat from his brow again. 'I beg your pardon, my lord,' he ventured quietly, when there was a pause in the conversation.

Henry turned toward him with surprise written on his brow. 'Yes, Master Tucker?'

'Well, sir. It's just . . . I thought this would be done sooner . . .'

'You can't rush a queen, Tucker.'

'Aye, that I know. But . . . I urgently need to get a message to my master.'

'Oh?'

'Aye. I can write it down for you.'

'Bless me, you can write?'

'Aye. My master taught me.'

Henry chuckled. 'Is there no end to the saintliness of Crispin Guest?' He laughed at his own jest. 'Tucker, go fetch a servant and have him bring quill, ink, and parchment.'

He bowed awkwardly and scurried to the doorway. To his surprise a page was waiting just within earshot. Jack didn't even need to say anything as the boy nodded and ran to comply.

'Sit here,' Henry was saying. He had risen and gestured toward a small table with a chair tucked into it. The page arrived just then and placed the items on the table, bowed to Henry, and left again, no doubt to hide in the archway, awaiting instructions.

Jack pulled out the chair and sat. He took up the quill, examined the nib, and dipped it in the ink. Looking over his shoulder, he noticed Henry hovering there. Did he wish to witness for himself the trained monkey aping his betters? Jack knew that was an uncharitable thought, but that's how it looked to him. He settled himself more comfortably on the chair, leaned his other arm on the table, and bent down over the parchment, tongue clenched between his teeth. With the quill, he slowly and carefully scratched in the words, telling briefly about Andrew and McGuffin and their exchange. When he'd finished, he took up the pounce-pot and shook the sand out onto the parchment. He blew the excess off and handed the paper to Henry.

Henry read it over with a whistle. 'What is this part here, "ach-ishkeh"?'

Jack shook his head. 'I know not, your grace. It was what I heard. I hope Master Crispin can make head or tail of it.'

'I agree that this should get to Crispin with all haste. I will make my own enquiries.'

'Thank you, my lord.'

Yet still Henry paused. Jack reasoned he was deciding if one of his pages should be seen sending messages to a traitor.

'I will take it,' said Lady Katherine, startling them both.

Henry awkwardly handed over the parchment. 'Lady Katherine, I . . .'

'I do understand, Henry,' she said softly. 'But *I* will send a messenger to convey it to Crispin.' She folded it and carefully placed it in her scrip. 'Please offer my apologies to her majesty that I could not greet her, but I know how urgent this message is.' She patted Jack on the shoulder. 'I will get it there in all haste, never fear.'

She said her farewells to Henry and was gone. Jack felt better about that, that his message would soon get to his master, but now he waited alone with Henry for the queen to come.

After another long time, Henry smiled. 'I was just recalling a time in my past when Crispin took me riding. I was a very young lad, I think. Seven or eight, perhaps, and I had fallen from my horse. I recall Crispin's face. Oh, he was terrified that he had allowed his charge to be killed. And I wept bitterly and loudly, though I had hurt little but my pride. He tried everything to calm me, for he did not wish to tell my father that I had fallen. I managed to cajole out of him a small bow that I had coveted but that my father had declined to give me. Poor Crispin. I'm afraid I was rather spoiled and, in his eagerness to indulge me, I made a nuisance of myself. Of course, my father did find out later about my having fallen and of my exacted gift, and he forced me to surrender it back to Crispin, with more crying and lamentation I am loath to say. What a wicked child. I have tried to learn from those memories, Tucker. I have tried to comport myself with fairness and with dignity. But . . .' He sighed. 'I fear the boy I was sometimes intrudes on the man I am today.' He studied Jack from his seat. 'You were naughty yourself today, Master Tucker.'

'And I heartily do apologize, my lord. I shall do my penance.'

'You were anxious, as any boy your age would be. And you have the sword of Damocles hanging over your head. How could I blame you?'

Jack squinted above him, but reckoned that the sword Lord Henry spoke of was some sort of adage. The queen's brooch had been a fine distraction. But now that it was done, he could not help but consider the morrow and whether Master Crispin was as good as his word. The fear he had kept at bay rushed in upon him, and he choked back a sob.

Henry was there beside him in a wink. 'I told you that story to take your mind from your troubles, but I think I did the very opposite. Forgive me, Jack.'

Jack shook his head. He couldn't speak.

Henry slid his arm around the boy's shoulders and gave him a squeeze before releasing him. 'I wouldn't worry. You know Crispin better than I these days. He will not disappoint you.'

'But what if he can't . . . can't find it, your grace?' He hated how small his voice sounded, but more would not come from the thickness of his throat. 'I don't want to die,' he whispered.

He held Jack tighter. 'I would plead for you myself, but I am out of favor with the king. I fear I'd only make it worse.'

Worse? What could be worse than execution? Jack nodded to Henry nonetheless. It was all he could do.

The door opened, and a page stepped through. 'Her majesty, our gracious Queen Anne,' he announced.

The queen entered with Lady Margaret, and Jack hastily wiped at his face and straightened his coat.

Henry bowed low and entreated the queen to sit. She did so but looked uncomfortable. The situation was awkward, Jack conceded.

After all, it wasn't as if the queen could readily admit what Jack had done for her.

Jack looked imploringly at the earl.

Henry smiled. 'It looks as if you have private business with her majesty and I must attend to my own duties. I hope, madam, that you will forgive me if I leave you here with your . . . your friend.'

The queen appeared suddenly grateful and she offered her hand to kiss, which Henry did with great aplomb. He bowed to her again and left without a backward glance. Lady Margaret seemed to see this as her cue to leave as well and she exited through an archway, giving Jack a wink. But Jack noticed her shadow lingering, as was proper for any lady's maid.

As soon as she had departed, the queen leaned forward, looking to Jack like all the anxious girls that Jack had ever known from any London parish, only far prettier and far more elegantly dressed. 'What have you discovered, my Goat?'

His excitement had momentarily washed away his fear of what tomorrow would bring. He pulled the pouch from his own scrip, opened it, and pulled out the small object wrapped in a cloth. He laid the cloth aside and looked for the first time at the jeweled brooch in his hand. For a moment, he saw the shield that was meant to look like the king's but then his eyes remolded it to one of the king's courtiers, one who was not in favor with his majesty. He flushed at it and quickly handed it to the queen.

Joy brightened her face. 'You found it! Oh, my Goat! You are a miracle.' She laughed and jumped to her feet. Clearly overcome, she launched herself upon him and embraced him tightly. Jack's jaw slackened, fell open. He dared not return the embrace. And it didn't matter, for she had quickly released him and paced about the room, looking down at the offending object. 'I should have that jeweler imprisoned . . . if I could find him,' she said.

'Aye, my lady. I would, too, if I were you. What will you do with it now?'

She tilted her proud head upward. The gold cage around her hair sparkled, and the veil fluttered from her horned headdress. 'Bring me that candlestick.' He looked to where she pointed and hurried to obey. It was heavy and he brought it to her.

'Now what?' he asked.

She placed the brooch upon the floor. 'I want you to beat the thing to a pulp.'

Jack stared at the gold and gems. 'B-beat it, my lady?'

'Yes. I don't want to look at the thing again. And it is too dangerous to keep intact.'

'Aye. Well . . . if that is your wish.'

She tilted up her chin. 'It is.'

Jack turned the candlestick in his now sweaty hand. How was he to . . . Oh yes. The bottom part was the heaviest. He plucked the candle from the holder and laid it aside on the chair that Henry had vacated. He turned the stick upside down and crouched on the floor over the cursed brooch. Cocking his hand back, he brought it down hard, and the jewel was instantly crushed and misshapen. He mourned the thing as soon as he had done it and looked up at Queen Anne for confirmation. 'Again?'

'Yes. Again and again until it is completely unrecognizable.'

'If that is your will,' he mumbled. Again he struck until gems scattered and the gold was bent and mashed. He picked it up, scooping up what gems he could find from the floor and handed them to her.

'That was a very fine job, my Goat. Very fine. I know what I will do. Will you take this as part of my thanks?' She plucked a mashed oval of gold and several loosened gems and drizzled them into Jack's open palm.

His eyes widened. 'My lady!'

'Please. You have done me a very great service. It is only fitting you claim your reward.'

'But I did not do it for any reward, my lady. I did it because you asked it of me.'

'And when you agreed, you did not even know who I was. Which is why reward is especially fitting.' Her smile was wide and bright. 'Please, Goat. Take it with my thanks.'

'But . . . you don't even know who *I* am.'

'Then who are you?'

Jack shook his head. 'My lady, it is not safe for you to know.'

She frowned. 'Oh. Is it . . . a very bad thing?'

'Aye, my lady. It is a very bad thing.'

She turned away slightly. 'I am saddened at these tidings. Very much so. And I will pray for your soul, dear Goat.' She took a breath and then faced Jack again. 'But I still want you to take my gift.'

Jack looked down at the bounty. It was a treasure indeed! His retirement was looking brighter. 'With all thanks, my lady.'

'I shall discard the rest of it. It's the cesspit for this.'

Jack groaned at the thought of such riches being tossed away.

The inner door opened and Jack saw Henry return. He looked uneasy.

Henry glanced at the dented floor, the now crooked candlestick in Jack's hand, but did not remark on any of it. 'Your grace, is your business done?'

She nodded. 'I have tarried too long. My husband would not approve of my being in your apartments, Lord Derby.'

'You are welcome, of course, as my dear cousin, but . . .'

'Then I shall depart. Thank you for allowing me here, Lord Derby. And I thank you with all my heart, my Goat, for doing me this service.'

'My lady,' said Jack with a deep bow.

Lady Margaret suddenly appeared, rushing forward with her veil trembling. She gave Jack a coquettish smile and Jack melted, smiling back.

The queen raised her head and was decorous again, allowing Lady Margaret to open the door and passing through it without a backward glance. Once the door was closed again and Jack and Henry were alone once more, Henry sighed. 'And now, Master Tucker . . .'

Jack deflated. It was true that he had a fortune now in his purse, but would he live to spend it? 'It's back to the storeroom with me, isn't it?'

'Can you promise me that you will stay there this time?'

'I have given you enough trouble, my lord. I give you my word.'

'And I trust—' he looked back toward the door through which the queen departed '—that I can rely upon that?'

'I will . . . do my utmost, my lord.' Jack offered a wincing smile. And then sent up a prayer for Master Crispin that he would succeed in time.

TWENTY-FOUR

Crispin left the abbey, leaving behind the passions and questions to the sheriffs when they arrived. There was only one day left. But that Crìsdean had been murdered weighed heavily on his thoughts. He was certain that the monk had been silenced, and that meant that one of the conspirators didn't want any loose ends. Did that mean they had the Stone at last?

He lifted his face to the wine-stained sky. One day left. He rubbed his eyes with the back of his hand. There was more to do with Westminster Abbey, he was certain of it. Yet the church and monastery had been thoroughly searched. Hope was slipping through his fingers. He needed to clear his head and he knew of only one way to do so.

He reached the gates of London well before Compline and hoped that the Boar's Tusk would still be open.

With relief, he passed through the doors of the tavern and into its familiar warmth, trudging to his customary spot before the fire, facing the door. He dropped onto the seat and let his head fall back, allowing the warmth from the fire to melt the chill that had crept into his bones.

He hadn't realized he had closed his eyes until he felt two someones plop down on the bench on either side of him. Eleanor on one side, blinking solicitously at him, and Gilbert on the other, pouring wine from a chipped jug into a horn beaker.

'Much thanks, Gilbert,' Crispin muttered, closing his hand around the beaker and bringing it to his lips. The wine – though not nearly as good as the abbot's – was nevertheless satisfying.

His friends silently watched him drink, refilling his cup when it was nearly empty. After Crispin felt the wine warm his belly and soften the ache in his head, he settled down and raised his face to each in turn.

'How goes it, Crispin?' Eleanor was the first to ask. 'What of Young Jack?'

The prickle of anxiety crept up his neck again. 'Young Jack is

still in King Richard's clutches, and the Stone is still missing. I fear
. . . I fear . . .' He sighed, turning the beaker first one way, then the
other. 'I fear that I might not be able to find it in time.'

'Oh!' Eleanor's fingers covered her mouth.

Gilbert's steadying hand closed over his shoulder. 'I know you
can do it, Crispin. Surely you must be close.'

Crispin slammed his hand to the table. 'Always close,' he said
harshly, 'but never close enough.' He drank another dose of wine.
'I am so close I can almost feel the Stone in my hand. But it is all
so muddled. I just need to think.' Wearily, he told them of his
investigations, of the factions, and of the dead monk.

'And they killed that monk to silence him, eh? You think he told
them where it was?'

'I think it unlikely that they would kill him without first knowing
where it was. It makes sense that the monks were in on the plan.
It was easiest for them to have access to the Coronation Chair. I
wasted so many days and now we are at an end . . .'

Gilbert poured more wine into his cup. 'One more day, Crispin.
That's enough time. I mean, if they've only just found the Stone
then maybe it's still in Westminster. Maybe even London.'

'Possibly.' His head suddenly throbbed and he scrubbed at his
hair. 'I can't think anymore. Perhaps it is time I go home. A fresh
start in the morning.'

Eleanor helped him to his feet with a strong arm. 'I think you
are right. When was the last time you slept properly, eh?'

He shrugged.

'That's what I thought. Come along now. And don't vex yourself,
Crispin. We all have faith in you. The good Lord knows where your
heart is and He is watching over you.'

He nodded, grateful again for their intervention. He bid his farewells and left the tavern. The thunk of the bar falling across the
door as they shut it up for the night made that final. He had been
the last to leave . . . again.

Trudging down Gutter Lane, he turned at the Shambles. The soft
clucking behind the shutters of the poulterer told him he was only
steps away from the tinker's shop and thence to his upstairs lodgings.
He grabbed the railing to his stairwell and lifted up each riser, feeling
heavy and weary. He hadn't realized how he had come to depend
not only on his apprentice's assistance but on his company, and it
left a hole that nothing – not even drink – seemed capable of filling.

He fitted his key in the lock and pushed open the door, expecting the dark and cold to greet him. Instead, a shadowed figure hunched over his chair by the small fire, turned at his step. His heart leapt for a moment before he remembered.

'John. I forgot you were here.'

'Thank you very much,' said Rykener with a good-natured chuckle.

He noticed with a sigh that John was still in his woman's gown but said nothing. Instead, he crossed to the fire and stood over it, warming his hands over the flickering flames.

A brisk wind rattled the shutters, and the rafters groaned briefly, but there were no other stirrings. Martin Kemp, the tinker, and his family had long ago gone to their beds and were quiet below. The noisy street with its busy commerce was also laid to bed and only the sound of a yowling cat disturbed its silence.

'What did you discover, Crispin?' said Rykener after a long pause.

'That Brother Crìsdean may not have been who he said he was, and that his Scottish compatriot – a Brother Andrew – is missing. I do not know if the man is also dead or the cause of Brother Crìsdean's death. Whatever the case, it might mean that the Stone is gone at last . . .'

John rose, took Crispin's arms, and carefully maneuvered him into the vacated chair. Crispin's limbs softened and he let his arms drape down. John dragged the stool forward and sat atop it next to Crispin. 'I've been thinking,' said John. 'I'd be willing to wager that the Stone never left the abbey.'

'It might have been there, but it might be gone now. Something *had* gone awry. One crucial message did not get out to the thieves who were to get the Stone. I believe these monks carried out the plan to spirit it away but never got word from the others as to what to do with it. That is, if these others – McGuffin, Findlaich, and Deargh – can be believed.'

'Then what of the m-murdered monk?'

'Something went awry again. Or one of the factions went searching for it and Brother Crìsdean either failed to give up the information or was no longer needed.'

'Then that would seem to exonerate this other missing monk, eh?'

'Possibly. He could have fled. Or be in hiding. So either the Stone is gone or the conspirators killed the wrong man and it is still in the abbey. What a choice!' He dropped his head in his hands. 'I can't think anymore. It is all too convoluted. In the morning, early, we will start again.'

'I think that a good idea, Crispin. Here. Let me help you.'

Crispin pushed himself up from the chair. 'Not necessary, John. I can do it myself.'

'Nonsense. I'm sure Jack helps you. Let me be your provisional squire.'

John, even in his woman's garb, wore an expression of kind concern. There was nothing of the playful tempter about him now. Crispin nodded.

John unbuttoned his cloak and tossed it over his arm while Crispin unbuckled his sword frog and belt. He laid his sword carefully across the table and draped his belt beside it.

John busied himself hanging the cloak on the peg by the door and fussed with the fire before returning to Crispin to pick up his discarded boots and carefully line them up under the bed. 'I must say, for an observant man, you are most inattentive when it comes to your own lodgings.'

'Eh?' he asked wearily, yawning so widely that his jaw cracked. 'What do you mean?'

'I mean this.' He spread his arm expansively toward the far corner where Jack's straw once laid. In its place was a modest cot and a scruffy mattress. A blanket and pillow lay tidy in their proper places.

Crispin halted unbuttoning his cotehardie. 'John! How did you—'

'I sought out a carpenter who turned out to know you well and offered one from his own servants at half the cost. And so the mattress and such were easily purchased. I'm sure Jack will be pleased.'

'I'm sure he will.' He stared at it in wonder, amazed at how far he had come in twelve years. The place was starting to look habitable. 'Thank you, John,' he said softly.

'My pleasure. But if you don't mind, I will test it out for him.'

'Staying again, are you?'

'Well, a lady shouldn't travel abroad this late.'

Crispin snorted and took off his cotehardie. He untied his stockings, stripped them off, and crawled into his own modest bed as John divested himself of his own garb down to his shift. He scratched luxuriously at his torso and, with unbound hair, looked like himself again.

'Ah me,' he said in sing-song. '"Eleanor" is put to sleep while "John" gets into bed.'

Lying with his head on his arms, Crispin stared at the gray ceiling. 'Does it ever get confusing, John?'

'For me? Oh no. Only for friends like you.'

'Friends like me,' he muttered.

'Think no more of it, Crispin. Dream.'

'Mmm,' he mumbled, and took that advice. And yet it seemed like so short a time. When Crispin awoke, it was to John's humming. The man had made himself at home, and still in only his shift, he stood before the fire, stirring broth in a kettle.

Glancing at the angle of the sun, Crispin suddenly sat up. 'It's late!'

'I let you sleep. You looked like you sorely needed it.'

'John!' He tossed the blankets aside and threw his legs over the side of the bed. 'I haven't time to waste! There is only today!'

John rested the hand holding the ladle at his hip. 'I know that, Crispin,' he said solemnly. 'But you can't think clearly if you do not sleep.'

He stopped yanking on his cotehardie to stare at his companion. 'What is the hour?'

'A few hours after Prime. There is plenty of time to sip a bit of broth and have a little bread before you trot off to Westminster again. Oh. And this message came for you last night.'

'A message? Why didn't you wake me?' He opened the parchment as he dressed. He recognized Jack's hand immediately. What was that boy doing? He read his apprentice's carefully written words:

Master Crispin, greetings. I am well and anxious. But I have not been idle and though I cannot yet tell you to what business I have been about, I must tell you of a situation. Two men, one a noble and the other a monk. One called McGuffin and the other Brother Andrew . . .

'I'll be damned!' cried Crispin so suddenly that Rykener nearly dropped the kettle.

'What is it?'

'It's from Jack. And the scoundrel has found out something. Well done, Jack Tucker! So Andrew is alive.' He read aloud:

The McGuffin fellow, a man from Scotland, had charged Brother Andrew to do a task at Westminster Abbey on that fateful day. That task was . . . the business I cannot relate to you. However, I believe the monk was also involved in secreting the Stone. For he was nervous about the death of another monk Brother Crìsdean. This might help you in your cause . . .

'Indeed it does, Jack,' he muttered.

. . . and he said he was sore afraid to return to – I assume – Westminster Abbey. I know he was a monk there, sir, for the deed he carried out – of my concern – placed him there. He begged help from this McGuffin as he feared for his own life, but the churl would not give it, for his task was not for the Stone but for another matter . . .

'As he had said,' remarked Crispin. 'Then McGuffin *was* telling the truth in *that* at least. Jack, what are you up to?'

. . . And so. He swore and said that his compeers could go to the devil – in so many words. And then he said something strange which I will recount here. He said: 'For it is secreted well and sound, and even an "ach-ishkeh" himself cannot find it.'

I didn't understand it, sir, but thought it might be important. I tried to give chase, but he got away and anyway, I could not leave the palace precincts as I had given my word to Lord Derby.

'Lord Derby? What the devil . . .?'

God keep you, sir. I await your rescue with confidence.
Your servant,
Jack Tucker

'With confidence. I hope it shall be deserved.' He read the missive again. 'What is an *ach-ishkeh*?'

'A what?' asked John, setting the bowl before Crispin.

'Here. It is what Jack says.' He showed the parchment to John.

John dipped a spoon into his own broth and peered at the letter. 'Some Scottish oath?'

'Not by context.' Crispin tore a hunk of bread from the stale loaf placed in the center of the table, crumbled it into the broth, and scooped it hastily with his spoon. 'We'll need to ask Domhnall its meaning.'

'Why?'

'Because this might be the clue as to where it is.' He spooned more of the meaty broth and slurped it up.

'Slow down, Master Guest, or you'll choke.' Just as he said it, Crispin coughed.

'Are you coming with me?' he said, clearing his throat.

John looked surprised and clasped his hands. 'Do you want me to come?'

'Well.' Crispin stirred the sops about in his bowl without lifting the spoon. 'You are clever and I could use your help.'

'Even dressed as a woman?'

Crispin scowled into his bowl. 'Make yourself ready or I will change my mind.'

It didn't take long for them each to finish and for John to dress. And there he was again, transformed into 'Eleanor.' Crispin shook his head at it. He had buckled on his sword, locked his door, and followed John down the stairs. 'I don't know how you—'

But they were met at the bottom step by Alice Kemp, his landlord's shrewish wife. Her face was screwed up and red, and she sidled up to block his path with her plump frame.

'Aha! I have caught you in the act of your sin. How dare you parade your strumpet down *my* stairs in the light of day!'

'Madam,' Crispin growled in warning.

But John pushed him aside and squared with Alice. 'What did you call me? I demand an apology!'

Crispin intervened. 'John . . . erm, Eleanor!'

'No, Crispin. This woman has accosted me in the streets. The streets! And I demand an apology. She knows me not. She does not know whether I am a client, a cousin, or your new wife and has caused a scene for her own vainglory.' He tossed his head, causing his braids to swing aside.

Martin the tinker skidded around the corner and took in Crispin, John, and his wife. 'Alice! What goes on here? Why are you harassing Master Guest?'

'Just look. *Look*, Martin!' She shoved a sweaty pink hand toward Crispin and John. 'Look what he does in the light of day without a care in the world for his soul or the good character of our household.'

'My dear,' said Martin in tight conciliatory tones, 'you don't know who this lady is or the manner of their coming and going. You know very well that Master Guest must entertain all sorts of clients at all times of the day and night.' He leaned into Crispin and offered a sheepish smile. 'I apologize, Master Crispin. And to you, good demoiselle.' He bowed.

John placed a hand at his breast and cocked his head. 'And you are a gentleman, sir. But as for your wife . . .'

Crispin shoved John none too gently forward. 'Let us go . . . *demoiselle*.'

Alice looked as if she would launch into another diatribe when Martin turned to her and, in hurried hushed tones, stoppered her every objection. Crispin and John were well away down the Shambles, but he could still hear her shrill voice behind him arguing with her husband.

'Such an awful woman,' John muttered, striding with head high beside Crispin.

'You have no idea.'

They headed again toward Westminster even as the bells tolled Terce, rolling and cascading down lane after lane as each church took up the call. London had been awake for hours, even if Crispin had not. The noises of animals and people and the clatter of wares sold in stalls and from peddlers' wagons all made up the sound of a brisk London. Everyone was going about their business, unaware of the turmoil flaring through Crispin in his worry over Jack Tucker. Yes, none were aware or even cared that a life lay in the balance between now and midnight.

Crispin and John said very little to one another as they made their familiar trek through London's streets and out onto the highway to Westminster. They passed the Temple Bar, Charing Cross, and were closing on the Great Gateway toward St Margaret's Street.

He put a hand out to John and they both stopped. 'What is it, Crispin?'

'This Brother Andrew. Jack said he is hiding in the monastery of St Stephen in the palace. I think I can find him there, but . . .'

'You can't go into the palace.'

'No. Richard . . . frowns . . . on that.'

Crispin searched across the top of the wall toward the rooftops of the monastery. Perhaps it might be possible to climb up and over the wall, directly into St Stephen's . . . but no. That would be foolish.

'What I need is a disguise.' He looked at John. John looked at him, until his eyes widened.

'You want *my* clothes,' he whispered.

Crispin sputtered. 'No, I do not!'

'But it's perfect! No one would suspect! And you keep yourself shaved.' He touched his cheek. 'More or less.'

Crispin batted his hand away. 'I will *not* wear women's clothes. I was rather thinking that if I had no disguise I'd send you.'

'Me? Into a monastery?'

'No. But I thought that, perhaps, you might know of a . . . a monk . . . from whom you could, er, borrow a cassock.'

Rykener settled a hand at his hip. 'Oh you do, do you? You think I know a monk here?'

Crispin sighed. 'I did not mean to offend, John. Forget it.'

'No, no . . . But will a priest do?'

Crispin pinched the bridge of his nose. 'No details, John. Just . . . get it if you can.'

'I'll be back in all haste!'

Off he went, and Crispin paced outside of court, making use of the wide avenue to make an extensive circuit. His gaze traveled over the walls and up to the stately entrance of Westminster Hall, trying not to remember the occasions that had caused him to be there, for good and ill.

It might have been a quarter of an hour, it might have been half, when John finally appeared again, a bundle slung over his arm. 'The things I do for you, Master Guest.'

'Details, John,' he muttered, taking the bundle. They found a quiet alley where Crispin divested himself of his leather hood and removed his cloak. With John's help, he shrugged into the cassock and handed the hood and cloak to Rykener.

'Much thanks, John.'

'What are you going to do? Arrest him?'

'I can't quite arrest anyone, but . . . well. I need to get him out of the palace.' He nodded curtly to the man and left the alley, heading for the Great Gateway.

The day was bright, with a blue sky that would ordinarily have put Crispin in a better mood with its searing color and lazy clouds.

Instead, he felt as black as a winter storm and just as cold, even as the sun warmed his cassock-clad shoulders.

With a cowl over his head and strange clothes on his back, he felt fairly anonymous but was still on his guard. He walked in measured steps across the courtyard and up the steps to the Great Hall. He kept his eyes down and made it to the doorway to the corridor and followed it to St Stephen's chapel.

He wanted to run but forced himself into a sedate stroll down the nave.

'Father! I beg of you, Father!'

He froze when he realized he was being addressed and turned toward the woman. She was a minor noble and a young and handsome woman. His eyes glanced over her and returned to the contemplation of the floor. 'Er . . . yes, my lady?'

'I would be shriven. I would be relieved of my sins.'

He raised a brow, and as much as he would have liked to hear her sins, he shook his head. 'I beg your pardon most humbly,' he answered softly, 'but I am called to urgent business.'

She looked disappointed and stepped back from him, hands clasped together. He gave her a reassuring nod and moved toward the sacristy. Once inside he looked around. An ambry, a tall desk and stool, a chandler brightly lit, and a sputtering hearth. The other door, he hoped, led into the cloister. The latch was free, but the door stuck. With a shove it opened and he recognized the arcade and carrels of the interior of the monastery. Of course, the man could be anywhere and he didn't know what he looked like. *Could have thought this out better*, he grumbled in his head.

A monk approached down the center of the arcade and Crispin decided it might be best to simply ask. Once the monk was upon him he stepped in his way. 'Forgive me, Brother.'

'Father,' said the startled monk with a deferential bow.

'I am strange to this convent but I am looking for a Brother Andrew, also a stranger here. Might you be able to point him out to me?'

'Such odd doings here,' he muttered.

'In what sense, Brother?'

'Well,' said the dark-eyed monk. His face was long, and his dark tonsure slashed across his forehead like Lenten ashes. 'Strange people have been entering the cloister yesterday and today. They aren't allowed in here.'

'Strange people? What sort of people?'

'People who aren't clerics. I chased out a young lad only yesterday. Everyone is in such a hurry.'

'Speaking of such, I am in a bit of a hurry myself, Brother.'

'Hurry, hurry, hurry,' he muttered. 'Brother Andrew, you say? The name is not familiar, but we get all sorts of visitors here, don't we?'

'Indeed.' Crispin was making ready to push past the tiresome fellow when the monk put a finger thoughtfully to his chin. 'There was a monk I did not recognize in the refectory this morning. Where did he go?' He walked back down the arcade, peering into each carrel and stopped at one nearest the corner.

Crispin followed and heard him address the man. 'Forgive the intrusion, my brother,' said the monk with a bow. 'But might you be Brother Andrew?'

The monk slowly set down the book in his hand and looked up. 'I . . . well, aye, Brother . . . er . . .'

A brogue. This was the man, then. Crispin stepped forward into the light.

'This priest wishes to speak with you.' Smiling at having accomplished his task, the monk bowed to them both and made his way back up the arcade, muttering about strange doings with a tick to his head.

Brother Andrew stepped from the carrel and eyed Crispin suspiciously. 'You were looking for me?'

'Yes. I have a message for you. You are to come with me.' *To a private place, preferably.*

The man hesitated. 'Who gave you this message?'

Crispin smiled. 'Now Brother, is it for you to question your superiors?'

'No-o,' he replied, still hesitant.

'Then come, Brother. We are wasting time.'

The monk emerged from the carrel and looked across the cloister garth. He pulled his cowl up over his head with a furtive flicking of his eyes. Crispin gestured for him to walk ahead and he did so haltingly.

'Where are we going?' he asked when they reached the door to the church.

Crispin opened it for him. 'A moment of prayerful contemplation.'

They entered and moved toward the rood. Crispin's only thought now was to get him outside and avoid his escaping into the recesses of the monastery. If he could get him to Abbot Colchester, then Andrew would at least be locked into a cell for safekeeping. A monk committing such a crime as the theft of the Stone was on the knife edge between an ecclesiastical court and the king's. And, due to the circumstances, the king might insist on his own justice. But not if the churl escaped.

Crispin grabbed the man's cassock perhaps a little too tightly, lifting him from his kneeling position. Andrew glared at him and stumbled after. 'I repeat, Father Priest, where are you taking me?'

They made it to the Great Hall and strode across it at Crispin's quickened pace. It was there Crispin pulled his dagger and jammed the point into Andrew's side. In a low growl he said, 'We are going back to Westminster, where you will be facing charges of murder and theft of the Stone of Destiny.'

Andrew jerked away, but Crispin held him fast and dug the knife point deep enough that the monk yelped.

With a fierce grip on the cassock, Crispin dragged the monk through the archway and to the courtyard. They moved even faster now. Crispin had to risk their being noticed for the safety of being outside the walls. He could see John waiting for him on the street beyond the gate.

He shoved Brother Andrew through once they reached the Great Gateway and when he looked as if he might run, John stepped in his way. 'Is this Brother Andrew, Crispin?'

The monk squinted at John, no doubt trying to reconcile deep voice to female appearance.

'Over here,' said Crispin, ushering them both to an alley. He wrestled out of his cassock and took his hood and cloak back from John. With his knife back in his hand, he leaned over Andrew cowering against the wall.

'And now. There is much we need to discuss.'

Andrew's eyes flashed from Crispin to John and back to the knife blade. But he said nothing.

'Well?' Crispin brandished his dagger. 'Must I use this? I admit, I'd very much like to for all the trouble you have caused me.'

'Who *are* you?' the monk managed to squeak.

'I'm Crispin Guest, and my apprentice has been held hostage by the king until the Stone is returned. Where is it?'

'The Tracker . . .' he whispered.

'I already know you are a false monk of Westminster and, along with Brother Crìsdean, the both of you were, perhaps, household clerics to Macduff?'

He threw his hand over his mouth. 'You mustn't say that name!' he hissed.

'Very well. That matters little at the moment. What happened to Crìsdean? Are you a murderer, sir?'

'Murderer?' Eyes wild, he glanced toward the open highway just outside the alley.

'Yes, for if just the two of you knew where the Stone was hidden, how much easier would it be to collect double the fee yourself?'

The monk cringed. 'God have mercy.'

'Well?'

'It's no for the fee,' he said in a shattered voice. 'He . . . he . . . he was going to tell! He was going to give in, you see, and confess all to the abbot and throw himself on the mercy of the king. Ha! As if there would be mercy. He was a fool. I told him so. But he would no listen.'

'And so you killed him.'

'It was an accident. I only meant to stop him from saying, but I . . . I . . . hit him too hard and . . .' He brought a trembling hand to his mouth and then becrossed himself.

'Then you must pay for that, too, and hang.'

'No! No, Master Guest, mercy! I'll bargain with you. You let me get safely away and I'll tell you where the Stone is.'

'I have no more patience for you deceiving Scotsmen.' Crispin grabbed the monk and shoved him hard into the wall. 'Tell me where it is now!'

'No, not until you promise. I will no say until you promise to let me go.'

Crispin turned an exasperated face toward John, but he offered no comfort in his stern expression.

Andrew pressed closer. A breathless desperation had overcome the fear in his eyes. 'You need the Stone, I know where it is. I'm the last one who knows. It was never meant to be like this. This is not what I was told would happen!' Tears glistened in his eyes. He did not bother to wipe them away.

Crispin sneered. 'Now you see where your own sin leads you.' The harsh words fell like lashes on the monk, and he cringed.

He nodded. 'I know. I know. I was loyal to my masters, as any vassal should be. I did what I was told.'

'You and Crìsdean stole the Stone of Destiny and replaced it with an explosive fake.'

'Aye, aye, we did. The powder was sent to us and we fashioned the imposter Stone. No harm was to come to anyone, and Crìsdean knew the powder well. It was going according to plan.'

'But no one came to claim the Stone and take it off your hands.'

Andrew stared with mouth dropping open. 'How did you know? We were fools to attempt this with you so near. I told them that. I warned them.'

'Was it you who told your fellow conspirators to divert me?'

He nodded. 'I heard the stories of you. I knew you would be in our way. But I see that it did no good.'

'How did you communicate, if you did not know your compeers?'

'I do not know how you know this . . . We were instructed to leave messages at Charing Cross. Folded parchments stuck into the crevices. That's how I received the powder. But I knew you would figure it out. I knew we had to get the Stone away quickly.'

'When did you steal it?'

'Two days before the Feast of the Virgin, God help us.'

'And you were told to set the explosive powder during the Mass?'

'I hadn't wanted to. Such sacrilege! But Crìsdean was urged to do so by . . . by one of our masters.'

'McGuffin.'

'You know too much about it, Master Guest.' He looked sharply over his shoulder before facing Crispin again. 'He wasn't interested in the Stone, but something else. He insisted he needed the explosive to go off at that time and that *I* was . . . I was to do another task.'

'What task was this?'

He shook his head so violently that his hood flew off and settled on his shoulders. 'Thievery. Like a common thief! But that's not important. What is important is my life!'

'The whole scheme seemed designed to cause disgrace to King Richard.'

'And his wife.' Brother Andrew all but threw his hands over his mouth when he stopped talking.

'The queen? What has this to do with the queen?'

The monk becrossed himself and shook his head. 'I said that this was only about the Stone, but others would hatch a plot to bring down Richard *and* his queen. I was against it. That is not an honorable thing to do.'

'What was the plot?'

'I . . . dinna wish to say.'

Crispin grabbed him by his arms and shook. 'You will tell me!'

'Peace, Master Guest!' He dropped his head to his chest and sniffed, weeping again. 'To discredit her. To distract the king.'

'And this was McGuffin's role?'

'Aye. It was. A plot of extortion and deception.'

Crispin nodded. More of it was falling into place. This was Jack's 'other business.' How did the boy get himself mixed up with the queen?

'I see. But the Stone. There was no one to take it off your hands?'

'No. I asked and I pleaded. And then . . . Brother Crisdean . . . You must help me, Master Guest. I can trust no one.'

'Do they have the Stone?'

'No. Not yet. There are too many masters wanting too many tasks. But once they know where the Stone is, they will kill me, I am certain. I want your word that you will help me get safely away.'

Crispin decided. What was one cursed monk to the life of his apprentice? 'You have my word. Where is the Stone?'

'Swear, Master Guest. I need that assurance.'

'Good God, man! Do you know me or not? I said you have my word and my word is my bond, as Jesus is my witness. Now where is the damned Stone!'

'It's—'

The monk cried out as if in pain. He arched his back unnaturally, and suddenly dropped to the muddy lane. An arrow stuck out of his neck and soon covered his cowl and the mud in a flow of crimson.

John let out a sudden shout and another arrow struck the wall next to Crispin's head. He ducked, and spun on his heel, crouching, searching the rooftops behind him for the archer.

He thought he caught the merest glimpse of a figure disappearing behind a chimney, but there was no more movement from above.

He flicked his gaze once toward John to make certain he wasn't hit before darting toward the buildings across the way. He ran along the lane, looking upward. A slate tile loosened and cascaded downward – the only evidence of a fleeing man – but he could see no one.

He stopped when he reached Charing Cross, scanning the rooftops but cursing when he saw nothing.

He looked back toward John who was bent over the monk. But as he approached his worst fears were realized.

John raised his tear-stained face and slowly shook his head.

TWENTY-FIVE

Crispin waited for the sheriffs to arrive. He paced, striding heavily back and forth along the stone-paved avenue while John bit at his nails.

'What will you tell them?' he asked Crispin.

Crispin continued to furiously pace. 'I don't know.'

'Well, you'd better think of something for they are coming.'

Stopping in his tracks, Crispin looked up. Four horsemen approached, not of the Apocalypse – *though they might as well be*, he mused. The soon-to-be ex-sheriffs flanked the new sheriffs. And not one of them looked pleased to see him.

Sheriff William Venour stopped his horse right before Crispin and glared down at him. 'Another dead monk, Master Guest? You have an uncanny knack for being nigh or the cause of a murder.'

Sheriff Hugh Fastolf pulled his mount up beside Venour. 'I weary so of Master Guest. I do not envy you, Thomas and Adam.'

The new sheriffs – twin blond heads and sneering faces – appeared to agree. 'What has happened here, Master Guest?' ventured Adam Carlylle.

'He was murdered as I was questioning him.'

'And why, pray, were you questioning him?'

'Because he and his fellow brother – also murdered – knew the whereabouts of the Stone of Destiny.'

Thomas Austin leaned over his saddle pommel. 'Why didn't you tell us this before!' he hissed, eyes darting toward the gathered crowd. 'Then the other death at Westminster—'

'I thought it might be obvious, my lord.'

'There is nothing obvious in your doings, Guest, for you deal in all sorts of dubious matters . . . for a *fee*,' he added disdainfully.

Crispin stood at the horse's head, tempted to caress the muzzle. *Better that than a bribe.* 'What else could so occupy my thoughts? There is only today before the Commons meet tomorrow.'

'Well then?' said Carlylle eagerly. 'Where *is* the Stone? Have you located it?'

Crispin gestured sourly to the corpse at his feet. 'He was the last who knew for certain where it was. And he didn't have an opportunity to tell me before he was killed.'

The all looked down solemnly.

'But I am certain,' said Crispin, 'that it is in Westminster Abbey.'

'The place was thoroughly searched,' said Venour.

'And yet, these two monks secured it where no one would find it.'

Fastolf dismounted and ambled toward the corpse, touching the tip of the arrow's fletching. 'What happened, Master Guest?'

Crispin joined his hands behind his back. 'He was shot. With an arrow.'

Fastolf gave him a withering gaze. 'I can see that for myself. I meant the circumstances, as you very well know.' He turned toward Carlylle and Austin with a world-weary tilt to his head. 'Do you see what we have to put up with? Disrespect.'

'Answer the question forthwith, Guest,' said Austin.

'We were talking, just here, and suddenly he was shot with an arrow. I chased who I thought was the archer. He ran along the rooftop there, but I never got a look at him.'

'Are we supposed to believe that?' said Carlylle.

John Rykener stomped forward, casting his skirts aside with his strides. 'But that is what happened! I saw it.'

'And who are you, demoiselle?' asked Venour, leaning on the saddle pommel toward John.

John wrapped his cloak about him and looked up at the sheriff through his veil. 'I am Eleanor, an embroideress. I saw it happen.'

'Did you see the culprit who did it?'

'No. No, God help me. I was too distressed when the monk was felled.'

'Of course. This is too unseemly for the likes of a woman. You may go.'

'Oh . . . but I am with Master Guest.'

The sheriff slid his gaze toward Crispin. 'Is that so?'

'She . . . is a friend,' said Crispin tightly, cursing John's choice of clothing for not the first time. He withstood the leer for as long as he could before announcing, 'If you are done with me I have more investigating to do.'

'Not so fast, Guest,' said Austin. 'Just where do you think you're going?'

'I am going to Westminster Abbey to search for the Stone of Destiny. With your permission,' he added through gritted teeth.

Carlylle waved him off. 'We don't need him.' He looked around absently. 'I hope someone has called for the coroner.'

Crispin almost turned away from them before he studied Carlylle. The neophyte sheriff narrowed his eyes. 'Why do you stare at me?'

'Your name is Carlylle.'

'What of it?'

'That is a Scottish surname, if I am not mistaken.'

Carlylle postured, but a red sunburst flushed his otherwise pale cheeks. 'What of it? What are you trying to make of that, Guest?'

'Nothing, my lord. Only . . . might you know of Scottish things, words? For example, the expression; *ach-ishkeh*?'

Carlylle hesitated. 'I don't make a habit of . . . This is absurd. I am English! My family has lived in England for generations.'

'I do not disparage it, my lord. It is merely a clue to the whereabouts of the Stone. If you know it, it would make my investigation easier.'

Carlylle chewed on his lip and snatched a look at his fellow sheriffs. 'Hmpf. Well. Do you by any chance mean . . . *each-uisge*?'

Crispin shrugged. 'It's as close as I could get to that pronunciation.'

Carlylle glanced again at his curious companions before looking away. 'Such a strange request. It's . . . a spirit, a demon. A man who turns into a horse, but stays close to the water. A water devil. So my grandparents said. A tale. They used to warn us as children to stay away from the water's edge or the *each-uisge* would drag us down. Foolish pagan nonsense.'

Crispin frowned. 'I see. Thank you.' He bowed and turned quickly.

'Guest!' called Carlylle.

Crispin stopped and barely turned.

'I don't know what you are about, and I don't know your character except by what these good men say.' He gestured toward the sheriffs. 'But I have heard other . . . rumors . . . about you.' He seemed embarrassed when he said, 'I pray that you *do* find it.'

He bowed slightly toward Carlylle. 'Thank you, Lord Sheriff. I shall do my utmost.' He said no more and hurried toward Westminster's north door, with John Rykener fast on his heels.

'What was that all about, Crispin?'

'I'm not sure. What did Jack say?' He withdrew the folded parchment from his scrip as they trotted up the stone steps to the Norman arched entrance. '*For it is secreted well and sound, and even an ach-ishkeh himself cannot find it.*'

'A water devil,' said John, finger tapping his assiduously shaved chin. 'Why would a monk speak of such curious things?'

'The Scottish are more prone to their pagan beliefs, even a monk.' Crispin smiled and slowed when he passed under the shadowed arch and stood in the cold entry. 'But I suspect that if he'd had more classical leanings he might have said Poseidon or Neptune.' John blinked at him. 'Don't you see, John? They've hidden it in *water*. And even this *ach-ishkeh* can't find it.' He poked his finger into John's chest and grinned. 'But otherwise could *because* it's in water.'

'Water!' He slid to a stop and peered into the font but shook his head when it proved to be just a font. 'But which water? I mean . . .?'

'Only so many places within a monastery. And think. Two men hiding it but having to retrieve it again. You wouldn't want to put it down a well. The horrid thing must weigh twenty-one, twenty-two stone. You'd not wish to haul it up.'

'A stew pond?'

Crispin shook his head, walking quickly through the church toward the cloister. 'Same problem. What if it got stuck in the mud? You'd never get it out.'

John winced. 'Surely not a privy or cesspit?'

'A little too disrespectful.' They reached the south transept and the door to the cloister. 'But close.' He reached out to grab the bell rope and pulled. The bells jangled while they waited for the porter.

John could not seem to stand still and strained his neck looking up in to the vaulted ceilings, the gated quire behind, the rood screen-covered sanctuary. 'You seem to know your way about here, Crispin.'

'I was friends with Abbot de Litlyngton.' He becrossed himself, thinking of the man.

'And . . . he is now gone from this life?'

'Alas. I miss him. He was a clever man and well-educated.'

'I am sure he is intervening for you in Heaven, Crispin,' John said softly.

Crispin smiled. 'I hadn't thought of that. I certainly hope so.'

A cowled monk shuffled from the shadows and greeted them at the door. '*Benedicte*. How can I assist you?'

'I need to get into the cloister.'

The monk stared at him. 'Only the monks are allowed into the cloister.'

'I am Crispin Guest. I am . . . acquainted with your abbot. You may consult him if you wish for my credentials.'

The monk he did not recognize bowed. 'I shall. Please wait here.'

Crispin muttered an oath and blew out an impatient breath. 'Ridiculous.'

John clasped the barred gate. 'Should they not all know you by now?'

'It is my own vanity that supposes it,' he grumbled.

'Never fear, Crispin. You are close to it now. You *will* save Jack.' John patted his shoulder. 'You have done well.'

'I haven't got it yet.' But he did feel suddenly better. Yes, he was close. Jack would be saved. His relief was immense, but he knew he mustn't put the cart before the horse. He had to have the Stone safely in his hands before he could begin to celebrate.

In his contemplation, he hadn't noticed the boy suddenly behind him, tugging on his cloak.

He turned and took in the bedraggled boy, looking much like Jack Tucker had when Crispin had first met him on the streets some four years ago. 'Are you Crispin Guest?' The boy spared a brush of his eyes over Rykener.

'Yes?'

'I have a message for you, sir.' He held out the folded parchment.

'From whom?'

The boy shook his head, trembling his overgrown locks. 'I don't know, sir. He gave me a farthing and told me to deliver it inside the abbey to you.'

Crispin's senses went on alert. Someone was watching him. But of course they were. He took the missive and broke open the blank wax seal.

We have your friend Eleanor. Yes, the true one this time. Bring the Stone and come to Queenhithe dock at Compline if you do not wish to see her die.

Crispin hadn't noticed he had been holding his breath. He let it out with a gasped, 'God's blood!'

'Crispin! What is it?'

Crispin let the parchment fall and grabbed the boy, who cried out at the rough handling. 'Show me the man who gave this to you!'

Mute, the boy nodded, eyes wide. Crispin held firm to his arm and dragged him to the archway. As they went down the steps the boy searched wildly about.

Crispin knew the answer ever before the boy spoke brokenly.

'I cannot see him, sir. He isn't here.'

'What did he look like?'

Expecting the description of McGuffin, Crispin knotted his brow at the pronouncement of another.

'And he spoke with a northern dialect?'

The boy, more at ease now that Crispin had calmed himself, replied, 'I know not of that, sir. But he spoke not as a Londoner.'

'Good enough.' He reached into his scrip for his money pouch and withdrew a farthing. 'For your trouble. I . . . uh . . . apologize for the . . .'

The boy clutched the coin in a dirty fist and bowed. 'No trouble, sir.' He fled down the street and never looked back.

Crispin marched back up the steps and met John Rykener there. He was reading the missive, moving his lips as he did. 'By St Katherine! This is ill done, Crispin. What do we do now? Should we not call in the help of the sheriffs?'

Should they? Crispin pondered it. They had never been much help before. 'I don't know,' he growled. He pushed past John, stomped through the church, and headed again toward the cloister door . . . where Abbot William de Colchester awaited, hands clasped before him.

'Master Guest,' he said, inclining his head. It was the first gesture of respect he had bestowed upon Crispin, even as subtle as it was. 'I was told you were here. Do you have tidings for me?'

'Yes. Some bad, some good. Your Brother Andrew was found. But he has since been killed. Murdered.'

'Jesus help us,' he whispered, becrossing himself.

'It appears that he killed Brother Crìsdean.'

'Then justice has been done,' said the abbot gravely.

'Indeed. But he managed to impart the news that the Stone is present here, in Westminster Abbey.'

'But we have searched, Master Guest. Most assiduously.'

'But not cleverly. Can you tell me the source of the water for your lavatorium?'

The abbot appeared startled but composed himself quickly. 'Come this way.' Crispin only then noticed his assistant, Brother Thomas, who had his hand on the gate and quickly turned to unlock the cloister door. They entered through and the abbot hesitated when John tried to follow. 'Women are not allowed in the cloister, demoiselle,' he said with a bow.

John looked to Crispin. It seemed so small a thing now. 'He is not a woman, Father Abbot,' said Crispin solemnly.

'Oh!' The abbot drew back, looked him up and down. He looked as if he wished to say something, but after a moment's pause seemed to reconsider. 'There must be a reason you are here with Master Guest and so garbed.'

'He is a good and loyal friend, my lord. And he has saved my life a number of times. In this instance, he has stepped into the shoes of Jack Tucker . . . albeit of a more . . . feminine sort.' He would not discuss further with the abbot what John was about, only that he needed him beside him. And the abbot, being the worldly man he was, merely nodded.

'Very well, Master Guest. This is not for me to sort . . . today.' He moved forward toward the study carrels and the corridor to the chapter house, dipping his hands into his sleeves without giving Rykener a backward glance. Brother Thomas, distaste plainly on his face, skirted wide around John to follow his abbot.

With a grateful but brief smile, John urged Crispin forward.

They all traveled along the arcade, their footsteps echoing off the windswept stone. The cloister garth in the center still sported a green lawn, herbs and hedges, and trees that had not yet succumbed to fall as it fast approached with a chill breeze and an icy morning. Their shade reminded of summer days, and Crispin well knew that the courtyard was often the place for the monks to take their leisure in games with a stuffed leather ball.

Today, all was quiet. And soon the monks would need to prepare for yet another funeral for one of their brethren, as loath as they might be to pray for such a man.

They turned the corner and reached the south covered walk. The long lavatorium trough ran almost the entire length of the passage, with its protrusion of brass spigots carefully spaced along the way. The refectory door sat at the end.

'This,' said Crispin, gesturing toward the trough, 'pipes its water from where, my Lord Abbot?'

The abbot turned to Brother Thomas. The monk addressed Crispin, studiously ignoring John Rykener. 'It is fed through lead pipes from a cistern.'

'And where is this cistern, Brother Thomas? Can you show me?'

The monk led the way through another passage that led to a gate behind the arcade. A large barrel the size of a tun, stood up on a raised platform. A leaden pipe snaked down from the tun and through the stone wall. A stairway led up to the platform where some tools lay scattered. A ladder leaned against it.

'We recently had some workmen here, Master Guest,' offered Brother Thomas, gesturing toward the tools. 'The pipes were in need of repair.'

Crispin examined the steps and the platform. Both had lines scraped through them with gouges and chips, all recently done. He climbed the stairs and stood on the platform, searching. 'Something heavy was dragged up here,' he said, warming with the sensation of confidence. 'Brother Thomas, have you a long hook of some kind? Something a workman might use?'

While the monk hurried away to comply, Crispin climbed the ladder to the top of the cistern and looked down into the dark water. He could see nothing in its depths. *It had better be here. I haven't any more ideas.*

And then there was Eleanor. This was not the work of McGuffin, whom he was convinced meant no harm. Though, apparently, that had not extended to Richard and the queen. That left Deargh or Findlaich. But he was inclined to consider Deargh. He was the fiercest of the lot, after all. Crispin had already fought with him. Whoever it was, he vowed to make them pay. How had they captured her? Had they injured Gilbert? No one hurt a member of his family, and all on the Shambles fell into that category . . . except, perhaps, for Alice Kemp.

And then there were still the sheriffs. Tell them or not?

It wasn't long until Brother Thomas returned with a workman carrying a long pike. 'The gardener,' he explained, urging the man up the steps toward Crispin. 'He uses it for dredging the stewpond, so he says.'

Crispin said nothing as the man bowed his head to him and set about his business of dunking its hooked end into the water. He swilled it around. Crispin licked his lips, becoming concerned when the man seemed to encounter nothing out of the ordinary. Until it snagged on . . . something.

'Something there,' said the man gruffly.

'Let me help you.' Crispin grabbed hold of the end of the pike but, try as they might, they could not budge whatever was down there.

'It will be too heavy to lift with this pike,' said Crispin. He thought a moment before he began unbuckling his belt and unbuttoning his cotehardie.

'Master Crispin,' said the abbot in a scandalized tone. 'What are you doing?'

'Someone has to go into the cistern, Lord Abbot,' he said, peeling first his hood then his coat from his shoulders and dropping them to the platform. He untied his stockings from his braies next, letting them sag around his ankles before he hopped on one foot to divest first one and then the other of his boots and stockings together. He untied the laces of his shirt and pulled it off over his head and stood in nothing but his braies. 'A boost would be most helpful, good master,' he said to the workman. He shivered slightly in the cold air but knew the water would be colder.

The man interlaced his fingers and lowered them to his thigh, balancing himself against the side of the cistern. Crispin clasped the man's shoulders and stuck his foot in the step he made with his hands and swung himself up until he straddled the top edge of the cistern. 'Here I go.' He plunged in. The cold water snatched his breath, clenched his muscles.

He surfaced and bobbed in the water a moment, getting used to the temperature. It wasn't so deep that his feet could not touch the bottom. He took one deep breath and dropped below the surface again.

Once the murk of the top layer of water dissipated and he accustomed himself to the lower light level, he looked at the bottom of the cistern and swam toward a dark shape. There. A square block on whose iron rings the pike had caught itself. Crispin ran his hands over its rough surface just to verify that he was seeing what was truly there. A sensation of deep relief and satisfaction washed over him. He pushed off from it toward the light from above and his head broke the surface. He gasped as the cold air hit his head. Wet hair plastered to his scalp.

Thomas peered over the side at him. 'Well, Master Guest?'

'It is there,' he said breathlessly. 'We will need ropes and some strong men to wrestle it out.'

'Let me help you out of there, Master Guest.'

'No, I am already wet. I can help.'

'But look. You are shivering. How would it be if you should drown once you had succeeded in your quest?'

Another monk had rushed up the stairs with a flannel and even though he protested, Crispin was pulled from the water and wrapped in the cloth.

The normally stoic abbot wore a grin. It seemed to score his face in unaccustomed creases. 'Well done, Master Guest! Come away. There is no need to freeze to death. We have some hearty servants who are adequate to the job.'

The man on the platform raised his brows, rolled his eyes, and reluctantly began disrobing.

Crispin stepped aside as more servants approached, eyeing him strangely. Ropes, pulleys, and iron hooks were gathered and carried up the stairs by several burly workmen, and set to the task as Thomas instructed.

Crispin tossed the cloth over his wet head and dressed quickly, helped by John Rykener who was smiling from ear to ear.

'You are a true hero, Master Guest,' he said quietly, helping Crispin slip into his cotehardie and assisting him to button it up.

'Be still, John,' he muttered. 'There is still the matter of Eleanor.'

John sobered. 'Oh dear! What are we to do?'

'My Lord Abbot.' He turned toward the monk below the platform. 'I must speak with you on a matter most urgent.'

'Anything, Master Guest,' he said in a jovial tenor. It seemed Crispin could now do no wrong in the abbot's eyes.

Crispin finished dressing and slung the flannel over his shoulders. He descended the stairs to join the abbot on the stone path. 'May we talk in your lodgings?' He watched the first workman gingerly lower himself into the water and the others gather around the top of the cistern with their secured ropes and pulleys. 'My Lord Abbot, might I ask that you not send word quite yet to the palace about the Stone?'

'Whatever for, Master Guest? Surely you are anxious to free your servant from his incarceration?'

'I am, but . . . we need to talk in private.'

'Yes, yes of course.' He left Brother Thomas to supervise the raising of the Stone and walked with taut strides back through the cloister toward his lodgings.

Crispin turned to Rykener. 'I need you to get a message to Jack Tucker.'

'Anything you like, Crispin. But how am I to do that?'

'He is in the care of the earl of Derby at the palace. Plead to get the message personally to Jack.'

'I will do as you say. What is the message?'

Crispin told him and John nodded. 'Here. You might need this.' He handed Crispin the ransom note. Crispin took it with quiet thanks and left John to follow the abbot.

Brother John Sandon was there at the abbot's lodgings to greet him with a stiff bow. He did not seem surprised to see Crispin, only that Crispin was still drying his hair with a cloth that he soon surrendered to the young monk.

The abbot ushered Crispin to the fire, for which he was grateful. He stood with his back to it, nearly sighing from the comfortable warmth.

'I must congratulate you Master Guest . . . Crispin . . . if I may be so bold as to call you so.' The abbot turned away for a moment before facing Crispin again. His cheek was flushed. 'I feel I must apologize. We . . . did not get off on the right foot when first we met.'

'You did not know me, Abbot William. I am . . . not an easy man to know.'

'And yet our dear departed Abbot Nicholas assured me of your constancy. Unfortunately, I was often away from the abbey, traveling on Church business. And I, alas, was suspicious of you and your dubious past. You see, he was an old man, and old men are likely to indulge themselves in fancies. After all, you were a . . . that is to say, you were not a friend to the king.'

'No,' he said drily. 'Not a friend. But now a loyal subject. For these past twelve years. But as you saw, it isn't an easy thing.'

'Yes.' The abbot stood for a moment before he went to the sideboard, pouring two goblets of wine. He returned to the fire with them and offered one to Crispin.

Surprised that the abbot himself would serve him, he took it without a word and sipped the Flemish wine, basking in the sensation of warmth flowing through his chest and belly.

'I understand you play chess, Master Crispin?'

'Yes, I do.'

'Perhaps . . . you would be so good as to indulge me sometime in a game. I remembered that you played with Abbot Nicholas.'

A bequeathed chess set which you reluctantly surrendered to me, he mused. 'I would be honored,' he said aloud, and bowed.

'And now.' The abbot sipped his wine and faced Crispin. They both stood at the fire as if they were equals. 'You wished to speak to me . . .'

'As I said. It is a matter of some urgency. There is this, you see.' He unfolded the ransom note and handed it to the abbot. The monk read it, brows arching.

'This is outrageous. Who is this Eleanor?'

'A friend. A very dear one. This man is very dangerous. I have no doubts that he will carry out his threats. I need to send some messages. And I also need to ask a favor of you, my lord.'

The abbot, usually composed, looked suddenly aghast. But when he saw Crispin smile, the abbot seemed to find his composure again.

TWENTY-SIX

Jack watched the sun set from the little window high overhead and, with it, all his hopes. Master Crispin had sent no word. No servant had come to give him tidings. It crashed in on him that he was utterly alone, and any fear that he had shuffled away while busy helping the queen now rushed back like a team of stampeding horses loosed from their reins.

Had his master abandoned him in his hour of need? But that wasn't like Master Crispin at all. Had something happened to him? That was even worse! Those evil men could have harmed him, and Jack wasn't there to rescue his master as he had done many times before . . .

He jumped when a key grated in the lock. Holy Virgin! They were coming for him. Should he fight? He looked around for a weapon, but there was nothing but a stool and a few sticks for the fire. He had his knife, but he'd only wound before they clapped him in chains. And would his master even wish for him to fight? Wouldn't he rather Jack saw to his fate with dignity, like a man?

He swallowed hard. Dignity was the last thing on his mind.

But as he stood back, hands clenched, and watched the door open, he tried – with a deep breath – to muster the strength to keep his chin high.

Hugh Waterton unlocked the door and, with an unreadable expression, said, 'You are to come with me.'

'Has . . . has there been word?'

Waterton clenched his jaw. 'You are to come with me.'

'Aye,' Jack breathed. He becrossed himself and slowly walked forward. He measured Waterton's iron expression as he passed him, but there was no hope in his eyes.

He followed the chamberlain to the main parlor and his heart battered his chest once he caught sight of both Derby and Lady Katherine.

I'm doomed. They've come to see me off.

He fell to his knees and folded his hands into a prayer. 'Lord Derby, Lady Katherine. I must beg your forgiveness for vexing you these past few days. I wish to confess to all here before God, that you have both been gracious and kind to me. May God and the Holy Virgin keep you and watch over you.'

'Arise, Master Tucker,' said Lady Katherine. Her face was as solemn as he had ever seen it.

He scrambled to his feet. 'Has there been any word, Lady Katherine?'

She glanced once at Henry, but his face was as stoic as a stone. 'We have heard nothing, Master Tucker.'

'The king has summoned you,' said Lord Henry. 'It is best we go.'

'Oh. Then . . . then it is all done.'

Lady Katherine laid her hand on his arm. 'There is still reason to hope, Master Tucker.'

'But . . . if my master has not come . . .'

She looked away, her cheek growing pale.

Doomed, he groaned inwardly.

The procession was quiet and somber. Henry and his retinue led, followed by Lady Katherine and her attendants, while Jack brought up the rear, with pages serving as guards. It was a long walk through the corridors to the Great Hall. Jack kept licking his lips. His throat had gone dry and his limbs quivered.

Dignity, Jack. Master Crispin would expect it. He tried to hold his arms close to his body so that they wouldn't tremble, but it wasn't working. Would Master Crispin be there at the gibbet, he wondered. It would be nice to see a friendly face. He supposed if it were at Tyburn or Tower Hill he'd be allowed to come just like anyone else.

Oh God! The whole of London would see it. He'd be dangling there, legs flailing, bowels loosening all over the gibbet. Hadn't he seen enough hangings to know?

He couldn't help the sob that climbed out of his throat, nor the tears that blurred his eyes.

The corridors seemed to go on forever, and his feet felt heavier and heavier. The king wouldn't demand it right now, would he? Jack wanted to say his farewells and thanks to Master Crispin, to be sure. But King Richard was a sorry young man and spiteful. He certainly wouldn't put it past the king to do so without Master Crispin being present.

Ah, but he knew he mustn't have these thoughts now. He needed to keep his mind on charity and praying . . . but he couldn't seem to. His thoughts were focused on death and humiliation, and how lost Master Crispin would be without him. *He can't manage it on his own. What will he do?*

At last the procession passed through the archway, and Jack could see that King Richard was holding court there. Richard was talking to a courtier sitting beside him, but he still seemed to notice when Henry Bolingbroke appeared. His face was aimed toward his courtier but his eyes followed Henry hungrily, with simmering emotion just below the surface. And though Richard's face showed to the world how he praised family and familial alliances above all, he could not seem to forgive his cousin's part in his own humiliation.

Or so Master Crispin had said.

The queen, demure and quiet beside her husband, was resplendent in a gown the colors of the king's quartered arms. Perhaps in defiance of her extortionists, she wore proudly that which should have been plain on that accursed brooch.

'Lo!' said Richard, and the crowd quieted. 'My cousin is here at last.'

Henry bowed low to Richard on his throne set up on a dais. 'Sire. I am sorry for any delay.'

'No need to apologize, cuz. I was assured of your imminent arrival. And so.' His eyes dismissed Henry, and, sullen that he had been discharged, Henry frowned and found his place at the foot of the dais, trying to look as if he was supposed to be there. But the bronzing of his cheeks told another tale.

Richard scanned the immense room. Fires in iron cages spaced along the floor warmed the courtiers, and the many chandlers and coronas glistened with flickering candles. 'We are gathered here tonight because I had charged the traitor Crispin Guest with finding the stolen Stone of Destiny.'

The room fell to absolute silence. Not a gown rustled. No banner on its pole dared creak.

Richard swallowed. 'Yes, the very same Stone of Destiny that belongs housed in my great-great-grandfather's Coronation Chair, stolen by vile rebels. Meant to humiliate England. And as England itself.' He gestured to his breast. 'We bear the burden of its shame.' He lifted his bearded chin to look about the room. 'And where is Crispin Guest? Has anyone laid eyes on him? Where is the Stone?'

Heads turned, but no one acknowledged that they knew anything.

The king drummed his fingers on his chair's arm, rings sparkling. 'No Crispin Guest?' He buried his smirk in his clenched jaw. 'What a surprise.'

'Your grace.'

Jack gasped as Lady Katherine stepped forward and curtseyed. Richard stared at her. Plainly she made him uncomfortable.

'I know that it was your desire to receive the Stone back before the Commons met in Cambridge, and your majesty, perhaps, believes that such a thing would bring dishonor to England. But we, your subjects' – she swept her arm, encompassing all present – 'know that your grace is not dishonored when a thief comes to the door. It is very like a man who is burgled. The master of the house sends his minions to go after the thief, cut him down, and return the goods. Yet this takes time. More than a brief few days. And so, might your majesty afford Master Guest more time to find the thieves and return the goods? It is a delicate thing, dealing with spies and rebels.'

The king leaned back in his chair, eyes hooded. 'Madam, do you suggest we forswear ourselves?'

'Not in the least, your grace.'

'And yet you would, Madam. For I have sworn that if Master Guest did not return the Stone at the appointed time . . . now . . . that the life of his traitorous apprentice was forfeit. And just where is my prisoner?'

It wasn't Derby's pages that pushed through the crowd and manhandled Jack forward, but the king's guards. And one was that Yorkshire man, who gritted his teeth and swore softly through them so that only Jack could hear his threats.

They shoved him forth and he fell onto his knees. When he dared look up, he glanced quickly toward the queen. Her hand trembled over her mouth. He was her 'Goat' no longer, but the prisoner Jack Tucker. Her eyes filled with all the confusion she could not express aloud. And seeing that, Jack lowered his face with the burden of guilt slicing through his heart. He had not told her who he was, and for that, too, he would pay.

Richard toyed with the laces on his tunic, looking at them instead of Jack. 'What's your name, boy?'

Jack swallowed, took a breath, then another. 'Sire . . . my n-name is Jack Tucker.'

'Tucker. And how does it feel to know that your master has deserted you?'

He looked toward Henry, but the earl's face was blank. 'He hasn't. I know he hasn't, your grace.'

'Loyal to the last, are you? I suppose traitors stick together.'

'I am no traitor, your majesty.'

Like a leopard, Richard launched from his seat to crouch over Jack at the edge of the dais. 'You are a traitor if I say you are, knave. And I see you are just as stubborn as Guest and just as arrogant.'

Jack cringed back, mouth firmly shut. Nothing could be gained by naysaying the king in his court, after all. And yet, if he were about to die, wasn't this the time to be brutally honest?

He screwed up his courage. 'I am not a traitor, your grace. And though my master *was* at one time, he is no longer. You will find no more loyal subject and servant than Crispin Guest. And I will always be proud to say that I served him. To my last hour.' Which was now, he supposed.

Richard stared at him, livid.

That's done it. Maybe a little humility was warranted. After all, though he was about to die, the king declared the manner of it. And quick was better than lingering.

'I . . . I mean, your grace, that he is *your* man, loyal to your majesty. And though he can be a bit . . . stubborn . . . it is because he is anxious to do your will. What a man might call arrogance is merely rashness. He will find the Stone, your grace, because he said he will. And my master rarely surrenders once set to a task. Even if . . . even if *my* time has . . . run out.'

Richard chewed on his lip, eyes lashed to Jack, even as he stepped backward until his knees touched the throne and he sat abruptly. Silence still reined in the hall and only the merest squeak of leather and clank of armor marred it.

Until Queen Anne suddenly shot to her feet. She faced the king and, just as surprised as anyone else, he could do nothing but stare at her.

'My gracious lord,' she said, gaze set on her husband. 'What is this boy to you? He is merely the servant of Crispin Guest. The failings of the master must not be visited upon the servant.'

'I . . . my dear madam, these are not matters for you to worry over . . .'

'But I do, my husband, for all the kingdom's subjects are like our children, and I would not see harm come to them.'

'Even if they are guilty?'

'But this boy is guilty only of loyalty to his master. Should that be punished?'

'If a master commits treason and his servants follow that master, then they are just as guilty of treason.'

She clasped her trembling hands together and pressed the tips of her fingers to her lips. 'But my kind and gracious lord, this boy has declared himself loyal to you.' The court gasped when the queen got down on her knees before the king and bowed her head. 'My lord and husband, I beg you to show mercy on this boy. His loyalty to his master and to you serves him well. And he has done you no ill. I fear that such an unworthy punishment would call down the wrath of God upon us and our people if we should enact so unjust a pain upon him. I beg you, my lord, to pardon him.'

Jack's jaw loosened, and he could not look away from the Madonna-like figure of the queen, pleading before a befuddled Richard.

Richard took in the breathless crowd. 'But my dear . . .'

'And the people shall shout in the streets at your benevolence, your mercy, your kindness. And they shall rise as one, as Englishmen against the rebels who would dare shake their swords at England's throne.'

The royal hand rubbed the royal beard, but his eyes still traveled over his wife with disbelief.

After a long moment, he fell back against his throne. 'Our lady wife, the queen would have mercy.' His fingers curled over the ends of the chair arms. '. . . and she has convinced us that mercy should be shown,' he added, reluctantly. 'Jack Tucker, you are released from your sentence.'

A collective sigh swept over the crowd. Jack gasped a sob and bowed his head.

'But! I do not release your master from his task. I want Crispin Guest found. I want to hear from his lips what he has been about.' He lurched to his feet and put out his hand for his queen. She rose serenely, catching Jack's eye for only a moment with the merest wisp of a wink, before she took the king's hand.

The crowd bowed as Richard stalked off the dais, escorting his wife away.

'You are the luckiest man alive . . . next to Crispin himself,' said the voice of Henry at his ear. 'It appears that the queen is now your patron. Whatever you have done for her has made you her vassal. I congratulate you. But I cannot say I am not pleased to see the back of you. Begone, Tucker, and bedevil me no more.'

Jack bowed breathlessly. 'With all due respect, your grace, I will be happy to!'

He whipped around toward Lady Katherine and took her hand, kissing it. 'My lady. Thank you!'

She shook her head, but her eyes were bright with tears. 'You silly boy. Go on. You are what Crispin needs, I am sure of it.'

'My lady.' He bowed, looked to Henry again – who couldn't seem to hide his smirk – and pivoted on his heel to depart . . . and ran right into a tall woman.

'Oh! Forgive me, my lady. I did not see you there—' The face was familiar and not altogether incongruous surrounded by a veil but it was not a particularly welcomed face. 'Rykener!' he hissed. 'What the hell—'

'Jack!' Rykener grabbed his shoulders, patted his forearms, his chest, then back to his shoulders again before Jack wriggled away. 'You are well and whole! Crispin will be so pleased.'

'You've been talking to Master Crispin?' Eyes darting, Jack wasn't certain that everyone couldn't see through Rykener's 'disguise.'

'I've been filling your shoes in your absence, and what big shoes they are. I do not envy you your apprenticeship, Master Tucker, for I am ill-equipped to do the task myself.'

'You've been what?' All this time he had lamented Master Crispin's solitude, his scrambling about without Jack, and instead, he had turned to the first substitute that entered his door!

But Rykener must have seen the hurt in his eyes.

'Oh Jack, fear not. Master Crispin misses *you*. Has done every hour of the day and night. No one could ever fill the hole you left, be assured.'

Jack adjusted his coat, letting the heat of his cheeks dissipate. 'I never doubted it, Master Rykener.'

'But I do have a message for you. Crispin has found the Stone!'

'What? Then why has he not sent word sooner? I was almost roasted alive back there.'

'Because these rebels have abducted Eleanor Langton to force Crispin to bring *them* the Stone.'

'God blind me! What's to be done? He isn't giving it to them, is he?' Jack rubbed his neck absently. The queen had intervened for him this time. If there was another instance of his capture, he doubted the king would see fit to relent a second time.

'Crispin needs help.'

Jack drew to attention instantly. 'Right.' He glanced once toward the main entrance toward freedom and turned his face away. Stalking back toward the palace corridors, he found Henry's retinue and called out, 'Lord Derby! Here! Lord Derby!'

He saw the stocky shoulders of Henry cringe upward. When Henry turned his face, his scowl was black. 'Tucker. Haven't you gone yet?'

'My lord, I must ask a favor.'

Jack could have sworn Henry was reaching for his sword.

TWENTY-SEVEN

Crispin heaved the cart with his heavy burden over the muddy ruts in the road, trying to keep it as quiet as possible. The Vespers bells had rung some time ago and Compline was nearer than he liked. He kept glancing toward the shop and house windows with their closed shutters, light leaking out around them in strips of gold.

He had prayed that Jack Tucker was well, that Abbot William's private message to the king would have arrived in a timely fashion, but he knew he must not think of that. He had wanted to go personally to Gilbert, to reassure him, but there had been no time. Just this. This cart with its cloth-covered burden.

His sword slapped his thigh, and it gave him grim satisfaction. He hoped he would get the chance to use it tonight.

All was quiet except for that damned squeaky wheel. He turned the corner at Vintry and stopped, lowering the cart. Pricking up his ears, he listened to the night. When he heard nothing he picked up the handles of the cart again, and trudged forward down the lane toward the dock.

The Thames was close. The odor of seaweed, privies, and fish all mingled into the smell he had come to know as the river. He trundled his cart along the street that opened wide into the docks. He slowed and paused when he saw the cog docked there with its lit lanterns bobbing fore and aft, but then he reckoned they needed to get the Stone away somehow, and a ship was the logical transport.

Crispin set the cart down again and pricked his ears, eyes scanning carefully not only along the flank of the ship, but up and down the docks. He saw no one, nothing. Even the rats seemed to be abed.

He watched the ship, rising with each swell of the river. Its hull creaked as it strained against the dock line. At once he saw movement, and a figure rose from below the castle to stand on the deck. He looked out over the water and Crispin saw the exact moment his presence was noticed.

The figure hurriedly moved to the gunwale and looked down.

And by the lantern light beside his face, where Crispin expected Deargh, he saw Findlaich instead.

'Master Guest,' he called, just loud enough for Crispin to hear. Crispin left the cart and moved closer to the ship along the wooden dock, stepping over coils of rope. The glitter of discarded fish scales along the planks was almost lovely by moonlight, but the smell brought any dreamy notions to a halt.

'Master Findlaich. I will not quibble with you. Have you Eleanor there?'

Findlaich smiled. 'You do get to the point. I like that about you, Guest.' He called back to an unseen compatriot behind him to the decks below. Presently, a henchman brought forth a woman, bound and gagged. Crispin recognized the dusky blond hair that caught the lantern and moonlight. She must have lost her wimple and veil. He had rarely seen her without it. Heart stuttering, he nevertheless breathed evenly.

'Eleanor, I am here.'

The figure twisted to look at him and relief broke through the reddened eyes.

'Ungag her. Let her speak.'

'Only if she will promise to behave.'

Eleanor's murderous glower caused Findlaich to hesitate. But he delicately reached behind her head and untied the rag. The first thing she did was spit at him. Findlaich observed her mildly and wiped his face with his hand.

'Crispin!' she called. Her voice was unsteady but otherwise strong. 'Where is Gilbert? Is he well?'

'Is he?' he asked of Findlaich.

'He is well. We no touched him.'

'Then that is well for you,' she huffed. 'For I shall not have to kill you now. Though I cannot speak for Master Guest.'

Findlaich laughed at that. 'She is spirited for her age.'

Eleanor kicked out, landing a hit to his shin.

Findlaich yowled and stumbled away from her. 'Madwoman! Enough of this.' He bent down to rub his leg and gave his henchman a bleary eye. The henchmen grabbed Eleanor's bound arms and yanked her back. 'Have you the Stone, Master Guest?'

'Do you take the Stone for your master or for yourself? Idle curiosity.' He ticked his head. 'There are all sorts of ways to commit treason, Findlaich.'

'And you would know.' The blow landed, but it didn't smart as much coming from such a quarter.

Findlaich laughed. 'How could I know the king would give you the impetus to harden your search? But I see you found the Stone at last. Tell me, Master Guest, is your apprentice well?'

Ashamed that he had no idea, he clenched his jaw. 'I don't know.'

'Oh? So this Eleanor means a great deal more than sorry young Jack Tucker? Oh ho! And she another man's wife. For shame!'

'You degenerate bastard!' cried Eleanor, wrestling with her guards.

'Release her and I will give you the Stone.'

'You think I'm a fool, Crispin Guest? Bring the Stone and I will release her.'

Crispin hurried back down the dock to the waiting cart, hefted it up, and rolled it forward. He stopped when he heard steps behind him.

'What, by Andrew's bones, is this?' cried Deargh. His men flanked him.

McGuffin came upon them as he turned the corner. 'Master Guest! Shame on you and your deception. You lied to me, sir!'

Findlaich gripped the gunwale so hard he was likely to break it. 'What have you done, Guest?'

'I thought it was high time that you all met.' He looked from one angry face to the other. 'My mistake. It seems you know one another very well.'

'He's a deceitful bastard,' said Deargh, pointing a finger at Findlaich. 'Greed is all he knows.'

'Look who's talking,' cried McGuffin. 'I have never met a more thieving bastard than Deargh.'

Findlaich laughed from his high perch. 'And you're the worst of the lot, McGuffin. Stealing your bauble from a *woman*. What's the matter? Afraid to face a man?'

Red-faced, McGuffin charged for the ship, but the presence of an archer aiming his arrow over the side at him stalled his progress.

'So it was you who killed the monk,' said Crispin. Again, he had been hoping for Deargh's guilt.

'He was expendable. All vassals are, Master Guest. Don't *you* know that?'

'Better than most,' he said ruefully.

He nodded to the cloth-covered item on the cart below. 'Uncover it.'

Crispin grabbed a corner and pulled it off with a flourish, revealing the Stone.

Findlaich gave a wide smile. 'And there it is at last. I see you managed to find it.'

'No thanks to you. Did you have to kill Brother Andrew *before* he told me where it was?'

Findlaich sent a searing look toward his archer, who shrugged.

The Scotsman grinned over the gunwale. 'Lucky for us that you are as clever as they say.'

'Yes. Lucky for us all.'

'Now then, Master Guest, if you would be so good as to step back so that my men . . .'

'Now hold, Findlaich.' Deargh strode forward. His burly men followed in lockstep. 'What makes you think *you* can take possession? We have all worked hard for our clan chief.'

'Because I clearly planned better than you did. Step aside, Deargh.' The archer on the gunwale pulled back the bowstring and aimed again.

Deargh grumbled and took a step back, but his hand was on his sword hilt.

One of Findlaich's men slid down the line tied to the dock and landed on the planks with a thud. He eyed Crispin warily.

'Are you going to pick that up all by yourself?' asked Crispin.

The man scratched his chin. 'Aye. I reckon not. Simon!' Another man leaned over the gunwale. 'Come down and help.'

The one called Simon had the intelligence to maneuver the gangway over the side until it slid down and touched the dock. He walked down it to meet his companion. Each grabbed one of the Stone's iron rings and pulled.

Nothing happened.

They pulled again, straining now, but the Stone would not be lifted from the cart.

'What sorcery is this?' asked Simon.

'No sorcery,' said Crispin, unsheathing his sword and flipping it around, so he held the blade but brandished the heavy pommel and hilt. 'Only the art of the plasterer. Is the paint dry?' He swung, and the hilt smacked Simon on the side of his head, sending him down flat to the dock.

The other man fumbled at his sword, but Crispin swung again, catching him on his jaw and down he went.

Crispin looked up at Findlaich. 'You're next.'

Findlaich frowned. 'You only delay the inevitable, Master Guest.'

'Do I?' By then the sound of horses reached their ears and all turned toward the mouth of the street.

The light was dim, but Crispin felt relief at the sight of Henry of Bolingbroke's colors on the destriers' trappers.

Henry, looking grim in his armor and open helm, merely pointed ahead and said, 'Get them.'

The horsemen rushed forward, fanning out to cover the entire width of the street, cutting off escape. Two ran down McGuffin's men, while two more peeled off to surround Deargh's supporters.

The last two galloped up the dock, slipped off their horses, and made their way up the gangway.

Findlaich quickly grabbed Eleanor and raced her up to the forecastle.

Crispin ran to the end of the dock. 'Let her go!'

'As you wish!' cried Findlaich. He shoved her to the edge of the gunwale and tipped her over the side.

'NO!'

Eleanor screamed as she plummeted toward the water.

Crispin leaped into the dark river. Blackness closed in around him and he could see nothing. But he felt the trail of bubbles against his face and followed it.

Down he dove, kicking his feet furiously, reaching wildly with his hands. Was it seaweed? Or . . . hair? He grabbed it, closing his fingers around the strands and tugged. He reached further and wrapped his arm around coils of rope bound tight around the woman. He raised his face upward toward the dim light of the lantern above and fought the water, kicking, until he reached the surface and broke through, pushing the woman up to breathe.

She gasped, mouth wide. Her light hair swathed her face, plastered against the pale skin.

Hands reached down and lifted her from him, then they were lifting him and he fell to the dock with a splat, just breathing. It wasn't long until a strong arm closed over his own and tugged him to his feet and he was face to face with Henry Derby.

'What took you so long?' Crispin said between coughs.

'There was a little matter of beating a servant of yours. Or rather, of wanting to.'

Crispin spied the servant in question over Henry's shoulder, cutting the binds off of Eleanor, just as Gilbert and John Rykener ran up to her.

'Jack!' Crispin didn't recall pushing Henry aside, but he traveled the short distance across the dock to pull his apprentice into an embrace.

The lad's arms encircled him in a crushing grip. 'Master Crispin!'

'Jack. Damn you, boy!' He hugged him tight for a moment more before pushing him back gruffly. 'Must you add so much vexation to my life? There is already enough.'

'I am glad to see you, too, sir!' Jack's voice wobbled.

Henry came up behind them, arms akimbo. 'Is this all of them, Crispin?'

Crispin looked over the sorry group of men being bundled together by Henry's knights. 'Yes. All except for Findlaich.'

'Look!' cried one of the riders, pointing to the bowsprit.

Findlaich stood on the edge, holding onto a line to steady himself. He looked as if he was going to jump, to swim for freedom.

But something black speared out of the sky. It screamed and flapped at his face, pecking at his eyes.

He bellowed, trying to bat the raven away. His hand slipped off the rope and over he went, plummeting not into the water, but down to the rocky shore. He landed headfirst, and everyone heard the crunch of bone.

When Henry and Crispin scrambled across the dock and down the bank, it was plain that he was dead.

Crispin combed the shoreline, and just there in the shadows stood Domhnall. He saluted Crispin, shouldered the bird, and disappeared back into the shadows.

TWENTY-EIGHT

Wrapped in a borrowed cloak, Crispin made his way back toward the Shambles with Jack striding beside him. With them was John Rykener and Eleanor bundled in Gilbert's cloak. He cooed to her with his arm encircling her tight. She laid her head on his shoulder, a broad smile on her face.

'What a night!' crowed Rykener. 'What a *night*! I've never seen anything like it.'

'And pray we never do again,' said Crispin, teeth chattering.

Gilbert seemed not to notice the cold without his cloak. He kept his wife close and that appeared to be all the warmth he needed. 'I hope you will all come back to the Boar's Tusk with us to celebrate. Food and drink for you three.'

Jack looked up at Crispin wearily.

'Perhaps tomorrow,' said Crispin. 'I am soaked to the bone and need to warm myself.'

'Tomorrow then.' Nothing could crush Gilbert's enthusiasm.

'How was Madam Eleanor taken?' asked Jack, checking on Crispin's cloak for the fourth time, making sure it covered him from the cold wind.

Gilbert sobered. 'I was in the mews, tending to the barrels when suddenly I was locked in. I called out for over an hour at least, until that wretched boy Ned let me out. He said someone had propped a chair in front of the door. It was another hour at least until we realized my Eleanor was gone.'

'An hour!' cried Eleanor. 'Well! I am glad to know I am so missed.'

'But my dear, Ned and I had cleaning up to do, and I thought you were busy elsewhere. How was I to know it was deadly mischief afoot?'

'Indeed, Eleanor,' Crispin placated. 'I only wish I had been more vigilant. They mistook John, here, for you when they abducted him the first time.'

Eleanor sized up Rykener. He postured. Crispin supposed the man was trying to look as appealing as possible.

'I look nothing like him,' Eleanor decided and snuggled into Gilbert's shoulder again.

'And you, my lad,' said Crispin to Jack.

Jack looked up expectantly.

'You are now friends with the queen, I hear.'

Jack flushed. 'Aye, sir. She was a lady in distress. I could not fail her.'

'And you were greatly rewarded for your honorable intentions.'

'More than you know,' he muttered, patting his money pouch.

'Was that all the gang rounded up, Crispin?' asked Rykener.

'Yes, I do not think there were any more conspirators. McGuffin's scheme was undone by young Jack here. It was only Findlaich who was out for himself under cover of the Mormaer's duty.'

'And he got his,' said Jack with a decided nod.

'The greedy do not prosper in the end.'

Rykener nodded sagely. 'And he killed that monk who had killed another. What sin it is when a *monk* kills. What wretched souls.'

They stopped when they arrived at Gutter Lane. 'You take care of our Jack, Crispin,' said Eleanor. 'And yourself.' She reached out and took him in an embrace once more, even planting a kiss to his cold cheek.

'I shall do what I can,' he said softly.

'Tomorrow!' said Gilbert cheerfully. 'We will celebrate together.'

'Yes,' said Crispin wearily. 'Tomorrow.'

The Langtons giggled and then shushed each other, gesturing toward the shuttered windows and the quiet street.

John yawned. 'And it is time I get back to my own home at last. I thank you, Master Guest, for your kind hospitality.'

'What?' cried Jack. 'Did you let him stay with you, too?'

Crispin approached his friend and grasped his arms. 'John, I scarce know how to thank you for all you have done for me.'

Even in the near darkness Rykener's blush was evident. 'You would have done the same for me, Crispin. And though I am not as fascinated by murder as you seem to be, the rest of it was . . . rather exciting.'

Crispin shook his head. 'Nevertheless. I owe you a great deal. You are a true friend.'

'And so are you. God keep you, Crispin. And you, Jack. Take care of your master.'

'I shall,' said the boy, chin raised.

Crispin gave a lopsided grin. 'Come along, Jack.'

They waved their farewells as each went their separate ways. Jack and Crispin hurried that much more to get in front of their fire and Crispin out of his wet things.

They reached the dark tinker shop and climbed the stairs. Crispin fitted his key in the lock and ushered Jack inside. The boy immediately went to the fire to stoke it from its covered ashes. When the hearth was bright again and the candle on the table was lit, Jack suddenly jerked to a halt.

'What . . . what is that, master?'

'That, Jack, is your new bed. You are soon to be a man. And a pile of straw simply will not do for the apprentice of the Tracker. Unless you would prefer straw, that is.'

Jack said nothing. His back was to Crispin as he faced the bed. All at once his shoulders drew up and a sob escaped him.

Crispin shuffled from one foot to the other while Jack dropped his face into his hands.

'Come now, Jack,' said Crispin softly. 'You have been through enough these past few days. Settle yourself and . . . and get you into bed.'

'Thank you, sir,' he whispered, and set about to disrobe. Gingerly, he touched the bedframe, smoothed his hands over the rough blankets and pillow. He stripped off his coat and set it carefully at the foot, folded and petted. A long silence ensued before Jack asked tentatively, 'Sir? I must confess . . . there was a time when I could have escaped, free and clear.' He slid his glance toward Crispin. Crispin raised a brow as he unbuttoned his wet cotehardie. ''Course, I couldn't have returned to you. They would have come here looking for me first thing. But that wasn't what stopped me. It was . . . it was that I had a duty to the queen. And more. To Lady Katherine for her kindness, and to Lord Henry for his charity. I . . . I felt it an obligation. And that my . . . my *honor* was at stake, if I can be so bold as to call it so.'

Crispin peeled off the wet coat from his shoulders and draped it over the chair by the fire. He began to unlace his soaked chemise. 'Of course you can call it so, Jack. Do you think "honor" is only for the nobility? Well . . . I must admit, I used to think so, but I have long since learned differently. You sacrificed yourself for something greater than yourself. For if a man cannot live by his principles, what is the point of living at all?'

'Aye, sir, you have said as much many a time, and I didn't quite understand the sentiment before. But now that I am nearly a man, I suppose I *have* learnt that lesson at last. I did think it the honorable thing to remain and fulfill my oath to the queen.'

'Rightly so, Jack.' Ringing out his chemise, he laid it before the fire. He took his blanket from his bed and draped it over his naked shoulders. He stared into the flames and said nothing.

'It's a sore thing carrying one's honor,' said Jack, hanging his cloak on the peg by the door. 'I see now the burden you have carried for so long, master.'

'It is not a burden, Jack. It is . . . myself.'

Jack nodded, continuing to disrobe.

'And now *your*self,' said Crispin. 'Dare I say the mantle is passed?'

Jack looked up, eyes wide with a deep flush blooming in his cheeks.

Crispin turned away, unfamiliar emotions roiling just below the surface. He wasn't as certain as Jack was as to whether it was a good thing to have taught the boy that lesson so well.

AUTHOR'S AFTERWORD

It's the oldest piece of furniture in Great Britain still used for the purpose for which it was created. It's over 700 years old and only used when a monarch of England accedes to the crown.

The Coronation Chair (not to be confused with a throne, for the Coronation Chair's *only* purpose is to anoint and crown the monarch) was created by King Edward I. Originally, it was to be a magnificent bronze chair to house his greatest relic, the Stone of Scone (pronounced, *scoon*), the celebrated stone of lore that every Scottish king was said to sit upon to get his crown. No one knows if it was housed in a similar chair in Scotland, but its capture in 1296 signaled to the Scots that England was now in charge. Edward still had battles to fight and needed money to do it, so the bronze chair idea was scrapped and he instead commissioned a wooden chair. Historians are not certain that his heir Edward II, or *his* heir Edward III, or even *his* heir Richard II were crowned sitting on the chair, but it is believed to be so. In fact, every monarch since sat on that chair except for the following:

- Edward V (one of the princes in the Tower) was deposed before a date was even chosen for his coronation.
- Lady Jane Grey was only *declared* queen and nine days later met a sticky end.
- Mary I sat in the chair for the homage but took a different seat for her crowning.
- For Mary II, her husband William of Orange got that privilege, and they made a special chair just for her, as they ruled together.
- And Edward VIII abdicated to marry Wallis Simpson before he could have his coronation.

Even Oliver Cromwell used it to become Lord Protector, and he had it removed from the Abbey to Westminster Hall to do the deed.

The first king that we know for certain to have been crowned sitting in that chair was King Henry IV, Henry of Bolingbroke.

The Stone of Scone has a lot of names: Jacob's Pillow, the Royal Stone, the Stone of Scotland, the Coronation Stone, and the Stone of Destiny. It is supposed to be the stone that biblical Jacob used as a pillow in Bethel. As legend has it, it was taken into Egypt with Jacob's sons and then the daughter of the Pharaoh, Scota (from which the name of Scotland was supposed to derive, but didn't – It comes from *Scoti*, a late Roman word used to describe the Gaelic regions), took it with her to Spain. From Spain it is said to have gone next to Ireland and to the sacred Hill of Tara. There it was supposedly called 'Lia-Fail,' the 'fatal' stone, or 'stone of destiny.' Irish kings were made by sitting on the stone – a very popular thing to do, apparently. Legend had it that it was supposed to groan if you had the right, and keep silent if you didn't. Finally, in the sixth century, Fergus Mòr Mac Earca, legendary King of the Picts and perhaps founder of Scotland, brought it to his western Scottish lands, where a later ninth-century King of the Picts and also supposedly the first king of the Scots, Cináed mac Ailpín, left it at the monastery of Scone in Perthshire for safekeeping.

It's not a very impressive rock. Gray, made of sandstone, carved and knocked about, it weighs 336 pounds, with two iron rings attached to it. It's 27 inches long by 17 inches wide by 11 inches high. In 1996, sophisticated tests proved that the stone's origins came from less than a mile from Scone. So much for the Egyptian/Irish tale.

For the purposes of this story, I took two fictional liberties (only two?): I moved up the date for Parliament to meet (so we wouldn't drag the story) and I had the Stone stolen in the fourteenth century (so we would have a plot). But it was never stolen, that is, not until Christmas Day in 1950 when it was taken by Scottish Nationalists. It really wasn't made for lugging around, and it had a deep flaw in it anyway, and the thing broke into two pieces. After four months on the run, the Stone was repaired and finally returned. And from then on it was placed in the same vault that kept it safe during World War II and only brought back out to the Coronation Chair in February of 1952 for Queen Elizabeth II's coronation.

In 1996, the British Prime Minister, John Major, announced that the Stone would be going back to Scotland with the proviso that it be returned when crowning a new British monarch. After all this time, the return of the Stone was greeted not with adulation by the Scots, but with a sneering sense of 'Really?' So if you wish to visit the Stone today, you will have to go to Edinburgh Castle. If you wish to visit the chair, you need to be in the opposite end of the UK in Westminster Abbey.

And this is all well and good, but there has been some question as to whether King Edward I actually got his hands on the real Stone of Destiny in the first place all those centuries ago. Did the monks hide the real stone and give him something like the lid to a cesspit, complete with its iron rings to carry it? After all, the stone is made of the same stuff that can be found around the abbey. Either all the other stories about the stone are fancies – and as we know from research into relics, they very well can be – or is there an even bigger conspiracy afoot, lost to the marches of time? Because some say that the seat of kings was made of basalt, and much larger, and decorated with carvings and the following inscription:

Ni fallat fatum, Scoti, quocunque locatum
Invenient lapidem, regnare tenentur ibidem
(If Fates go right, where'er this stone is found
The Scots shall monarchs of that realm be crowned.)

Was Edward duped all those centuries ago? Even *he* was suspicious and sent his knights back to the abbey two years later to tear the place apart, looking for the *real* stone. None was found. It might be buried at Dunsinnan Hill, where the real King Macbeth secreted it. It might be in Skye. Or at the bottom of the sea.

Or it really is the same stone. It's the kind of thing where no one will ever really know the complete truth.

In this book, we also finally meet Katherine Swynford. She was the sister-in-law of Geoffrey Chaucer, and that was, no doubt, how Katherine met John of Gaunt, the duke of Lancaster, as Chaucer lived in his household. By all accounts by her contemporaries, we can extrapolate that she was witty, charming, able, and dignified. But the details of her life are sketchy at best. We don't even know what she looked like.

She married Hugh Swynford when she was about twenty and had two children from him, Blanche and Thomas. When Hugh died in 1371 in Aquitaine under Lancaster's command (very David and Uriah), Katherine's association with the Lancaster household only deepened. She had started as lady's maid to his first wife, Blanche, and was already governess to Lancaster's daughters – Philippa and Elizabeth – when it is believed somewhere around 1372, a year or so after Katherine's husband died, that she became

John of Gaunt's mistress. They had three children together, and all, by law, were considered bastards. This sort of activity was not uncommon, but a deeply religious man such as King Richard found it distasteful. He was utterly devoted to his own first wife, Queen Anne of Bohemia, and even though they had no children, Richard is not known to have any bastards of his own.

Katherine had a brief falling out with John for a few years, but then resumed their relationship. And when John's second wife died – a match made purely for land, profit, and prestige – Gaunt had nothing more to prove and, like Charles and Camilla, married his longtime love at last. (Heck, he was already the richest man in England. What more did he need?)

The children sired by Gaunt were declared legitimate by King Richard, but they were barred from ever inheriting the throne. However, Gaunt's eldest son by Katherine Swynford, John Beaufort, had a granddaughter, Margaret Beaufort, whose son became Henry VII and took the throne from the last Plantagenet, Richard III. And Henry VII in turn married Elizabeth of York (who was also related to John of Gaunt), thus ending the York and Lancaster feud known as the War of the Roses. Their descendants inherited the throne after all.

In fact, Katherine's descendants are not just great in number but great in prestige. Her descendants include five American presidents – George Washington, Thomas Jefferson, John Quincy Adams, Franklin D. Roosevelt, and George W. Bush – as well as Princess Diana, Sir Winston Churchill and Alfred, Lord Tennyson. How's that for a legacy for a person about whom history knows very little?

Now let me just say one thing about the book *Katherine* by Anya Seton, by which many of us were introduced to Katherine Swynford. The book, written in 1954, would seem to be the definitive word on Katherine, when in fact, much of it was speculation. As I have mentioned before, we don't know much about Katherine, even to the year she was born. I did not refer to the novel for my own characterization of Katherine or John of Gaunt. I read it too many years ago to remember it, and I don't find that novels are good places to do research. Instead, I took the contemporary accounts of each character and drew my visions of them from that. Seton's Katherine will always be well-loved, but it can't necessarily be gospel.

And then there is John Rykener. We first met him in *The Demon's*

Parchment. John Rykener is a real fellow from fourteenth-century London, cross-dressing and serving as a male prostitute as well as spending time as an embroideress. So there *was* diversity in London all along, even though the term 'homosexual' was a long time away and understanding one's orientation even further. John got in trouble with the law not for his homosexuality or even for prostitution but for his cross-dressing, a distinct no-no for men as well as women; one was not to dress as the opposite sex.

Crispin and Jack, as usual, had a lot to contend with in this book and there is no end of trouble as their story continues in yet another tale of mayhem and death in the next installment, *A Maiden Weeping*.

GLOSSARY

Aventail A curtain of mail, it is affixed to the bottom of a helm and cascades down, protecting the chin and neck.

Bascinet A conical helm onto which one can affix any number of visor styles, so that the head and face are completely covered.

Cog Compact one-masted medieval ship designed for trade.

Destrier Warhorse.

Diseisement To be dispossessed of title, properties, and rights.

Each-uisge Literally 'water horse' in Gaelic. A deadly water spirit or demon.

Ekename Nickname.

Explosive Powder Black powder, gun powder.

Fitheach Gaelic for raven.

Forecastle A raised area at the bow of a ship, a place to observe oncoming enemies, perhaps. Today it's pronounced fo'c'sle, but in Crispin's day it was still pronounced as it is spelled.

Gonne Fourteenth-century spelling for the newest weapon and soldier, 'gun' and 'gunner.'

Gunwale Edge of the hull of a ship, where one might lean over the side in a case of *mal de mare*. Today it's pronounced gun'l, but in Crispin's day it, too, was still pronounced as it is spelled.

Mormaer A medieval high steward of a province in Scotland. English equivalent to 'earl.'

Pavior A man who lays pavers.

Plinth A heavy base at the bottom of a column, statue, or tomb.

Pluralis Majestatis The Royal 'We.' Referring to oneself in the plural. Literally, 'the plural of majesty.' King Richard was fond of this formality to set himself apart from others.

Rood Screen Architectural partition in a church that separates the quire (choir) or chancel (the area around the altar) from the nave (the long corridor down the center of the church where the laity stands for services). It might be a wooden screen or even a set of stone arches. The rood is an Old English term for cross or crucifix.

Trapper A colorful cloth covering, or leather or metal covering for a horse.

Tyler A man who covers a roof with tiles.

CPSIA information can be obtained
at www.ICGtesting.com
Printed in the USA
LVOW08*1459281116
514772LV00006B/52/P